Achille wheeled his bicycle around a curve to be surprised to see a new black Mercedes parked beside the road. The last sort of car Achille expected to see on a back road near Galliate in northern Italy. He rode closer to see a young woman sitting on the running board and smoking a cigarette. She stood when Achille came to her.

"Buongiorno signorina," Achille said. "Posso aiutarla?"

The young woman frowned. "Sprechen Sie Deutsch?"

Achille shook his head.

"Parlez-vous le Française?" she asked in the most wonderful accent that Achille had ever heard.

"Oui," Achille said.

"Ah good," she said in French. "My car has stopped and I'm stuck."

"What happened?"

"It just stopped and everything went dead."

"I can fix your car."

"Merci."

Achille loosened the straps and folded the bonnet back to search for the battery, for surely a faulty battery would cause a car to stop and everything to go dead. But there was no battery under the bonnet, so he unlatched the box on the side of the running board and found the battery there. The battery terminals were secure so he traced the cables down, and got onto his back beneath the car to check further. While Achille was under the car, the woman sat on the running board again, and he saw her legs from his vantage point. Long, slim, shapely. Achille smelt her cigarette while she smoked, and then he traced the battery cables where one had parted. He re-connected the plugs, and climbed from under the car while brushing dirt from his clothes. She stood and Achille was surprised that she was as tall as he. Tall and slim, flawless fair complexion, lovely blonde hair, dark red lips and amazing, deep blue eyes.

"Your car should be fixed now," Achille said. "It was an electrical problem."

She climbed into the driver's seat, pressed the button and the engine started. She climbed down. "How much do I owe you?"

"It's my honour."

She kissed his cheek. "Danke young man."

She got into her car while Achille fastened the battery box and bonnet. Achille stood back and watched her drive away. She was beautiful, and if he was older he would have kissed those dark, red lips. He would have indeed.

Achille woke from his daydream, wondering why, after so many years, he remembered that moment of his youth near his home; a long way from Caffè Sforzesco in Milano. Achille gazed out of the window to spot her. Not tall, slim and blonde but just as beautiful. Very beautiful. He dropped coins into the bowl to pay for his coffee, and then he went to the petite young woman and half-bowed.

"Buongiorno signorina," he said. "My name's Achille Varzi," he said in Italian.

"Buongiorno signore Varzi," she said. "My name's Norma Colombo."

"Buongiorno signorina Colombo."

"You're not supposed to be doing this," she said, and laughed.

Achille knew he was being forward. "I saw you and I just had to," he said.

"And now that you've introduced yourself?"

Achille glanced at his watch. "It's a good time for lunch, and I know a cafe that makes great coffee and excellent foccacia."

"Let us have coffee and foccacia."

Achille took signorina Colombo's arm and guided her inside Caffè Sforzesco, which was busy, bustling and smelled of fresh coffee. He took her to the table by the window, and the waiter departed with orders for coffees and foccacias.

"Has anyone told you how beautiful you are, signorina Colombo?"

She chuckled. "No, they haven't."

"That means I'm the first to tell you that you are beautiful."

"You are and grazie. What is that you do, signore Varzi?" Norma asked.

"I'm a racing car driver," Achille replied.

"I don't know anything about racing cars, but I suppose it's a man's sport."

"Some men follow car racing and some men don't, and some women follow car racing and some women don't."

"I suppose this is true. What car do you drive?"

"I just bought an Alfa Romeo."

Norma nodded. "I know this name."

"I expect to have great success with this car."

"I hope you do. Is it exciting to race cars?"

"It is, and there are good rewards for those who are successful."

"Well I hope you do well with your Alfa Romeo."

Their lunch came; they ate and talked while Achille liked Norma Colombo. She was down to earth, easy to talk with and she accepted his forward introduction. He thought that he could get to like Norma even more, and he hoped that Norma could get to like him too. Maybe that was the purpose of his dream. If so, it was a dream worth having. Achille glanced at Norma who was really beautiful – surely fate had dealt him a lucky hand that day.

Other Works by Mark Morey

The Red Sun will Come - June 2012

Souls in Darkness - August 2012

The Governess and the Stalker - July 2014

Maidens in the Night - September 2014

One Hundred Days - September 2015

The Adulterous Bride – October 2016

No Darkness – March 2017

In Our Memories – November 2017

Blood Never Sleeps – March 2018

Ketsumeidan – December 2018

Yuejin – Aim High! – July 2019

Wenge – Destroy The Old! – July 2019

Ice – February 2020

Across the Border – July 2020

Burrangong Creek – January 2021

Overreach – May 2021

Thunderbolt – November 2021

Into Smoke – March 2022

Upon The Sea – October 2022

Poor Girls – November 2022

Friends, Boyfriends and a Sister – March 2023

The Young Romantics – June 2023

Lulu – September 2023

Invisible Chains – January 2024

The Temple Priestess – September 2024

The Last Great Race

by

Mark Morey

Mark Morey

http://markmorey.blogspot.com.au

Copyright ©

978-0-9944171-5-2

Published In Australia

April 2016

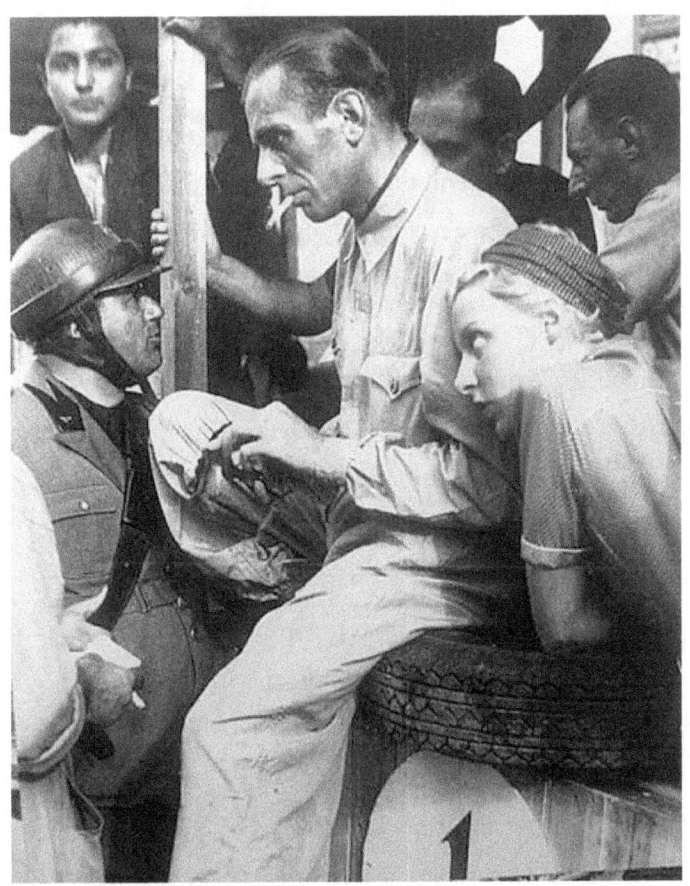

Achille and Ilse, Circuito di San Remo, July 25, 1937

Chapter One

Achille leaned against his blue Bugatti and smoked a cigarette. For the first time ever, the grid was formed in order of practice times, with Achille fastest and on the inside of the front row. Team manager Meo knew to keep his distance while Achille surveyed the dark blue and white Alfa Romeo of Louis Chiron, second fastest. Scuderia CC, Chiron and Caracciola, was reduced to one car after Rudi Caracciola's practice crash near the tobacconist's shop, which was a bad crash indeed. Immediately behind Achille's Bugatti was the red Alfa Romeo of Tazio Nuvolari, with Tazio and team manager Enzo Ferrari talking quietly. Tazio also crashed in practice at the tobacconist's shop but only damaged his car. Typical Nuvolari luck. For the race Ferrari had enlarged two of his Alfa Romeo's engines, those for Tazio and for Baconin Borzacchini. Achille wondered how those cars would perform during more than three hours of racing.

Starter Charles Faroux held up the three minute board and many drivers made nervous, last minute adjustments to overalls, caps, gloves and goggles. Achille finished his cigarette while remaining cool and calm. It was to his advantage if his competitors saw that he was relaxed. But Achille wasn't, of course, particularly as the Grand Prix de Monaco had, in five short years since the first running of the race in 1928, become one of the premier events on the motor sport calendar. A difficult circuit with steep climbs and descents, many tight curves and even a tunnel. The Circuit de Monaco wound between the shimmering blue Mediterranean under a cloudless sky on one side, and sandstone buildings clinging precariously to the sides of the steep cliffs of Monte Carlo on the other. A big crowd crammed into every possible vantage point, including balconies of apartments and hotels.

Two minutes and Achille climbed into his Bugatti while the mechanic started the engine to get it to temperature. Soon the engines of eighteen racing cars, Bugatti, Alfa Romeo and Maserati, made the most ear-piercing racket, muffled by Achille's ear plugs.

One minute and mechanics and team managers cleared the grid. It was down to the drivers, and unusually this Monaco race didn't need refuelling stops, so mechanics had no further part to play unless a car struck trouble. Achille studied Faroux readying the blue and yellow flag of Monte Carlo. Faroux raised the flag, Achille increased revs to six-thousand, Faroux paused, revs still six-thousand, Faroux nudged the flag and Achille dropped the clutch and made the most magnificent start. Also quick away was Baconin who loomed large in Achille's mirror when they rounded Sainte Dévote and commenced the steep climb to Casino Square. Fast but neat past the casino and down to Station Hairpin, hard braking before turning, and onto the short straight leading to the two right-handers under the railway bridge, drifting towards the outside of the circuit and into the tunnel; momentarily driving in near-darkness while focussed on the light at the end. Hard braking and left then right through the chicane and along the harbour side to the tobacconist's shop, braking hard before taking the left-hander, and keeping it neat for the run along the quay. Hard braking into Gasometer Hairpin and onto Boulevard Albert, and past the finish line with the pits on the right, where Achille checked the car's gauges to see everything was good.

The Bugatti was nervous and darting, and needed a graceful, easy touch to point it in the right direction. Too fast or too loose cost time sliding sideways, and ran the risk of clipping a sharp, concrete curb and a flat tyre, bent wheel or worse. In the cockpit, despite engine noise and vibration, bashing and crashing over bumps, manhole covers and the tramline, and seventeen drivers waiting for the slightest mistake, time slowed in the most amazing way. A tenth of a second took twenty seconds, twenty seconds took a minute, a minute seemed like 30 minutes. Every insignificant detail was clearly visible: a woman in a red dress on the right as he went past the casino; a fireman in dark overalls leaning against the wall just before Station Hairpin; spectators watching the race from yachts tied up at the quay. Past the pits and Meo held out the board. Achille knew Baconin was only a second behind, but was surprised to note that Tazio was third. Third already. Achille knew that one, red Ferrari-entered Alfa Romeo would soon be replaced by another.

Sure enough Tazio passed Baconin on the run to the Gasometer Hairpin on lap three, and eased his Alfa past Achille's Bugatti on the climb out of Sainte Dévote. The Alfa had more power and speed on the steep hill where Achille had no answer for that. Fast the Alfa was, but Tazio struggled badly at Station Hairpin, and struggled more on the curves leading to the tunnel. Next time around Achille used his momentum into the tunnel to pull inside Tazio and pass him into the chicane. From there it was easy, and Achille eked out a tiny gap to lead across the finish line. Again on the climb out of Sainte Dévote, Tazio powered past but Achille was relaxed about that. It was a long race and if he stayed no more than a second behind, he could overtake the red Alfa whenever he wanted.

On lap 19 they came to lap a slow Bugatti, and with a moment's hesitation Achille was past both of them, led the way to the Gasometer Hairpin and across the finish line to begin lap 20. They stayed locked together for ten laps before Tazio passed on the climb to Casino Square again. Achille sat right on the tail of the red Alfa to pressure Tazio to make a mistake. Someone else made a mistake at the chicane, with displaced sandbags as a testament. Past Casino Square where Tazio lost control of His Alfa and spun onto the footpath. Achille ducked inside the gyrating car and continued down the hill to Station Hairpin with a clear lead. Not for long because Tazio rejoined in second and his lap boards showed lap times of two minutes and two seconds. Achille concentrated on shaving precious tenths to match Tazio's times, but it wasn't possible to continue at that speed without risk. Tazio closed so that by lap 50, half distance, Tazio's Alfa was less than a car's length behind the Achille's Bugatti. Eight laps later Tazio passed on the climb from Sainte Dévote, so Achille sat close to keep pressure on his rival. For twenty laps, until Tazio got untidy under the railway bridge and Achille swept past. But not for long because Tazio powered into the lead a few laps later. This time Achille eased off to rest and recover, before working to close the gap to be right behind Tazio by lap 97, and then he swept into the lead through the tunnel. Again Tazio passed on the climb out of Sainte Dévote, where every time it was when Achille changed into fourth. Achille realised that to win he had to rely on his Bugatti's engine being strong enough. Achille passed in the tunnel, and again, on lap 99, Tazio powered into the lead on the run up the hill to Casino Square. Achille followed close to Tazio to start lap 100, and this time Achille held third gear all the way from Sainte Dévote to Casino Square, with the Bugatti's engine so far into the red he didn't even look. Past Tazio into the lead, down the hill to Station Hairpin, where Achille checked his mirror and got the greatest surprise for Tazio wasn't there; the Alfa had slowed or stopped. Achille recovered from his shock and raced the remainder of the final lap to take the chequered flag.

Achille cruised around the Monte Carlo circuit at half pace on his slowing down lap, with marshals cheering and applauding, while just after the tunnel, Tazio Nuvolari pushed his still-smoking Alfa Romeo towards the chicane. Clearly he took his engine past its limits but it had broken. Achille drove to the Bugatti team pits where Meo Costantini, the mechanics and Norma all waited to greet the victor. They gathered around the blue Bugatti while Achille sat on the tail and lit a cigarette.

* * *

Paul looked down from the balcony of his hotel room at the driver in white overalls casually smoking a cigarette while his team gathered around the winning car. It had been an amazing race, and probably the best race ever run. He leaned against the balcony rail and contemplated how a chance viewing of a motor race at Phillip Island changed his life. The excitement of man and machine on the limit was unmatched, but motor racing in Australia was strictly for amateurs, so if he wanted to see the best and write about the best he had no choice but to move to Europe. Therefore Paul did, where his first Grand Prix was three hours and twenty-eight minutes of non-stop action. The battle between Achille Varzi and Tazio Nuvolari, and also Philippe Étancelin's spectacular fight-back to third after an indiscretion at the chicane, before the rear axle of his Alfa Romeo failed.

Of the drivers Varzi impressed the most. He was always in contention for the lead, despite his Bugatti lacking speed on the straights, and he never looked like making a mistake. Tazio Nuvolari gave all but he made mistakes, and even though his engine blew-up he was almost certainly destined for second place. Étancelin, who raced with his cloth cap turned back to front, made one mistake on an unforgiving circuit, but he made up for that with his dramatic recovery to third, passing a Scuderia Ferrari Alfa Romeo in the process.

Paul returned to his room to sit at the desk. He had two articles to write from his notes: a long one for motor sport journals and a short one for newspapers. Briefly he pondered about being an Italian-Australian who spoke both languages, and also spoke French, in a French-speaking country writing race reports in English. But then, that was why he was there. He fed a sheet of paper into his typewriter and wrote 'The Greatest Grand Prix Of All Time'.

Chapter Two

Achille was annoyed. What was the point of a team manager who managed to get the cars and drivers to the circuit, but didn't manage to submit the entry on time? He let Meo know that he was annoyed in no uncertain terms, and Achille overheard Meo muttering about bad temper when Achille left the pits. He travelled all the way to Alexandria and even practiced, only to be told he wasn't starting in the race. More fools the organisers who denied their spectators a chance to see a top driver because of a technicality.

Achille lit a cigarette and sensed someone nearby. He caught the eye of a tall young man, dark-haired and dark-eyed, dressed casually yet neatly with black trousers and a white shirt open at the collar, topped with a broad brimmed khaki-coloured hat of a style that Achille had never seen before, but practical for the sun. The young man approached with a big smile.

"Buon Pomeriggio signore Varzi," he said cheerfully. "My name is Paul Bassi and I'm a new journalist following the races," he continued in Italian.

"Buon Pomeriggio signore Bassi," Achille replied.

"I saw your race in Monaco and I want to congratulate you for your victory."

That comment pricked Achille's interest; it was rare for journalists to show more than a passing interest in events past. "Grazie," Achille said. "Which journal do you represent?"

"I represent journals and newspapers in England and Australia."

"Austria?" Achille asked, confused.

Paul Bassi smiled even more brightly. "No signore Varzi, I write articles for Australia, on the other side of the world."

That made even less sense to Achille. He looked Italian and he spoke perfect Italian.

"I'm from Australia," Paul Bassi said. "And I'm part-Italian and part-Australian."

Achille thought that made sense. He was forward, more forward than any Italian.

"I heard you're not racing tomorrow," Paul Bassi said.

Achille drew on his cigarette. "Our entries were late to the organisers."

"That's too bad. I'm sure the spectators would wish to see the winner of last weekend's great race."

Achille nodded in silent agreement.

"Well, there's Tripoli next week and the lottery," Paul Bassi said. "They draw the ticket holders today. Six million lira for win and place."

Just then Tazio appeared. "Tazio Nuvolari, this is Paul Bassi, a journalist from Australia."

"Buon Pomeriggio signore Nuvolari," Paul Bassi said.

"Buon Pomeriggio signore Bassi, and your Italian is excellent," Tazio replied.

"He is Italian," Achille interrupted.

"Of course, there are Italians everywhere. Even in Australia."

"I don't want to waste your time," Paul Bassi said. "Good luck for tomorrow signore Nuvolari. Do you have a two-point-six litre engine in your car, by any chance?"

Tazio chuckled. "Well, one of the new engines was damaged last weekend, but there might be another available."

Paul Bassi nodded. "Grazie for that signore Nuvolari. I should go. Buon Pomeriggio signore Varzi e signore Nuvolari," the young journalist said before leaving them for his next conquest, Baconin Borzacchini.

"Achille," Tazio said. "I want to talk to you about next weekend at Tripoli. The lottery...."

"Six million lira for win and place," Achille interrupted.

"I have a plan. The most likely winners at Tripoli are you and I, and we can use this to our advantage. We can make an agreement with the men who draw our numbers to pool their winnings and share this amongst us."

Achille couldn't see the sense in that. "Why would the men who drew our numbers agree to such a thing?"

"It's a guaranteed prize of one million, seven hundred and fifty thousand if one of us wins, rather than a fifty-fifty chance. And an even bigger prize for them if we finish first and second."

Achille saw the possibility of that.

"I've spoken to Baconin and he's interested as well," Tazio said.

"Three drivers and three lottery ticket holders, and we split the earnings six-ways?" Achille clarified.

"Yes."

It was a lot of money, an immense amount of money in fact. The money was worth it but it had to be done properly. "We need a legal agreement with everyone as a signatory, and notarised as well."

"I can organise this. Let's say we meet in Roma on Monday."

Achille nodded. "You'll have it easy tomorrow seeing as I'm not here to beat you!"

Tazio grinned. "Your turn will come at Tripoli."

Achille lit another cigarette. "Goodbye friend," and he headed to the hotel to pack his things and arrange a ride to the airport.

* * *

The newly-built Autodromo di Mellaha was, in a word, breathtaking. The recent crushing of local resistance against Italian rule in Libya resulted in the Italian Government increasing their development of the colony, including building the best motor racing circuit in the world as the venue for the richest motor race in the world. Governor-general and motor racing fan, Marshal Balbo, arranged for a State Lottery to be held throughout Italy. For the small investment of 11 lira, the holder of the lottery ticket which corresponded with the winning car of the Gran Premio di Tripoli would be a millionaire many times over. The income from the lottery paid for the Autodromo, and enable truly massive prizes for the top-placed cars and drivers.

The autodromo was adjacent to the city of Tripoli, between the desert and the sea with a massive, brick and concrete grandstand beside the broad start and finish straight, and spacious pits opposite; also in brick and concrete. The circuit had a starting light system: red, yellow and green, and a photo-electric timing system feeding a timing tower for the benefit of teams, spectators and journalists. And speaking of journalists, Paul was more than impressed by the spacious accommodation within the grandstand for newspaper and radio journalists. But the pits were where the stories were to be found as Paul headed to the sterile building

cowering behind a sterile, concrete apron. There he found a face
he recognised from pictures of times past: Sir Henry or 'Tim'
Birkin. Just like his photos with wispy hair and a small moustache
– one of few British drivers to race in Europe and certain to be of
interest to Paul's English readers. He went to the pit with a green
Alfa Romeo Monza sparkling in the sun, and with Sir Henry
smoking a cigarette in the shade of the awning which sheltered the
counter.

"Good morning Sir Henry," Paul said in English for once.

"Please call me Tim," Birkin replied with a lisp.

"Of course. My name's Paul Bassi, and I'm a journalist
representing a number of journals and newspapers in England and
Wales. I thought my readers might be interested in your opinion of
your chances this weekend."

"The car's running well and my chances are good. I'm
determined to beat the cheaters...."

"Pardon?" Paul asked; surprised by that comment.

"Nuvolari, Varzi and Borzacchini have made some sort of
deal."

Paul was stunned. "Are you saying the race is fixed?"

"You should ask them. I'm determined to win on Sunday, and I
will do everything I can to wreck their grubby plot."

Paul was even more startled. "I will talk with these men if I can,
and of course I wish you all the best with your racing this
weekend."

Tim Birkin didn't acknowledge Paul's good wishes, which left
Paul to find one of the three. In the shade of the Bugatti team pits
was an immaculately dressed Achille Varzi, smoking as usual. A bit

shorter than average, about five foot seven, with dark eyes and jet black hair, immaculately parted. He had hard features but still was a handsome man, and always well presented. His overalls fitted just so, were always crisply pressed, and he even had his initials embroidered on the pocket. In a way he dressed as fastidiously as he drove. Some drivers and most of the press thought he was aloof and arrogant, but Paul thought Varzi took his racing more seriously than most.

"Buongiorno signore Varzi," Paul said.

"Buongiorno signore Bassi," Achille Varzi replied.

"I spoke with signore Birkin and he told me something," Paul continued in Italian.

"About our agreement?"

"Yes."

Achille Varzi frowned while he drew on his cigarette. "Three lottery ticket holders and Tazio, Baconin and I have agreed to pool any winnings that might result from our performances in the race."

Paul digested that and it seemed alright, although of questionable judgement. "So the race isn't fixed?"

"We are free to race as we see fit."

"Can I print this?"

"You can."

"Grazie signore Varzi and good luck for the race."

Achille Varzi flashed a brief smile. "Grazie signore Bassi."

"Your Bugatti lacked speed on the straights at Monaco, and this circuit is fast with long straights."

"But not steep hills."

"Even so...."

"I know. The Monza with two-point-six litres is going to be a challenge."

"Buongiorno signore Varzi."

"Buongiorno signore Bassi."

Paul headed towards the grandstand with a great opening paragraph for his articles about practice for the Gran Premio di Tripoli.

* * *

By race day Paul knew there was antagonism by most of the drivers towards Nuvolari, Varzi and Borzacchini. Giuseppe Campari and Luigi Fagioli from Maserati were particularly hostile while Tim Birkin's animosity hadn't abated. If anything Birkin was more determined to win the race, and maybe that would spur him to greater feats in European racing than he'd achieved to date. Maybe. In a special roped-off area in the grandstand, thirty lottery ticket holders were feted by the military government of the Italian colony. The governor-general of the colony, Marshal Balbo, was in attendance, and looking resplendent in his sand-coloured uniform with epaulets and colourful medal ribbons; and with his distinctive beard immaculately trimmed. Balbo was a high-ranking founding member of the Fascist Party and formerly a Secretary of State for the Air, before being appointed Governor-general of Libya, which showed how important the colony of Libya ranked in the Italian scheme of things.

Sand was an appropriate colour for Autodromo di Mellaha mid-afternoon under a baking sun, with the temperature close to forty or a hundred, depending on which part of the world you came from, and with a hot wind blowing from the desert. Paul was grateful he wore a light, cotton shirt without a tie, and was shaded by his trusty Akubra hat. It was hot, as hot as his hometown of Shepparton in mid-summer; hot for the drivers and hot for the cars. Surely such heat would affect reliability, particularly with lap times averaging close to 170 kilometres per hour.

The weather hadn't put off the spectators and the huge grandstand was full. If the true purpose of Gran Premio di Tripoli was to encourage potential migrants from Italy to visit the conquered colony and remain as settlers, the scorching heat wasn't helping. But for sure with such a large field, the racing was bound to be fascinating.

Starting order was picked by ballot, which resulted in Luigi Premoli in a privately entered Maserati on pole with Tazio Nuvolari second on the five-abreast grid, and Achille Varzi was in the middle of the second row, in position seven out of 29. The cars lined up in scorching heat, drivers were shown the three, two and one-minute boards, starting lights flashed from red to yellow to green, and Carlo Gazzabini led away from the outside of the front row into the desert and palm trees. But it was Tim Birkin in the lead at the end of the lap, ahead of Nuvolari and Campari. Varzi was in the middle of the field with the engine of his Bugatti running roughly; perhaps on seven cylinders. Campari, one of the drivers most annoyed about the deal struck by the six, passed Nuvolari and Birkin, and then he pulled out a decent lead until, on lap 14 out of 30, he pitted for fuel and attention under the bonnet of his car, which cost a lot of time. Birkin also pitted for fuel – his stop was routine except he burned his arm on his car's exhaust while picking up a cigarette lighter. Nuvolari led the race from Varzi as usual, until Nuvolari eventually pitted for an extremely quick fuel stop on lap 23. Varzi continued while Nuvolari in second chased hard after the leader. Nuvolari reduced the gap until, on lap 28, Varzi slowed dramatically and Nuvolari swept by before Varzi picked up speed again.

Over the last two laps the red Alfa and the blue Bugatti swapped and re-swapped the lead, and often raced along the straights side-by-side. It was shades of Monaco only at double the speed, and Paul was surprised to see both drivers shouting and gesturing at each other. He wondered if the race really was meant to be fixed but the agreement was broken by one of them, perhaps in the rush of battle. They started the last-lap-side and stayed that way most of the way around the circuit until, at the last turn, Varzi braked later and cornered faster than Nuvolari. But it wasn't over because Nuvolari then used the Bugatti's slipstream to close, and Varzi crossed the line officially two-tenths of a second clear, but to those in the grandstand it was as near to side-by-side as made no difference. Third, about one minute and thirty seconds behind the leading pair, was Tim Birkin.

Paul put down his binoculars and tried to concentrate enough to finish his notes, but all he could think of was the mastery of Achille Varzi. His coolness under pressure and the unrelenting pressure he brought to bear on drivers ahead. Everyone knew of Tazio Nuvolari, even in Australia, but Achille Varzi was the best of the best.

* * *

With his grand trophy in one hand, Achille sought out Norma from the crowd, but she was petite with dark hair and hard to pick from those around her. He pushed his way to his companion in a floral dress and a straw hat that wasn't exactly fashionable, but at least practical for the sun.

"There's a special dinner this evening for drivers and teams," Achille told her.

"You go," Norma said. "Fancy dinners aren't for me."

Achille was disappointed. "Are you sure?" he asked.

"I'm sure."

Achille led Norma away from the crowd and towards the car park. "I made a lot of money today; nine-hundred and thirteen-thousand lira."

Norma put her hand over her mouth.

"I won and Tazio came second, so we get one-sixth of the first and second place lottery prizes, and I get my share of the prize money for a win."

"Congratulations Achille."

They reached their borrowed car where Achille got inside for the short drive to the Grand Hotel. He had to bathe and dress to be feted as the winner of the richest motor race of all time, although he really would have preferred a quiet night playing cards with his friends.

Chapter Three

Achille was pleased to have a two week break before the next race at Avus in Berlin. He was even more pleased to park his Lancia and unlock the door to their apartment on Via Della Spiga. Home was a place he didn't see as often as he wanted, and he had plans at least for the next few hours. And other plans for that night.

Norma came through the door carrying her own bag because she travelled as light as he. She was a practical woman. Norma went to the bedroom and unpinned her hat where Achille joined her with two glasses of Cinzano Bianco.

Norma took one. "Celebration?" she asked.

"It's to get us in the mood."

Norma laughed that boisterous laugh of hers. "I don't need Cinzano to get into the mood!"

Achille knew that well enough. Norma drank rather than sipped her drink, and then went to the bathroom. Soon Achille heard taps running.

"Come on Achille; you know there's room for two," she called.

Achille put his half-empty glass to one side, removed his tie and went to join her.

* * *

Achille lay on his stomach in the midst of wrinkled sheets and a quilt draped onto the floor. He looked up at the alarm clock and it was six already. He got up and stretched before lighting a cigarette.

"Are you going out?" Norma asked.

"Yes, to Ristorante Bagutta," Achille replied.

"I'll join you for a meal."

Achille went to the wardrobe and picked a cream linen jacket, black trousers, a light brown shirt and a darker brown tie and laid them on the rumpled bed. He pondered before putting the shirt and tie away. He flicked through his clothes and found a pale yellow shirt and laid it on the jacket and contemplated it. Then he found a light brown tie with fine, pale yellow stripes and laid it over. Tie matched shirt and shirt matched jacket. He dressed and returned to the wardrobe to find a pair of black leather shoes. He held them so they reflected the light and they were spotless. He sat on the chair and used a horn to slip them on, to avoid crushing the leather, and tied laces neatly. A quick visit to the bathroom to oil and comb his hair, parting it just so, and he returned to find Norma in a simple, light blue striped dress and a darker blue hat pinned into place.

"Are you immaculate enough?" Norma asked with a big smile.

Achille nodded and slipped his arm through hers, and together they descended the stairs to head to Ristorante Bagutta.

Milano bustled at six-thirty on a Monday night, with workers rushing home and early diners heading out. Achille liked Ristorante Bagutta: it was unpretentious, the food was excellent and the service was good. It was his home away from home, and if it was late and they were still going he could bring them home. Mario, immaculate in black and white, greeted them both and held the door for Achille and Norma to enter the smoky, crowded room. Ristorante Bagutta was a cafe of red, brown, dark timber, flickering candles, tall ceilings and line drawings, paintings and frescoes. Mario showed them to a large table in the second room away from the other diners, and left with orders for Cinzano

Bianco and a glass of gin. Drinks were then exchanged for orders of ossobuco and casoncelli, which arrived promptly as Achille preferred.

Achille had just finished his meal when Pietro appeared, and both Achille and Norma stood to be greeted before Pietro took one of the spare seats. Didi was next – congratulating Achille for his win in more ways than one. Didi raced in Alexandria but wasn't entered by Ferrari at Tripoli. Tonino then joined the table, and like Didi he raced at Alexandra but not at Tripoli. Mario took orders for drinks and meals. At that point Norma finished her gin and wished them all good evening before leaving. Achille said he was going to his estate in Galliate for a few days hunting and they were free to join him, to which all agreed. Achille reached into his pocket for his deck of cards, and they spent the next few hours playing scopa with Achille winning, as was usually the case. Mario kept the cafe open past normal closing time, but Achille was tired after the day's travelling so they left a bit after ten with an agreement for Achille to pick up Pietro, Didi and Antonio the next morning, when he got around to it.

* * *

Achille woke, glanced at the clock which showed eight, and then he sat up and lit a cigarette. He felt movement in the bed and Norma, who liked a long night's sleep, lifted her head from beneath the quilt. She rubbed her eyes and Achille handed the Camel packet and his lighter to her. She sat up and lit one.

"Are you going to Galliate?" Norma asked.

"Yes, with Pietro, Didi and Tonino," Achille replied. "Do you want to come?"

Norma shook her head. "No thanks. I'll leave the vagabonds to hunt, drink, play cards and talk about cars."

Achille nodded. He knew her preferences.

Norma butted her cigarette and kissed his cheek. "Let's have a present before you go."

Achille nodded before butting his cigarette. Norma removed her nightdress in one, swift move and started on Achille's pyjamas. Achille slid down the bed and relaxed as he let Norma make love to him. It was something she did very well.

After they bathed, Norma left Achille to contemplate his wardrobe while she cooked breakfast. After Achille dressed in a pale brown shirt, darker brown trousers, cream pullover and brown leather boots, he joined Norma for brassadei and a cup of strong, black coffee.

"How long are you going for?" Norma asked.

"Just a few days," Achille said. "We're going to the villa."

"You should see your parents."

"I'm at the villa with Didi, Antonio and Pietro. I'll see my parents some other time."

Norma nodded and Achille sensed she had something on her mind. "What is it Norma?" he asked.

"It's been a long time since you saw your parents."

Achille looked his companion in her eyes, and she was right. "We'll stay at the villa for a few days and then I'll bring them home. You and I should go on Sunday. I'll ring Mama and let her know." Achille got up and kissed Norma's cheek. "I must go. I'll see you Friday."

Achille went to the bedroom to pack his bag for three days away, and then he headed down the stairs to where his Lancia was parked. Three days of hunting, cooking, playing cards, drinking and talking about cars. And of course a visit to Corrado Galliate. Norma was right. If Mama knew Achille was in town and he didn't see her, she would be hurt. He would ring Mama as soon as he could.

Chapter Four

After two days travelling, Paul was relieved to eventually arrive in Berlin to cover the next major race at Avus. However, his taxi ride to the Hotel Augustinenhof on Auguststrasse dampened Paul's mood. In the evening, men in dark and shabby clothes had already gathered in doorways of shops and business to sleep rough. Crowds filled a park; men, women and children, again to sleep rough. The taxi driver turned onto a narrower road lined by grubby, smoke-stained buildings, with many women standing on the edge of the footpaths – prostitutes of all ages. The taxi driver turned onto another street and there were more prostitutes; indeed the city teemed with women selling sex. Sex for sale wasn't unique, there was a lot of part-time prostitution in Australia by desperate mothers or daughters, but prostitution on the scale of Berlin was indicative of an economy in a bad way, and an economy in worse shape than Paul's homeland or what he saw during his time in England and Wales. Paul wondered how badly Germany had fared from the Depression. For sure the economy of France wasn't so badly off, while what he saw during his journey through Italy was reasonable. For some reason Latin countries were doing well while Saxon countries suffered.

Paul checked into his hotel which was large, four-storey brick and stucco in a broad street of large, four-storey, brick and stucco buildings. After unpacking he had a meal at a cafe before heading to bed early. He needed a good sleep.

The next morning Paul dressed in a shirt, tie, pullover and freshly ironed trousers and then had breakfast at the same cafe. Later, Paul spent a few hours writing to his parents and his uncles.

He had much to tell beyond mere car racing, although he briefly described the races for Uncle Antonio's benefit. Paul asked reception for directions to a bank and a post office, but the young woman didn't speak English, French or Italian. Paul resorted to sign language but he couldn't understand her directions, so the woman drew a sketch map for Paul to follow. He went to the bank to exchange British Pounds for German Marks, and then to the post office to mail his letters. Berlin during the day was a city of hustle and bustle with packed trams rattling by, cars fighting for space and pedestrians also fighting for space. Paul went to a cafe for lunch where he bought a roll and black coffee, again by using sign language. The tables were taken but there was a large bench around the perimeter of the room with several stools and one unused. He took his purchase to the bench and sat beside an attractive woman a few years older than he.

"Guten Tag," she said as a greeting, which Paul had worked out to meet 'good day'.

"Guten Tag," Paul replied and glanced at the young woman in a charcoal grey dress and black hat. There had to be someone in Berlin he could talk to. "Excuse me; do you speak English, French or Italian?"

"I speak a little English," she said in a quite lovely accent.

"My name's Paul Bassi and I'm new in Berlin. I'm staying for almost two weeks."

"Good day Herr Bassi, my name is Corinna Engel."

"Good day Miss Engel."

"Where are you from?"

"Australia."

"Austria?" she asked, frowning.

"No, Australia. On the other side of the world."

"Ah."

"I'm here on business."

"I hope you enjoy your stay in Berlin, Herr Bassi."

"This is my first day." Paul pondered what to say next before it came to him. "Miss Engel, do you have any recommendations of what I could see?"

She turned to face him more directly. "The night life of Berlin is interesting, and it is open every night of the week. You should see some good, Berlin cabaret."

"I'll see some cabaret tonight."

"There is a good cabaret club on Gartenstrasse, which isn't far from here."

This was going well. "Do you like cabaret, Miss Engel?" Paul asked.

She pursed her lips. "Sometimes."

"Would you like to go with me tonight?"

Silence. "Yes, I can go with you tonight," she eventually said.

"Thank you."

"I have never met an Australian before. What is Australia like?"

Paul drew a big breath. "It's a young country and very big. I think it's almost as big as Europe, but there are only six and a half million people."

She looked at him with eyes wide. "That is not much more than the population of Berlin."

Paul nodded. "Australia's really boring."

She laughed lightly. "I can imagine – there would be no cabaret or night life or anything."

"Yes."

"Will you be going to Australia when your business is over?"

"After Berlin I'm going to the Eifel Mountains for a few days and then I'll travel to France. I have no plans to return to Australia."

"You will like the Eifel Mountains. Where are you staying, Herr Bassi?"

"You can call me Paul and I'm staying at the Hotel Augustinenhof on Auguststrasse."

"You can call me Corinna and I will meet you at your hotel at eight."

* * *

Corinna was punctual while her evening attire was attractive and distinctive: a silvery-blue-grey dress and a black fedora hat with a brim, which looked great against her fair complexion and chestnut-brown hair. Paul had pressed his suit and decided his Akubra hat wasn't suitable for an evening out. So hatless he went, as he offered to take Corinna's arm when they went outside.

"Berlin is affected by where it is located," Corinna said while they walked along a street just as crowded as the middle of the day. "The atmosphere of Berlin is, and I don't know the right word for this in English, but in German we would say Berliner luft." She frowned. "Berliner air in English."

The street was busy with many couples walking arm in arm together. Paul and Corinna rounded a corner and came across yet another street lined with prostitutes.

"This is what comes from the Berliner luft," Corinna said. "You can have anything you wish; just ask and it's yours. There are many sex clubs where Berliners and tourists enjoy decadent pleasures: women and girls to satisfy every conceivable fetish, boys for men, women for women, take your wife and have another man's wife while he has yours, watch others, be watched; it's all there."

Paul didn't know of more than one pleasure, which he thought was more than pleasurable enough.

Several soldiers approached where the manner of their uniforms reminded Paul of what he'd seen in Napoli. Their uniform jackets were cut well, and were matched with long boots and riding trousers. The soldiers joked with each other and flirted with women, and one half-bowed towards Corinna who briefly glanced in his direction before turning her head away.

"Nazis," she murmured when they were out of hearing range.

"Fascist?" Paul asked.

"Yes."

"I saw similar in Italy."

"The economy of Germany has been bad for as long as I can remember, and Nazis promised to fix this. They did well at the last election and then their leader, Adolph Hitler, was made chancellor. Since the Reichstag fire in February we have been under a state of emergency, more or less, which I know will be permanent."

"What do you think of this?"

"If Nazis make the economy better, this will be good because many have suffered for far too long. But all power with one person and one party is dangerous," she said in a soft voice.

"How do Nazis plan to improve the economy?"

"They will spend money on programs and works like roads, railways and the military."

Paul nodded. "This might work," he said. "In Australia the government cut spending and they also cut people's wages, and that made the depression there worse."

"I hope Nazis make things better. One thing I don't like," she said in a soft voice. "Is the idea of Germany only for Germans. This is dangerous. But those who have no job, no money, not enough food and nowhere to live, do hope Nazis improve the economy. I am lucky because I have a job."

"What work do you do, Corinna?"

"My family owns a brewery and I work in the office. My family has been lucky. What work do you do Paul?"

"I'm a freelance journalist."

"So you are travelling for a story?"

"Yes I am."

They rounded another corner into a brightly lit street of cafes and apartment buildings. They went along a lane beside an unpretentious three storey block of apartments built in red brick, to an equally unpretentious-looking building opening off a courtyard. That second building had a small sign: Kolibri Festsälle.

"This is it," Corinna said. "There will be a variety of acts, and some of the comedy about German politics you will not understand, but other acts will be entertaining and typical of the Berlin way of life. It is quite tame. It is not so much affected by the Berliner luft."

They went inside to a restaurant with cabaret where Corinna handled the reservations she previously made. They were shown to a white table with white, leather-covered chairs in a large dining hall with an arched roof. The room was decorated in green and brown and had a stage at one end, recessed into a part-arched alcove. The room echoed with the sound of many couples and small groups eating and conversing. The waiter spoke with Corinna.

"Paul," Corinna said. "What would you like to drink?"

Paul knew one thing about Germany. "I'll have a glass of beer. Your family's beer if they have it."

Corinna smiled briefly, and only then did Paul realise how serious she was for a young woman, perhaps in her late twenties. The waiter took their orders for drinks and left two menus.

Paul pondered the menu but none of it made sense. "Corinna," he said. "Do you have any recommendations?"

"If you have an appetite you can try königsberger klopse with kartoffelpuffer, meatballs with potatoes and rather nice. I am having eierkuchen, pancake."

"I do need more than pancake."

The drinks arrived and they ordered their meals.

"What did you do for entertainment in Australia, Paul?" Corinna asked.

Paul sighed. "I lived on a farm a few miles or a few kilometres from a town called Shepparton. We sometimes went to Shepparton to see movies, but when I was older there wasn't anything more than the pub, or hotel, which serves beer in a room for men, and women have different drinks in another room. A few times I went to a bigger city called Melbourne, but Melbourne wasn't any more interesting than Shepparton."

"This is very different to life in Europe."

Paul looked deep into Corinna's eyes. "My family's Italian and this is part of the reason why I came to Europe. My aunt Bianca told me a lot about Italy and she taught me to dance. Sometimes there were dances in Australia."

The waiter brought their meals where Paul's meatballs with potatoes were both filling and quite flavoursome. Tasty meals were another difference from Australia, with boring chops, sausages or steak, always accompanied by mashed potatoes. In the background the cabaret started with a master of ceremonies spruiking the crowd in German and getting a warm response. The acts followed over the next few hours, from jugglers and acrobats to a comedy routine which caused much laughter, and even with Corinna, but the comedian didn't interest Paul. A woman singer with a husky but attractive voice followed, and she stayed for a second, upbeat song accompanied by a chorus line of young women in tight blouses and tiny dresses. Even skimpier was a dancing routine which followed, for it consisted of seven women wearing nothing but brief shorts and high heels. During the dance Corinna told Paul there was some Berliner luft in that cabaret. More Berliner luft followed in the form of a song by a bare-breasted singer who wore a long, plain skirt split to her waist and clearly nothing underneath. She sat on a bed on the stage, and later lay down while singing her languid song beneath a sign which spelt the word 'Kokain'. Paul knew what the song was about although he would have gained more if he understood the language.

The final act was all performers accompanied by the chorus line now topless in their tiny skirts. The symmetry of their dance steps was quite amazing and much more colourful than seeing similar on film, although never near-naked. The audience took to their feet for applause at the end while performers took bows three times. Paul felt it was a pity the show was over and they had to join the throng filing out of the hall.

"I hope you enjoyed the show," Corinna said.

"I did very much," Paul replied. "And thank you for accompanying me."

She took his arm. "There was a little Berliner luft for the young man from Australia."

"It does no harm," Paul replied, and that was true. "I wish they had shows like that in Australia."

"They only have pubs, movies and dances."

"That's right. Do you like dancing Corinna?"

She paused. "Yes, I do," she eventually said.

"Do you have plans for tomorrow night?"

Again she paused. "No I do not. I know a lovely dance club. I can meet you at eight at your hotel again."

"I hope this isn't any trouble."

She squeezed his arm. "Of course not my young man from Australia."

* * *

Paul lay in his bed but couldn't sleep. He had one thing on his mind where it seemed Berliner luft was affecting him. Maybe it was the near-naked women at the cabaret. Maybe it was cool Corinna who was beautiful but also unobtainable, at least in one week. More likely it was the length of time since London. Although that hadn't been love or even friendship, it was something he would never forget. But it had been a long time. He rolled on his side and thought about the streets and what was available. He sighed and hoped that sleep would come.

Chapter Five

Corinna was on time as always, and as always she was beautifully dressed – this time in a long, white dress and a matching white hat with a dark brim, worn angled just so. In a way she was rather stunning and made Paul feel self conscious that all he could do was wear his dark blue suit, white shirt and a blue tie. It was made to measure but not really evening attire.

"Shall we go?" Corinna asked.

"Of course."

Paul took her arm, they joined the crowds and passed street prostitutes, some of whom were rather young. More bizarrely, Paul thought he saw women and teenaged girls working together as pairs. Paul thought of mother and daughter but dismissed the idea. Such a thing wasn't possible. A car pulled up and one of the pairs of woman and girl went to the driver's window.

"We are going to the Resi," Corinna said, breaking into Paul's thoughts on incestuous debauchery. She squeezed his arm and Paul got a shock. "You will be amazed, my young man from Australia."

That pricked Paul's interest.

"We will catch a tram here," Corinna said.

The brown tram rattled to a stop where Corinna forced herself into the crush, for it was busier at night than in the day. Paul pushed and shoved and just managed to get a handhold. As was the case sometimes in Melbourne, the conductor had no hope. It was a free but uncomfortable ride for several blocks until they disembarked. They took a short walk to a large building from a past age with bright, neon signs proclaiming that it was 'The

Residenz-Casino'. They followed the crowd up several steps and into a wide entrance before entering the massive, dining and dancing hall. And massive it was, with a hundred or more tables surrounding a dance floor big enough for several hundred or more.

The tables were on different levels while some tables for five or six were surrounded by small partitions. What surprised Paul were telephones on each table and also around the room. Corinna found their table, 74, which was shared with a middle-aged couple. Paul contemplated language difficulties while 'guten abends' or 'good evenings' were exchanged.

Their company for the evening were Herr and Frau Lindt who didn't speak English, French or Italian. But Paul wasn't there for casual conversations; instead to eat, drink and dance.

"Would you like a drink, Corinna?" Paul asked after noticing where the bar was. Like everything else at the Resi, the bar on the far side of the room was massive.

"Ein, sorry, a glass of white wine," she replied.

"I can get your drink."

"Ein glas weisswein bitte is what you should ask for. What do you want?"

"I'm part-Italian so it has to be red wine."

"Ein glas weisswein und ein glas rotwein bitte."

"Ein glas weisswein und ein glas rotwein bitte," Paul repeated; pleased he was learning more German. "I'm good at this!" he exclaimed before heading to the bar. He returned with two glasses and realised they had privacy, despite being cheek-by-jowl with another couple. He sat and sipped his wine which was reasonable, and then he contemplated the phone again. "Corinna," he asked. "What's the phone for?"

"Well, if you see someone who takes your interest, you can ring his or her table to ask for a dance." She turned in her chair slightly. "See that tube there?"

It was in brass and fashioned like a snake's head. "Yes."

"You can go to a gift station and buy a present, and then send the present in the pneumatic tube to your fancy!"

Paul leaned closer to Corinna. "In Shepparton we had a barn with a band which played guitars, banjos, fiddles and whatever else they could get their hands on. Woman stood around the wall where you asked the girl who took your fancy for a dance. The girls who were left without a dance were called wallflowers. Most Australian men drank too much beer which meant more dances for me!"

"Do any women here take your fancy?"

Paul looked around the room with pretend studious intent until his eyes fell on his lovely companion. "Frauline Engel, would you like to accompany me to the dance floor, bitte?"

"Ya, danke."

Paul took Corinna's hand and placed one hand on the small of her back to guide her, but for more than that. It was even nicer to hold her for a modern waltz and for a foxtrot.

"This is good," Paul said. "Danke."

"It is my pleasure. I am enjoying this as much as you."

"I'll have fond memories of my week in Berlin."

"What are you reporting on?"

"I'm covering the motor race at Avusring. I cover many major races, and after Berlin is the Nürburgring in the Eifel Mountains. Would you like to go to Avus?"

"I don't like big crowds."

"How about the Nürburgring?"

"The Eifel Mountains are lovely, so thank you or danke for the invitation."

"This is my pleasure."

After three dances, including applause for the orchestra at the end of each song, Paul and Corinna returned to the table, where Corinna bought more drinks and then she showed the way to the buffet. That was new for Paul: dishes of food kept warm and always available. While Paul ate he contemplated the phone, and he would have without hesitation, but for the language problems. He contemplated that phone again.

"You should do it," Corinna said.

"Do what?" Paul asked.

"Who takes your fancy?"

Paul looked around the room and spotted a lovely, dark-haired woman who really took his fancy. Older than Corinna even. "Table fifty-seven," he said.

"Go on, ring her. It's just a dance."

Paul dialled 57 and saw her pick up the phone. "Guten abend, I'm table seventy-four and do you speak English?"

"Nien," she said.

"Parla Italiano?"

"Nein."

"Est-ce que vous parlez le Française, peut-etre?"

"Ah, oui."

"Bon." Paul smiled because he could say anything and Corinna wouldn't understand it. "Vous êtes trèz belle et j'aime bien danser avec vous."

"Merci, et j'aime bien danser avec vous aussi."

"Ji vais en ce moment." Paul hung up.

"What happened?" Corinna asked, looking really confused.

"I have a dance," Paul said. "You should ask someone."

"I will, but I can't ask like that."

"En Française?"

She shook her head. "Nein."

"I won't be long."

Paul guided his dark-haired beauty to the dance floor where they enjoyed two slow waltzes together. They conversed but Paul kept away from his Australian past because it confused people. For two dances he was Paolo and Italian and she was Brigitte from Berlin. At the end he bowed and offered 'merci beaucoup et au revoir' and received the same in reply.

He returned to Herr and Frau Lindt while Corinna returned after a dance with someone who took her fancy, and she sat all flushed and finished the last of her wine.

Paul looked around. "I could stay in this place forever."

"It is good."

"I'm getting to like Berlin." He got up close to Corinna. "Frauline Engel, would you like another dance?"

"Danke."

They danced a foxtrot where Corinna felt truly delightful in his arms. Paul wanted more, much more, but didn't know what to say, and then he did. "Je t'aime," he murmured.

"Pardon?"

"I love you."

"Ich liebe dich."

"Do you?"

"Tonight I do."

Paul's heart beat fast. "We should go,' he said.

"Yes we should."

He took her hand and led her to the street. All the way on the tram he held her tight, tighter than on the dance floor and tighter than necessary in the crush. They kissed in reception and staggered up the narrow stairs arm-in-arm. He loved her that night and the next day would take care of itself.

* * *

Paul woke in bed naked with his arm draped around Corinna, also naked. She was asleep and he didn't want to disturb her, which wasn't hard given his single room actually had a double bed. He moved slightly and she murmured before stretching.

"Good morning," Paul said while gazing at her lovely face.

"Good morning," Corinna replied.

"Je t'aime."

"Do you?"

Paul thought about that. "Darling Corinna, we have grown together these past two days, and in time maybe I could love you."

"But we don't have time."

"We have a week here and more time in the Eifel Mountains."

"And then...?"

Paul wouldn't mislead her; not then and not ever. "I'm a motor sports journalist where most motor races are in France and Italy and I speak French and Italian. I don't have a home but I will find a place to live, and it will be somewhere else."

Corinna looked deep into Paul's eyes and she had the most beautiful, deep blue eyes. "One evening my ex-husband took me to the Resi where I saw the telephones, and like you I was curious. So I rang someone and we talked, and then we danced for a while. When I got back my ex-husband dragged me outside. The bruises healed soon enough but scars stayed with me for longer. Things hadn't been going well between us and that was the end of it for me."

"I'm sorry to hear about this," Paul said while understanding Corinna's coolness and maybe her transformation, although Paul felt she would always be measured, although in an attractive way.

"Thank you young man from Australia for showing me the good side of men again, and I know if I spent more time with you I could fall in love with you, which is why we must part."

Paul didn't understand that. If they got on well together, which they did, then why should they part?

"My heart was broken that night, and I'm not ready to have my heart broken when you leave."

Paul understood. "I really enjoyed our time together and I know I will remember you for a long time, and I will remember last night for always."

Corinna grabbed his face and kissed him hard. "You are a wonderful young man."

Corinna slid out of bed while Paul admired her – tall, fair, slim and delightfully feminine. He rolled on his side and propped his head with his hand while Corinna gathered clothes strewn all around the room. "What are your plans now, Frauline Engel?"

She turned to face him. "It is time for me to find a good man."

"I will be jealous of him."

She smiled brightly. "You do say the most wonderful things."

Paul sat up. "I know what to do," he said excitedly. "When you find your man who I will be eternally jealous of, you must take him to the Resi. And when you're there you must ring someone who takes your fancy and have at least two dances with that man, or maybe more."

Corinna laughed brightly. "This is a good idea. Is it signore?"

Paul nodded.

"Signore Bassi, when you find a place to live and a wonderful woman to share your life with, I will be eternally jealous of her!"

When Corinna said that Paul wondered if he could make Berlin his home. It seemed so pointless to part when they had wonderful rapport. Corinna dressed while Paul sat cross-legged and watched her. When she finished she bent down and kissed his lips. "Goodbye Paul Bassi and good luck for your future."

"Goodbye Corinna Engel, and good luck for your future too."

She left the room. Paul would have liked to spend more time with Corinna, the rest of the week and the Eifel Mountains too, but two great days and one wonderful night was more than he expected. Or maybe it was the Berliner luft. Either way it had been – wonderful.

* * *

After a spectacularly close preliminary race for 1,500cc supercharged Voiturettes, dominated by privately-entered Bugatti Type 51s, the main Formula Libre race on the high-speed Avus circuit was going to be a close-fought affair between the four special words Bugattis with five litre engines for Achille Varzi, Stanislas Czaykowski, Kaye Don and Williams. Ferrari's entry of Alfa Romeo Monzas for Tazio Nuvolari and Baconin Borzacchini was likely to be overshadowed by Bugatti, while an interesting outlier was Manfred von Brauchitsch in a works-entered Mercedes-Benz SSKL sports car with a modified seven litre engine and special bodywork. And so it proved to be with Varzi content to let Czaykowski lead in the early stages of the race, probably to preserve his tyres, before closing to pass Czaykowski to win Europe's fastest ever motor race by a slim margin from his team mate, with the rest of the field lapped. The Mercedes-Benz suffered multiple tyre failures and never was in contention while the Alfa Romeos were too slow. However, the high-speed battle between Varzi and Czaykowski, who drove a great race, had everyone on their toes.

Chapter Six

The Eifel Mountains were unlike anything Paul had seen before: towering, forbidding; covered with lush pine forests and with an eerie ruined castle up high, looking down on everything below. It was the most unlikely place to build a motor racing circuit, and yet in a few short years the Nürburgring had become the ultimate test of both man and machine. A lap that swooped, climbed and curled through desolate countryside for 23 kilometres, with 88 left hand bends and 84 right hand bends. Paul wondered how drivers were able to remember each curve of each lap, not to mention dealing with the notorious Eifel weather. Rain and fog were common, even in summer.

Facilities near the circuit were surprisingly rural while the Ringhaus Hotel was truly rustic. A quaint hotel in white stucco with extensions leading off in different directions all higgledy-piggledy, two-storeys with an extra level of rooms set into a high-pitched roof. If it was rural, rustic and friendly like his hometown it would have been a pleasant break after the hustle of Berlin, but by then Paul realised Germans weren't warm when dealing with customers. Officious and to the point was a better description. Some Germans spoke English, more spoke French and many spoke neither language.

The Eifelrennen attracted a moderately healthy field of 16 Formula Libre cars, including the Ferrari team with Tazio Nuvolari, Louis Chiron, Piero Taruffi and Eugenio Siena, and a factory Maserati for Luigi Fagioli. Unfortunately the Bugatti team were absent after their exciting race at Avus, but their five litre cars would have been unsuitable for the Nürburgring. Run concurrently was the Voiturette Eifelrennen with a small field of five, and an 800cc race for 12 laps with only two entrants. Maybe 23 cars were enough for long laps of the Nürburgring. Maybe.

Paul paid the taxi driver and grabbed his clipboard and hat from the back seat. Rugged up with pullover and a coat despite it being late May, Paul looked up at cloudy skies before setting off to discover what was what.

The start and finish straight was massively wide, running south and downhill to a broad, semi-circular curve that brought the cars uphill to the north before curving left and snaking over hills and valleys to disappear into the distance. On one side of the straight was a huge timber grandstand. Opposite, behind a broad, concrete apron, were the pits with open viewing areas on top. The paddock was on the grandstand side of the circuit while an underpass led to the pit apron opposite, while just past the northern left curve was a link road to form a short, warm-up circuit.

Paul had his pass inspected by a uniformed policeman before being allowed into the paddock which had lock-up garages. Not much was happening except for two Alfa Romeo Monzas, one in red with white stripes and the other in white with red stripes, being tended by three men with a young woman looking on. Paul went to the foursome: two men in driving overalls, a grease-stained mechanic and the woman.

"Hello," Paul said. "My name is Paul Bassi and do you speak English?"

"Nein," the taller of the men said.

Paul sighed. "Est-ce que vous parlez le Française, peut-etre?"

"Ah, oui."

"My name's Paul Bassi and I'm a journalist from Australia." Paul said in French.

"My name's Paul Pietsch, he's Charly Jellen, our mechanic is Sigfried Lang and this is Ilse Hubitsch," Paul Pietsch said; glancing at the young woman. A beautiful young woman: tall and slim with delicate features, a perfect complexion and platinum blonde hair. Marlene Dietrich at the Nürburgring.

"Bonjour Monsieur Pietsch, Monsieur Jellen, Monsieur Lang and Mademoiselle Hubitsch."

"Charly doesn't speak French," Ilse Hubitsch said while moving closer and holding Charly Jellen's hand. "He's originally Polish."

"We pooled resources to run our cars," Paul Pietsch said.

"And I'm team manager, lap scorer and number one fan!" Ilse Hubitsch said enthusiastically. "I like motor racing."

Paul was surprised. It wasn't unusual for racing drivers to attract beautiful girlfriends, but it was unusual for beautiful girlfriends to be interested in the actual racing. More luck Charly.

"What do you think of your chances this weekend?" Paul asked.

"Ferrari is here and that will make it hard," Ilse Hubitsch said. "We'll be happy if we score a placing in the top four or five. One driver to look out is Manfred von Brauchitsch in the Mercedes SSKL."

Paul was surprised; a massive Mercedes sports car seemed unlikely to do well on the twisting, winding Nürburgring. "Are you sure, Mademoiselle?"

"The SSKL has good acceleration out of slow corners and von Brauchitsch is a true talent."

Paul visited paddocks to pick up snippets of information, and for once he heard something useful. "I will look out for the Mercedes and I'm sure it will be spectacular. And good luck Monsieur Pietsch and Mademoiselle Hubitsch, and tell Monsieur Jellen good luck from me."

"Au revoir Monsieur Bassi," the beautiful and surprising Ilse Hubitsch said as a farewell.

Paul then went to the grandstand to wait for practice, and soon after heard the sounds of racing cars warming up in the paddock before being driven to the pits. There was a scurry of activity while plugs were changed. One by one drivers took to the circuit, around the south curve and then the left hander, over crests and around more curves before disappearing out of sight. With near to eleven minutes per lap it was impossible to time more than two cars at once, but it seemed Nuvolari was fastest and von Brauchitsch was several seconds slower, which would add up to a fair margin over fifteen laps.

The Voiturette class was even less inspiring, with one Delage for English driver Francis Howe and the rest being small-engined Bugattis. Howe did a lap in 11 minutes and 20 seconds but Paul didn't have a chance to time any of the other class runners. Because it would be of interest to his English readers, Paul intended to use Howe's time in his article on practice.

Day two of practice was equally uninspiring while Paul wondered why he was there in the cold when he could have been in the dining room of the hotel by the fire, albeit alone. After he noted more times and observations he returned to his room, turned up the heater and typed his article before heading out to get it telegraphed.

Sunday was cool with light rain when racing at the Nürburgring opened for motorcycles. Later in the morning, Paul made his way to the journalist's area of the grandstand and greeted his compatriots. By that stage the rain had stopped, the track was slowly drying, the grandstand was full to capacity and there were more spectators visible around the circuit. After lunch, cars were warmed up on the loop behind the pits before being readied on the grid. Although the different classes were supposed to have staggered starts, they all lined up on the grid from Formula Libra at the front to the smallest at the rear. Then everything stopped and Paul didn't know why until a hundred or more uniformed Nazis gathered into a formation in front of the grandstand, where they held a memorial or service which was broadcast to the crowd over loudspeakers. Those Nazis eventually marched to grandstand seats cordoned off from the rest of the spectators.

An almighty great cannon was used to signal the start the race, very Germanic, where Chiron tore into the lead from Nuvolari and the Mercedes of von Brauchitsch. A timing tower and the public address system informed spectators in the packed grandstand of race placings telephoned from several timing points on the lap. After an age, Chiron flashed past at the end of the first lap followed by Nuvolari and von Brauchitsch, much to Paul's surprise. Ilse Hubitsch's tip was spot-on. Nuvolari took the lead on lap two and gradually extended it for three long hours. Chiron lost time at the pits with a leaking fuel tank, Fagioli dropped out and Charly Jellen pulled into the pits to retire on lap 13. Nuvolari ran out a strong victor with von Brauchitsch almost six minutes, or more than half a lap behind in second, Taruffi was three minutes further behind in third with Chiron a much-delayed fourth. Paul Pietsch managed a distant sixth. By keeping track of the positions through the timing tower, Paul was able to type his articles as the race dragged on. Fortunately the race for the 1500cc class was close, where Howe won by the smallest of margins from German driver Ernst Burggaller in a Bugatti. That was something of interest for Paul's English readers. Paul finished his articles while the packed grandstands emptied, and then he headed off to get them telegraphed. German weather ended up being lousy and Paul couldn't wait to leave for France. He had a race at Nîmes the next weekend, and then the original Grand Prix, the Automobile Club of France, at Montlhéry near Paris.

Chapter Seven

Achille smoked a cigarette and contemplated the red Maserati – the 8CM monoposto model with a three litre engine. To date it hadn't achieved much but that was before Maserati got Tazio. He broke his contract with Ferrari after Reims, and a week later in Belgium at Spa-Francorchamps he was with his new team.

"Buongiorno Achille," Enzo Ferrari said.

Achille turned around. "Buongiorno signore Ferrari," Achille replied.

"You'll have trouble winning now."

Achille shrugged his shoulders. There was no point swapping to Ferrari for 1934; the Alfa Romeo Monza was no faster than his Bugatti, and Bugatti had a larger engine under development for later in the season.

"If I can get a Tipo B for you...," Enzo Ferrari said.

"I'm not a man to break a contract."

"I know this, Achille, which is why I'm talking with you."

"If you can wait until next year."

"I can wait until next year for the best driver."

"But only if you get a Tipo B."

Ferrari rubbed the back of his neck. "We have done well enough with the Monza, but if Maserati start winning then Alfa Romeo might look at things differently."

Achille nodded slowly. The Alfa Romeo Tipo Bs, the fastest racing cars of all, were languishing unused since the Alfa Corse factory team withdrew from racing the previous year. But if the Tipo Bs were released to Scuderia Ferrari then that would enable Ferrari-entered Alfa Romeos to beat Maserati.

"I'll be talking with you soon enough," Enzo Ferrari said before he wandered off.

Achille contemplated the red Maserati again. In practice he hadn't been able to get closer than 2.8 seconds, which was a lifetime slower. Even worse that Spa was one of the fastest circuits and he did better on faster circuits. He would be lucky to finish three minutes behind. He lit another cigarette and waited for the three minute board.

* * *

Paul watched Achille Varzi talking with Enzo Ferrari and guessed what that was about, but there was little point in Varzi driving a Ferrari-entered Alfa Romeo Monza. Paul doubted that Varzi would do that; he didn't have the manic desire to lead every lap of every race like his countryman. The starter held the three minute board as Paul jotted the date and time in his notebook: the ninth of July at one in the afternoon, Belgian time. Paul needed somewhere to live; a home between visits to hotels. Somewhere in France made sense. For the previous several weeks he travelled north and south through and out of France: Nîmes, won by Tazio Nuvolari in an Alfa Romeo Monza, Montlhéry near Paris, won by veteran Giuseppe Campari in his privately-entered Maserati, Montjuic at Barcelona in northern Spain, a race of attrition won by Juan Zenelli in a privately-entered Alfa Romeo Monza, Reims won by Philippe Etancelin in his Alfa Romeo Monza, and now Spa in Belgium. But for some reason Paul didn't feel at home in France, and then there was the travel distance to races further afield such as Sicily or North Africa. France wasn't what Paul was after.

* * *

Achille got out of his Lancia and looked around the near-deserted Circuito di Montenero. He saw a number of red cars where one was slimmer and sleeker than the others. The Alfa Romeo Tipo B, which won everything in the short time that it raced. Achille grabbed his bag and went to the Ferrari pits.

"Buongiorno signore Ferrari," Achille said.

"Buongiorno Achille," Enzo Ferrari replied.

"You were right, as always.

"Spa, the Coppa Ciano, Nice...."

Achille nodded. For the past month Nuvolari won everything with ease, and as Enzo Ferrari predicted, Alfa Romeo gave the unused Tipo Bs to Scuderia Ferrari. Ferrari already had Luigi Fagioli, they signed Giuseppe Campari, and one of those two would win on Sunday. But true to Ferrari's word Achille had a test drive, and if he set a faster time than Fagioli or Campari he would be racing it in 1934. It was all down to one, fast lap.

Achille went inside the Ferrari pits to change while the mechanics warmed the Alfa. Achille emerged in clean, white overalls, and he smoked a cigarette while waiting for the mechanics to shut the engine down and change plugs. He lit another cigarette before getting into the red Alfa and checking it for reach and comfort. Hands to the wheel and feet to the pedals were all good, so he switched the magneto and the mechanic started the engine. Into first with the stubby lever between his legs and out onto a long, 25.5 kilometre lap. He thought one lap at eight-tenths to get a feel for the car and then two fast laps would do it. At the Coppa Ciano on the same circuit two weeks previously Nuvolari did 13 minutes 27 point something during the race in the wet, but Achille didn't know Nuvolari's dry lap time.

The car felt good and having a single, central seat made a big difference. Plenty of power, good throttle response, decent handling and good traction although not quite as nimble as the Bugatti. No car was as nimble as a Bugatti, but the Alfa had noticeably more power. Achille ended a long lap and flashed past the pits at top speed and gave the car all. It responded better when driven harder, which was unusual but comforting. And hard he drove it all the way around, and hard again for a second lap. He crossed the finish line for a third time, eased off and braked before turning the car and returning to the Ferrari pits. He shut the engine down and the car smelled of hot metal, hot oil and burning brakes. Achille got out, lit a cigarette and went to the mechanic with a clipboard. Hand-timed at 10 minutes 27 and 10 minutes 27. Achille looked into the pits and spotted Enzo Ferrari in the semi-darkness.

"Am I fast enough?" Achille asked.

"You know you are," Enzo Ferrari said,

"Do you want me?"

"That depends."

"Two-hundred thousand lira plus half of prize money."

"What!" Ferrari bellowed. "Do you take me for a fool?"

"Two-hundred thousand lira."

"One-hundred thousand lira."

"Two-hundred."

"You will drive me out of business!"

Achille sighed; it was the same game every time. "If Fagioli and Campari can get within five seconds of my time, you can have me for one-hundred. But they can't and you know it."

"One-hundred and twenty-five"

"One-hundred and seventy-five."

"One-hundred and twenty-five, and I will have to cut my own wages."

Ferrari always regarded drivers with disdain, but he had the fastest car. There might have been more reasons for Nuvolari leaving Scuderia Ferrari other than the slow Monza. "One-hundred and fifty thousand lira, and half of prize money."

"Alright, one-hundred and fifty thousand lira, and half of prize money."

Achille nodded; it was what he wanted and more than he earned at Bugatti, while he had the fastest car for 1934. All in all it was a good morning's work.

Chapter Eight

Milano Centrale Railway Station was magnificent. Paul walked from the dark, smoky and sooty train hall to the arrivals area; open and airy in sandstone with a towering glass-roofed ceiling, and offices, the luggage hall and a large cafe set into each side. The open space echoed with hundreds of conversations in Italian, of course. Paul went outside on a lovely, autumn day with the sun shining brightly from a cloudless sky, and with a gentle breeze to temper the heat. He turned to look at the massive facade of Centrale which was a combination of architectural styles from ancient Rome to the latest, modern look. Paul crossed a large plaza with different colours of porcelain and marble set into patterns. He went to the first taxi in the line just off Piazza Duca D'Aosta, where the smartly uniformed driver emerged from his black Fiat saloon to help with Paul's suitcase.

"Buongiorno signore," Paul said. "I want to go to Alfa Romeo at Via Arona, 25," he continued in Italian.

The driver opened the rear door and Paul climbed in. The driver checked the road was clear before they headed into Wednesday afternoon traffic. The big city in northern Italy was busy, bustling and purposeful, and also attractive to the eye with many, delightful sandstone buildings. For some reason Milano felt like home although he'd been there only for a few moments. They arrived at a modern building with a glazed street frontage, and with lovely cars clearly visible inside. Paul paid the driver the meter plus a small tip, received 'grazie' in reply and then Paul took his suitcase into the dealership.

The showroom had four Alfa Romeo saloons, while the only sign of life were two men in dark suits at two tables in the far corner. Paul waited for attention, because buying a new car was quite different to most purchases in life. One of the gentleman; mid-thirties, quite tall, and immaculately dressed in a dark blue double-breasted suit came to Paul.

"Buongiorno signore," the salesman said.

"Buongiorno signore," Paul replied. "My name's Paolo Bassi and I received a letter from Alfa Romeo." Paul reached into the inside pocket of his jacket, extracted the envelope and handed it across. He watched the salesman read it with no obvious signs of surprise. The salesman nodded and handed the letter back.

"Signore Bassi, my name's Angelo Gianni and we have been expecting you. Your car is prepared and registered, but first you must sign some papers. If you would like to come to my desk."

Paul followed signore Gianni to one of the desks and took a seat. It took about ten minutes to sign the registration papers, insurance papers and get a receipt for the car. Paul handed the last paper across and signore Gianni gave Paul his copies of registration and insurance, and two keys on a ring which Paul slipped into his pocket.

"You are a journalist, signore Bassi?" signore Gianni asked.

"I report on motor sports." Paul was curious. "Has anything like this happened before?"

"Yes a few: singers, actors, writers and dignitaries. No journalists though. Alfa Romeo doesn't have the facilities to prepare and register cars as easily as we can, so people come here rather than to the factory."

"I understand," Paul said. "What's the arrangement with this car."

"The car is yours for as long as you wish it to be. And when you are finished with the car you must return it here."

Paul was shocked and eternally grateful. It would make getting around so much easier.

"The car has a full tank of petrol, there is a map book of Milano under the driver's seat, and now I will take you out the back."

Paul followed signore Gianni through a door and along a short corridor lined with timber doors to a door at the end. They emerged into a cramped yard containing a red Alfa Romeo 6C1750 Gran Sport Zagato Spyder. Paul knew the basics of the car: it had a 6-cylinder twin overhead camshaft engine designed by Vittorio Jano, which formed the basis of later 8-cylinder engines that had won many Gran Premio and endurance sports car races over the past four years. The chassis, steering and suspension were all competition-based, and the supercharged version of the 6C Gran Sport had been raced.

"The first service is one thousand and five hundred kilometres," signore Gianni said. "And then every five-thousand kilometres after this. You must check oil, water, brake fluid and tyre pressures regularly, say every week, and if you do this and service this car regularly it will run reliably for many years. The choke is there," signore Gianni said, pointing to a black knob. "Use full choke on a cold start and then push it in until the engine runs smoothly, and all the way in after a few minutes of normal driving. Drive gently until the oil temperature rises to about sixty degrees, and then you're right to drive normally. Water should stay at seventy and no more.

That's all and you have the keys and documents, so this car is yours now."

Paul opened the rather small boot, but large enough for his compact suitcase. He climbed into the driver's seat and immediately noticed he was on the wrong side of the car with the gear lever to his right. He pulled the choke, put the key in and turned, and pressed the button to start the engine where the raspy exhaust echoed in the small yard surrounded by tall brick buildings. Paul put his hat on the passenger's seat, selected first and eased out of the yard and into the lane. Something other than a narrow lane could have been easier for his first drive sitting on the wrong side of a car. He reached the end of the lane and stopped because he'd forgotten to check where he was going. Paul reached under the seat, pulled out the map book and went to the index. He found Via Rovello, turned to the page and traced all of the left and right turns. With the map book on the passenger's seat, Paul headed into Milano's mid-afternoon traffic.

Paul concentrated on traffic and where he was going, and he was surprised that driving from the left and changing gear with his right hand wasn't difficult at all. In fact it came naturally although he concentrated when turning at intersections. When stopped at traffic lights, Paul liked what he saw. Milano was a lovely city in the European style of high-rise apartments with shops and business close by, rather than the bleak desolation of sprawling suburbs that passed for cities in Australia. There were shops for everything and many cafes – the city was affluent and had a genuine cafe culture. Trees on broad boulevards had leaves turning to golden brown, which added to the beauty because autumn was the best time of the year. And then it struck Paul; in Milano he was home. He was Italian with his descent from Lombardy, and now he was home in the largest city in Lombardy.

Paul kept up with the traffic to reach the city centre, and after briefly getting lost he found Hotel Giulio Cesare on Via Rovello. It was an unpretentious and rather narrow street lined with tall apartment blocks and small business, while the hotel was a modern, red brick building overlaid with fake, Roman-style columns in concrete. Paul parked his car in a nearby laneway, grabbed his suitcase and went to check-in. He was staying for three weeks and struck a special deal. He had a few things to do and some races to report on, and in general was looking forward to staying in one place for a while.

* * *

Paul left the outskirts of Milano to speed along a sparsely trafficked road lined by small farms, guided by the map that reception at the hotel obtained. He passed paddocks fenced by ancient stone walls, and whitewashed farm houses and other buildings dotted at regular intervals. Crops of wheat rustled in a light breeze; there were orchards of fruit trees near many of the farm buildings and grape vines as well. Orchards and fruit trees would normally have reminded Paul of home; his family owned a farm on which they grew peaches, pears and oranges, but the undulating landscape of northern Italy was very different to the flat, desolation of the Goulburn Valley in Australia.

Paul drove through the small town of Calcio which had modern apartment blocks, mostly painted white, lining broad streets. People gathered at a small marketplace in the midst of several, small shops. Older men in well-worn dark suits and cloth caps, older women dressed in black with black shawls, younger men were in shirtsleeves, younger women wore bright clothes and children ran about the same as the world over. After about an hour's driving, Paul reached Chiari, a medium-sized town of small shops and apartment buildings. Paul drove along that broad street until he reached several shops shaded by awnings, where one had men sitting outside drinking coffee while playing chequers and smoking cigarettes.

Paul parked his Alfa, crossed the road, acknowledged those at the alfresco dining area, and went into a darkened cafe smelling of fresh coffee.

"Buongiorno signora," he said to a young woman old enough to be married. "Cerco Via Vittorio Venetto per favore.

"Ah si. Si va al terzo as sinistra."

"Grazie signora."

Paul got into his car and drove the last few hundred metres to his destination; number twelve. He got out and knocked on the heavy, timber door with massive, iron hinges and handles. Thick walls muffled any activity resulting from an unexpected visitor, until the door squeaked open.

The middle aged man frowned for a moment and then his face changed. "Signore Paolo Bassi?" he asked.

"Si," Paul said; not understanding how he knew.

"You look a lot like your father and your uncle when they were younger," he said in Italian. "Come in."

Paul followed signore Ruggeri into his cosy home. A stairway on the right, a corridor ahead, a sitting room to the left with bulky, grey velvet-covered sofas and armchairs, and a fireplace with a thick, heavy mantel above holding many souvenirs acquired during years of travel.

"I came to thank you for everything you have done," Paul said.

"Ah, it was nothing."

"No, it was everything. Lending me money for the steamship ticket, the advice you gave Uncle Antonio who gave those letters to me. I wouldn't be here without your help."

"Take a seat...."

"Paul," Paul said.

"And I'm Mario. Take a seat."

Paul sat on the sofa and Mario sat in one of the large chairs. Just then a woman entered the room and Paul stood, as did Mario. "Paul Bassi, this is my wife Helena."

Paul greeted Helena.

"You're the young man who I have heard so much about," she said.

"I came here to thank you both."

"There's no need to do this. Paul, are you staying for lunch?"

"If it's no trouble."

"It's no trouble. Mario, I'll go to the shops."

She left and the two men sat.

"I can't thank you enough for the loan for the steamship ticket," Paul said.

Mario smiled with lines around his eyes making his face brighter. "Your uncle Antonio and I were car crazy for as long as I can remember. Your father was more serious and practical, so he was the one who suggested they look beyond Lombardy for a life for their children to come, even though he wasn't yet married. But Antonio was the car enthusiast, so he and I wrote to each other about cars, and he knew I was travelling to races to report on them. Then he discovered there was a race in Australia and he took you all; his children and his nephews there. From there you know what happened."

"I liked that race and I wanted to see more, but there are few races in Australia and they're only amateurs racing whatever they can get their hands on. So Uncle Antonio suggested that if I wanted to see more races I should go to Europe, and to earn enough to travel I could write about the races I saw."

"Antonio said you wrote well in school."

"Uncle Antonio gave me your letter suggesting I write to newspapers and motor journals in English-speaking nations, and contract to write articles about races. Now, here I am."

"How has it been?"

"It's been fantastic!" Paul looked at Mario. "I have seen so much and not just races, and I have met many of the drivers and some of their wives and girlfriends."

Mario looked startled. "You know the drivers?"

Paul nodded. "Achille Varzi, Tazio Nuvolari, Louis Chiron, Baconin Borzacchini and some others."

"Who's the best?"

"Achille Varzi."

"Not Nuvolari?"

"Tazio Nuvolari is fast and likeable. Varzi is different: he's thinks about race strategy and I believe he races without risk. Rather than take a chance and possibly make a mistake, he pressures his rivals from behind to take chances and possibly make mistakes. He's as fast as any, as long as his car has enough performance."

"Which the Bugatti doesn't have at the moment."

"Over the last few months Bugatti hasn't."

"Racing was different in my day."

Paul pondered that. "Racing might have been different but it's always the same."

Mario laughed. "That's true. I'm glad you came here Paul."

"I came to Milano after Marseilles to take a break before the Gran Premio d'Italia and the Gran Premio di Monza, and I'll stay until it's time to go to San Remo."

"Do you like Milano?"

"It's my home," he said softly.

"I understand. Now, what was I saying? Ah yes. You write in English, of course, and your articles are published in newspapers and journals. I thought there could be an opportunity to deal with more newspapers and journals for very little effort on your part. There are many English-speaking nations, so you might be able to get your articles published in New Zealand, South Africa, North and South Rhodesia and Kenya. These are wealthy countries with English-speaking populations who will be interested in European motor sport."

For sure they would all have newspapers and some would have motor journals. But how to contact them? And then it came to him. "I'll write to my contact at The Star in London and he might know about newspapers, and I'll write to my contact at Motor and Sport and he might know about journals." Paul wondered because he lived a transient lifestyle. "Do you mind if I ask them to write to me care of you here? I don't have a home at the moment, only hotels."

"No, this won't be a problem."

"Thank you Mario, and thank you for the advice. I'm sure this can work out, and then all I have to do is telegraph the same articles to more destinations."

"I would like to read what you have written but I don't understand English."

"I would like you to read what I have written too. English is my first language but I seldom use it, except for writing. I'm grateful my French has been good enough."

Paul heard the door in the background and Helena came into the room. "Mario, there's a sports car in the street," she said, smiling brightly.

Paul felt flushed and turned to face her. "It's mine on loan."

"What do you have?" Mario asked.

"An Alfa Romeo 6C 1750. When I was in Pescara for the Coppa Acerbo, a salesman from Alfa Romeo visited me at my hotel. They gave me the car without saying why, but I think it's to do with my articles in England."

"They want you to write about the car for publicity?"

"One free car to a journalist is nothing compared to what they spend on racing, but I'm not sure what I should write. I've only really driven it today and it's a lovely car, and the least I can write is that it's a genuinely lovely car to drive."

"The 6C is not so expensive by Alfa Romeo standards."

"It's a Gran Sport with a twin overhead camshaft engine," Paul said quietly. "Do you want to see it?"

Mario jumped to his feet. "Of course!"

They went outside where the red Alfa was surrounded by small boys, some on bicycles, and one of them asked Paul if it was his car. He said it was before opening the door for Mario to climb inside.

"Very nice," Mario said. "You can pretend you're Achille Varzi driving the Mille Miglia!"

"If it had a supercharger I could, but it's a lovely car regardless."

Mario got out and shut the door, and then he put his arm around Paul's shoulder. "Come with me, Paolo Bassi, and let's see what Helena's preparing for lunch."

Chapter Nine

Paul spent most of Friday writing letters to Motor and Sport, to his mother and father, to Uncle Antonio and to Uncle Lelio. He also wrote to Neville at The Star to ask for details on newspapers in various countries, and also if they could send copies of articles about the Italian economy over the past three years. After his journey to Germany, Paul was interested to find out what was really going on, while assuming that in a military-controlled state the local newspapers would be economical about what they printed. On Saturday he gave his grandparents the greatest fright because they had no idea, and Paul was disappointed that his father hadn't written and told them. Paul's grandparents were pleased to see their grandson and he spent the day with them, although it wasn't easy. They were from a very different place and time.

On Monday Paul bought a jacket with matching shirts and ties, and he also visited a few real estate agents to get a feel for rentals, availability and areas in the city where he might like to live. Later in the week he drove to Monza and walked around the park, peaceful and quiet on a cloudy and fresh day. On Friday night he went out to try his luck where Via Rovello was bustling. Renata Minozzi was at the bar of Caffè Letterario where they got to talking and not about cars or racing. Paul then wanted to dance, but she was weary after a day at work, so they left with a promise to meet at the same cafe the next night. On Saturday Paul told Renata more about what he was up to and she was genuinely interested. During his visits to Libya and Pescara, Paul knew soccer was the number one sport in Italy, as he expected, but he was surprised to find motor sport was almost as popular. However with Renata they didn't go further than a half-hearted promise to meet sometime the following week, where Paul knew the sign. But nothing ventured and nothing gained.

A parcel arrived at the hotel and Paul spent most of Friday digesting the stories Neville sent him. Benito Mussolini split with the Italian Socialist Party over the question of Italy remaining neutral during the First World War. After serving in the war, Mussolini established the Italian Fasci of Combat which promoted the idea of states always being ready for armed conflict, and all citizens in a state must be able to be mobilised for war or to support war. To achieve this, a totalitarian dictatorship was essential. The Italian Fasci of Combat attracted many unemployed war veterans, where Mussolini organised them into armed squads known as Black Shirts who terrorised their political opponents. The Italian Fasci of Combat was renamed a number of times before becoming the National Fascist Party of Italy. Following more than a year of conflict between fascists and socialists, in 1922 a march on Roma by Fascist Black Shirts led to the appointment of Mussolini as Prime Minister by King Victor Emmanuel III, who feared civil war. This led to one party rule where the overriding philosophy was Italy for Italians, and re-establishing Italy as a great European power. Benito Mussolini was known as Il Duce, the supreme ruler who could do no wrong. Then followed an upgraded war effort against Libya, and victory there in recent times. One area of concern to Paul was the systematic brainwashing of school students with the dogmas of the ruling party. The Great Depression hit Italian industry, as it hit industry all around the world, and that led to banks coming to the aid of businesses in trouble and the subsequent collapse of those banks. Banks were then nationalised which avoid the dreadful outcomes of Paul's homeland which saw millions lose their jobs, and millions lose every penny they owned when banks folded one after the other. In the end Italian industry was saved by the banks and the banks were saved by the government. Italy's big agricultural sector continued because everyone had to eat, which was Paul's family's saviour. Unemployment in Italy peaked at less than ten percent which was a better outcome than the dire poverty and despair prevalent in Australia, Britain and Germany. But even so, one party rule by force had many risks.

Although the grids for the Gran Premio d'Italia, and the Gran Premio di Monza held the same day, were drawn by ballot, Paul decided to attend the Saturday practice session to gain an appreciation of relative speeds of the competitors. But first he needed a coffee! On a pleasant, autumn Saturday, Paul headed towards Via Dante to see what offered. On his left was the almost hole in the wall Caffè Sforzesco, which looked unpretentious enough to serve a good brew. He went inside to a compact timber-panelled room with long, timber cabinet on the left, and behind that cabinet against the wall were shelves with bottles of wine. The barista was hard at work with his espresso machine, the cafe smelled of the lovely aroma of brewing coffee, and it buzzed with dozens of quiet and not so quiet conversations. Unfortunately every table was taken so Paul was just about to leave when he spotted someone. She wore a simple, dark blue dress with matching blue gloves, and a black velvet beret. Fair skin, big dark eyes and wavy, jet black hair. She was beautiful and at a table for two near the window. Paul approached and she looked up.

"Buongiorno signorina," Paul said. "Questo sedile è preso?"

"No," she said.

"Posso condividere il vostro tavolo per favore."

"Si."

Paul took a seat and a waiter in black and white with a chequered apron approached. Paul greeted the waiter and ordered a coffee.

The waiter left for the kitchen and Paul glanced across the table at the beautiful young woman who had a coffee of her own. "My name's Paul Bassi," he said in Italian.

"My name's Pia Donati," she said while reaching across the table. Paul lightly shook her hand. "You're not from here."

"From here?" Paul asked innocently.

Pia studied him. "You look like you're from here, but there's something that says you're not."

"I'm from Australia," he said and waited for her reaction.

"Austria?" she asked, looking surprised.

"No, I'm from Australia on the other side of the world."

"Ah. So what brings you to Milano?'

"The race at Monza."

She smiled brightly. "Men and their cars...."

Paul's coffee arrived along with a glass of water, as it should be. He sipped the espresso and then some water. "It's my job," Paul said. "I'm a sports correspondent for English and Australian newspapers."

Pia frowned. "That seems complicated."

Paul was surprised. "How so?" he asked.

"You write articles for English and Australian newspapers."

"I was raised in an English-speaking country, and I can speak Italian because of my family."

"I understand." She sipped her coffee. "Is this a good job?" she asked.

Paul nodded. "It is." Paul sipped more coffee while glancing at his companion. Pia was extraordinarily attractive; especially her mesmerising dark eyes and lovely figure. Paul wondered, but nothing ventured and nothing gained, and motor racing was a national sport of Italy. "Signorina Donati," he said. "Have you ever been to Monza?"

She shook her head. "No I haven't."

"Would you like to go, if you have the time?"

Pia tilted her head. "Today?"

"Today is practice so we can meet some of the drivers. We can see the cars trying for fast times, and you might find it interesting for a few hours."

Pia finished the last of her coffee. "Well, I planned shopping for clothes but this can wait." She looked into his eyes. "I have heard a lot about Monza so I would like to go there," she said firmly.

Paul was pleased. More than pleased. "I have a car near here," he said. He finished his coffee and stood to help signorina Donati with her chair. He left his money in the bowl on the counter and together they headed into busy Via Dante. It took only a few minutes to walk to the hotel where the Alfa Romeo waited in the lane. He opened the passenger door for Pia.

"Oh my!" she exclaimed. "You have your own racing car!"

Paul tried to stop grinning, unsuccessfully. "Alfa Romeo loaned this car to me," he said. "I think they want me to write about it."

"Will you?"

Paul opened his door and slid behind the wheel. "I'll thank Alfa Romeo for lending me a lovely car that's a pleasure to drive."

"It is a lovely car."

Paul started the engine where the raspy exhaust echoed between tall buildings. He selected first, they pulled out of the lane into Via Rovello for the short drive to the large park in nearby Monza, and one of the classic racing circuits of the world. Driving the same route as the previous week, but with a map book under his seat just in case. It was a pleasant drive on a Saturday morning.

"What's it like growing up in one country, and then driving across a city like Milano in another country far away?" Pia asked.

What a question! "It's like a dream come true," Paul said honestly. "Especially Milano. I've only been here a week and I love this city."

"You must do a lot of travelling."

"I do."

They reached the park where a uniformed policeman manned the boom gate. Paul pulled up, the policeman strolled to the car while Paul fished for his pass from the inside pocket of his jacket. He held it out and the policeman opened the gate. They entered the park which was too beautiful and peaceful for a racing circuit. Large and formal, with many tall trees shading lush, green grass, and with these lawns bisected by footpaths and the race circuit. Paul followed the access road to the car park at the end. Ahead were the pits, which was a long, timber building partitioned into spaces for each car for each team; with a roofed spectator area above for important people like sponsors and journalists. Hoardings displayed advertisements for fuel, oil, tyres, sparkplugs, wine and spirits, while many colourful pennants fluttered in the light breeze. Outside the pits were mostly red and a few blue cars glinting in the sunshine. The main straight was very broad and about three times the width of most circuits. The cars started on the western side of the straight and headed between trees to Curva Grande and the road circuit. The cars returned on the eastern side of the straight adjacent to the pits before taking to the banked oval which crossed the road circuit on a bridge. The oval then looped around the outside of the road circuit to bring the cars to the western side of the straight again. On the opposite side of the main straight were one large and six smaller roofed, timber grandstands with seating capacity for many thousands, set two metres high on brick bases so that spectators standing in the open area closer to the track wouldn't block the view of those seated behind. Paul clambered out of his car and grabbed his Akubra hat before opening the passenger door. Pia joined him and looked around.

"It's very quiet," she said.

"Practice is due to start soon," Paul said. "Let's find out what's up."

Paul led the way to a well-known driver walking towards the Maserati pits; dressed simply in brown trousers and a yellow pullover with his trademark turtle emblem.

"Buongiorno signore Nuvolari," Paul greeted.

"Buongiorno signore Bassi," Tazio Nuvolari replied. "You have a friend, I see," he said.

"Signorina Donati, this is signore Tazio Nuvolari."

Pia stood with her mouth open for a few moments before struggling to get out a quiet "Buongiorno signore Nuvolari."

He shook her gloved hand.

"Signore Nuvolari," Paul said. "What are your chances for tomorrow?"

"Ferrari has two of the Tipo Bs for Fagioli and Chiron. So it's going to be a close race with our three Maserati Monopostos and the two Alfas, but I think we can win." He turned to face Pia. "Signorina Donati, are you coming to the Gran Premio tomorrow?"

Pia actually looked down to Nuvolari because she was about five foot six, and taller again with two-inch heels, to his five foot three. "I hadn't thought about it. I could come."

"You must come. The race is five-hundred kilometres and anything could happen."

She looked at Paul. "Signore Bassi…?"

"You can come with me," Paul said.

"I will see the Gran Premio tomorrow."

Tazio Nuvolari grinned. "I will look out for the pretty signorina in the grandstands."

Pia went bright red. "Grazie," she said quietly.

"We must go," Paul said. "Good luck signore Nuvolari."

"Grazie."

Paul spotted a familiar figure in crisp, white overalls smoking near the doors to the Ferrari pits. Paul led Pia to where Louis Chiron butted his cigarette.

"Bonjour Monsieur Chiron," Paul said, switching to French. "This is my friend Mademoiselle Donati."

"Bonjour Monsieur Bassi et Mademoiselle Donati," Louis Chiron said before kissing Pia on each of her cheeks.

"You have an Alfa Romeo Tipo B?" Paul asked in French.

"And Fagioli has the other one," Louis Chiron said, grimacing.

"How is Monsieur Caracciola?"

He sighed deeply. "This is off the record."

"Of course."

"He's in a bad way. We don't think he can race again."

Paul was startled. "Whatever happens this weekend pales into insignificance."

"Well said."

A beautiful woman came from inside and Louis Chiron glanced towards her.

"Bonjour Madame," Paul said.

"Bonjour Monsieur," she replied. "Cheri," she said.

Louis Chiron glanced at his watch. "I must get ready."

"Of course. Good luck."

"Merci."

"We should get ready too," Paul said to Pia, switching to Italian. "It's better to be in the grandstand, opposite the start and finish line."

"I didn't understand your conversation, but that man was Louis Chiron," Pia said.

"Yes, and he's driving one of the fastest cars in the race, with Luigi Fagioli in another."

"He was unhappy with Luigi Fagioli; is he Calabrian?"

"He's Abruzzian."

Pia looked out of the corners of her eyes at him.

"My family comes from Lombardy," Paul said.

"What about Caracciola?" Pia asked. "I know that name."

"Rudi Caracciola had a bad crash in practice for Monaco earlier this year, and it's unlikely he'll race again."

"Oh, the poor man. Was that woman Louis Chiron's wife?"

"That was Louis Chiron's mistress, Baby Hoffman."

Pia stopped walking. "Mistress?" she asked slowly.

Paul wondered what to say. "The rules are different here. It's like a travelling circus going from city to city for each race – drivers and their wives or mistresses, team managers and their wives or mistresses, journalists and their wives or…"

"Mistresses?"

Paul nodded. "Yes, sometimes."

They continued walking. "I don't know anything about car racing but I do know of Nuvolari and Chiron and even Caracciola. How do you…?"

Paul thought he knew the answer. "I'm born and raised in Australia, which is the most egalitarian country in the world. Everyone is equal, from the Prime Minister to a rubbish collector, and I think drivers like it when a journalist treats them as an equal, rather than hired help as the English press tend to do, or as Gods who walk on water as Italians tend to do. The drivers are talented, of course, but more importantly they are men who make their living from racing cars."

"Yes, this makes sense."

Paul liked that matter of fact acceptance. "I could turn you into an Australian, signorina Donati," he said.

She looked him in the eyes. "You can call me Pia."

"And I'm Paul."

"What's your real name?"

"Paolo, but I'm called Paul."

Paul then noticed an immaculately dressed Achille Varzi, smoking as always.

"Buongiorno signore Varzi," Paul offered.

"Buongiorno signore Bassi," Achille Varzi grumbled while frowning and smoking. And then he realised and his demeanour changed entirely – his face opened up while Pia matched that. "Buongiorno signorina….," he said lightly and delicately.

"Signorina Donati," Pia said just as Achille Varzi discarded his cigarette and kissed her gloved hand before a long, lingering look into her eyes.

"Signore Varzi," Paul said. "You're not practicing."

He sighed. "Management in Molsheim says the new car isn't ready."

"That's a pity."

"We'll have to wait for Spain."

"Yes, of course." Paul glanced at his watch and they didn't have much time. "Buongiorno signore Varzi."

Achille Varzi gave Pia one last, lingering look. "Buongiorno signore e signorina."

They continued around the rear of the pits towards the car park where Paul grabbed his clipboard with stopwatches, and his portable typewriter, before heading to the tunnel under the main straight.

"I've heard of Achille Varzi," Pia said. "I've seen his picture but I didn't realise he's such a handsome man."

"I believe he's the best driver of the moment and it's a shame that he doesn't have a car for this weekend."

They used the tunnel, and emerged to climb steps to the central grandstand, to join a few thousand enthusiasts who knew racing was for a weekend and not three hours on a Sunday afternoon. Paul set up his typewriter and studied the entry list on his clipboard.

The first car starting shattered the peace and quiet. Several other cars were started by mechanics in overalls who brought them to temperature. Paul grabbed his typewriter and wrote a paragraph about the track, weather and the three Bugattis of Varzi, Drefus and Williams not starting, and also missing were the private Alfa Romeo Monzas of Charly Jellen and Paul Pietsch. Paul remembered Ilse Hubitsch, Jellen's beautiful girlfriend, who was unusually fascinated with motor sport. One by one the engines were shut down for the mechanics to change sparkplugs. Piero Taruffi in his works-entered Maserati monoposto was out first and quickly disappeared from view around the north turn of the banked oval.

"The cars are very loud," Pia said.

Paul reached into his pocket and gave her two of his spare ear plugs. "These will help when more cars are running." He put plugs into his ears and Pia did the same.

Fagioli and Chiron took to the circuit just before Taruffi appeared on his flying lap. Paul timed him and then the two Ferrari-entered Alfa Romeos. Taruffi did a good time, three minutes twelve, while Fagioli was faster then Chiron which was interesting. Nuvolari did several laps but couldn't match Taruffi's time, which was also interesting. Goffredo Zehender in the third Maserati Monoposto was a little slower than Nuvolari, which wasn't surprising. During the session Paul explained his practice times to Pia who found them informative. He finished typing his article and then contemplated the rest of the day. Clearly he was escorting Pia to the Gran Premio the next day, and that was an excellent opportunity courtesy of Tazio Nuvolari. Dinner together, maybe. He put the cover on his typewriter.

"Have you finished?" Pia asked.

"Almost," Paul said. "Next I take my article to the telegraph operator in Milano, and he sends it to five Australian newspapers, six English, one Welsh and two motor sports journals."

"That seems like magic," and she laughed.

"It's easy for today, but tomorrow for the race I must type two articles. A longer article for the two journals and a shorter version for the newspapers. But it all works out in the end." He glanced at Pia who was truly lovely. No wonder Achille Varzi was taken by her quintessential Italian beauty highlighted by dark eyes, darker hair, slim build and long legs. "Pia, do you have any plans for this evening?"

"No."

"Would you like to share dinner with me?"

"Yes, I would like this."

"I can take you home and pick you up later."

"I don't want to put you out."

"It's no trouble."

"I share an apartment with my sister at La Vittoria, which is close to where you parked your car."

"That's close to my hotel."

"So we can meet at, perhaps, La Felicità."

"It's an early start tomorrow so we should eat early. Would seven be alright?"

"Seven will be good."

* * *

Paul entered a hushed dining room and was glad he dressed in a suit and tie. The restaurant was luxurious, from carpeted floors and heavy drapes to absorb the noise, and proper, starched white tablecloths. A bar along one side of the room had many bottles of wine – quite different to the pub and beer culture of his homeland. La Felicità was finished in shades of green: lighter for the walls and darker for the carpets and drapes, contrasting against the mahogany bar and matching, mahogany and green velvet chairs. Early on a Saturday night had only a few tables taken with Pia alone on the far side of the room, and dressed in a beautiful blue striped evening dress. Paul went to her, she stood and he lightly kissed her hand. They sat and then a waiter came and laid out thick, starched tablecloths. The waiter left with an order for a glass of beer and a glass of Campari. For once Paul decided beer would go down well after a busy day.

"Pia, have you been here before?" Paul asked.

Pia nodded. "I have. It's good, and better that they have local cuisine."

"It's not a coincidence that my heritage is from Lombardy, and this means I feel home at my true home, but I'm new here and I don't know the local cuisine terribly well."

"I forget you come from the other side of the world. I can order for you, if you want."

"Yes per favore, and the expertise of a local lady would help with a drink to accompany."

"Of course."

The waiter returned and Pia ordered their meals and a bottle of red wine, which was delivered and opened with a flourish, and poured ever so professionally. Paul inhaled the scent which it told him Milano really was his spiritual home. Although for a moment he missed his real home, or he missed his family. He hoped replies to his letters would arrive soon.

"And so Paolo or Paul, how has this year been for you?" Pia asked.

"This year has been very busy," Paul said as an understatement. "I arrived in Britain in March and visited the journal and each of the newspapers who agreed with my proposal, and then I went to Monaco for the Grand Prix in April. Since then there's been a race meeting almost every weekend, from Belgium in the north to Tripoli in the south, and a few races in Germany as well."

"And what are your plans now?"

"The last race for the season is at San Remo in Spain in two weeks, and the next race will be Monaco in April next year. So I need somewhere to live and a job for a few months. I looked at different cities, where Paris is too far from Sicily or North Africa, and then I came here."

"So you want to live in Milano?"

"Yes I do," Paul said. "It's a lovely city and has a great ambience, and it's central to most of the racing circuits in Europe. It's ideal for me."

"And a job for summer?"

"Do you have any ideas?" Paul asked, realising that dinner with a Milanese woman had many advantages.

"You write about sport," Pia said. "You could write about basketball. It's very popular, especially in Milano, and the season runs from October to May."

"Do you follow basketball?"

"I have been to games of Assi Milano."

That was a good option if he could make it work. "I'll be staying here for a while so I'll see what I can do. I can look for an apartment as well."

"With a parking spot for your racing car," and Pia laughed lightly.

"Yes, I need a parking spot for my racing car," Paul said while smiling in agreement. "Tomorrow the race starts at nine-thirty and we'll be in the spectator area above the pits. We must get to the circuit on time, so I should pick you up at seven-thirty."

"Yes, of course. I live at Viale Umbria, eighty. Apartment twelve with my older sister."

"Do you work?"

"I help design dresses and I prepare new designs for models."

"And your sister?"

"Daniela is a seamstress where I work, but she's getting married next month. I must look for somewhere to live. I can't share a small apartment with Daniela and her husband."

Paul pondered that but it was much too early, although it would be delightful.

"What of your family, Paul?" Pia asked.

"My father and his two brothers are from near here, and they settled in a state in Australia called Victoria where they're farmers," Paul said. "My mother is Australian, I have an older brother who works on the family farm and my other, older brother works in the nearby town, and I have cousins too."

"My family is from Soncino, which is a small town near here. My father's a mechanic with his own business, and I have an older sister and an older brother. My brother's married and lives in Soncino, working for my father, and he and his wife have two children."

"My father and my uncles came from Chiari."

"Chiari is close to Soncino."

The waiter brought their steaming, hot meals, where Paul was treated to cotoletta alla Milanese with risotto and vegetables and Pia had la cassoeula, which was a meat and vegetable stew. That stopped conversation for a while Paul wondered. It would be a special treat and if he didn't ask he would regret it. "Pia, do you think you could take a few days holiday from work the week after next? Thursday through to Tuesday?"

"Why?"

"Well, the Gran Premio di Spagna is at San Remo in northern Spain, and I'll be driving there. It's a lovely journey along the Riviera Ligure and the Côte d'Azur, and we could stay the night somewhere in Provence on the way."

Pia touched her cheeks with her fingers in excitement. "Oh, that sounds wonderful!" she exclaimed.

"You will need a passport and visas, but I think there's time if you arrange it on Monday."

"It sounds nice but..."

Paul's heart beat fast.

"Will I be your mistress like that woman today?" Pia asked.

Paul looked deep into her dark eyes. "You will be my friend."

"Good. My family's old-fashioned and they wouldn't understand things like mistresses for racing car journalists."

Paul was disappointed by that, but glad that Pia was accompanying him. "You'll enjoy the journey."

"I'm looking forward to it already," and she smiled brightly, and Paul thought he might have a future with the lovely young woman he met in a café.

Chapter Ten

It was a cloudy and damp morning when Paul drove to Viale Umbria, but rain had stopped by the time he left his hotel. Pia carried an umbrella while Paul made do with an overcoat over his usual attire of a pullover and trousers, and his Akubra hat of course. Early on Sunday made for a quiet drive to Monza Park, where they arrived with 30 minutes to spare before the start of the race.

Paul escorted Pia to the journalist's viewing area and introduced her to journalists he liked: Françoise from Paris, Alain from Nice, Stéphane from Marseille, Gilles from Lyon, Corrado from Roma and Ignazio from Napoli. Then he introduced Pia to some of the journalists he didn't particularly like such as Charlie from London and Jack from Birmingham. Paul and Pia went to the viewing area while Paul overheard Charlie mumble something about 'bloody wogs', which didn't surprise him. The English were even more racist than Australians, while Paul's journalistic success in their country made things worse. And then he accompanied a beautiful Italian woman to the track. At least Pia didn't understand that English insult.

The grandstands filled and engines were started and warmed just below. Mechanics pushed cars to the grid accompanied by drivers. There were cheers for all of drivers, with the biggest cheer for Nuvolari. A great driver and a genuinely lovely man, where what you saw was what you got, regardless of his incredible successes. Start time approached, the starter was ready and right on nine-thirty, 26 cars thundered from the grid in a cloud of blue tyre smoke. Although Nuvolari was on row three of the grid, as dictated by his race number, it was predictable that he led at the end of the first lap chased by Fagioli in the Alfa Romeo Tipo B and Taruffi in the second Maserati Monoposto. Fagioli took the lead at the end of lap two, and over the next seven laps Nuvolari and Fagioli swapped the lead back and forwards until Fagioli pitted to refuel, indicating Alfa Romeo speed was attributable to a light fuel load. Nuvolari and Chiron then diced for the lead although both had unscheduled stops to change tyres. Chiron retired with engine failure which left Nuvolari well clear of Fagioli, until Nuvolari's Maserati suffered a flat tyre only two laps from the end. Fagioli's Alfa Romeo flashed past and Nuvolari resumed the chase, but it was too late and he finished 40 seconds behind. Although the middle section of the race had been dull, it ended spectacularly.

During the lunch break, dark clouds drifted across the circuit and there was some drizzle which made the track wet for the Gran Premio di Monza. That was to be run over three heats and a final using the banked circuit only, with the first heat scheduled to start at 14:00. Nuvolari withdrew from the afternoon's racing because of his tyre problems, which would have been disappointing for many in the crowd. The first heat became a battle between Count Carlo Trossi in a red Ferrari-entered Duisenberg and Stanislas Czaykowski in one of the Bugattis from Avus, until the Duisenberg engine broke and dropped oil on the south, banked curve. Czaykowski won from Guy Moll in a Ferrari Alfa Romeo Monza, who spun on the oil on the last lap and protested to the officials about the condition of the track.

The cars lined up for heat two with Giuseppe Campari receiving a bigger ovation than Nuvolari, which was fitting as Monza was his last race before the great driver retired to become an opera singer. And a great driver he was since his first race in 1914; scoring many successes including the Gran Premio d'Italia, twice winning the Grand Prix de France, twice winning the Mille Miglia and three times winning the Coppa Acerbo. Young Baconin Borzacchini was also popular with the crowds, and both Borzacchini and Campari had front brakes removed and slick tyres fitted. The start was delayed while the track was swept and sand spread to soak up the oil, while drivers were warned in writing of the conditions. In the meantime the impatient crowd shouted, whistled and stamped their feet. Eventually Campari and Borzacchini led away, but at the end of the lap it was Renato Balestrero, Lelio Pellegrini, Mademoiselle Hellé Nice and nothing. The three drivers kept racing while nobody knew what was going on, except nurses and mechanics ran to the south and ambulance sirens could be heard in the distance. Paul knew it was bad so he held Pia's hand. Eventually, organisers announced that there had been a serious accident, and about 30 minutes later Paul heard that Campari was dead and Borzacchini was gravely injured and unlikely to survive the night. Paul felt terrible; especially that nothing could be done for Giuseppe Campari except to pray for his soul.

A driver's meeting took place before five drivers assembled for heat three which was then aborted for another driver's meeting. Eventually after two hours of jeering, whistles and cat-calls the third heat was underway, but Paul had lost the heart for it. If his car hadn't been trapped inside the circuit he would have taken Pia home, but sadly he couldn't. Marcel Lehoux won in a Bugatti.

The siren announced the starting time of the final for 11 competitors, which English driver Whitney Straight led from the start in his green Maserati. Soon Czaykowski in the fast Bugatti took the lead and held it until lap eight, when Lehoux led past the pits and Czaykowski was missing. Sadly a column of smoke told the story and there had been yet another crash on the south banked curve, when the engine of Czaykowski's Bugatti blew-up. There was no hope for the driver and the race was flagged off. Paul was shocked to see winner Marcel Lehoux so shaken by the events that he had to be lifted from his car. Indeed, Paul's own hands were shaking so much that he could barely read his scribbled notes. Not that he wanted to read those notes, except where he wrote that never again should a race be run on the Monza banking.

* * *

They trudged to the car in silence with Paul still confused about the tragic events of the second heat. Was it all down to an oil slick? Racing with slick tyres and no front brakes on a still-damp circuit? Driver mistakes? Paul opened the door for Pia before placing his clipboard and hat behind the front seat. He started the engine and followed the other cars out of Monza Park and towards Milano.

"What are you plans Paul?" Pia asked.

"I have two stories to type from my notes, and they get telegraphed as usual. I'll ring a friend to gather more information about those who died so I can write brief obituaries."

"At least you will be kept busy."

Paul signed. "It can only take me a couple of hours because I have deadlines to meet. After this I don't know. I can't face eating alone to be honest."

"I know what you mean. Daniela has gone away and I don't feel like eating alone either."

Paul thought it seemed wrong, but it was the lesser of two bad choices. "I don't want to sound callous, but we should eat together." He looked across at Pia for a moment. "Something casual, and together we can come to terms with what happened."

Silence and Paul glanced at Pia again. "You're right," she said. "You say two hours?"

"Yes, about two hours."

"We can meet at Caffè Sforzesco. If you leave me near there I can make a booking for us for nine."

Paul thought the casual Caffè Sforzesco was suitable for such a meal. He drove through busy but fast-moving traffic towards the centre of Milano, to leave Pia at Via Dante and then park his car at the Hotel Giulio Cesare around the corner.

Paul rang Mario, briefly explained his situation and how little time he had. With pad at the ready he got the information he needed, and had his two articles written by eight-thirty and on their way before nine. He walked to the cafe to see Pia waiting at the table by the window. Their table. He went to her, she stood, and he kissed her hand before sitting. The waiter came where Paul asked Pia to order a local red wine. The waiter left two menus and departed with an order for two glasses. Paul studied the menu because he was surprisingly hungry. The shock had worn off; especially after the evening's rush.

The waiter brought their glasses. Paul ordered ossobuco while Pia ordered pollo with risotto.

Pia sighed deeply. "It was such a lovely day and then it was spoiled so badly."

Paul agreed. "It was tragic," he said without being able to find the right words. He raised his glass. "Let us hope that it's not in vain."

Pia raised her glass and they clinked them together. "Let us hope," she said.

Paul sipped his wine.

"How can their deaths not be in vain?" Pia asked. "They died in racing cars, as happens."

"It's the circuit," Paul said, knowing the cause – a world-wide scramble to build the fastest circuits in the world. "There have been too many deaths on banked circuits, but if they change Monza and take out the banked part then their deaths will not be in vain."

"I hope they do that."

"I'm sure they will."

"While I was alone in the apartment waiting, I thought they died doing what they loved. Many men live grey and bleak lives, but these men are larger than life. They're true heroes and even gladiators of the racetrack."

Paul agreed with that. "I know some drivers, as you know, and they must know the danger, but they wouldn't do anything else." Despite the tragedy Paul hoped their plans were not in ruin, although he felt terribly selfish for such thoughts. "I hope this hasn't put you off going to San Remo?"

"Is that circuit banked?"

"No."

"Then I will go to San Remo. Nuvolari will be there and I want to see him win!"

"He had bad luck today and he deserved to win. Varzi should be at the next race, but his Bugatti may not be competitive. But next year..."

"What's Varzi doing next year?"

"I'm not sure," Paul said, but he pictured a scenario which would work. "Alfa Romeo withdrew the Tipo B so Ferrari was forced to enter the older, slower Monza model, against which Varzi did well with his Bugatti. Nuvolari then broke his Ferrari contract and signed up for Maserati, and shortly after Alfa Romeo gave some Tibo Bs to Ferrari. Varzi is not a man to break a contract, but next year he might be looking for a better drive."

"In the Ferrari Alfa Romeo Tipo B?"

"Very possibly."

"That would be interesting."

Paul couldn't believe it and was most amused.

"What's so funny?" Pia asked while looking perplexed.

"I've turned you into a car racing enthusiast!"

Pia crossed her arms. "I'm not a car racing enthusiast," she said indignantly.

"Tifosa...."

"Who for?"

"Tazio Nuvolari. Try this. Next year Mercedes-Benz returns to Gran Premio racing with a new car, and there's another new German car designed by Doctor Porsche who's a top racing car designer. It's called the Auto Union."

"So there will be Varzi in the Tipo B, Nuvolari in the Maserati and new German cars?'

Paul nodded. "Yes."

"This will be interesting."

"Do you want to see races next year?" Paul asked half-innocently and half-not.

"As your friend?"

"Yes."

"We can travel to France and Germany and other places besides?"

"If you want to."

"The drivers and their mistresses will think I'm…"

"It doesn't matter what they think," Paul interrupted. "You're a beautiful young woman and of course they will think you're my mistress, just like Alice Hoffman, Norma Colombo, Ilse Hubitsch and others besides."

Pia sat there with her mouth open and was bright red and flushed, and Paul realised he went too far.

"Do you think I'm beautiful?" she asked quietly.

Paul leaned forward and as close to Pia as he could get. "You're the most beautiful and the most pleasant woman I have ever met." Paul knew he had her interest and contemplated what to do next, and then it came to him. And then it didn't because after the day's tragedies, anything more than a meal together would be wrong. But he knew their attraction was built on both being Italian, while Paul was more outgoing and Pia quieter but quite lovely. Paul couldn't wait to go to Spain with Pia, because he felt she might the one for him if she felt he was for her.

Chapter Eleven

Paul left the outskirts of Milan behind and cruised along the highway south to Genova. It was a lovely autumn day with the sun shining from a near cloudless blue sky. The Alfa drove a treat and Paul knew he had to write more about the car in his articles. He'd driven average-type saloons where the Alfa Romeo 1750 was in another league. If more people had a chance to drive an Alfa Romeo, there would be more Alfa Romeos. It was as simple as that.

"What are you thinking about?" Pia asked.

"What I should write about this car," Paul said.

"Your racing car is lovely."

"It is."

It was steadily downhill from the mountains to the sea, with lush, green pastures bordering the road. After a bit more than 90 minutes they reached the outskirts of Genova, where Paul used Via Borzoli to skirt to the west, with glimpses of the blue Mediterranean visible from time to time. Once past the suburbs, they continued along a road between mountains and the sea. In an open car the fresh, smell of a salty breeze was unmistakeable, but as driver Paul couldn't really admire the scenery. At least it wasn't busy in the morning mid-week and other cars mostly moved at a decent speed. Even though Riviera Ligure was a holiday area, September obviously wasn't the peak time for the beach. The weather was nice enough for it, with lovely sunshine and mid-twenties temperature. After two hours driving by the clock on the dashboard they reached Vado Ligure and stopped for coffee. It was a town of factories and ships tied up at an ugly port.

Back on the road where the drive was uneventful, until they reached the border with France. Paul stopped for passport and visa checks, and custom's officials gave a brief glance at the Alfa Romeo's small boot before they were able to continue. The road continued much as before, and then diverted into the hills above tiny Monaco. They wound down to the coast again and headed towards Nice. Nice was a sizeable city set between hills on one side and the sea on the other. It was a pleasant drive along broad boulevards lined with lovely, French-styled buildings, while palm trees reminded Paul that he was at the Côte d'Azur. They left the city behind to continue along the road adjacent to the coast, with an eye on the clock until signs showed they were only ten kilometres from Cannes. It was time for lunch.

Cannes was smaller than Nice while Paul spotted a cafe with parking out the front.

After the warmth and bright light outside, the cafe was cool and dark. Simple inside with wooden tables and chairs, no tablecloths, polished timber floors and white-coloured rough-hewn walls. As always in Europe there was a bar at one end stocked with bottles of wine.

"Now that we're by the sea," Paul said to Pia. "I recommend a seafood lunch with local white wine."

"This sounds great," Pia said.

"I come from an inland town like you, so I make the most of journeys to the seaside."

"It has been a beautiful drive in your racing car, and I enjoyed the scenery."

They took a table by the window where the waitress brought two menus, and departed with an order for two glasses of white wine.

"What are these foods?" Pia asked.

"Moules au Roquefort is mussels with cheese, while Lobster au Gratin is lobster topped with breadcrumbs."

"Then we will have one of each."

When the waitress returned he gave her their orders.

"Do we have far to go?" Pia asked.

Paul did some quick arithmetic based upon the distance reading of the car. "We have about 170 kilometres or about two hours to go. I booked a hotel in Provence which is inland, but it's on a lake. My friend told me it's quite scenic."

"How did you learn this language?"

"In Australia they always teach French in school, and I think it's a tradition from British education where Britain is close to France. In Australia, speaking French is next to useless."

"Unless you move to Europe."

Paul nodded. "Yes." From his travels he realised many British spoke French but French didn't speak English so much. Paul glanced at his watch. "We're close to the sea and we have plenty of time, so we could walk along the beach after we eat."

"Oh yes!"

Their food arrived smelling delicious, while Paul asked the friendly waitress for extra plates so they could share. After, they finished with coffee.

Paul helped Pia with her chair and took her hand. Together they walked towards the sound of restless surf and found a broad beach with beautiful, clean, white sand. The tide was going out where sand was damp and firm which made walking easier, while a gentle breeze tempered heat from the sun. They walked without talking, with the only sound being the surf crashing close, and the screech of seagulls diving for fish. It was magnificent. After about 20 minutes they reached a rocky outcrop, and from there they headed back to the car.

"I could get used to travelling for a job," Pia said.

"It's better when you have company."

"I could get used to having company too."

They reached the car where Paul held the door for his companion. He drove out of Cannes before heading inland using the highway towards Aix-en-Provence, entering a region of rolling hills, small villages, small farms and healthy crops. It was a scenic place and a scenic drive, while Aix-en-Provence was a sizeable, regional city. Slow moving, gently paced and easy on the eye. Paul stopped in the main street and they walked through a market.

"Life here is like Soncino," Pia said.

"Do you miss your home?" Paul asked.

"A town like this is pretty to visit, but soon every day becomes the same as every other day and you feel like you're wasting your life."

"I understand."

"You would."

They returned to the car, where Paul checked the map book before starting the last part of their drive to Rognac. Those 30 kilometres didn't take long and the hotel was on the main road through the town. When he drove past the Hotel le Royale

Provence, Paul didn't think much of it, but when he turned into the car park he was impressed. The hotel stood on the narrow strip of land between Rue Quartier Les Bosquets and the blue waters of Étang de Berre, with hotel windows overlooking the lake. It was even better to reach their destination after more than 500 kilometres of driving.

Paul opened the small boot, and they took respective bags to the glazed door which Paul held it for Pia. Reception was small, as expected for a small hotel, with a couple of leather chairs and a polished, timber counter with a book and a bell, and behind that were pigeon holes and a door. Paul went to the counter and rang the bell, for a middle-aged woman to come through the doorway a few moments later. Paul sensed Pia watching from near the door.

"Bonjour Madame," Paul said to the receptionist.

"Bonjour Monsieur," she replied politely.

"Je m'apelle Paolo Bassi et elle s'apelle Mademoiselle Pia Donati."

"Ah, oui Monsieur." She ran her finger down the register, although reading upside-down, Paul saw there were few bookings for that night. "Oui viola." She took a pen, handed it to Paul who signed against his name.

Paul turned around and Pia closed. She signed her name and the receptionist too two keys from pigeon holes behind to place them on the counter.

"Chambres quatre et cinq," the receptionist said.

"Merci Madame," Paul replied.

Paul took the keys and gave room five to Pia. They carried respective bags while climbing the narrow staircase to a narrow corridor in dark red and burgundy, with eight brown doors, all with brass numbers. Pia unlocked door numbered five and opened it wide. Paul opened his door and placed his bag into a dark room when Pia nearly screamed, "Paul, look at this!"

Paul went into Pia's room where she pulled the curtains wide, opened the windows and leaned against the window frame looking towards the beautiful, blue lake. Paul joined Pia and took her hand.

"This is wonderful!" she exclaimed before kissing him on his cheek. "The drive was wonderful and I saw so much, and the lunch was wonderful and I have never eaten food like that before. The walk on the beach was wonderful and now I have this wonderful room; I just can't describe how wonderful this day has been. Grazie for inviting me."

Paul squeezed her slim hand just so. "Grazie for coming. It's been great to have company."

She nodded. "This wouldn't be much on your own."

"A place like this is made for sharing," Paul said without thinking. But it was true and he put his arm around her waist and held her lightly, and she rested her head on his shoulder. They stood in silence with a light breeze ruffling Paul's hair while his heart beat fast. He wondered what to say and realised he didn't need to say anything, but then he needed to.

"Grazie for being my friend," Paul said quietly.

"Grazie for being my friend," Pia said equally quietly.

Paul squeezed her. "If I could be more than your friend, I would."

Pia sighed and Paul wondered if she was ready.

"I'm glad you were forward in the café last week, and I'm glad you invited me for this weekend. An Italian man would never do such things." She eased away and Paul looked into her dark, dark eyes. "There is one way," Pia said quietly. "Ci sarà avere sesso anale."

Paul was startled. "Will you?" he asked.

"Si."

Pia came beside him and he took her hand and contemplated her smooth skin and slim fingers. Still holding Pia's hand Paul said very softly, "We will make love."

"We need some oil."

"I'll get some from the receptionist."

"You mustn't ever tell my family."

"I won't."

Paul raced down the stairs and rang the bell. The receptionist came through the doorway looking surprised.

"Madame, Je voudrais un peut d'hulle, s'il vous plait," Paul said.

"Oui. Ji vais en ce moment."

The receptionist, who Paul guessed owned or managed the hotel, took only a moment to return with a small bottle of olive oil. Smiling brightly, she handed it to Paul.

"Je voudrais une salle seulement, chambre cinq, s'il vous plais," Paul said while he placed the key for room four on the counter.

"Bien sur," she agreed, smiling even more brightly.

"Merci Madame," he said before climbing the stairs without rushing, even though he wanted to. He entered Pia's room which was light and surprisingly spacious. Bright from pale beige walls and the afternoon's light from the large windows, still open. It had a double bed with a golden cover, one side table, a compact wardrobe, a dressing table and a gold-upholstered chair.

Paul put the small bottle on the side table, went to Pia and took her hand. He wasn't sure what to do next, so he hugged her to make sure she really wanted to make love with him. She held him lightly as they stood together in silence with Paul noticing the buttons on the back of her slim-fitting dress. Slowly, almost surreptitiously, he loosened those buttons one by one. Pia didn't flinch, not even when the last button came free and Paul slowly, gently, peeled the dress from her shoulders. With her dress hanging from her waist Pia started on the buttons on Paul's shirt, and soon shirt, shoes and trousers were dealt with. Paul knelt and removed Pia's shoes and they faced each other where Paul touched her smooth, satin slip and fantasised about even softer beneath. He didn't have to fantasise for long because Pia removed her slip and also removed her lacy underwear – she was amazing, especially her lovely round bottom and her legs so long! Naked in his arms she was indescribably gorgeous. He held with his heart racing fast, and felt warm despite the light, salt-laden breeze filling the room with freshness. Pia pulled away and folded back the cover, blankets and sheets. Paul removed his cotton underwear to join her in a spacious bed made for love. They held each other where the sensation of skin against skin was divine, but not as divine as what was coming.

"I want to make love with you," Paul said.

"Yes, but slowly."

Paul turned to get the small bottle while Pia rolled onto her stomach with legs nearly together – Paul was surprised.

"This will be better," she said.

Paul admired the delightful curve of her back blending into her feminine bottom blending into her long, shapely legs. He applied some oil and then he cast his thoughts back to that first time when she knew it all, of course, and it was better when it was relaxed and unhurried. He knelt outside Pia's hips, and at first gently but soon more firmly. Pia sucked the air and Paul went slow; slowly and slowly and slowly, and it was quite lovely – in fact just as good if not better.

Pia breathed out long and languid as Paul absorbed her softness with the insides of his thighs. He bent down while Pia turned her head so they could kiss. They kissed, skin against skin, with the light breeze caressing two lover's bodies.

* * *

Pia lay on the bed while Paul admired the delightful curve of her back blending into her feminine bottom blending into her long, shapely legs. She turned her head and propped it with one hand. "I wish we could make love properly," she said.

Paul briefly kissed her on her lips. "We made love properly and it was wonderful for me, and I hope it was wonderful for you."

"It was wonderful, and I'll never forget this afternoon for as long as I live. You should bring your bag into this room, amore mio."

"Yes of course, amore mia."

Chapter Twelve

Achille paid the taxi driver and was surprised to see the journalist from Australia arrive at the Maria Cristina Hotel in a new Alfa Romeo Spyder, and accompanied by the young woman he took to Monza. More luck him: a beautiful car and a beautiful companion. Achille had just asked for the key for his room when they arrived with a little luggage, as befitted a car with little luggage capacity.

"Buon Pomeriggio signore Bassi e signorina Donati," Achille offered.

"Buon Pomeriggio signore Varzi," they replied in near unison.

Achille considered the car and there were two possibilities. "You have a reward for the success of your news articles," he said.

"Yes I do," signore Bassi replied. "Next year we'll have something in common."

"We have more than one thing in common. We both have beautiful, Italian women as companions." Achille turned to face the fair signorina with the mesmerising, dark eyes. "Signorina Donati, you will brighten the paddock tomorrow and Sunday."

She blushed lightly. "Grazie signore Varzi," she said quietly.

"Signore Bassi, in answer to your question, I'll be driving for Scuderia Ferrari next year, but in the meantime there's a race to be run on Sunday and I'll be doing my best, as always. The Bugatti Type 59 has not proven fast in testing so I don't expect to trouble the leaders. However it might rain so anything could happen."

They both thanked him and went to check in. Achille went to his room where his, beautiful Italian companion waited. He might as well make love with Norma because there was little else to be gained from a weekend in the north of Spain.

After a wet Saturday practice where Williams crashed his new
Bugatti rather badly, Paul was glad to see that race day was cloudy
but dry. Paul and Pia left the Maria Cristina Hotel early and drove
to the start and finish area at Oria. The little village of Oria was
surrounded by several hills, where time had stood still for a century
or more. But for the different architectural style of Spain, the
cluster of shops, villas, apartment buildings and churches could
have been any village in Italy. They occupied a cafe adjacent to the
race circuit, which wound its way through the centre of the village,
and opposite were the pits located on a grassy reserve. Crowds
streamed into the village which was full by midday, for an unusual
rolling start from behind a pace car. Fagioli led from Chiron and
Tazio Nuvolari who started well back on the grid. Nuvolari
predictably took the lead on lap two and gradually extended the
gap. Even in the early laps the two remaining works Bugattis of
Varzi and Drefus were struggling for speed, even against the older
model Type 51 of Monza winner Marcel Lehoux. Chiron took
second from Fagioli while the race set into a pattern as skies
darkened.

Just after two, or just before two-thirds distance, the rain came,
and soon cars trailed plumes of spray when they passed the cafe. A
few laps later, Chiron came past well in the lead and Nuvolari had
disappeared. Paul went to the pits where he discovered Tazio
Nuvolari had crashed badly but suffered only minor injuries. He
then called by the Bugatti pits to see what was up but nobody was
talking, although Norma was out the back smoking.

"Salve Norma," Paul offered.

"Salve Paul," she replied. "Are you and Pia still dining with us tonight?"

"If Achille finishes the race in time."

Norma burst out laughing so hard that she almost choked. Eventually she recovered. "Their carburettors are working loose, so either they run on reduced power or lose time to have them tightened. Achille decided to continue without stopping."

"I understand. Grazie Norma."

Paul headed back contemplating the consequences of loose carburettors, and was well-soaked when he arrived at the cafe. He ordered another coffee and brought it to the table.

"What happened to Nuvolari?" Pia asked.

"He crashed but isn't hurt," Paul replied. "I know your tifosa for...."

"I'm not!"

"Alright. But he's crashed a few times and it's a wonder he's still alive. Achille Varzi is quite different. He's never crashed a racing car."

Pia tilted her head. "That can't be so for a top-level driver."

"Nuvolari's crashed twelve times now and Varzi never. Oh, and the Bugattis are suffering from loosening carburettors, which would make their engines run lean, losing power, or even burn their valves. I met Norma."

"Are we still eating with them?"

"Yes, and I hope you like playing cards. Achille has a reputation that things go his way, and if he wants a meal with Italians and his friends aren't here, then that's what happens. And if he wants to play cards, then that's what happens too. But we're not dining until eight and...."

Pia giggled. "Yes, of course."

Paul expected that. He wrote notes on his clipboard while Louis Chiron hurtled past with his Alfa Romeo trailing a great plume of spray; set for another win.

* * *

It was quite late when they eventually arrived at the Hotel Du Musee in Arles, which was a little more than half-way to Milano. It had been a long drive, about 700km, where Paul looked forward to a bath and changing before having something to eat. They had a big lunch and Paul hadn't done much for the day except for driving, so he didn't want to eat much. They wandered the local streets and found a cafe, where glasses of wine with baguette and cheese suited well. They headed back to the hotel hand-in-hand.

"This is our last night together," Paul said. "Do you want to see more races next year? The first race of the new season is at Monaco which is an easy, day's drive."

Pia sighed. "This will be good."

Paul didn't know what to say, because they were lovers and yet it was hidden from Pia's family. How far could they go and for how long? Up the flight of stairs to their room where Paul closed the door behind. Pia slid the curtains and turned to face him.

"This is our last night and I want to make love with you," she said. "It's time for us to make love properly."

Paul was surprised. "We have made love properly."

She held his hand. "I mean, you know, but don't come inside me."

Paul nodded and he felt oddly nervous. He didn't know why; he's made love with other women and he made love with Pia three times already. But it was her first time for this, he supposed. Pia undressed and sat on the bed, and Paul undressed and sat beside and kissed her. He held her and kissed her and kissed her more, and felt her relaxing. Relaxing and relaxing as she moved from his embrace and lay on her back. Paul took his breath away, and he couldn't believe she was his. It defied time, space and reason.

"You are the most beautiful woman in the world," he said quietly. "Ti amo."

"You are the most handsome man in the world. Ti amo."

Paul moved as she spread her legs to give him room. He lay between and kissed her and he felt her delicate fingers. He knew what she wanted and went with her touch, where it felt indescribably gorgeous like always, until Pia winced.

"What is it?" Paul asked.

"Relax amore mio. The first time can hurt for a moment, but you must do it for us."

Paul went as slowly as he could and suddenly it felt different and Pia gulped the air. Again he stopped but her face said something different. He kissed her cheek and moved slowly while she put her fingers on his buttocks, drawing him to her, and he went with what she wanted; face to face for the first time.

Paul kissed her. "This is making love," he murmured.

"It is making love," Pia said quietly.

Paul made love to her; gazing into those mesmerising dark eyes. Eyes that sparkled with joy. He made love to her and didn't want it to end, even though he sensed it was the first of many times. He made love as he felt it building. Closer and closer and he remembered what she said. Closer and closer until he slipped out and slid across her soft, smooth skin just when his pleasure burst free. He lay still and kissed her, and she held him just the way he wanted to be held.

* * *

Paul lay on the bed and Pia ruffled his hair lightly. That felt delightful. They moved their relationship to another level but it was happening fast. "Are you alright, amore mia?" he asked.

"Yes of course amore mio. I'll remember these past days forever."

"I'll remember them too," Paul said. "What do you want to do now?" he asked.

"What do you want to do?"

He looked into Pia's eyes, and even though she was sitting on the bed still naked beside him, he felt such yearning, such an overpowering ache of desire for her. He didn't want to lose her, but it was only a week and two days.

"I want time to love you and I want to know you better, and I want time for you to know me," he said. "And then…"

She tilted her head. "Time is good and then we won't make a mistake." She ruffled his hair again. "Giorgio asked Daniela to marry him, but ever since then, things haven't stopped for her. Papa wants a big wedding for his daughter, so she's inviting many relatives who she hardly knows and it's been too busy. Instead we're in a lovely hotel in France, it's wonderful here and we enjoyed making love. This is why I will always remember these past days."

Paul nodded. "I think we will marry."

"I think we will marry, but now is Daniela's time. Later we can get engaged, when the time's right."

"This has been good, as you said. We've learned more about each other and we've made love too."

"It's a pity that other couples don't have a special time like this. Racing car drivers know about more life than how to race cars."

Paul agreed; realising that separating love from sex was a good way to come to terms with the mysteries of attraction. "Yes they do."

Pia moved to sit up against the bed head and look down. "I heard it at the practice sessions, and with waiters and receptionists. The language of the French is lovely."

"It is," Paul agreed. "Je t'aime ma cherié, I love you my darling.'

"What do I say?"

"Je t'aime mon cheri."

"Je t'aime mon cheri."

"Je t'adore ma cherié."

She smiled brightly. "Je t'adore mon cheri."

"J'aime beaucoup faire l'amour avec toi maintenant. Now."

Pia chuckled. "J'aime beaucoup faire l'amour avec toi maintenant, but don't come inside me."

Pia slid down the bed where Paul hugged and kissed her. He loved her and he knew he would marry her.

Chapter Thirteen

Paul parked his car in Via Vittorio Venetto in Chiari and knocked on the big, thick door. So thick it muffled all noise until Paul was surprised when it swung open.

"Ciao Mario," Paul said.

"Ciao Paul, but I can't get used to your name," Mario replied.

"I'm called Paul in Australia because they're racists!"

"I know. Come in. How was the race in Spain?"

"It was wet. No, Louis Chiron drove to the conditions and deserved his victory."

"And Nuvolari didn't?"

"I believe he hit water running across the track, but at the same time he was so far in front he could have eased off and given himself a greater margin for error."

"I think you're right. Take a seat."

They both sat in the sitting room; Paul on the sofa and Mario in an armchair.

"On the phone you said you met someone," Mario said.

Paul nodded. "We met in a cafe in Milano and I took her to the race at Monza, which was bad as you know. But we already agreed to go to San Remo together and we did."

"So you'll be living in Milano?"

"Yes I will, and I expect to be engaged to Pia when the time is right."

"That's marvellous news! You'll have a home and soon will have a fiancee."

"Yes I will." Paul was glad that Helena was in the kitchen preparing lunch. "I want to give the woman I love the best I can in all ways. We both know how to, of course, and Pia knows more from someone, perhaps her older sister. But I want to make everything special for her."

"Of course my friend, and this is a conversation that is hard for a father to have with his son. The most important thing is to treat Pia as the centre of your life and always make sure that she knows you love her. Kiss her whenever you see her, hold her for no other reason than you want to, and always tell her that you love her. As for other things this is not so hard. Women are different to men, and their bodies are more attuned to love than ours. Every part of her will respond to your touch, from her earlobes to the side of her neck, her breasts of course, and even her feet."

Paul was surprised by that.

"Oh yes, suck her feet and she will nearly die with the pleasure," Mario continued. "But do everything gently, if you can understand what I'm trying to say."

Paul understood, and he pictured Pia naked on the bed and how he would gently ravish every part of her.

"Now there is one place that is queen above all others, and from this she will get the greatest pleasure of all – like what men experience but actually more. But to do this you need her help and guidance, because if you do it right it will be heavenly for her, but if you do it wrong then it will feel like nothing."

"Pia is by nature quiet," Paul said.

"And you're more outgoing, so you have a good match. But what you will have to do is gain her confidence to put aside her quiet ways and help you, and in return you both will be rewarded.

She will gain great pleasure, and you will enjoy her pleasure as much as she does."

Paul was surprised. "Is it this simple?"

Mario nodded. "It is." He stood. "Let's go into the yard and I will tell you all, and even more."

Paul went with Mario to the yard and they sat at a table shaded by a large apple tree. Mario told Paul about it all and more, and when he recalled his sheer pleasure and how Pia could enjoy the same pleasure, or more, he was determined to do it, with her help. He couldn't thank Mario enough.

"When's the big event happening?" Mario asked.

"Her sister's getting married on Sunday and I'm meeting her family. It's not far, Soncino. Once the wedding's over I'll ask Pia."

"That's good news, and you must bring Pia here to have lunch with us."

"Yes I will do this. She can meet my grandparents, of course." Paul tilted his head and looked at Mario. "She will feel at home when I bring her to your home, just as I do."

"You're family, and family always feels at home with family."

* * *

It wasn't hard to tell that a wedding was happening in Soncino that day. There were people everywhere, looking lost in the centre of a tiny town that hadn't changed for 100 years. Utilitarian brick apartment buildings and villas, shutters at each window, shops at the ground floor. Clean, simple and style-free. Pia led Paul to the austere brick church adjacent to Via Tenelli, where more waited for the Sunday mass and a wedding. Pia left to change into her bridesmaid dress. Apparently it was traditional to have ten bridesmaids, but a younger, unmarried sister would always be the number one bridesmaid.

Men smoked and talked, women gossiped, youngsters ran about but didn't make much noise. It was a little like standing outside a church in Shepparton, but also quite different and not just the language. The buzz rose and Paul followed gazes to see Giorgio arriving with his family the Aconis, at which point everyone went inside the church. Paul knew he had to wait for the bride to be late, of course. Paul went into the most amazing church where every surface, wall and ceiling, had been transformed by fresco paintings depicting hundreds of biblical scenes. He sat near the back and was first to see Daniela in her long, white dress; face concealed by a lacy veil, escorted by her father. Behind were her ten bridesmaids looking radiant in white. The wedding party went to the front of the church where the priest spoke at length about marriage before vows were exchanged. At that point the wedding ceremony was over and the wedding party occupied vacant front pews, while Pia joined Paul. Then followed a normal, Sunday mass.

After, Paul remained on the fringes because it was time to take photos, and Pia was involved in that of course. An austere brick hall served as the venue, where Paul watched the large wedding party posing while a dozen or more pictures were taken. When that was finished, Pia sought Paul and took his arm. They went to Daniela with veil folded back; the shorter, almost twin sister of Pia, and with Daniela was her husband Giorgio, tallish and seemingly too muscular for his suit, as you would expect for a fire fighter. Paul kissed them both, as was the way with family.

"Grazie for coming to my wedding," Daniela said.

"Grazie for having me," Paul replied.

"It's good that you can meet our family, but there's so much family!" and she laughed. "Pia will look after you and you can meet our parents, and our brother and his family, and then...." and she shook her head. Paul gained the impression that Daniela was more outgoing than quiet and contemplative Pia.

Pia took Paul's hand. "Today is your day," Pia said to Daniela. "I'll introduce Paul and then we can enjoy lunch."

Pia led Paul away while Paul admired his beautiful companion, who looked especially radiant in her white dress and hat. He met signore and signora Donati, Giovanni and Clara. Signore Donati was darkish and bulky while signora Donati was slim and svelte – and Paul noticed the resemblance between mother and daughters. He also remembered advice given by Mario; if you want to know what your wife will look like in 30 years time, look at your mother-in-law. Next was Antonio, dark and broad like his father, and Claudia. And their children Giovanni and Camilla. In one way the wedding was an opportunity to meet Pia's family, but it was a wedding day and little chance to get to know them except by name.

"What work do you do?" signore Donati asked Paul.

"I'm a journalist and I report on car racing," Paul said.

"Paul knows Tazio Nuvolari," Pia interrupted.

"Do you?" signore Donati asked, sounding surprised.

Paul nodded and then he wanted to say more about Pia with Achille Varzi and Norma, but he couldn't of course. "Pia came with me to Monza," Paul said to clarify things.

"Does your job pay well?"

"I'm freelance and contracted to newspapers and journals, and I hope to have more journals and newspapers for next year."

"Paul writes his articles in English and they're published world-wide," Pia said.

Paul nodded in agreement.

"Well, that is interesting," signore Donati said.

Paul decided his Australian past could wait for another day.

Pia grabbed Paul's arm and steered him away. "I'll introduce you to my uncles and aunts and cousins," she said.

"And after you can quiz me on their names."

"Pardon? Oh, yes," and she laughed.

"You're treading on dangerous ground by mentioning Nuvolari."

"I didn't think until I said it. Grazie for being discreet."

"Our turn will come."

"I know."

Paul met them all, and he even remembered some of their names, more or less. In the meantime trestle tables were covered in white sheets and burdened with food and glass flagons of home-made red wine. It looked like the women of Soncino had cooked for a week. It was lovely and homely and very special, especially with his pretty, Soncino girl at his side. Paul was suddenly curious.

"How was it that we were able to meet like that in a cafe?" he asked.

"Ah yes, that was lucky. I finished school and I got a job in a haberdashery shop here, but it was really quiet. Daniela moved to Milano, and when I visited her I just had to move to the city. It was good because I got a job where she worked and I was able to pay half our rent. I went out and met some boys, but none interested me until I met Gino. Gino was Milanese and smooth and sophisticated, and maybe he impressed a country girl like me. We went to dances and movies, and sometimes picnics with Daniela and Giorgio. We came here and my parents were sure. But when that happened, Gino started taking me for granted, although he always took me for granted in a way. It was always 'I want this' and 'I want that', but when he demanded what I wasn't prepared to give him, I decided he wasn't the man for me. So we had our usual Saturday evening date with a dance to follow, and I told him we could dine and we could dance, and after that I wouldn't see him again."

"And then I came along?"

"Yes. You're different, but more importantly I feel differently about you. I think it's called love."

"It is."

Paul grabbed his glass tumbler and drank some more of the rough wine.

"I'm sorry about that," Pia said, glancing at the glass.

Paul didn't mind. "I'm used to it," he said.

"I keep on forgetting."

Paul nodded and then it hit him. "Next weekend I'm taking you to meet a family friend and his wife, and I'm sure you'll love them both. And while we're there we can meet my grandparents."

Pia grabbed him. "Oh, you wonderful man!"

"I am."

"And modest."

"Yes, I know."

Chapter Fourteen

Paul knocked on the door of apartment twelve and Pia, who was alone given Daniela and Giorgio were away on their honeymoon, answered promptly. She looked surprised but didn't say a word. Of course she guessed what was happening.

"Where are we going tonight?" she asked.

"Ristorante Bagutta," Paul said.

Pia locked the door and accompanied Paul. It was only a short walk to where a waiter held the door before showing them to their table in that classy and yet informal restaurant. The waiter, Mario, departed with an order for two glasses of red wine.

"This is good here," Pia said.

"It is," Paul agreed. Still she didn't mention that he wore his suit. Paul decided they would eat, and over coffee he would ask. He knew the answer.

Paul ordered ossobuco and Pia ordered prosciutto and sausage. They waited and then Mario returned.

"Excuse me signore Bassi," Mario said. "Signore Varzi would like you to join him at his table."

Paul couldn't believe it! He looked to where the waiter glanced and saw Achille, Norma and Count Trossi, with Carlo Trossi smoking a pipe as always. "Tell signore Varzi grazie, and we'll join him when we finish our main course," Paul said.

Pia giggled.

Paul looked into her big, dark eyes sparkling with humour. He reached out and took her hand. "Pia Donati," he said. "I knew I would be asking you this the day we met. I would like you to be my wife."

Pia got up and went around the table and briefly kissed Paul's cheek. "Yes, amore mio."

"Grazie."

"Should we go now?"

"We'll eat and then we'll play cards."

Main course arrived shortly after. Paul reminded Pia about their weekend away, because Mario agreed they could stay at his house. Paul wondered what his grandparents were going to think; one day they met their grandson and a few weeks later they would meet his fiancee. After they finished eating, Paul ordered a glass of sweet, white wine and Pia ordered Cinzano Bianco. Paul helped Pia with her chair and then they went to the other room separated by an arched opening.

"Buonasera Carlo, ciao Achille and Norma."

"Buonasera Paul e Pia," Carlo Trossi replied.

"Something's happened," Norma said.

Pia nodded. "We're engaged to be married."

Norma got up and kissed her cheek. "Congratulations. Will we see more of you next year?"

"Yes you will."

"I'm going so you can take my place."

Norma left while Achille got the cards out for a typically noisy game of Scopa. "Paul and Pia against Didi and I," he said.

"We can't stay for long," Paul said.

Achille nodded. "I understand. Three games only."

Chapter Fifteen

Achille leaned against the still and looked through the window. The fresh snow was immaculate; clean and unmarked. Only nature could produce something so perfectly smooth and perfectly white.

Norma came to the window to hand Achille a cigarette and his lighter. "It's a good day. Are we bobsleighing?"

Achille lit his cigarette and gazed out of the window again. "The snow's too good. Do you want to ski?"

Norma nodded. "Yes, cross-country."

"We'll go to Tre Croci Pass." Achille turned to look at her. "Breakfast Norma?"

"Yes."

The hotel dining room was only half-full early on a Monday morning. They took a large table in case the others showed, and they ordered after Achille scolded the waitress for not setting the table correctly. A cappuccino made for an excellent start, while in the background the fire crackled invitingly. The others appeared couple by couple and were given the opportunity of skiing for the day, which Tonino and his girlfriend Luciana agreed to do. Achille thought that although they were new together, Tonino and Luciana were close, although a racing driver should never marry because that would slow him, although being married hadn't slowed Tazio or Carlo.

After breakfast, Achille, Norma, Tonino and Luciana met outside, dressed in waterproof jackets, trousers and gloves, with ski boots, beanies, scarves and tinted goggles. They trudged through soft, deep snow away from the settlement to the start of the run to the pass, and there they donned their skis.

"Remember there are two women and this isn't a race," Norma whispered.

Achille nodded. "We can race on bobsleighs tomorrow."

"And get beaten again?"

Achille didn't reply to that, but next time he had to make sure that Pietro worked closer as a team. There wasn't much in it, two seconds only, and he was sure they could make that up.

* * *

Paul watched Pia slide out of bed and find her night dress discarded the previous night, and he wished she didn't put it on. Their room was warm enough. She showered, and after she finished Paul climbed out but didn't bother with pyjamas. He showered while Pia dressed. While he sorted through the wardrobe, Pia opened the curtains and the snow looked particularly inviting. It was their second day of lessons.

The restaurant was delightfully rustic with simple white walls and ceiling contrasting against polished maple tables and chairs, a maple counter for food and a maple bar for the evening meal. After eating, they dressed in layers of clothing and joined the small class of six, where four of the six were honeymooners. They spent several hours perfecting turning, stopping and returning to the top of the slope, which was easier on fresh snow rather than the ice of the day before. Paul felt he was getting to grips with skiing. After another lesson he could do the basic slopes on his own, and maybe explore further by the end of their fortnight at Cortina d'Ampezzo. Despite sub-zero temperatures, the combination of layers of clothing, a cloudless sky and exertion had made him quite hot.

They returned to the hotel for a late lunch, and spent the rest of the day playing scopa. Pia won and Paul insisted her let her.

Dinner had local fares with regional wines grown further down the mountains. Desserts were delightful while coffee rounded out a second, great meal at the Hotel Meuble Oasi. Paul went to the bar and bought a sweet, white wine and a Cinzano Bianco for Pia, and they relaxed at their table.

Pia sipped her drink and leaned close to Paul. "I told you my story with Gino at the wedding lunch, but I don't know your past."

Paul pondered a cold, wet winter four years before. "In Australia," he said. "They're quite racist. They treat the native aboriginals very badly, there are some Chinese there and Australians call them names, while we Italians are called wogs and Australians mostly don't want much to do with us. Even if a girl liked us, her family would never approve. But even bigger than their racism is their sport, where they have a local brand of football that's quite different to here. It's like a cross between football, basketball and a riot. Like basketball it's better when you're tall, and I'm tall and I'm an accurate kick, so when they put me forward the school team started winning games. This was mostly because of me and I became popular, and then they called me wog but in a nice way."

"How can that be nice?" Pia asked while looking puzzled.

"You don't know Australians. Because of this, in my last year of high school, some girls showed interest, and that's when I got to know Alice who looked a little like my mother with fair skin and red hair. We went to movies and to dances, I had dinners at her place and she came to mine, and in summer we went on picnics together. When I left school I joined the town's football team, and they found me a job just to keep me in the town, even though a third of men are unemployed in Australia."

"They really are keen on their football."

"They are," Paul agreed. "By this stage one part of me wanted to make love with Alice, but another part said that if we made love she would take that as a sign that we were close to being engaged, but the last thing I wanted was to marry Alice! Instead, I came up with the idea of moving to Europe." Paul thought about London with the 34 year old prostitute and decided not to tell Pia. "I travelled by ship to London, and after that I went to Monaco and North Africa, and then I went to Berlin for two weeks. I met Corinna, who was a few years older and divorced. She took me to a cabaret and a dance, and after the dance we spent the night together." Paul looked at Pia who was really entranced by his story. "The next morning Corinna said we could fall in love and we shouldn't see each other again, because it would hurt her when I left. At the time I understood the words, but not the emotion until I met you. And then, on our weekend away together, that was the best."

Pia leaned looked around before leaning forward and speaking to Paul in a soft voice. "I spoke with Daniela and she told me about anale and how to do it. Then I thought we should make love properly, so we did."

That was wrong. "We made love properly each time that weekend, just differently some times to others. Besides, we can use anale at those times of the month, and other times when we want something different."

"Yes, you're right, we will."

"I enjoyed it."

"I did too."

Pia had obviously enjoyed sesso anale. Soon they would go to their compact painted in simple white, and there they would make love.

* * *

Achille contemplated the bobsleigh run dropping down and curling away out of view. They had to do it in one minute seven or better. That was Tonino and Didi's time from their best run just finished.

"On three," Achille said to Pietro. "One, two, three," and he pushed as hard as he could. They went over the crest where Achille jumped in, and they went away down the hill. Faster still and into the left curve with Achille steering low on the banked turn for maximum speed. Down the hill and left, right, left a big one-eighty degree right, then right, right and straight. Faster and faster, more curves flashing by, each curve taken on the fastest line. Faster and faster nearing the end of the run, and it was all down to their line through the last curve to the left. From there it was gravity as they flashed past the beam where Achille felt their brakes bringing them to a rough stop. He breathed hard before climbing out.

Achille walked carefully on icy snow to the timing beam and the numbers read 1.06. They did it but there was one run left. Up the top Tonino and Didi would be ready for their last run while the sleigh at the bottom was pulled out of the way. Once the 'all clear' was telephoned they would be off. Shortly after Achille read the time: 1.05. Achille's last run counted for all. Achille and Pietro carried their sleigh to the top and put it in place.

"We have to be quicker still," Achille said.

"I'm doing my best," Pietro said.

"You have to do better."

Achille went to the front bar and readied himself. "One, two, three," and he pushed hard to get underway. Achille concentrated intently as he lined each curve to the ideal line. Down and down, curves and straights and across the finish line. Tonino glanced at the timing beam where his body language said it all. Achille won. Achille checked his time and it read 1.03. That was unbeatable no matter how many runs were left.

They trudged up the hill towards the Hotel Cortina d'Ampezzo, where as they closed, Achille spotted a familiar couple burdened with skis and stocks. He left his companions, and the couple must have sensed him because they turned and their gazes met.

"Ciao Achille," they both said.

"Ciao," Achille replied. "Obviously you're having a skiing holiday"

"This is our honeymoon," Paul replied.

"This is a great place for a honeymoon."

"It is."

Achille wondered if Paul knew, but being on a honeymoon he probably didn't. "Did you hear about Charly Caracciola?" he asked.

"No, what happened?"

"She was killed in an avalanche a few days ago."

"Oh, that's terrible! I don't know Rudi but I know of him, and now this."

"Louis and Baby are with him at the moment."

"He will be in my prayers," Pia said.

Achille nodded towards the young lady – that was remarkably respectful. "Would you like to play cards tonight?" Achille asked.

"Yes, grazie," Paul said.

"Pia, you can keep Norma and the other women company."

"That's fine," she said.

"Eight at Hotel Cortina d'Ampezzo."

"Grazie Achille."

Achille returned to his colleagues but he didn't mention the couple. For some reason the journalist from Australia interested him. He was Italian and not Italian, which was an unusual combination. That, and he wrote well from what Achille had been told. He attended races, unlike Giovanni who wrote his articles from a teleprinter. Norma liked Pia, which was most important. And he played cards well and joined in the fun.

Chapter Sixteen

Pia mopped the sweat from her brow. It was May 1934 at Tripoli, and hot of course. For the second year in a row, Monaco had been a great race with an unexpected victory for young Guy Moll on the last lap. Also it was good to see Rudi Caracciola drive a lap of honour before the race started. All in all it had been a great weekend starting with a pleasant drive along the coast, and a hotel room with a good view to the pits and to the circuit. Alessandria followed with Varzi scoring a solid win in a wet and tragic race, where Carlo Pedrazzini crashed and was killed in one of the heats. In the final, Tazio Nuvolari over-drove his Maserati while trying to keep up with the Alfa Romeos and crashed badly on the first lap, breaking his leg. Pia was no longer his tifosa.

They reached the grandstand at Mellaha. "You should go to the journalist's area and I'll catch up later," Paul said.

"Trying to find which Ferrari-entered Alfa Romeo will win?" she asked.

Paul shrugged his shoulders. "Wait until the new German cars appear later in the year."

Pia nodded and walked away while rummaging through her bag for her pass. Paul guessed the winner would one of the four Tipo Bs, either Varzi, Moll or Chiron, while the fourth car for Mario Tadini was very much an outside chance. Nuvolari wasn't racing, but Maserati had an interesting twin-engine car for Piero Taruffi which could be in contention, especially on a high-speed circuit made faster with some partly-banked curves, something that Paul thought was unnecessary.

Achille Varzi waited in the shade behind the pits, smoking a cigarette as usual. "Ciao Achille," Paul said.

"Ciao Paul," Achille replied.

"Is your car fixed?"

He nodded. "A new engine was flown in overnight. Idiotic Bugatti drivers."

Achille damaged his car avoiding Dreyfus towing Brivio's car back to the pits, but practice had ended and Varzi was still travelling at maximum speed. Paul didn't mention that.

"Good luck Achille."

"Grazie."

Paul then headed off to check out the two, American Miller cars. The four-wheel-drive five litre of Peter de Paolo and the 3.8 litre car for Lou Moore. Built for Indianapolis oval racing neither car stood a chance, but they were interesting.

Paul rejoined Pia in the relative coolness of the luxurious and spacious journalist's area overlooking the start and finish line. Pia was in a chair adjacent to the counter next to big, glass windows. Paul came alongside and she looked up.

"I want to be more help," she said. "It's a long lap here, so I'm going to the far side of the circuit, and there I can write what I see."

Paul looked out of the window into the harsh sunlight. "Are you sure?" he asked.

Pia pointed into the distance. "Over there is a lake with palm trees, so I'll have shade. I'll take a bottle of water and I'll be fine."

Ignazio obviously overheard the conversation. "I have a spare clipboard," he said.

"Thank you Ignazio," Paul said. "I have extra paper and pencils, so you're all set. Next time we'll be better prepared."

"When does the race start?"

"It starts in 30 minutes."

"In a straight line that's about three kilometres, so I'll be there in time." Pia stood, took her supplies and a wine bottle filled with water. Paul watched her show her pass before trudging across the broad track and into the desert.

Paul took Pia's seat and got ready for the race. Racing engines being warmed shattered the peace and calm, and soon cars accompanied by drivers were pushed onto the grid. As always, drivers were cheered before they got into respective machines. Then everything stopped because race number allocations were then drawn for the lottery, with the organisers taking no chances. Eventually starting lights went from red to yellow to green and the 1934 Gran Premio di Tripoli was underway. The two-motor Maserati separated the Alfa Romeos of Chiron and Achille until Taruffi put that car through a beer advertising hoarding. Achille took the lead when Chiron pitted for fresh tyres, so Moll moved into a watching second place. Moll increased speed over the last 10 laps to close on the leader, and it was shades of the last laps of 1933 only with Moll chasing Achille. Like 1933 Moll aimed to out-brake Achille into the last corner, but Achille was having none of that as he closed the door quite firmly. That left Moll to slipstream Achille down the straight until he draw alongside, but not quite and Achille won by two-tenths of a second; the same margin as the previous year. The Autodromo di Mellaha was a circuit made for close racing and close finishes.

Paul waited for Pia who emerged from the desert about 30 minutes later; hot and flushed.

"I need a bath," she said.

"I need a bath too," Paul said. "Was the race good?"

She nodded. "We don't need many different makes of car to have an exciting race. Which race is next?"

"The Targa Florio in Sicily."

Pia stopped walking. "Are we going?" she said quietly.

"I have to. Why?"

"Mafiosi."

"It's only a race, although not much of a race. You don't have to come."

"I don't really want to go. What's after that?"

"Berlin and then the Eifel Mountains in Germany."

"Are we driving?"

Paul shook his head. "It's too far. We'll go by train."

"I haven't been on a long train trip before."

"I'll book a sleeper."

"Ah, good."

Indeed, they would make love on the train, no matter what.

* * *

Over the previous year Berlin had changed under the National Socialist Government. The streets were no longer lined with prostitutes, and doorways and parks were no longer sleeping places. Paul wasn't certain if the change was due to a booming economy or uniformed Nazis keeping the streets clear of unfortunates. He suspected it was a bit of both. He also suspected that the sex clubs Corinna mentioned were still around to satisfy demands for various fetishes, and he pictured uniformed Nazis partaking of mother and daughter pairs and all the other things that happened in those places. Paul and Pia went to a cabaret where political satire was off the agenda, as was toplessness. The Resi was good once they were able to sort out the language problems for Pia. She picked a man who took her fancy, so Paul wrote a note in three languages and sent it in the air-tube system. She got her dance! Paul found an attractive, thirty-something blonde Berliner who spoke English. Monika was pleasant company and an accomplished dancer.

Apart from improving the economy, moving undesirables on and clothing formerly naked performers, Nazis had changed things in unfortunate ways. Books by Jewish authors, from Karl Marx to popular fiction, had been burned. Indeed, Jews, Gypsies and others were persecuted in a number of ways. Berlin went on as if nothing had changed, and although many Jews had left, Paul was sure that many more Jews, although not authors or academics, stayed because they had nowhere else to go. People who were different were often persecuted, as Paul once experienced.

The race at Avus was a disappointment for the many Germans in attendance, including hundreds of uniformed Nazis. The Mercedes-Benz was a sleek, silver racer, while the silver Auto Union with a rear engine was longer, lower and even sleeker. By comparison to the two German cars, the Alfa Romeo Tipo B looked vintage, including the lumpy, streamlined version driven by Guy Moll. Mercedes had fuel pump problems during practice and withdrew from the race, while Hans Stuck in the Auto Union built a massive, one-minute lead on the first lap in the wet, but fell behind when he pitted for tyres later in the race, and then the clutch on his car, failed allowing Guy Moll to win some distance ahead of Achille Varzi. Paul thought the driving talent for Mercedes was solid with von Brauchitsch, Fagioli, and Caracciola if he was physically capable, but Auto Union only had Stuck and inexperienced drivers to back him up.

Paul and Pia then travelled to the Eifel Mountains where it rained. Pia stared out of the window of their hotel room at heavy fog and drizzle. She sighed and turned her back on the bleakness outside.

"Only Germans could build a racing circuit in a place like this," she said.

"Not only man and machine against the circuit, but also against the environment." Paul checked his watch and grabbed his overcoat. "We must go, despite the rain."

"We're here for a job."

"That's right."

Despite rain and squalls of hail there was a healthy crowd in the big grandstand. It didn't matter that they reached the grandstand early because the atrocious weather delayed racing for hours. During the wait they continued Pia's French lessons – it was the universal language of Europe and not hard for an Italian to learn.

Eventually rain eased, cars were warmed and then pushed onto the grid. For 1934 the three classes were started separately, but all the interest was for the big cars. Mercedes-Benz didn't disappoint on their racing debut with Fagioli taking the lead from von Brauchitsch and Stuck, where the three, silver cars easily led Chiron at the end of the first lap. Given the track was winding and wet, German speed was partly attributable to better traction from independent suspension. Fagioli was given a sign to yield the lead, and at the end of lap three the race order was von Brauchitsch, Fagioli and Stuck.

At half-distance the two Mercedes pitted for fuel and tyres, and Paul used his binoculars to see Fagioli arguing with Mercedes team-manager Alfred Neubauer. After their big argument, Fagioli set off trailing Stuck and von Brauchitsch, and then closed on and harried the leading Mercedes without actually passing, and was called into the pits and there was another furious argument. Stuck stopped for fuel, tyres and plugs; probably fouled from running cold in the wet weather. Eventually Stuck got away in third place which became second when a still-furious Fagioli simply abandoned his car out on the circuit. And that was the end of the race, with von Brauchitsch winning from Stuck and a distant Chiron. Paul Pietsch scored a solid fourth place in his elderly Alfa Romeo.

It was quite late when they trudged to the Ringhaus Hotel, but at least the rain had stopped some time previously.

"Are you sure Luigi Fagioli isn't Calabrian?" Pia asked.

"He's Abruzzian."

"Mercedes-Benz should hire Achille."

"Can you imagine Achille following orders to let his slower, team mate past?"

"He just wouldn't."

"What do you think of these, new cars?"

"I don't like the scream of the Mercedes, but the new cars are fast and they make the red cars look old-fashioned."

That was the truth of the matter.

Chapter Seventeen

Achille leaned against his car and smoked a cigarette. He stood
little chance of victory based upon speed alone. During practice
Achille watched the cars rounding the rough, Montlhéry banking
for the Grand Prix de l'A.C.F, where the Alfa Romeos of his team
mates jolted, bounced, darted about and looked quite dreadful. By
comparison the Mercedes-Benz and the Auto Unions seemed to
float across the uneven concrete and that showed in their times.
Manfred von Brauchitsch smashed the lap record in his screaming
Mercedes-Benz, ahead of Louis who did a single, quick lap, then
Fagioli in another Mercedes and Hans Stuck in the Auto Union.
Achille felt that Auto Union were short of driving talent, with
August Momberger and Hermann zu Leingingen anything but
potential race winners. Rudi Caracciola made his return to racing
and managed good practice times. Bugatti were in disarray, but
Tazio had no choice because Maserati chose not to enter.

Two minutes and Achille climbed in, switched the magneto on
and the mechanic started the engine. Achille was on the front row
of a grid decided by ballot which gave him a good chance of
leading. But the Grand Prix of the Automobile of France was a
long race, 500 kilometres, and anything could happen. One minute
and Achille adjusted his goggles and got comfortable. The starter
unfurled his flag while Achille raised engine revs. Up went the flag
and the Alfa Romeo stuttered for a moment – Achille was
swamped by Chiron, Fagioli, Caracciola and Stuck. In fifth place,
Achille decided to play a waiting game while those ahead fought
amongst themselves. It didn't take long for Stuck to take the lead
in the Auto Union, but soon his tyres wore out and he fell back to

fourth. Achille lined up to overtake when Stuck headed to his pits instead.

That left Louis in the lead with Fagioli and Caracciola battling hard for second, and Achille was surprised that Rudi had strong pace despite his injury. Then the two Mercedes-Benz pitted and Achille noticed them being pushed away. Stuck surprised Achille that after his tyre stop, he didn't catch the leaders again. Clearly something was wrong with his car. Achille held station behind Louis; Montlhéry was his track and his race while Achille had already won four times that season. Achille then passed Stuck's Auto Union stationary at the pits while the mechanics worked on a problem. But to no avail and the silver car was pushed away.

Enzo Ferrari showed the 'in' sign and Achille pitted the next lap. It had been thirsty work on a hot, sunny day and he was more than a minute clear of Moll, so he climbed out and drank water from a bottle and lit a cigarette. The mechanics topped up fuel and changed rear tyres, and then Achille got back in and continued while still smoking his cigarette.

The crowd stayed to watch Louis Chiron win the French Grand Prix, which obviously went down a treat, and Achille heard the roar from the crowd when he finished an unhurried second. The three Alfa Romeos had beaten the dreaded, German cars, but Achille knew Mercedes-Benz and Auto Union would deal with their reliability issues and then they would be unbeatable.

* * *

Achille surveyed the low, sleek silver Auto Union in the shade of the pits at Monza. His meeting with signore Ricordi was about to pay off.

"C'est voiture spécial," Herr Walb said in rough French.

Achille knew it was his only choice for 1935. Alfred Neubauer and Rudi Caracciola had a partnership going back many years, and no other driver at Mercedes-Benz stood a chance. It would always be Rudi first, and if not Rudi then another German driver like von Brauchitsch. At Auto Union they had Hans Stuck and some lesser drivers, while Willy Walb wasn't so much wedded to Stuck. At Auto Union Achille could win races. The car was more than fast enough and he could beat Stuck. But Achille feigned indifference while the mechanics finished changing spark plugs on the 16-cylinder engine. They fastened the engine cover.

"Je vais conduire maintenant," Achille said while grabbing his cap, goggles and gloves from the counter. He would do a couple of slower laps to get used to the machine, and also find his away around Monza shortened and made much tighter in the aftermath of Black Sunday the previous year. Achille climbed into a hot cockpit just behind the radiator, and surrounded by frame tubes carrying hot water. A mechanic attached the steering wheel while Achille was surprised by a tachometer red-lined at a mere 3,500rpm. He flicked the magneto switch, gave a sign and the starting motor was applied to the rear. The engine caught immediately, Achille selected a baulky first gear and eased onto the straight. He rounded the tight Rettilinio Tribune hairpin and quickly picked up speed towards Curva Sud. Around the broad, banked curve before braking hard for the chicane part-way along, and exiting between concrete curbs in an easily-controlled power slide to continue onto the back straight. Shortly after he turned left and then left, and onto a short straight before another broad hairpin with a chicane, which led onto the straight past the pits. The Auto Union felt different to any other car Achille had ever driven; the front wheels went exactly where he pointed them while the rear pivoted from the front. In a way it was like racing a motorcycle, which always stuck at the front and slid at the rear. The engine had solid pick-up from as low as 2,000rpm, which was handy on slow, tight Monza, although wheel spin was easily provoked and the gearchange was awfully stiff, probably because of the linkage from the cockpit through the fuel tank and past the engine to the gearbox at the far rear.

On lap three Achille opened the big car up and it responded well. The trick was to squeeze the throttle out of the curves to maximise traction, and without wheel spin the car surged forward like an arrow shot from a bow.

Achille did many laps while feeling more and more comfortable behind the wheel, until he noticed the mechanic holding a board with an arrow. Achille completed one further lap at three-quarters speed before drifting slowly to the pits. He flicked the switch, released the steering wheel and wriggled out of the tight cockpit. Only then did he notice Walb looking over the shoulder of the mechanic with the clipboard and stop watches. Achille strolled towards them to notice his lap times started at two fifteen and dropped to two-thirteen, or the fastest yet recorded on the revised Monza. Walb's expression gave nothing away but Achille knew.

"Je suis plus rapide," Achille said. "Champion of Italy and winner of six Grand Prix this year," he continued in French. "I will win races for you. Two-hundred thousand lira plus half of prize money," Achille said.

"Are you sure?" he asked.

Achille knew Auto Union had a small racing budget and would be pleased to get a top driver for that amount. Achille also knew Tazio was interested in racing for Auto Union, and while Achille could beat Tazio on the road he couldn't compete with his good humour in the pits. They drove for the same team once, and it failed when mechanics put their effort into one car only. "I will win races in your car, but I won't accept Tazio Nuvolari in the team."

"I can't agree to this."

Achille got close to Herr Walb. "Your car has a lot of low-down power, as you know," he said, knowing that Walb had raced in his younger days. "If you don't use that power wisely you can wear rear tyres in no time, and you can't win races from the pits. You need a patient driver."

"I know your driving style and I agree to your request, but I must get final permission from the board." He put his hand out and Achille shook it.

Unlike Enzo Ferrari, Willy Walb was an employee of a big car manufacturer, but Achille had no doubt that he would be driving for Auto Union in 1935. Two hundred thousand lira would be sufficient, and he would have the fastest car for 1935. He was pleased by this.

* * *

It didn't seem like a year since Paul took Pia to the Gran Premio d'Italia at Monza, where they enjoyed a classic race followed by tragedy. For 1934 Monza was much altered, with part of the road circuit and part of the banked circuit connected by a new roadway, and with chicanes on the banking, and on one of the new curves, to further slow things down. Paul would have preferred the road circuit only, with a diagonal run across the start and finish straight to Curva Grande. The new, hybrid circuit was even tighter than Monaco. Paul thought the only reason they raced there was because of the excellent facilities at the track, and the big crowds who came from Milano and nearby Torino.

After mechanical failures at Montlhéry, Mercedes and Auto Union proceeded to dominate the next two races they entered. The Gran Premio di Germania where Stuck won from Fagioli, and the Coppa Acerbo where Fagioli won from Nuvolari in a dramatic and tragic race where Guy Moll was killed, probably from over-driving his outclassed Alfa Romeo Tipo B. Ferrari entered and won a number of other races, with Achille scoring two further victories to become Champion of Italy, and with Carlo Trossi winning at Vichy and Biella. For a wealthy playboy Trossi was a fine driver. For Paul's newspaper and journal articles about practice, he reported that Achille Varzi tested an Auto Union on the Monday before the race.

Maserati debuted the new 6C-34 model which was so heavy all fluid had to be drained from the car so it could pass the 750kg weight limit, and mechanics even drained its brake fluid. Practice times were terribly slow on the tight circuit, and Paul estimated the race would take close to five hours for 500 kilometres. Pia decided to spend the day with Daniela.

At Monza the cars were pushed to the grid escorted by their drivers as usual, where all German and Italian drivers gave fascist salutes to uniformed dignitaries on their way to the grid. Stuck led away while Caracciola got into second. Achille was best of the Italians while Nuvolari tried everything against his great rival until his Maserati suffered obvious brake problems. Stuck pitted and was relieved by zu Leiningen which put Caracciola into the lead, until he had a routine stop and had to be lifted from his car. The strain of endless, heavy braking and hundreds of gear changes had taken its toll. Fagioli who previously retired then took over the leading car while Achille got his Alfa Romeo into an amazing second place, before the gearbox wilted under the strain and he retired.

It was a messy, scrappy race, and it showed that while the German cars had an advantage, the old-fashioned Italian cars were not so far behind. The problem was the red cars were at the limit of development potential while the silver cars would only get faster.

* * *

Daniela and Giorgio were still with Pia when Paul arrived home, after delivering his articles to the telegraph operator. Paul greeted them and kissed both on their cheeks.

"How are you both going?" Paul asked.

"Good," Daniela said.

"You look good," Paul said and she did too. Radiant, as mothers to be always were. "How are you feeling?"

"Better now. No more sickness. When's your turn?"

"We're trying very hard," Paul said as meekly as he could manage.

"Paul!" Pia snapped.

"We are," he said.

"It's in God's hands," Pia said.

"Paul, how was the race?" Giorgio asked as if to change the subject.

Paul sat in the chair; feeling exhausted by the thought of it. "It was like a marathon. Not only did the circuit break the cars, it broke most of the drivers. Luigi Fagioli and Rudi Caracciola shared the winning Mercedes."

"And Achille?" Pia asked.

"The gearbox of his car broke when he was in second place."

"We must go," Daniela said. "I'm sure Paul was busy today, and he has more work coming for tonight."

Pia went all red.

They kissed and departed with ciaos all around, and Paul fell back into the armchair when they left.

"I want to talk to you about things," Pia said.

Paul turned to face her. "I'm sorry about that but Daniela is good fun."

"No not that; I know you. It's been nearly eight months."

"There's only one chance a month, amore mia, and it can take time. We'll get there I'm sure."

"How do you know?"

"Well...," and Paul really didn't know.

"I think we should get checked."

Paul thought it was too early. "Antonio my brother took eight months after they married, so I think it's normal."

Pia didn't look convinced.

"We should try for a few more months, and if nothing happens then we can get checked," Paul said. "Two more months."

Pia still looked unconvinced.

Chapter Eighteen

Achille was pleased that Auto Union eventually confirmed their agreement, and after a drive across the Alps to Zwicau and a big ceremony, he had a contract for one year with an option for a second year in his pocket, for the reichsmark equivalent of 200,000 lira plus half of prize money. He knew he could earn more elsewhere, but with Auto Union he would win races. The biggest problem was Germany had currency trading restrictions and the money could only be dribbled to Achille in small amounts.

Norma was away for the day so Achille went Caffè Sforzesco for focaccia and coffee for lunch. At a table by the window was the journalist Paul Bassi looking rather glum. Achille went to him where Paul stood and greeted, but still looked sad.

"Sit, per favore" Paul said.

Achille sat and, the waiter came and Achille gave his order.

Paul sipped his coffee. "Congratulations on your Auto Union drive," he said.

Soon that would be known all around the world, not that it mattered. The Italian public wanted Italian racing drivers to race Italian cars, but a racing driver's job was to win. But still Paul looked miserable. "Are you well?" Achille asked.

"Yes, I'm well." Paul sipped his coffee and some water and then looked up. "No, I'm not well. We've been married for a while now and Pia wanted us to take tests. I just found out I can't be a father."

"I have the same problem," Achille said.

Paul looked shocked. "I am sorry," he said.

"There are worse things in life."

"I know."

That was a bad blow for the young couple. "From now you must put you and your wife first, because you are all that you have. Is there family you could see? Maybe this will take your mind off your problems."

"My family's a long, way away."

Achille's lunch arrived and he sipped some water.

"It's nearly Christmas where we will be with Pia's family," Paul said. "After, I think we should go on holiday together."

"Cortina d'Ampezzo?"

He nodded. "Yes."

"Norma and I will see you there. We can play cards again."

"Yes, we can."

"Does Pia know?"

"I haven't told her yet."

"Tell her that you and I share the same affliction. This should help."

"I will and grazie Achille."

* * *

Milano was restless early on December twenty-four. Many were departing for La Vigilia di Natale celebrations near and far. Paul and Pia walked to the secure parking for his car.

"I don't know what to say to my family," Pia said.

"We shouldn't say anything."

Pia looked at him. "We can't do this."

"Christmas isn't the right time for this."

"When should we say something?"

Paul wondered. "I write to my mother every month, as you know, and I don't know what to do. If I was with her I would know what to say, but if I write this and she reads my letter thinking it will be all good, as it often is, she will get a terrible shock. When you tell your parents it won't be as bad as this."

Pia nodded slowly. "Mama, I met and married the most wonderful man in the world, we travel to places near and far and live the most wonderful life together. We live together, we work together, we love together. But sadly we can't have children together."

Paul was astounded. "Yes, that's just right for when the time comes. And if you don't mind I'll borrow your words for my next letter."

"It will be hard on your mother because she doesn't really know how much we love each other, and what a great life we live together."

Paul agreed with that, and he also recognised the great strength of their marriage. He was more of a thinker while Pia had the heart and soul of their relationship. They were good together.

"We should visit your family one day," Pia said.

Paul disagreed. "We could have Christmas in Australia, although it's a long way to travel. If we did, you will know that despite a few bad things here, we really are well off."

"How so?"

Paul cast his mind back. "It's terrible; there's so much suffering. Many men have given up hope and gone onto drink, or just cleared out and left their families. Wives and mothers scrounge work as best they can, or maybe prostitute themselves for rent and some stale bread for the next meal. Daughters prostitute themselves for their families, and some have lost everything and live in shacks where it's freezing in winter and boiling in summer. There are many suicides."

Pia gasped. "That's terrible. Things aren't so bad here."

"There are political prisoners and you must be careful of what you say." Paul thought about the one thing that worried him above all others. "I don't like children being indoctrinated with fascist ideology at school. I worry for your brother's children and I worry for Daniela and Giorgio when their time comes. Despite this, we shouldn't go to Australia."

"Why?"

"It's a long way, it's terribly expensive and there are family issues that I prefer to leave on the other side of the world."

"Surely it's not this bad?"

"It is this bad and my mother will hate you."

"Why would she hate me?"

"Because you're in love and happy and she's not."

Pia looked at Paul. "I don't understand but I trust you."

"Grazie." Paul then realised he wasn't going to live in Australia ever again – he'd been living on a two year's work permit renewed for a further two years, but there was another option. "I'm going to become an Italian citizen."

"Can you?"

"Italian citizenship is automatic for me. If I ever need to travel to Australia, I can get a visa like you would have to."

"Amore mio, you'll be truly Italian."

They reached the garage where Paul unlocked the door. Soon they were on their way to Soncino where many decorations brightened houses and apartments. The greetings at the Donati house were loud and raucous, as to be expected in a house full of Italians. For all his being raised in another country, Italian get-togethers were something that Paul was familiar with. Women then prepared dinner collectively leaving men to talk about men's things, and as Paul was there they talked about car racing for a while. Paul didn't mind but was careful not to appear to brag about aspects of his job. In fact he dismissed it as just a job. But while they were talking Paul spotted Pia with her nephew and niece, Giovanni and Camilla. She was a natural with children, as you would expect from someone with a good heart, and it was sad to see that.

For dinner they ate seven different types of fish, as was the tradition, and after they had pannettone. Then the extended family went to midnight mass where the small church was full of worshippers. It was a fitting end to a great La Vigilia di Natale.

Chapter Nineteen

Paul was amazed that it was his third visit to North Africa. So much had happened in such a little time. More recently in February, Daniela gave birth to a girl who she named Clara after her mother. The first race in Africa for 1935 was the Grand Prix de Tunisie on the pleasant Circuit de Carthage, located between the desert, the sea and the city of Tunis. Tunis was a meeting place of two cultures and the city reflected that. Many houses and shops were simple, rectangular mud brick painted white, always with a flat roof, while other buildings in the city centre wouldn't have looked out of place located on a boulevard in Paris. Interspersed were mosques, identifiable with domed rooves clad in copper, and corroded brown from the proximity of the city to the sea. Auto Union entered a single car for the Grand Prix, with Achille Varzi lining up against Ferrari-entered Alfa Romeos, Scuderia Subalpina-entered Maseratis and works Bugattis. It was quite a strong field, with Achille about a second a lap quicker than Tazio Nuvolari in the two-motor Alfa Romeo. Benito Mussolini forced Ferrari to take Nuvolari back so the quickest Italian racing car would be driven by the quickest Italian driver, but the Bimotore had three tyre failures and Nuvolari reverted to a Tipo B for the second practice session, and for the race.

Paul went to the rudimentary pits after practice where Auto Union had Willy Walb and two mechanics inside, and Achille out the back smoking a cigarette. For that meeting he was staying alone in the hotel, which was unusual.

"Ciao Achille," Paul said.

"Ciao Paul," Achille replied.

"Congratulations on your practice times. Can you tell me for my readers which car you have?"

Achille frowned. "Do they want to know?"

"Yes."

"It's a 1934 chassis updated with new water piping to the radiator, and it has a 1935 engine."

"Grazie. Pia was on the far side of the circuit and noticed your car looked unstable on the back straight."

"There were strong, gusts of wind and they moved the car around. It's manageable as long as I keep to the windward side of the straight."

"How's Norma?" Paul asked.

"She decided not to come. It's too hot and she's been here before."

"Grazie. Ciao Achille."

"Ciao Paul."

Paul then went to the Ferrari pits to talk with drivers there, especially Gianfranco Comotti who was a surprise selection in place of the more experienced Tonino Brivio.

On a grid decided by practice times, Achille easily achieved pole from Tazio Nuvolari in a larger-capacity Tipo B, and Wimille in a Bugatti. In the race Achille led away and gradually stretched his lead while Nuvolari retired with engine problems after only five laps. It was a two hour and twenty minute procession with Achille seemingly content to nurse the updated Auto Union to a near four-minute lead from Wimille, with Étancelin in a 6C-34 Maserati one lap down, and still racing with his cloth cap turned backwards.

* * *

Achille went down the stairs and into the dining room where Tonino was already at a table. The dining room only had guests at one other table, and Achille ordered a red wine before joining his friend.

"How did you find the wind in yesterday's practice?" Achille asked Tonino.

"It was unsettling," Tonino replied.

"Carthage is a magnificent circuit, but I would like it a lot better if there wasn't as much wind."

"It's the desert."

"Desert or not, the wind makes driving difficult."

"It does."

After an early lunch and a long afternoon, Achille was famished and ordered a steak, medium, and Tonino ordered veal with pasta. Achille ordered another red wine and waited for his meal. And waited and waited for his meal. He looked at his watch and was about to say something when the waiter came to their table.

The steak seemed half-cold and Achille cut the surface to see the meat cooked right through. Merda! He calmly put the knife and fork down, put his napkin on the table, got up and marched into the kitchen. There, looking smug was the big, fat cook, if he could be called a cook.

"Lei boiata busone testa di cazzo!" Achille grabbed for the cook's throat. "Si è ucciso!" Achille shook the cook whose eyes bulged with terror. And then Achille felt hands on his shoulders, pulling him.

"Achille, Achille...."

It registered. Tonino. Achille let the cook go.

"What is it Achille?" Tonino asked.

"He murdered my meal! Cooked it right through! Well-done and tough."

"Cook another one," Tonino said in French. "Quickly! Do you know who he is?"

The cook shook his head; still looking terrified.

"Achille Varzi. Just do it."

The cook nodded and went to the stove while Tonino guided Achille to their table.

"It won't take long Achille."

Achille was still fuming. "It better not take long."

It didn't take long and the second steak was just right. He knew how to cook a medium steak, the stronzo!

Chapter Twenty

Achille sat on a chair in the corner of the Auto Union pits.
Outside the weather was typical for the Nürburgring; sunny one
minute and raining the next. He wondered about his stomach pain;
it was so bad he couldn't practice on Friday. Despite the extra time
his car wasn't ready for Saturday and mechanics worked out the
front. It wasn't good enough. At least his pain was better although
he still felt unsettled.

Achille woke from his near-slumber by the entrance of a tall,
young man in racing overalls accompanied by beautiful, blonde
woman almost as tall. Achille was truly startled by the woman of
his past. He fixed her car, he admired her legs when she sat to
smoke a cigarette; he admired the way she spoke. She kissed his
cheek and he fantasised about kissing her lips. But it wasn't her
because that was many years ago. The young man noticed Achille
as he crossed the pit with his cap, goggles and gloves in one hand
and his beautiful companion in tow.

"Guten Morgen Herr Varzi," the young man said.

Achille groaned.

"Je suis désolé," the young man said. "Bonjour Monsieur Varzi,
my name is Paul Pietsch and I'm here for today's practice," he
continued in French.

Achille recognised his name as the other new driver. "Bonjour
Monsieur Pietsch," Achille replied without much enthusiasm.

"I wish to introduce my wife Ilse."

Achille stood and took the young woman's hand and kissed it
lightly. "Bonjour Madame Pietsch," he said.

"Bonjour Monsieur Varzi," she replied in the most delightful, sweet voice with exactly the same, lovely accent. Achille held her hand as she kept her gaze on him in a way he'd never experienced before.

Herr Walb stomped into the pit and snapped at Paul Pietsch, before thrusting a clipboard with stopwatches in Ilse Pietsch's direction and instructing her in German.

Paul Pietsch vaulted the counter and strode to Auto Union numbered three while slipping the earplugs he carried in his pocket into place. Next he fastened his cap, goggles and gloves before climbing into the cockpit. Then the steering wheel was attached and a sign given to the mechanic who applied the starting motor to the rear of the car. The ripping cacophony shattered the peace while Pietsch blipped the throttle to bring the engine back to temperature. Ilse Pietsch climbed onto the counter beside Rudolf recording the times for Rosemeyer, where she studied the car beneath her. Achille waited for Pietsch's noisy getaway before climbing onto the counter beside Ilse Pietsch. They sat with the only noise being the car on the warm-up loop before it closed, closer and closer, until the noise level rose to a bellow and the silver car adorned with red threes flashed by. Frau Pietsch clicked her stopwatch and then looked up. "Excuse me Monsieur Varzi...," she said in French.

"Call me Achille, s'il vous plaît," he interrupted. "You're part of our team now."

"You can call me Ilse. My passion is racing cars and I'm glad Paul has this drive. Auto Union is a great team and I'm pleased to be part of it."

Achille nodded. Ilse would keep the lap times of her husband, like most wives and girlfriends, but he was surprised that racing was her passion.

"Paul never told me even though I asked him," Ilse said. "What's it like to race a car like the Auto Union?"

Achille looked into her blue eyes while remembered thoughts from long ago. "A racing car such as an Auto Union is unlike anything else made by man. It's an extension of you, the driver. It responds to the slightest tug of the steering wheel and the slightest nudge of the throttle. And you, the driver, are an extension of the car. You hear it, you feel it through the seat and pedals, you smell it, you taste it. It's intimate and sensual." Achille paused for effect and he saw on her face that she understood. "But there's more to racing than being one with the car," Achille continued, still gazing into her lovely eyes. "What comes with victory's not easily explained."

The sharp scream of Caracciola's Mercedes passing the pits caused Ilse to wince, while Achille was surprised that he revealed his innermost thoughts to a young woman he barely knew.

"I understand," Ilse said after the noise receded.

Achille discreetly studied Ilse Pietsch. Tall and slim, fair skin, short, curled blonde hair and deep red lipstick – strikingly attractive, especially in a simple but fashionable white dress and black beret. "Tell me Ilse, why is it that beautiful women are attracted to men who race cars?"

She laughed lightly. "Maybe I had the choice of being the wife of some boring manager; sending him to work in the morning and waiting for him to return at night; always late of course. Or I could be sitting on the counter of a pit, discussing the sensual appeal of racing cars with the most successful and famous driver in the world."

Achille decided not to reply.

"Are you staying near the circuit?" Ilse asked.

"I'm staying at the Ringhaus Hotel," Achille replied.

"We're staying there. Perhaps you could dine with us this evening?"

Achille had to keep his distance from Paul Pietsch: team mate and rival. "No, I can't intrude," Achille said.

"Do you have someone here? Perhaps we can share a table."

"My companion isn't here."

"You can't dine alone."

Something about Ilse Pietsch fascinated him. She was beautiful, charming, and she liked car racing which was unusual for a young woman. More than that he had waited fifteen years to kiss her lips. He wanted to spend more time with her but he couldn't dine with her husband. "I must have an early meal and an early sleep so I'll be fresh for the race tomorrow."

She nodded while the sound of Rosemeyer's car passing made talk impossible for the moment. Achille then noticed mechanics pushing his car, number two, into place. They started the engine where the bellow of sixteen stub exhausts meant the end of his conversation with Ilse Pietsch. Mechanics raised the engine cover to change to racing plugs while Achille grabbed his cap, goggles and gloves, jumped the counter and strolled to the car to check it out. He slowly walked around the Auto Union while slipping his gloves on, and everything was in good order. Into the cockpit where a mechanic attached the steering wheel. Achille flicked the magneto switch, put his finger up and the starting motor was applied far to the rear. The engine caught, Achille selected first gear and eased onto the straight. He rounded the South Curve and continued along the warm-up loop before turning onto the main straight and passing the pits at speed.

* * *

Race day was a mixture of sun, cloud and showers of rain, but it was dry in the journalist's area of the grandstand. Paul used his binoculars to study the pits where he got the biggest surprise. At the Auto Union pits was Ilse Hubitsch from an Eifelrennen some years before. Her companion of the time, Charly Jellen, was killed the previous year so Paul assumed that Ilse was the companion of the new Auto Union driver, Paul Pietsch.

"Who are you looking at?" Pia asked.

"Nobody," Paul said as innocently as he could manage.

"Give me those binoculars."

Pia focussed and scanned the pits. "Aah," she said. She put the binoculars down. "That German lady."

"She's not as beautiful as you."

"What is it then?"

"She gave me a tip a few years ago which turned out to be right. That's unusual for the mistress of a driver."

"She's beautiful."

"She is."

"Her name's Ilse Pietsch and she's the wife of Paul Pietsch, the new Auto Union driver. My French is proving useful."

Ilse being married wasn't a surprise, while Paul now was curious that Pia knew. "Are there any other driver's wives you know, beyond Norma and our other friends."

"A few, and mistresses too. Alice Hoffman is lovely and she's very much in love with Louis Chiron, but he won't marry her. All women want love, and I think women want marriage as a commitment of love. Paula Stuck's delightful and I have spoken with many others." Pia looked towards the timing tower. "There's 30 minutes until the race so I must leave." She kissed Paul on his cheek and departed on foot for the Hatzenbach section of the track, rugged up with an overcoat and waterproof hat.

Mercedes-Benz had a full team for the race with Caracciola, Fagioli, von Brauchitsch returning after his crash the previous year, and former racing mechanic and motorcycle racer Hermann Lang making his car racing debut. Auto Union had four cars for Hans Stuck, Achille Varzi, former motorcycle racer Bernd Rosemeyer and Paul Pietsch. Ferrari had two cars for Louis Chiron and René Dreyfus, with Nuvolari away doing speed record runs in a bimotore.

Coloured lights replaced the cannon to signal the start, and during the course of the race many cars were in out and out of the pits changing spark plugs. They suffered ignition problems from the wet track and the variable weather. Manfred von Brachitsch led until the engine of his car blew-up which let Caracciola into the lead, while new driver Rosemeyer worked his Auto Union into second place. Achille struggled for speed and pitted after thee laps to hand his car to Hermann zu Leiningen. Paul was surprised to see Achille grabbing his stomach in obvious pain. Caracciola won at his favourite circuit from Rosemeyer in only his second car race, and the German crowd was most impressed with both drivers.

Pia returned about 30 minutes later and sat beside Paul.

"Von Brachitsch's car was misfiring like many of the others," Pia said, "So when he went past me he revved it harder to make up for the lack of power."

That explained why his engine blew-up.

"What happened to Achille?" Pia asked.

"He was sick and in some pain."

"That's a shame and Norma's not here to look after him. I hope it isn't serious."

Paul thought there would be nothing worse than being alone in a hotel feeling sick and they must check on him. Paul led the way out of the grandstand, now emptying.

"We must find Achille's room and offer to help him, if we can," Pia said.

"I thought the same thing," Paul said.

"You can type and telegraph your articles while I'll see him."

Paul thought that was an excellent idea. He reached their own room, unlocked and went inside. Pia returned about half an hour later.

"Achille has a sore stomach, but he's feeling better now that he had a chance to lie down. He thinks he'll be able to drive to Milano tomorrow where he'll visit his doctor."

"What if he can't drive?"

"I offered that he could travel with us by train, and to see us over breakfast if he wants this."

That was a good idea as Paul returned to his typing. He hoped Achille's health problems weren't too serious, seeing as this was a busy few weeks of racing.

Chapter Twenty One

Achille lay on the narrow table while the doctor poked and prodded for several minutes. Doctor Bari then turned his back leaving Achille to sit up and pull his shirt on.

"You have appendicitis signore Varzi," Doctor Bari said. "You need an operation."

"I can't. My next race is at Paris on Sunday and I need to be there on Thursday. Is there any other way?"

The doctor sighed. "You should get it treated but I know your commitments. If we deal with your pain you should be alright, but you must have an operation, because if you appendix bursts you could be in trouble."

Achille's contract was only for a year, and he needed to do well and not languish in a hospital bed.

"Morphine will deal with your pain," Doctor Bari said. "Be careful. It will affect your judgement, it will make you tired and it can be addictive. Only use it when you absolutely must, and never more than five milligrams." Doctor Bari went to a cabinet, grabbed a little vial, and then he went to a cupboard to get a syringe. He put the vial on his desk and Achille went there.

"Pull the syringe back to five, insert it through the rubber bung on the vial, press air into the vial, turn the vial upside down and pull the syringe out slowly until you get five milligrams." Achille watched the doctor draw five milligrams and then he did it himself.

"Inject the morphine into muscle, like your leg," Doctor Bari said. Doctor Bari sat in his chair and wrote a prescription. "Take this to the pharmacist when you need more, but remember what I

said. Don't use morphine more than you have to, and see me to
schedule an operation as soon as you can."

"I will."

"This is important."

Achille took the syringe, vial and the prescription away.

* * *

Montlhéry was quiet and calm, but it was a calm that wouldn't last.
Soon, fifteen cars would be started for practice in 30 minutes time.
Achille crossed the bridge where he found an earth bank
surrounded by trees. He sat in peace and smoked a cigarette.
After, while he walked slowly to the pits, he came across Paul and
Ilse Pietsch heading along the concrete path. For the race Paul
Pietsch was the reserve driver and Achille hoped that he wouldn't
be needed.

They greeted one-another while walking slowly.

"Cette année a l'air d'un rêve," Ilse said. "Paul's racing the best
of the best: Nuvolari, Caracciola, Stuck, Chiron, Dreyfus, and I'm
part of the team," she continued in French. She turned her head.
"Who is the best driver, Achille, apart from you?"

"Tazio Nuvolari is the maestro," Achille said without hesitation.
"We can only achieve what our cars are capable of giving but
somehow Tazio achieves more than this. He has won races in cars
that had no right to win."

"Tazio Nuvolari and Achille Varzi; two great Italian drivers.
Which are the best cars?"

"Mercedes-Benz has developed their car over the off-season
and Rudi is driving at his best, so they're the greatest competition
to Auto Union. Alfa Romeo, Bugatti and Maserati are struggling,

and over time I'm sure they'll be left further behind. They're working with engineering from last decade."

"Why do you think these other manufacturers will slip further behind?"

Achille thought that was a good question. "Alfa Romeo, Bugatti and Maserati have progressively developed and refined their cars over the last dozen years, and now they must build all-new cars to remain competitive. But the economic situation outside of Germany means these manufacturers will have difficulties to find sufficient money for design, development and testing."

"Surely Italy won't want to be left behind after dominating racing for so long?"

"The German government gave Mercedes and Auto Union grants to develop new racing cars, but the cost to build and race these cars is much more than these grants. Alfa Romeo and Maserati must invest their own funds in addition to any government grants, but such funds might not be available."

All the time they walked, Ilse gazed at Achille while Paul hadn't contributed to their conversation. Perhaps he just got into his cars and raced without considering which car was the best, why that car was the best, where each car's weaknesses lay and how to exploit those weaknesses. For sure the Auto Union's key weakness was poor traction, and on tighter circuits the more nimble Alfa Romeo P3 could be an embarrassment. Especially at Montlhéry in 1935 with new chicanes.

"Achille," Ilse said. "I understand what you said about racing when we spoke last week, but surely you must think it's dangerous."

"Ilse knew a man who was killed last year," Paul said. "Charly Jellen introduced us."

"I more than knew Charly," Ilse said before turning to look at Achille again. "I met Charly Jellen just after my divorce when I went to a local motor race meeting. But he didn't want to marry me and Paul did. And then, later, Charly crashed and was killed."

Achille was surprised. Ilse and Paul were in their mid-twenties, and yet she was married, divorced and had a lover for a time. He thought that was interesting more than surprising. An interesting young woman with a fascination for car racing.

They reached the pits where his car number eight waited. The morphine made all the difference and he felt no pain. Soon he set good times, eventually getting down to 5 minutes 21.3 which was excellent given the chicanes. Achille knew he could better that time on Saturday.

* * *

Achille lit a cigarette and pulled Le Ambizioni Sbagliate from his luggage. He sighed while he momentarily contemplated nights in hotel rooms. It was always better when Norma accompanied him or when his friends were around. But racing had changed and the cost of developing new cars meant fewer entries, fewer drivers and fewer friends. He sat in the velvet armchair in the corner of the room and turned to the first page, just when he heard knocking at the door. Achille put the book down and opened the door to be surprised by Ilse Pietsch. Momentarily startled he then realised she ought not be seen there. "Ilse," he said. "Entrez, s'il tu plais."

"I saw your times from practice today," Ilse said in French after she closed the door behind her. "They were good."

Achille nodded while puzzled to have her in his room.

"That isn't why I came here," she said. "During the time you were practicing I thought about your comment on Tazio Nuvolari. I know that any driver can drive fast, and any driver can drive beyond his limits and perhaps crash and break his leg, or even kill himself. A great driver and an even greater man is the man who knows where his strengths and weaknesses lay, and how far he can go to achieve his ambitions without going too far and sacrificing all."

Achille stood stunned – Ilse understood him like nobody else.

"Achille?" she asked.

"Pardon?" Achille said, still confused. He looked at her eye to eye for she was as tall as he. "How do you know this?"

"So I'm right."

"You knew you were right."

"I wanted to hear it from you."

"Why?"

"You're a great man more than a great driver, and I know you've been misunderstood. I heard talk of arrogance but they don't understand you. You're a deep thinker who analyses all options before deciding on a course of action."

Achille was again startled. Ilse knew more, much more, about him than his racing. He wondered how she could do that, and especially a woman so young.

Their conversation faded to silence and Achille suddenly felt an intense ache of desire for beautiful and insightful Ilse Pietsch. A yearning, a longing, an almost overpowering urge to ravish her. He never felt such strong feelings before and he liked them. He liked them a lot, except she was unobtainable. Perhaps that was it. She understood him and yet he couldn't have her. No, such feelings were something else and he guessed what it was. After two brief meetings he'd fallen in love with another man's wife. He didn't love Norma and never had, but he never expected to find love in a hotel in Montlhéry. Achille butted his cigarette in the ashtray and all the time Ilse stood there, close but not too close, and Achille knew the significance of that. He wondered, but it was too far too fast. For many years he wanted to kiss those lips, but he knew if he started he wouldn't be able to stop. He gazed at beautiful Ilse Pietsch, he smelt her soft perfume, and knew he shouldn't.

"You should go before people realise," Achille said.

"Of course," Ilse replied.

She left his room and quietly closed the door behind to leave Achille pondering whether he should have asked her to stay.

Chapter Twenty Two

Achille stared out of the window with his thoughts far away. In Frankfurt where he'd never been, but where a beautiful young woman lived. He fantasised about holding her, sensually unbuttoning her tight-fitting dress and then removing her slip to reveal her slim body. Holding her naked and knowing what was coming; passion shared with the only woman who'd ever understood him. That thought made him feel light-headed; she understood him and their passion would be much more intense for that. He wondered how it would be. Two souls merged into one? Heart to heart, mind to mind and body to body? He knew what they would share was beyond his comprehension.

"What's wrong Achille?" Norma asked. "You've had that game of chess for an hour, and haven't made a move against yourself."

"Pardon?" Achille asked, and then it registered. "I'm distracted."

"You've been distracted for a week. What do you want to do?"

Achille couldn't think straight. He had one thing he wanted to do but that had to wait, if it happened at all.

"Do you want to see a movie?" Norma asked.

Achille shook his head.

Norma came and stood between the table and the window, and Achille looked up at her standing with her hands on her hips. "You and I are going to make love, and then we're going to eat at Ristorante Bagutta and then we're going to see a movie."

Achille nodded. After making love he might think clearly again. "Yes, we'll do this."

By the time Achille went to their bedroom Norma was ready, and he quickly undressed and joined her. He knew every centimetre of her, as he closed his eyes and ravished her like she'd never been ravished before. From her lips to her feet and all besides, until she cried out, and then he took her where she lay. Hard, rough, aggressive. Harder and harder and not registering what was happening. Nothing was happening until he saw someone else. Tall, slim, fair, blonde. With him, wanting him, wanting him to take her. Taking her, filling her, loving her. He came.

Achille rolled onto his side and Norma ran her fingers through his sweaty hair. "Are you alright?" she asked.

"I'm fine," Achille said without thinking.

"You seemed distant."

Achille rolled onto his side and looked into Norma's brown eyes, and then he knew. In practice at the Nürburgring in three week's time. He touched Norma's cheek lightly. "I'm feeling better now."

Norma went to bathe while Achille sat in the midst of rumpled sheets. Ilse Pietsch was beautiful, intelligent, and she alone understood him. Nobody understood him except for Ilse. Until Ilse his life had been sensible and orderly but now he felt like he was losing control. Achille wondered if that was good or if that was bad. But good or bad it was something he had to do.

Chapter Twenty Three

The narrow streets of Nürburg were hard for the bus driver to navigate. From behind, Paul watched the driver working hard at the big steering wheel while feeling glad he wasn't driving. Slowly and slowly until the familiar Hotel Ringhaus loomed in the distance. The driver pulled up at the stop just along the road as Paul stretched, stood, grabbed Pia's handbag from the rack and gave it to her before holding the back of the seat in front and climbing down the stairs. Outside, a middle-aged man in a shabby suit and a shabby hat unloaded their luggage, which was German efficiency at its finest, although Paul was surprised that a middle-aged man had such a menial job. Paul stood with arms crossed while watching the porter aged in his forties, with receding black, curly hair grey at his temples. The porter turned around and caught Paul's eye.

"Was wollen Sie?" he asked.

"Sprechen Sie Englisch?" Paul asked as a first option.

"Yes I do," the porter said in accented English. "What do you want?"

"Nothing," Paul lied.

The door of the bus slammed shut with a hiss of air, and then gears ground before the bus lurched away in a cloud of smoke and a cacophony of noise.

"I hope you enjoy the racing this weekend."

Paul looked up at the cloudy sky threatening rain and thought the weather might be a challenge, as usual.

"Where are you from?" the porter asked.

"My name's Paul Bassi and I'm a journalist from Italy."

The porter nodded slowly. "My name is Ludwig Broder and I was once a journalist."

"What happened?"

"It's the way of things."

Paul wondered the way of what things, until he realised. He looked around and nobody was close. "Persecution?" Paul asked quietly.

Herr Broder nodded his head.

"I'm sorry to hear about your misfortune, Herr Broder."

"It was only a newspaper in Koblenz, but...."

Paul was sure that persecution would get worse. "Should you leave?" Paul asked quietly.

"To where? My family has lived in this region for more than four generations."

"If you leave, one day you can come back when it's better." Paul thought about options. "You speak good English. Go now, while you can." Herr Broder demurred. "I was born and raised in Australia and then I moved to Italy two years ago," Paul said. "Because I speak Italian, Italy became my home."

"Where are you staying Herr Bassi?"

"We're staying at Hotel Ringhaus. We can take our luggage; it's not far." Paul opened his wallet and took out a twenty mark note. "Thank you for your trouble, Herr Broder."

"Thank you," Herr Broder said before placing the note in his pocket.

Paul picked up his case and bag and Pia, looking baffled, grabbed hers.

"One day it might be too late," Paul said. "Goodbye and good luck."

"Enjoy your racing Herr Bassi."

Paul headed towards the hotel with Pia alongside.

"Che cosa?" Pia asked.

"He's Jewish," Paul said in Italian. "I told him to leave now, while he can."

"People shouldn't have to leave their country just because they're Jewish."

"If you were Jewish; what would you do?"

"I would leave."

"He used to work for a newspaper, but as you know...."

"No public servants, no teachers, no writers, no academics, no journalists."

"I'm sure this will get worse."

Pia shrugged her shoulders while Paul wondered how much worse it could get. Whatever that was, Paul was sure it would get worse.

* * *

Achille strode to the Auto Union pits where four improved cars waited out the front – for Stuck, Rosemeyer, Pietsch and himself. But Achille wasn't worried about the cars. He went into the pits and straight to Ilse.

"Room fourteen," Achille whispered in her ear.

She nodded. "Tonight cheri."

Achille left for his car.

* * *

Pia stood with her hands on her hips and looked across the wide straight towards the pits. Cloudy skies threatened rain, as always.

"I know you were excited about these German cars, but this hasn't been a good thing. We have to come here twice a year, for a start."

Paul agreed about these German cars not being a good thing. "Mercedes-Benz is off-limits to journalists and I haven't said more than three words to any of their drivers. Auto Union aren't so bad; we know Achille, and Hans Stuck is genuinely lovely."

"Paula Stuck is lovely too."

Things had changed, and what was once intimate and friendly had become deadly serious. However, they were at the Nürburgring for practice for the Grosser Preis von Deutschland where the silver cars were out in force. Auto Union had four entries for Achille Varzi, Hans Stuck, Bernd Rosemeyer and Paul Pietsch, while Mercedes-Benz had five cars for Rudi Caracciola, Manfred von Brauchitsch, Luigi Fagioli and junior drivers Hans Greier and Hermann Lang. Ferrari had four large-capacity Tipo Bs for Tazio Nuvolari, Louis Chiron, Tonino Brivio and René Dreyfus, while Scuderia Subalpina had newer Maseratis for Philippe Étancelin and Goffredo Zehender and older models for Euginio Siena and Pietro Ghersi. There were a few privately-entered Alfa Romeos and Maseratis, and an ERA for Raymond Mays which stood no chance. Despite the modernity of the meeting, grid positions were drawn by ballot. Nonetheless practice was interesting, especially with Nuvolari surprisingly competitive on a circuit that demanded the utmost in driving skill.

When Paul returned to the hotel with Pia, he expected to find Achille smoking and playing cards with his friends Tonino Brivio and Pietro Ghersi, but the dining room was all quiet. That was strange.

* * *

Achille sat on the end of his bed smoking a cigarette. He tried to feel calm but it wasn't working. He listened for the slightest noise, until the rapping startled him. He slowly butted his cigarette, stood, checked himself in the mirror and went to the door. He nodded at Ilse, and closed and chained the door when she came into his room. He turned around and almost gasped in wonderment. Dressed in white as she often did; simple, sophisticated and attractive against her fair skin, deep blue eyes and light, blonde hair. He cupped her buttocks through thin cotton as their lips touched.

It took a life of its own, without time, space or reason. Ilse's dress all but torn from her body, her slip bunched around her waist where Achille pushed her onto the bed, he kneeling above her still half-dressed while sucking her gorgeous breasts, her fingers on his belt to loosen his trousers, his underwear in the way until he momentarily rolled away so she could rip them off and toss them aside. Entering her still wearing his shirt while she unbuttoned it. Her soft, slim fingers running through the hair on his chest while he sat up to pull his shirt free, and she sat to kiss his chest while murmuring slightly, and with him still inside her. She fell back and he went with her, kissing the side of her neck, she turning her head to give him room. A big hand on her firm breast, the sleek softness of her skin, her legs above him locked at the ankles, drawing him deeper, deeper, deeper. Deeper into her heart and soul. She took him completely, utterly, totally until he came, and in sheer exhaustion he lay above her while she held his shoulders and kneaded the muscles of his arms. He slowly returned to the here and now while kissing lip to lip with a brief touch of tongues to remind them both of what happened. He lay with her and didn't want to let her go.

But he had to let her go, as Achille lay beside Ilse while absorbed the electrifying softness of her skin through his fingertips. She brushed his firm muscles; chest, stomach and lower where he was calm and still sensitive.

"Achille, Je t'aime," she murmured.

"Je t'aime cherié," he whispered in a hoarse voice with his throat parched.

Ilse moved and Achille looked around a small room littered with clothing. He briefly smiled with the recent memory. Ilse sat up. "I must go cheri." She bent down and kissed his lips lightly. "I will be back."

"When?"

She half-smiled. "Tomorrow." She kissed him lightly. "Sleep well cheri, and set good times tomorrow."

Achille lay in his bed, watching Ilse straighten her slip before dressing, and then she unchained the door and slipped out of his room. Tomorrow would be different, better, but nothing could be better than what they just shared.

* * *

It rained on Saturday night and race day dawned foggy with dark clouds. The crowd streaming into the main spectator area was truly massive, and when Paul reached the grandstand he used his binoculars to see hills in the distance dotted with many thousands more. Pia departed for Hatzenbach while Paul waited for the ten-thirty start on a wet track.

The starting light flashed from red to yellow and the noise was incredible, and suddenly a mechanic ran from the Auto Union pits to Hans Stuck's car just before the light changed to green. All cars surged forward except Stuck on pole, while Paul watched horrified as Achille Varzi from the fifth row tore through the cloud of tyre smoke, oil smoke and water spray to hit the mechanic tending to Stuck's car. The poor mechanic was tossed aside like a rag doll, and after the rest of the field cleared the grid, other Auto Union mechanics ran to carry him away while Stuck's car was push-started. Tazio Nuvolari led away from the grid until Rudi Caracciola took the lead on the run to the South Curve. Fagioli held third ahead of von Brauchitsch and Mays. Trailing the field were three Auto Unions of Stuck, Varzi and Pietsch!

Part-way around lap one Nuvolari spun the Alfa, fortunately without hitting anything, and Rosemeyer in the Auto Union passed car after car to move into second and harry Caracciola for the lead. Stuck also drove well to get into fourth but Varzi drove at the tail of the field while Paul guessed he was affected by the accident at the start, even though he was blinded by smoke and spray.

Rosemeyer lost time having a tyre replaced, and Varzi in eighth place was caught by Paul Pietsch and then got into the swing of the race, banging wheels with his younger rival and closing the door to overtaking at every opportunity. That sort of driving was slow and neither Auto Union was able to close the gap on the rest of the field. The race was headed by the three Mercedes of Caracciola, Fagioli and von Brauchitsch, followed by Nuvolari in fourth and Rosemeyer in fifth.

Nuvolari got inspired on lap nine to overtake two Mercedes, and then he put pressure on Caracciola before taking the lead. Rosemeyer used his fresher tyres to take second ahead of Caracciola and von Brauchitsch, before the top four pitted on lap 11 for fuel and tyres. Von Brauchitsch was away first from Caracciola and Rosemeyer, while Nuvolari was out of his car and jumping up and down with anxiety or anger while mechanics refuelled his car by hand. That left von Brauchitsch in the lead from Rosemeyer, until the Auto Union retired. Caracciola struggled for speed while Nuvolari drove like a man possessed, even hanging his arm out of the cockpit and whipping his car with nervous energy. He surged past Fagioli to move into a distant second to von Brauchitsch who was given signals to slow, but Paul noted that he kept the same lap times.

Von Brauchitsch started the last lap with a 35 second lead over Nuvolari while continuing at the same, demented pace until the Karussel where he blew a tyre and Tazio Nuvolari swept past. Then a second tyre blew on the run to the finish line where the stunned crowd silently watched the red Alfa Romeo take victory before they broke into a massive cheer for a truly, amazing victory. Second was Stuck, followed by Caracciola, Rosemeyer, von Brauchitsch and Fagioli. Geir and Varzi were one lap down in seventh and eighth and Pietsch was a further lap behind in ninth. Paul was amazed to see von Brauchitsch crying at the end of the race, and thought it would have been better to have pitted again for tyres, or slow and ease the wear.

All in Paul had an amazing story to write for his newspapers and journals, and Tazio Nuvolari was a truly, remarkable racing driver.

Chapter Twenty Four

Achille lay on his back and Ilse rested her head on his chest. He touched her pretty, blonde hair. She was beautiful and sophisticated and strangely vulnerable. She was everything. But a few hours every few weeks when they met at races wasn't enough. It could never be enough. He wanted more; he needed more. He needed her forever.

"Je t'aime Achille," Ilse murmured. He cupped her buttocks and squeezed her with affection. "Your hands are so big and strong," she said quietly in French.

"I want you," Achille said. "With me always."

She sat up and looked down on him. "My future's with you."

"When?"

"Tomorrow's your race and then there's Brno which is the last race of the season. I'll tell Paul when we arrive at the hotel and I'll leave with you."

"Brno next week."

"Where will we live?"

"Milano. Norma can have my apartment, she deserves this, and we can stay in a hotel until we find an apartment. We can live in a suite."

"I like Milano."

"It will be good."

* * *

The Circuito de Lasarte at San Remo for the Gran Premio di Spagna suffered from many loose stones during practice. Jean-Pierre Wimille of Bugatti told Paul that he feared for what might happen during the race. On the other hand Tazio shrugged the danger off, while Achille departed for the Maria Cristina Hotel in an amazing rush and Paul didn't get a chance to talk with him. Paul sensed something was up. Norma stayed away from North Africa because of the heat and that was understandable, but she hadn't been seen at a circuit since then. They saw her in Milano when Paul took Pia to Ristorante Bagutta, and Paul ended up playing a noisy game of scopa while Pia and Norma drank together and talked in dialect for a few hours.

On race day loose stones continued to be a hazard where Achille suffered first, pitting at the end of the first lap with a broken windscreen on his car and blood streaming from a cut on his face. Reserve driver Paul Pietsch took over Auto Union number six while Achille disappeared out of sight.

About 10 minutes later Achille appeared at the pits; arguing most vociferously with Willy Walb. Paul Pietsch pitted for a replacement windscreen, and Achille nearly dragged the young German out of his car before departing sideways while still smoking a cigarette. He was followed out of the pits by Wimille in his Bugatti, where the French driver stayed close to the faster Auto Union for 15 laps and their speeds dragged the Bugatti into a surprising fifth place. Not so Achille who pitted on lap 25 with black smoke pouring through the louvers of his car's engine cover.

Caracciola won from Fagioli and von Brachitsch, and in doing so Rudi Caracciola was Champion European Driver for 1935. Jean-Pierre Wimille finished fourth and less than three minutes behind the three Mercedes-Benz, which was the best performance by a Bugatti for many years.

Paul and Pia ate in the dining room of the Maria Cristina Hotel, where Paul overheard Jean-Pierre Wimille tell his companions that he learned more from following Achille Varzi for 15 laps than he learned in all of the races he'd ever contested. Paul knew by the speed he showed and the successes he earned that Achille was special, but he never realised that he was *that* special.

The Velká cena Masarykova at Brno, Czechoslovakia was held the weekend after Spain, where there was no choice for Paul and Pia but to fly from San Sebastian to Paris, and then to Prague. They stayed for two nights in Prague, which was a truly beautiful and cosmopolitan city straddling the Vitava River. Much of the inner city was quite ancient, with Medieval churches, cathedrals, squares, bridges and other buildings, while other parts of the city dated to the seventeenth and eighteenth centuries. They enjoyed a wonderful night where the concierge recommended a good ballroom for dancing, and the next day they explored on foot including the delightful St Vitus Cathedral. They then flew to Brno where they reached the Grand Hotel by midday Thursday. The Grand Hotel was grand too; a large and lovely building, somewhat French-styled. It was the place to stay at Brno, as drivers for Mercedes-Benz, Auto Union and Ferrari all were there. Paul hoped the race would be worth it. At least the last race of the season was in Italy where he could drive.

The paddock on Friday had a strange atmosphere but no drivers were talking to journalists. Until Paul spotted Tonino, and checked that nobody was around before he closed on him.

"Ciao Tonino," Paul greeted.

"Ciao Paul," Tonino replied.

"Do you know if anything's wrong?"

A pause before he got close. "This isn't for publication," he said quietly.

"Of course."

"Achille's fallen for that German woman Ilse, wife of Paul Pietsch. Ilse told her husband she's leaving him for Achille."

A few things then made sense, like Achille disappearing at race meetings and Norma not being around. Paul didn't know what to say so he didn't say anything. It was safer that way, given he was honorary Milanese.

"Grazie Tonino. Ciao."

"Ciao Paul."

Paul went to find Pia and tell her the news, where she was at first shocked and then realised their affair must have been happening for the past few months.

"It's not the first affair in the world and won't be the last," Paul said.

Pia frowned and then, of course, agreed. In the meantime Paul had a major story on his hands, but he couldn't do anything with it. All he could do was report that although Mercedes entered, they withdrew from the race leaving Auto Union versus Ferrari, like at the Coppa Acerbo. And like that race it would almost certainly be an Auto Union walkover. He could also report Paul Pietsch left Brno for personal reasons.

The dining room was hushed when Paul and Pia ate a meal together without wanting to be overheard, although there were few Italians at the meeting so it didn't really matter what they said. But somehow it seemed wrong.

Saturday practice was more normal because everyone knew, and of course the priority was setting times for the Gran Premio and the Voiturette race to be run in conjunction. After, Pia had disappeared so Paul walked to the hotel room to type his articles.

* * *

Pia walked along the corridor where a floorboard creaked, and then she heard something else – a woman crying. Pia went around the corner to see Ilse sitting on a black leather bench in the corridor, gently crying.

Pia closed. "Qu'est-ce que c'est?"

Ilse wiped her cheeks. "Do you know about Achille and me?" she asked in French.

"I do."

"Do you hate me?"

"Of course not!"

"The other women hate me. When I went to the paddock, they all left."

"Oh no; I'm so sorry!" Pia sat beside Ilse. "I've known Achille for a long time, and Norma too, but whatever happens is their and your business, not mine. If Achille loves you, I'm happy for him and of course I'm happy for you."

Ilse smiled. "Thank you."

Pia realised Ilse won't be able to help in the pits, unless the other women changed their minds. "Whenever you come to a race, you know you'll always be my friend."

"Thank you so much. I must go because Achille might know what happened."

Yes, he would. "You can tell Achille that I'm happy for you both."

"I will; thank you."

Ilse left while Pia knew the other wives and girlfriends assumed Ilse abandoned a relationship with an unsuccessful driver to lure a successful driver into having a relationship with her, which was wrong. The first time Pia met Achille, she was shocked by the way he made her feel. Several times, no many times, she'd fantasised about being ravished by Achille, having him ride her the same way he drove his cars, so confident, so masculine, they being one like she'd never experienced before: the sexual experience of her life. Pia felt hot and flushed and wet inside.

Pia got up from the bench while hoping Paul didn't notice, because she didn't want to tell him about Ilse. That was sad, because more than any other wife or girlfriend, Ilse got genuine pleasure from being part of the team, which was now denied to her. That was truly sad.

Pia walked away – hoping time would heal, but every time wives and girlfriends saw them together, that would remind them, even though that was wrong. Achille was very attractive, especially sexually, and any woman could fall for that. Pia could, no matter that Paul was marvellous and probably wondering where she was. Pia continued on her way to their room.

Chapter Twenty Five

Achille sat in the chair in the corner of their bedroom; watching Ilse in the faint light. The only sound was her gentle breathing. It was as if she had been put on earth to bring joy and happiness to those who knew her, and she'd spent many years searching for a man worthy of her affections. It was their first morning together and the first morning of their new life.

Ilse stirred and murmured before rolling over, and then she sat up. "Qu'est que c'est?"

"Je t'aime ma cherié," Achille said.

"Je t'aime mon cheri." She rubbed her eyes. "What have you planned?" she asked in French.

"For what?"

"For everything."

"This year has been good in some ways, where I had strong wins in Tunis and the Coppa Acerbo. But the car has let me down many times and I don't like driving for a German team. Language difficulties are a bigger problem than you can imagine. I can speak with Walb and Rosemeyer speaks a bit of French," and Achille shrugged his shoulders. "It's difficult and I have trouble getting my money out of Germany. I tested a new Maserati but it was slow, so I signed for Auto Union for next year."

"Whatever you think is best, I'll support you"

"I heard about what happened to you at Brno."

"Don't worry about that. What's important is that we're together at last. You'll be racing a lot mon cheri, and I'll travel with you even if I have to stay in hotels."

Achille appreciated that. "That's next year. For now, do you like skiing?"

Ilse sat up beaming brightly. "I love skiing!"

"That's good. Each January we go to Cortina d'Ampezzo, and in February we're doing a bobsleigh exhibition at the Winter Olympics. Carlo Trossi who we know as Didi, Piero Taruffi, Franco Cortese and I."

"Will your friends tolerate the German home-wrecker?"

Achille wondered, and remembered that many of his friends had problems with Norma being unsophisticated in their eyes, although Norma didn't much care for how they felt. Ilse was sophisticated but at the same time she was sensitive. "I hope they like you my darling."

"I hope so too."

"You met my brother Angelo at the Coppa Acerbo, and in the meantime we'll visit my family and especially my uncle Hercules. We'll have a big, noisy Italian Christmas together, and then we'll go to the Alps. After this we'll be testing cars for the new season, here at Monza, and racing starts in April at Monaco."

"I like Monaco, and we can book a room that overlooks the circuit so I can see you win."

Achille liked that idea. "Yes, from the hotel you can see me win." Milano was a new city for Ilse, her new home, and there was much to do. "Do you drive?" Achille asked.

"I do."

"I'll buy you a car. What would you like?"

"I don't know. I never thought I would have my own car."

"You can have your own car and more besides. We'll go shopping and you can have anything you like."

"There's just one thing I want cheri; you."

Achille went to the big bed. "Yes cherié."

"How do you say 'Je t'aime mon cheri' in Italian?"

"Ti amo amore mio."

"Ti amo amore mio," Ilse said.

Achille knelt on the bed and removed his gown. "Ti amo amore mia."

* * *

Achille cuddled up to Ilse who had a lovemaking style that reflected her nature. Close, intimate, loving. With love shared, nothing else mattered.

"Now that I'm living in Italy I must learn Italian," Ilse said. "The journalist's wife Pia told me that learning French from Italian wasn't hard, so I hope learning Italian from French isn't hard either."

"She's right," Achille said. "It won't be hard for you."

"I like Pia; she was nice to me the other day."

"She would have been," Achille agreed, knowing Pia to be a real lady. And then it made sense; Pia was young, younger even than Ilse, and devastatingly beautiful. Achille was certain that if Pia left her husband and began an affair with a driver, she would be treated the same way despite being a well-liked part of the circus for some years. "You have something in common with Pia."

"What?" Ilse asked, frowning. Then her face changed. "Oh, yes."

That made sense because there was no real difference between Ilse having an affair and then leaving her husband, and Baby having an affair with Louis and then leaving her husband. Achille then wondered because Baby was beautiful, but in an older, mature way. It must have been the combination of youth and beauty. That was it.

* * *

Paul was glad to park the car after the last race of the season at Cosenza, which had been a long drive. Just over a thousand kilometres with an overnight stay at Napoli, and Pia quite rightly didn't bother to come along. Paul reached home and let himself into their comfortable, two bedroom apartment. They were lucky to find it, in immaculate condition in a pleasant neighbourhood. Their own home, furnished just so.

Paul kissed Pia. "Ciao amore mia."

"Ciao amore mio," she replied.

Pia seemed distracted. "Is there anything wrong?"

"No. Yes. Would you like to eat out tonight?"

After so much travel? "No thanks."

"We could go to Ristorante Bagutta."

Paul understood and Pia was good to think of that.

Ristorante Bagutta was quiet as to be expected on a Tuesday night, when Mario showed them to a table and left with an order for two glasses of red wine. Paul had his back to the other room. "Can you see anything?" he asked.

Pia nodded. "Achille and Ilse alone."

"We should eat, and if Achille's friends don't show up then we can go there."

Paul and Pia ordered and ate, and nobody came which was rather cruel. They went to the other room where the couple sat at a large table, with Ilse gazing intently at Achille. Paul could almost reach out and touch her love, or adoration because her gaze was more intense than mere love.

"Bonsoir Achille et Ilse," Pia said.

"Bonsoir," Paul echoed, still fascinated by the intense connection between the couple.

"Bonsoir," Achille said. "Assis, s'il tu plait."

They sat. "Are you both well?" Pia asked in French.

"We're both well and we have much planned," Ilse said, turning to look at Pia. "I'm having Christmas with Achille's family, and then we go to the Alps with Achille's friends to practice for a bobsleigh demonstration at the Winter Olympics."

"This sounds wonderful," Pia said.

"Are you going to Cortina d'Ampezzo?" Achille asked.

"Yes, we'll we go there after Christmas with my family."

"I'm looking forward to meeting Achille's family at Christmas."

"You haven't had a Christmas until you've had an Italian Christmas."

"This makes me even more excited. Paul, you're lucky to have Pia's family here, seeing as you come from far away."

"I know I'm lucky."

"You love each other too."

Paul turned his head – yes, always. "I adore Pia."

"I know what this feels like, now."

"Do you want to play cards?" Achille asked.

That's the last thing Paul wanted after a long drive. "Yes I do."

"Couple against couple."

That was appropriate. Achille dealt while Paul knew Cortina d'Ampezzo and the bobsleigh demonstration was pre-arranged, and Achille had been removed from his circle of friends. Possibly for abandoning Norma, who some didn't have a high opinion of anyway, but it might have been that Ilse was German and she didn't speak Italian, which changed the group dynamic. It wasn't fair because Ilse was lovely and they adored each other, which was all that mattered. The whole thing was terribly unfair, as Paul contemplated his hand.

Chapter Twenty Six

Achille grimaced, pulled off his gloves, reached into his pocket for the packet of Camels and lit a cigarette. Their best was one minute and seven seconds which wasn't fast enough. It wasn't anywhere near fast enough and their demonstration would be an embarrassment. Two choices. He could continue bobsleighing or he could go skiing with Ilse. Shadows were long and afternoon light was fading when Didi and Franco trudged up the hill. They all stood in a circle.

"What do you want to do?" Piero asked Achille.

"I'm skiing with Ilse tomorrow. Anyone who wants to come with us is welcome."

They didn't, of course, so next morning Achille and Ilse headed to Tre Croci Pass, where alone in the snow made Achille feel like they were the only couple alive on earth. The peace and quiet gave Achille time and space to think. It was clear that things weren't going to be the same as before, and if that was the case then so be it. He would rent an apartment in Milano, arrange Italian lessons for Ilse, spend more time at Galliate and they would travel together to each race. He could hunt with Angelo and Analects, when their busy schedules at the textile factory allowed for this, which would be hardly ever. They reached the end of the pass and Achille took a break.

"C'est beau," Ilse said.

Achille nodded. "Oui, c'est beau."

"I'm sorry about your friends."

Achille thought about them. "They're hypocrites. If they were good enough to earn a drive for Auto Union, they would sign a contract tomorrow. And if they fell in love with a beautiful German woman, they would. Every one of them."

"It'll be better when I learn Italian. Soon molto feline," Ilse said. *I'm very happy.*

"So chef site." *I know you are.* At least they had the journalist Paul and his wife Pia were staying nearby, although Achille couldn't annoy them evening. "We should go."

They turned and headed back to Cortina d'Ampezzo.

Chapter Twenty Seven

Monaco was a wet race full of incidents, where Rudi Caracciola won in an all-new Mercedes-Benz with a more powerful engine and shorter wheelbase, from a distant Achille Varzi in one of the short wheelbase Auto Unions constructed specifically for Monaco that seemed to be more difficult to handle.

For the second race of the 1936 season at Mellaha in Tripoli, Mercedes-Benz had entries for Rudi Caracciola, Manfred von Brauchitsch, Luigi Fagioli and Louis Chiron, who debuted for Mercedes at Monaco. Auto Union entered Hans Stuck, Achille Varzi and Bernd Rosemeyer. Ferrari entered Alfa Romeos for Tazio Nuvolari, Tonino Brivio, Mario Tadini and Carlo Pintacuda. There were several private entries which stood little chance for even a top three placing, making 26 cars to match the 26 lottery tickets to be drawn on race day.

Tripoli on Friday was hot with a strong wind blowing from the desert, which swirled sand and dust restricting visibility to about 200 metres. Paul went to the pits where Achille wasn't to be seen at Auto Union, so Paul confirmed with new team manager Dr Karl Feuereissen that they were continuing with their upgraded C model with a six litre engines, and they had reverted to regular wheelbase chassis. Paul went to Mercedes-Benz where Rudi Uhlenhaut spoke excellent English, where Mercedes-Benz was continuing with their W25K model. Able to get close for the first time, Paul checked out the new car which had an extremely cramped cockpit. He wondered how a taller driver like von Brauchitsch would fit. Paul greeted Tazio Nuvolari and then spoke with Enzo Ferrari to discover three of the new 12-cylinder Alfa Romeos were to be driven by Tazio, Tonino and Mario Tadini and there was an older, 8-cylinder car for Carlo Pintacuda. Even though they were trying, the Alfa Romeos were lumpy and upright compared to the sleek German cars.

The first practice session began at 15:00 where it was obvious that the new Mercedes handled poorly on this high-speed circuit, then Caracciola pitted to have a differential changed. Nuvolari ran off the track, burst a tyre and his car overturned, fortunately throwing Tazio clear. Complaining of a sore back he was taken away in an ambulance. Practice continued where Mercedes-Benz was in trouble with their cars washing wide at the front.

Weather was still grim for Saturday afternoon practice, and Rosemeyer set fastest time from Chiron, Varzi and Stuck. Fagioli, Caracciola and Brivio were next. Nuvolari qualified eighth fastest in a plaster cast protecting cracked ribs, despite being warned not to race.

Race day was hot and windy, but fortunately the wind blew from the west rather than from the desert. Pia headed to her palm tree oasis on the far side of the circuit where the cars came out of a sequence of curves before accelerating up to speed on the back straight. Paul got ready for what he expected to be a race hard on tyres, with the most likely outcome being the three Auto Unions battling amongst themselves for victory. The drivers waited in their cars in the heat while lottery numbers were drawn, and a few minutes later the starting lights flashed red to yellow to green and the race was underway.

Stuck made an excellent start, as did Nuvolari who came from the third row of the grid to take third place behind Chiron, while

Achille's car bogged down and he was swamped. At the end of the first lap Stuck led Rosemeyer, Nuvolari and Chiron while Achille worked his way up to eighth. Caracciola passed Nuvolari who might have been in pain, and Achille continued to make up ground as he moved into fifth. Rosemeyer passed Stuck for the lead and Achille moved into third place.

On lap eight tyre stops began, where the 12-cylinder Alfa Romeo proved to be hard on tyres or its Englebert tyres weren't up to the fast pace. Stuck retook the lead from Rosemeyer while Achille continued to close the gap to his team mates ahead.

Achille pitted for tyres and had a slow stop, especially when he accelerated away, while quicker tyre stops followed for Stuck and Rosemeyer. A few laps later Rosemeyer's car caught fire and he pulled over, jumped out and heaped sand on the flames. Despite his slow tyre change Achille caught Stuck and then seemed content to remain in second place. On lap 30 out of 40 both Auto Union drivers were shown green flags to slow their pace, and three laps later Achille pitted to replace his left, front tyre in a quick stop. Stuck continued to cruise as Achille closed on the leader, and then passed into the lead on lap 36 and pulled out a 15 second gap. Achille then slowed his pace and Stuck gradually closed the gap, and at the start of the last lap Stuck was right behind Achille who then set a new lap record to win by 4.4 seconds from Stuck, with Fagioli and Caracciola next.

With Achille feted as victor for the third time in four years, Paul didn't know what to make of the race. He waited for Pia to emerge from the desert and meet him in the journalist's area. She drank some of her by now hot water before taking a seat.

"I noticed Achille wasn't changing gears," she said. "All the other cars went third, fourth, fifth as they closed and passed me but Achille was in one gear all the way. He was slower than the other Auto Unions on the back straight so I think he was using fourth only."

Paul pondered that. "He was battling gearbox problems and that would explain his slow start."

"He went for second or third and it wasn't there."

Paul nodded. "But with a slow-revving six litre engine, using one gear wasn't such a disadvantage."

"What about the lap record?"

"Maybe he used risked using fifth on the last lap."

Pia gulped more water. "If so then it was a great victory."

"Why did Stuck slow and let Achille pass and pull out a gap?"

Pia frowned. "Team orders?"

"Then Stuck had second thoughts but Achille had enough in hand."

"Might be."

"The new Alfa Romeo was a disappointment. It was beaten by the old car."

"The new Mercedes wasn't any better."

"Auto Union's looking good for the rest of the year."

"I would like to talk with Achille, but he's kept out of the way and I don't know if Ilse's at the hotel."

Paul glanced at his notes. "I'll write what I saw and also mention that Achille Varzi had gearbox problems and mostly was using fourth gear only." He looked his darling wife deep into her amazing, dark eyes. "Thank you so much for helping me, especially today."

"I like races and I liked this race. The Gran Premio di Tripoli always has an exciting finish, which makes the heat, wind, sand and flies worth it!"

Paul laughed. "Why do we do this?"

Pia laughed and shook her head. "I have no idea."

* * *

Achille lay in a lukewarm bath still confused by what happened. He was shown a green flag which was the Auto Union signal to slow, although the other teams had worked out that green meant slow years before. So he slowed and then pitted when canvas started to show, and then he was shown a red flag to go fast, which he did. Right into the lead, followed by green again, and then Stuck closed so green flag or not, he decided to chance using fifth to make sure he won. Obviously Auto Union wanted him to win or else he wouldn't have been shown red to go fast into the lead. He wished he had Ilse to talk with, but like Norma, North Africa in May was not an attractive prospect. Few journalists bothered to come but Achille noticed Paul and Pia Bassi attending, with Pia in the middle of the desert shaded by a few palm trees. That was keen.

Achille climbed out his bath and towelled himself dry before inspecting the clothes he brought with him. He hated the ostentatious banquet with self-important governor Balbo in his garish palace, overdone with marble, fountains, mirrors, gold leaf, columns, arches and even an illuminated, indoor swimming pool. Always, less was more. And the crowd of hundreds, where most had no interest in motor sport or the race just run. Achille dressed formally because the banquet was black tie, even though it was ridiculous to wear heavy clothing on a hot evening.

Marshal Balbo sent a black Fiat for the victor, and Achille was surprised to share the big car with Hans Stuck. They were driven to the Governor's residence which was more like a palace, and escorted by uniformed aids to the banqueting hall. Achille was to share the victor's table with Hans Stuck; one at the left and one at the right leaving a space in the middle. The Air Marshal appeared from a side doorway, greeted both men, and then he stood between them, took a bottle of white wine from an ice cooler and poured some. He raised his glass, and despite a room of hundreds it was hushed.

"I want to congratulate the true winner of the 1936 Gran Premio di Tripoli," Balbo said before turning to his left. "Hans Stuck!"

Everyone stood to toast Hans and Achille couldn't believe it. He won the race; he won it despite using only fourth gear, and Stuck was being feted for finishing second! Achille looked around the room and everyone who was anyone in motor sport was there; including Caracciola, Chiron, Nuvolari, team mate Rosemeyer and everyone else. Team managers too, including Enzo Ferrari, Neubauer and that idiot Feuereissen. Watching him being made a fool! How could he share the victors table with Stuck feted as winner? How could he be humiliated in front of those men he'd beaten over the years? Achille got up and left through the open door to the side.

Humiliated; completely and totally humiliated. How could he ever face those men again?

"Excuse me signore Varzi?" a young man in a uniform asked.

"I must go to The Grand Hotel," Achille said.

"I'll arrange a car for you signore Varzi."

"Grazie."

The journey was a blur – Achille couldn't remember getting his key from reception or entering his room. But he was in his room, alone. It was better to be alone, although he missed Ilse. He needed her support, but sadly she was a long, way away. Tomorrow, Achille thought. Tomorrow he would fly to Milano, but first he would ring Ilse. For the second time that evening he picked up the phone, dialled nine and asked to be put through to the Hotel Cavour in Milano.

* * *

Achille used the key from reception to let himself into their suite. He unpacked and hung his clothes and wondered what came next. For the moment he traded one, empty hotel room for another.

He heard light tapping on the door and went to let Ilse in. They hugged and just holding Ilse made him feel better. He needed touch to bring him back to reality.

"I can't believe they did that to you" Ilse said.

Achille had gone over it a hundred times and it came out fluently. "The team signalled me to pass Stuck to take the lead, and I held the lead to win. Later at the banquet, Air Marshall Balbo toasted Stuck as the real victor, in front of the other drivers, team managers and everyone else who was there."

Ilse put her hand over her mouth. "That's terrible."

"I signed onto Auto Union because I knew I could beat Hans Stuck, and I have, many times. We were ordered to slow when Stuck was in the lead, while I followed orders expecting him to win. But somebody decided I was to win."

"Do you know who and why?"

"Someone wanted an Italian driver to win a race held in an Italian colony."

"Nationalist governments...."

Achille nodded in agreement. "Team orders happen all of the time, but the bigger thing is how can I front the other drivers after being humiliated like that?"

Ilse squeezed his hands. "You will go to Tunis, you will be the fastest and you will win the race, and you will show them that you deserved that win. I've followed your career for years and I know you're the best."

"They're just words."

"Words followed by action mon cheri, and I will be there so you will know you have my support."

Achille knew that was why he came home. "I didn't sleep last night and I'm very tired."

Ilse let his hands go. "You're a proud man Achille. This time you must let your pride go or it may hurt you."

"I am what I am."

"I know, and I know your pride is makes you a great driver. Whenever Tazio Nuvolari or any other driver closes on Achille Varzi, they know they have a battle on their hands, because your pride tells you that they will not get past. But this time things were out of your control, and you must let your pride go."

Achille wasn't sure.

"You did nothing wrong," Ilse said. "Everything that happened was out of your hands."

Achille he knew what Ilse said was right, but it was very hard to put aside a life lived one way. He hoped he could.

They ate in the hotel dining room, while Achille was terribly tired so they went to bed early. He dreamt of faceless men laughing at him. He woke – the room was dark and Ilse was fast asleep. Despite his tiredness, despite going over what she said, he couldn't sleep. He waited until early light seeped through the curtains, and then he had a bath and two cups of coffee with breakfast. He went through the day so tired, after no more than one or two hour's sleep in more than two days.

"We should make love," Ilse said. "This will make you tired and give you a good sleep."

Although Achille was tired, he made love with Ilse, slow and intimate the way she liked. He came hard, like he always did with her. Now Achille would sleep; he had to, because on Thursday he would to fly to Tunis to show them. But despite making love, sleep never came.

Achille bathed and dressed before Ilse woke. "You didn't sleep again," she said.

Achille looked at her.

Ilse sat up. "Before you had your operation, sometimes you took morphine. And sometimes that made you tired."

Achille couldn't believe it. "No," he said. "It's dangerous."

"If you don't sleep you won't be able to show them, and if you don't show them you won't be able to sleep. If you have one good, long sleep, you'll be better."

Achille pondered those words. Just once. Just once and he would be fine.

"I'll draw the curtain, put out the sign and leave you to sleep," Ilse said.

Achille nodded.

"Do you have any morphine left?" she asked.

He had some left over from his operation, in the second drawer beside his bed.

"I'll bathe, dress and go out, and you can sleep while I'm gone," Ilse said. "And when you wake you'll be better."

Achille waited for Ilse to finish in the bathroom, only he didn't want to be alone. "Stay with me," he said while she dressed.

Ilse looked at the vial and the syringe on the table beside the bed. "I'll stay with you mon cheri."

Chapter Twenty Eight

Achille left for Milano early the next morning, and Paul wasn't surprised given what he was told about the banquet. He only hoped Achille would return and show them in Tunis, especially that he raced well at Carthage.

"I think he's too proud," Pia said.

Paul barely believed that. "You know what happened," he said.

"I know and I still think he's too proud."

"He's Piedmontian, close to Lombardy where you come from. Of course he's proud."

"He is Piedmontian so I know, and if he doesn't put that insult aside it will destroy him."

Paul hoped Pia was wrong, but in the meantime they had a boat to catch to Tunis, and later that afternoon they checked into the old and delightful Hotel Majestic. A grand, French-styled hotel in a French-styled area of the city; a lot like a scaled-down version of Paris. The city centre of Tunis was truly beautiful.

Over the next few days they visited markets where Pia bought lovely, bargain fashions, and Paul found a marvellous bookshop where he bought some lovely, bargain novels. Their camel ride through the desert to an oasis was a treat, even though the weather was hot. Practice started on Friday while Carthage was a walk, although a long walk from the hotel. The circuit had been altered with two new chicanes, probably to give lesser-powered Italian and French entries a chance.

Like Tripoli, practice was held in the afternoon and like Tripoli, it was hot and windy. From a distance Achille looked fine. Paul spoke briefly to him at the paddock, and he was looking forward to the race and there was no mention of Tripoli, of course. Pia reported that Ilse was staying at the hotel, which Paul thought was a good idea. Neubauer wasn't talking to reporters but Paul noticed Mercedes for Caracciola and Chiron only. Tazio Nuvolari wasn't there, as was to be expected, so Ferrari had entries for Tonino Brivio and Carlo Pintacuda only. Bugatti brought a Type 59 for Jean-Pierre Wimille to race at this French colony.

Rosemeyer set fastest practice time from Varzi, Caracciola, Stuck, Chiron and Brivio, who was a handy driver.

The race was scheduled for 15:00 in the afternoon on another hot and windy day. Pia was brave enough to head to a shaded oasis along the back straight for about two hours and 30 minutes of racing. At the start Achille muscled into the lead and slid his Auto Union through the chicane at the end of the first lap, which was not his usual smooth style. Clearly he was making a point. Following were Rosemeyer, Caracciola and Stuck. The race set into a pattern with Varzi in the lead and pulling away on the near 13 kilometre long circuit, ahead of Rosemeyer and Caracciola, while Stuck pitted and retired with the engine of his car smoking badly.

On lap 15 Rosemeyer sped past the start and finish line while Varzi was nowhere to be seen. Some said he crashed but those reports were unconfirmed. The race dragged on while Paul was surprised to see Pia trudging towards the open seating area, which was the best spectator facility at the circuit. She held her floppy, broad brimmed hat to stop if blowing away, sat and drank hot water from her bottle.

"Achille crashed," she said and drank some more. "I've never seen anything like it. He was the only driver taking the banked curve at the end of the straight flat-out. Each lap I heard the exhaust note of his car never wavering as he took that curve with his typical, stylish precision. And then on lap fourteen a massive gust of wind came in from the desert, swirling dirt and debris. I held my hat and glanced at the Englishman nearby, just as the wind caught the front of Achille's car and lifted the front wheels from the track. The car rose higher and higher like an aeroplane, flying away from the track until the rear of the car hit the ground and then the front, and it rolled over and over with the most terrible noise. Over and over until it stopped on its wheels in the middle of an orchard. Arab men dressed in robes ran to the car, while I was on the wrong side of the circuit so I checked that nobody was coming before I ran to it as well, and so did the Englishman." She drank more water. "I thought he must be dead, nobody could survive a crash like that, but he climbed out of the wrecked car and brushed dirt from his overalls. He looked around and saw me but I don't think it registered."

"Is he alright?" Paul asked, worried.

"He's fine although shaken. He didn't even light a cigarette, and then he fainted. The Englishman, Raymond Mays, helped him, and he drove us back here in his car."

Paul contemplated what he heard, and that would have been a terrible thing to see.

"I've never seen anything like it," Pia repeated, and Paul hoped that Achille really was alright. If he was taking that curve flat-out he would have been doing about 300.

Paul was there for a job, and he noted that on lap 23 Rosemeyer pulled over with his car on fire for the second race in a row, and this time his car was destroyed. That left Caracciola to win in the ill-handling Mercedes-Benz from Carlo Pintacuda and Jean-Pierre Wimille.

Late afternoon was still hot with the wind blowing from the desert, when they left the circuit for the near 40 minute walk to the old and delightful Hotel Majestic.

* * *

Achille sat on the bed and wondered why he was there and how he managed to bathe and get changed. The room came into focus although much of the previous few hours were indistinct. He remembered leading the race and he remembered looking at the Englishman and the wrecked car, and then somehow arriving at the pits. There, Dr Glässer checked him and drove him to the hotel.

"Achille?" Ilse asked.

"Oui," he replied automatically.

"Are you alright?"

"I think I was nearly killed."

She sat on the bed and held his hand. "A wind gust blew your car off the circuit."

"Yes." It was a shock and something he never thought would happen. "I thought that if I drove a certain way, fast enough to win or even be champion but no faster, I wouldn't be hurt or killed. But today I was nearly killed and I'm lucky to be alive."

"I know my darling. I heard you crashed and I knew I was to blame. I pressured you to win to show those men from Tripoli, and then you went too fast and crashed." Ilse drew a deep breath and choked a sob. "Only later, when they brought you to the hotel, did I find out what happened."

"You weren't to blame."

"I feel terrible."

Achille noticed that her face was red and her eyes puffy. He felt sad. "You need something," he said, and he knew what he meant.

"But should I?"

"It will take away the pain and give you the sleep of angels."

"Do you have pain Achille?"

"Today I was nearly killed. I need the sleep of angels."

Chapter Twenty Nine

After a three-week break in Milano, it was great to attend a race where they could drive, to Barcelona for the Gran Premio de Penya Rhin. A night at the Hotel le Royale Provence on the way brought back great memories. Like almost all European cities Barcelona was breathtakingly beautiful, and with a colourful, cosmopolitan lifestyle that made a four-night stay not anywhere near long enough.

The Circuito de Montjuic was tight and twisting, running through parkland around a hill above the city's harbour. It was a magnificent circuit, and likely to be a leveller for the cars, placing a premium on nimble handling rather than power. Paul was interested in practice because he felt the long wheelbase Auto Union might be at a disadvantage. He went to the paddock before the first practice session on Friday to come across a surprisingly dishevelled Achille Varzi. Hair uncombed, his shirt grubby, a few buttons not done up. It was startling.

"Ciao Achille," Paul greeted Achille.

"Ciao Paul," Achille replied before looking around. "This is the most amazing circuit, don't you think? It's so pretty and even has birds in the trees. It's a shame to run a motor race here. I think we should call it off."

"Yes," Paul said, taken aback by their conversation. Achille was normally a man of few words. "But we are racing and what do you think of your chances?"

"Ha, the same question as always! I will win, of course. I told Auto Union to bring the short-wheelbase car that we used at

Monaco, and they did. For sure I'll win in this car. How's your lovely wife?"

"Pia's fine. How's Ilse?"

"She's waiting at the hotel, but we have practice first." He looked at his wrist but wasn't wearing a watch. "What time is it?"

Paul checked. "It's almost two."

"Ah, I must get ready. It's been good talking to you Paul."

Achille went towards the pits, presumably to get changed.

Pia was sightseeing in Barcelona, so Paul went alone to the grandstand to time the cars. The two Mercedes of Caracciola and Chiron looked terrible – the car didn't turn into corners and they also wallowed and pitched. The Auto Unions were little better, and then Rosemeyer crashed which put an end to his session. The short wheelbase Auto Union was like the Mercedes, and it wallowed and pitched as well. There were only two Auto Union entries, and one driver was hurt and one car didn't perform. Ferrari looked good with their 12-cylinder car a chance for victory in the hands of Tazio Nuvolari, recovered from his crash of a month before.

After the session Paul walked to the official car park where he witnessed a furious argument between Dr Feuereissen and Achille Varzi, although neither spoke each other's language. Bernd Rosemeyer was in the middle translating French to German and back again as best he could. The argument was that Achille didn't want the short wheelbase car, but Rosemeyer hurt his knee and couldn't fit into it. Achille then said he wouldn't drive at all and walked away, got into a Horch sedan and left the circuit.

So one Auto Union would start the race, or probably junior driver Ernst von Delius would be allocated the short wheelbase car. Paul got into his Alfa Romeo and left for the beautiful Majestic Hotel, located right in the middle of a beautiful city in a country being torn apart by conflict between Republicans and Nationalists who were fascists. War in Spain seemed inevitable.

The key wasn't at reception so Pia was in their room. Paul knocked on the door and she let him in.

"How was practice?" she asked.

"Interesting," Paul said, still mulling over events.

"Whenever you say 'interesting' that means something strange happened."

"Well the two Mercedes didn't handle, but you would expect this, and Auto Union had a regular car for Rosemeyer and a short-wheelbase car for Achille. He didn't like it so he refused to drive it, and that was that."

"What do you mean 'that was that'?"

"I mean he left the circuit and won't be driving in the race. And he was really strange when I spoke to him; talking about trees and birds. Something has happened."

Pia frowned before sitting on the bed. "He's been through a lot of stress the past several months and he's a man who keeps his emotions bottled up tight. All men keep their emotions in check, but none more than Achille."

Paul sat beside his beautiful wife. "Do I keep my emotions in check?"

"You relieve your stress with sarcastic humour." Pia smiled. "If you keep doing this, you'll be fine."

"I'm worried about Achille and I wish we could help him in some way."

"Ilse's lovely, but I don't think she has enough experience to guide someone strong-willed like Achille Varzi. I wouldn't have enough experience if I was in her place, so that's no bad reflection on Ilse."

Pia was right. "I don't think can help in any meaningful way."

"His family can best help him."

That was true and Paul hoped that would happen.

* * *

Achille unlocked the door to their suite in the Hotel Cavour. He looked around their spacious suite, but it was just a hotel room and a hotel room wasn't a home. It was time for change. Ilse went to the table beside the bed and slid the drawer open, and then rummaged through it desperately. Wide-eyed she looked up at Achille.

"We've run out," she said.

Achille briefly wondered what they ran out of and then he knew, although he had enough in his bag for a few days. That was good; he didn't want those bad feelings to return. But he used his last prescription and it was worse that he felt stressed. He glanced at the clock and it was only 14:00, so he had time.

"I'll get some," he said, knowing that he was a motor racing champion and he could get whatever he wanted. "I won't be long."

He went outside into the cool, cloudy day for the short walk around the corner to Via Bigli. He didn't have an appointment but the receptionist fitted him after the next patient. Doctor Bari was in his chair when Achille sat in the visitor's chair, separated by a messy desk covered in paper.

Achille greeted his doctor formally and Doctor Bari greeted Achille in response.

"How are you?" Doctor Bari asked.

"I'm well," Achille said. "But I need a prescription for morphine."

Doctor Bari looked over the top of his glasses. "We removed your appendix and we dealt with your abscess, so what's the problem now?"

Achille sighed. "I have bigger issues." Much bigger issues, he thought.

"You're addicted to morphine."

"No, but it helps me deal with problems."

Doctor Bari crossed his arms. "I can't give you a prescription for morphine unless you have genuine pain. So I'm sorry, signore Varzi, and if there's nothing else you can settle your account with my receptionist on the way out."

"Morphine helps me deal with problems," Achille said, knowing that to be true, and knowing a doctor's duty was to deal with all sorts of illnesses.

"You should leave signore Varzi."

"I have problems Doctor."

"I cannot help you, signore, so go, per favore."

That was that, although the pharmacist knew Achille so he went to the shop in the next building. Achille greeted his chemist and then glanced at the two customers waiting for their prescriptions. "Is there somewhere we can talk privately?" Achille asked.

Signore Pelino led Achille through a door into a small and quiet laboratory.

"Signore Pelino," Achille said. "I need another prescription of morphine."

"Your last prescription ran out," signore Pelino replied. "Do you have a new prescription from your doctor?"

"No I don't, but you know who I am."

"I know who you are but I can't help you. I could lose my licence."

"Surely you can," Achille said, not believing that he wouldn't be helped.

"I'm sorry signore Varzi."

"Grazie signore Pelino," Achille said, and in the narrow street between tall buildings, he didn't know what to do next.

"Signore Varzi," someone said, and Achille turned to face a young man dressed in a white laboratory coat. "I overheard your conversation and I can help you." He gave a piece of paper to Achille. "Ring this number in Roma, and tell the man who answers that his cousin Elio sent you."

"Why would you do this?" Achille asked.

"I know who you are."

"Si, grazie."

Achille left for the Hotel Cavour and went to their suite which had a phone. "I must make a phone call," he told Ilse before asking the operator for the number. It rang several times before being answered by a man with 'pronto'.

"Buongiorno signore," Achille said. "Your cousin Elio told me to ring you because you have something that I need."

"What do you need, signore."

"I need morphine."

Silence. "This will cost you."

"I have money."

"If you come to Roma you can have what you want."

"I'll be there tomorrow."

"Meet me at Via Cola di Rienzo, 257, apartment seven."

He hung up.

"What was it?" Ilse asked, because she wouldn't have understood some of their conversation in Italian.

"We must go to Roma," Achille said. He looked around their spacious suite which wasn't a home. "We'll rent an apartment in Roma," he said.

"Should you?"

"There's nothing for me in Milano anymore."

Chapter Thirty

Achille lay on the sofa in the atrium while admiring the fountain and thinking Villa Francesca was one of the most beautiful houses in Italy. A tiled entrance with marble floors led to the atrium, a full two stories high with a glass ceiling, and with a lovely fountain of a cherub gushing water which echoed through the entire house. Beyond were the formal rooms: a sitting room and a huge dining room with space for a dozen around a carved, mahogany table. Beyond that were the kitchen and the quarters for servants, where Achille had a maid and a part-time cook. Upstairs were five bedrooms leading off a balcony which circled the atrium. The rooms were light with off-white coloured walls and thick, dark green carpet. Their bedroom had a truly massive bed on a platform, an inbuilt wardrobe with ornate, white-painted timber doors and the minimum of furniture, all of which was gloss white. A brass chandelier provided light, as did big windows overlooking the nearby park. It was a home where you could spend all day inside and never want for more. It was a home that Achille had earned after many years of hard work.

Achille heard noise and looked up at the balcony with handrails in sparkling brass, where Ilse came around and down the stairs. Slowly and gracefully she sat on the end of his sofa.

Just then Achille heard knocking and Ilse went to answer. She returned with Valente and Michel smiling brightly. Achille rose, kissed their cheeks and they exchanged greetings. Valente placed the vials on a glass-topped table at the end of the sofa, and Ilse took them and went upstairs. She returned moments later and handed Valente a handful of notes which he stuffed into his pocket. Achille lay on the sofa and Ilse sat at his feet while Valente and Michel sat on the sofa opposite. Achille felt that lying on a white leather sofa still dressed in his bathrobe was rather comfortable. Ilse dressed in simple white as she often did, in a figure-hugging dress that was most enchanting.

They conversed for a while in Italian which Ilse could mostly follow, and then she left for the kitchen. Ilse returned a few moments later, and Maria the maid brought tray with four cups of coffee. Maria placed the tray on the glass-topped table and Achille sat up to drink. Just as he finished there was knocking at the door so Ilse went to answer. She returned with Dr Glässer.

The Doctor was agitated as he spoke harshly in German, although Achille felt that German always sounded harsh even when it wasn't. But his voice and his face were angry as Ilse translated to French that the Doctor had just driven from Pescara where Achille was supposed to be practicing for the Coppa Acerbo. Achille was amazed that the race slipped his mind. Glässer looked around the room, and at Valente and Michel, and then he spoke with Ilse again. Apparently Dr Glässer wanted to examine him.

Achille rose. "I must prepare for a race," he said. "Ciao Valente, ciao Michel." They kissed cheeks and departed. "Ilse, tell Dr Glässer that I will dress, and he can examine me if he wants, and then we can go the race."

She spoke in German while Achille climbed the stairs, where he dressed and packed a bag for a few nights away, and of course the bag contained all that he would need. He heard knocking on the door and opened it to let Dr Glässer inside.

The doctor placed his brown bag on the white dressing table and extracted his stethoscope while Achille removed his outer layer of clothes. He was examined with the stethoscope, with a light into his eyes and ears, asked to stand on one leg and the other with his arms outstretched, and then made to sit before Dr Glässer tapped each knee with a small hammer. In the background, Ilse watched with her arms crossed.

The doctor put his things into his bag and clipped it shut, and he spoke with Ilse. In the meantime Achille dressed again.

"Dr Glässer says you can go in his car to Pescara," Ilse said.

Achille went to his love, held her tight and kissed her, and he whispered in her ear that he wouldn't be long, just long enough to win the race. He grabbed his bag and followed the doctor down the stairs for a short drive to Pescara.

* * *

For a second time Achille Varzi was missing. He didn't appear at the Nürburgring for a race run in the most atrocious weather conditions, even by Eifel mountains standards, and from what Paul understood, he wasn't at Pescara for the Coppa Acerbo. Since the Nürburgring, Achille raced in the Coppa Ciano at the new Circuito di Livorno, and was leading when forced to retire with brake problems. And two weeks after that he was missing again.

Auto Union had four entries for Hans Stuck, Achille Varzi, Bernd Rosemeyer and Ernst von Delius, with the young Rosemeyer looking likely to be European Champion in only his second year of car racing. Ferrari had cars for Tazio Nuvolari, Tonino Brivio and Nino Farina, while Mercedes-Benz chose not to appear in preference to developing their cars for the race in Switzerland the following week.

Paul learned that Dr Glässer set off for Roma to find Achille, and in the meantime the rest of the competitors got down to the first day's practice. Hans Stuck had a serious crash when a wheel came off his car just before the chicane and he had to jump out. He wasn't hurt but was badly shaken, and Dr Feuereissen announced that he wouldn't be taking part in the race.

Late on Thursday, Dr Glässer returned with Achille who checked into the Esplanade Hotel. Friday continued to be hot while Achille immediately was at his best, and set fastest practice time to take pole position from Nuvolari, Brivio, Rosemeyer and von Delius.

Saturday was even hotter, where it was 43 degrees for the start of the race at 14:00. It was surely going to be a race of attrition for cars and even harder on tyres. Tazio Nuvolari led followed by Achille, Rosemeyer and von Delius, and for four, long laps Tazio held the lead until the engine of his Alfa Romeo sounded rough and he was passed by the three Auto Unions. Achille then set fastest lap but he had to pit for tyres, which let Rosemeyer into a lead he kept until the end of the race. Nuvolari eventually pitted to retire on lap 10 of 16 by which time Achille had pitted to change tyres a second time, where his immaculate, tyre-preserving driving style seemed to have left him. The race dragged on in extreme heat, with Rosemeyer a worthy victor who only changed tyres once, and finishing seven minutes ahead of his friend von Delius who changed tyres twice. Achille was third about 40 seconds behind von Delius after changing tyres four times, with his fifth lap the fastest of the race. Tonino Brivio finished in a good fourth only a few seconds behind Achille, showing the value of nursing a car and its tyres on that circuit in the heat.

Chapter Thirty One

Achille sat on the counter of the pits while contemplating his Auto Union adorned with red eights. In practice he did 2 minutes, 39.5 seconds which wasn't good enough. Rudi did 2 minutes 37.9 in an improved Mercedes that still didn't handle. Achille wondered if he should make another attempt for fastest lap, because there was prestige in that and an advantage into the first corner, but decided not. He doubted his car had much left to go faster. For some reason Dr Feuereissen wasn't around so Achille wasn't going to be pressured to go faster anyway.

Achille waited for the final practice session to end and then he changed. He walked the kilometre and a half the Bellevue Hotel in the city proper, went upstairs to their room and knocked. Ilse immediately opened the door and she looked terrible.

"What happened?" Achille asked, shocked by her appearance.

"Dr Feuereissen came into the room where he saw the morphine and syringe," Ilse blurted.

Achille barely believed. "How?"

Ilse took his hand. "I don't know. I was lying in bed because there wasn't anything else to do, and he unlocked the door and came in."

"He had a key?"

"He must have."

Achille thought Feuereissen must have bullied reception to give him a housekeeper's key. He would do that, which wasn't something that Willy Walb would ever do. Now their secret was out. Achille drew Ilse to him, and held her while she shook with fright or worry. He gently patted her back. "Don't worry my darling, it will be alright."

"You'll lose your contract," she said quietly.

Racing had changed since Tunisia. "There are worse things in life than losing a contract, like being killed through no fault of your own. Do you know what I mean?"

"Yes."

"If that were to happen, we wouldn't have each other."

"I know mon cheri."

"So don't you worry about Karl Feuereissen, because none of this matters as long as we're together." He eased Ilse away and looked into her beautiful, blue eyes. "I never knew love until I met you."

"I never knew love until I met you," she said.

Achille held his darling Ilse again while thinking the visit by Feuereissen might have been a good thing.

* * *

Paul paused in front of the building housing Gazzetta Dello Sport where for some reason he felt like he didn't belong there. But there were pressing issues involved so he went inside to a spacious reception area with lovely timber panelling and a parquetry floor, and to the young woman behind the dark, timber reception counter.

"Buongiorno signorina," Paul said. "My name is Paolo Bassi and I would like to meet with signore Giovanni Canestrini."

"Can I ask why you wish to speak with signore Canestrini?"

"I'm here about signore Achille Varzi."

"Take a seat, per favore."

Paul sat on a black, leather sofa while the receptionist spoke on a telephone, and shortly after the lift doors opened to reveal the middle-aged motor sport journalist. Paul stood and they greeted each other.

"Come with me, per favore," signore Canestrini said and led the way to the lifts, where they went to the fourth floor and along a narrow corridor into a large, open office with a dozen or more men at desks with typewriters. Signore Canestrini took Paul to a small office, simple and sparse with the minimum of clutter. The furniture consisted of a desk, a large chair and small table with two more chairs. Signore Canestrini gestured for Paul to sit at one of those chairs and he took a seat opposite.

"Why do you wish to talk with me?" signore Canestrini asked.

"You'll know that I'm an acquaintance of signore Varzi for the past three years, and I also attend the majority of races to write articles for English-language journals and newspapers," Paul said. "I've been concerned about signore Varzi's state of mind for some time, especially when he missed the recent race at the Nürburgring, and more recently when he had to be fetched for the Coppa Acerbo. His problems appear to be related to the morphine found in his hotel room at Bern."

"I'm aware of these issues and that his driving is less than it used to be. I believe his problems to be the making of Frau Ilse Pietsch."

"I'm not so sure," Paul said. "For sure his first blow was his friends abandoning him, which came from his relationship with Ilse, but we can't blame her for this, or for the issue at Tripoli and what followed in Tunisia. I've have seen Achille and Ilse together many times, and it's clear he genuinely loves her and she loves him. We kept a relationship with the couple where we found Ilse to be genuinely kind, and although quiet she was good company, but this came to an end when they no longer dined at his favourite restaurant, and now we know he's living in Roma."

"I heard about Roma and this is when his problems became significantly worse. Nonetheless he's taking morphine and probably is addicted, and probably Ilse as well."

"This is a sad outcome for someone I admire as the greatest racing driver of his time, and also as a decent man who has a strong, competitive urge with everything he does."

"I would like to get him out of Roma and back here where we can look after him."

"This is why I came to meet with you, signore Canestrini, because I believe that if one man in Italy can bring Achille Varzi home, you can." The two men went back a long way, and Giovanni Canestrini did more than report on motor sport. He helped organise and promote the first Mille Miglia and subsequently the lottery at Tripoli, which resulted in a great racing circuit and one of the most important races on the calendar.

"I'll seek the assistance of Marquis Brivio with this. He's a gentleman, as you know, and I'm sure Achille will take notice if one of his best friends offers support if he returns to Milano."

"Regardless of how we feel, Ilse has to be a part of this."

"You're right on this, and I believe we'll never learn what really happened."

Paul went to stand. "I wish you luck with your quest, signore Canestrini."

Signore Canestrini showed Paul to the lifts. Paul felt he had to do something, but if Achille and Ilse were actually addicted to morphine, that wasn't something friends could help with.

* * *

Achille switched on the light and placed his bag on the floor. The suite of the Hotel Cavour was too familiar and it had to be temporary. Ilse closed the door behind her and Achille turned around.

"I'll find a home as soon as I can," he said.

She looked around the room. "I hope you can."

"It won't be Villa Francesca because we don't have houses like that in Milano, but it will be home for us."

She held his hands. "Home with you is all I need."

Achille knew that. "I'll start now."

Achille went to the corridor, downstairs, through reception and outside. It was familiar territory where he knew a real estate agent just a few streets away. He went into an office, empty but for a young man in a smart suit.

"Buongiorno signore," Achille said.

"Buongiorno," the young man replied.

"My name's Achille Varzi and I want to buy an apartment."

"Certainly signore Varzi; take a seat, per favore. My name's Bruno Fabri."

They sat at a desk devoid of everything but for a telephone. "I want an apartment close to here, within a kilometre or two, and it must be spacious, bright and comfortable. Two bedrooms or even three would be suitable. Do you know of such an apartment?"

"I'll look for you signore," as the young man reached into a drawer and pulled out a slim folder of loose pages. He flicked through those pages and stopped. "We have the apartment you're looking for," he said. "It's nearby in Hajech."

Hajech was a good area.

"I'll get the key and we can look at it," signore Fabri said.

He opened a small cupboard fastened to the wall and took keys from a hook. They walked four blocks to Via Camillo 27 to reach a stucco over brick building of four storeys. The apartment was one of four in the top storey – it was light, bright, spacious and in excellent condition. Achille went from room to room where he was pleased with what he saw. He would get decorators to furnish it, and then he had a home. It was something he should have done long before.

"Are you interested in this apartment, signore Varzi?" signore Fabri asked.

Achille nodded. "Yes I am." Once he would have argued and haggled over the price but that time had long passed. As long as he got what he wanted without fuss, then he was satisfied.

"This is a good apartment," signore Fabri said. "Now, with lawyers and contracts it will take a few weeks, maybe three. Do you have a lawyer?"

"Latini and Partners in Galliate."

"Well, we should return to the office and get this process underway."

Achille looked around the empty sitting room. "In the meantime can I borrow the key for decorators to furnish this for me?"

"Of course signore."

"Grazie. We should go."

.Achille was pleased that in three weeks or maybe less he would have a home.

Chapter Thirty Two

Paul suggested they celebrate after the last race of the season, the Circuito di Modena, but he had another motive. He knew Achille and Ilse had returned to Milano and were staying in Hotel Cavour, and he also knew Achille bought an apartment in nearby Hajech. Achille might be dining at his favourite restaurant again.

Mario greeted them both and showed them to a table, and departed with an order for Cinzano Bianco for Pia and a glass of beer for Paul. Later they ordered their meals, and while they ate, Paul noticed Achille and Ilse entering, and being shown to the other room, followed about 10 minutes later by Tonino Brivio. When they finished eating, Paul ordered a glass of red wine and went to that room with Pia.

Achille, Ilse and Tonino were there, and superficially it seemed familiar with Achille smoking a cigarette and drinking Cinzano Bianco. But it was quiet compared to times past, and when Paul got close he noticed Achille and Ilse had strange, glazed expressions. Paul greeted in French where Ilse replied in Italian, so he used that language, as did Pia.

"It's good to see you again, Achille," Paul said.

"It's good to be here," he said.

Paul waited for more but it wasn't coming. "Pia and I will be holidaying at Cortina d'Ampezzo in January, after Christmas. We're looking forward to this, as always."

"There are many difficulties driving for a German team," Achille said. "Next year I'll race an Italian car."

"Can I publish this?" Paul asked.

"You can."

Paul wasn't surprised about Achille's decision, given Bernd Rosemeyer was European Champion Driver for 1936, a title that could have gone to Achille had he not become addicted. Achille had no future at a German team against a talented German team mate. Paul avoided that, they talked about not much and didn't play cards. After an hour or so Paul made excuses and left with Pia.

"Achille and Ilse are addicted," Pia said when they reached the street.

"I don't know much about addiction, but maybe they drift along until the next high," Paul said.

Pia sighed loudly. "What can we do? What can Tonino do?"

"It's up to Achille's family now. I thought that if he moved to Milano he'll be closer to his family, and when they realise what has happened, they can help him."

"I hope they do. This is more than Achille Varzi, once a great racing driver. This is Achille Varzi, a shadow of the man he once was."

"And Ilse too. She was bright and vivacious, and she's a shadow too." Paul wondered. Everybody blamed Ilse for what happened. If Achille's family got involved and tried to separate the couple, that would fail because Achille loved her. And if they got together again, Ilse would still be an addict unless she was treated. That would be a bigger failure.

"What are you thinking of?" Pia asked.

"I hope that someone, somewhere has the goodness of heart and the influence over them both to get them treated for their addictions, and I hope this turns out right in the end."

They continued their walk home.

* * *

Achille was startled by hammering at the door, so he slid out of bed and pulled his robe on. He opened drapes on his way to the door, and was surprised to see Uncle Hercules. They exchanged greetings and Achille invited him in.

"Sit Uncle, per favore," Achille said.

They sat in the leather armchairs. "I was disappointed the family didn't see you this Christmas," Uncle Hercules said. "I knew you were in trouble, but I didn't realise your trouble was this deep."

Achille listened but wasn't interested.

"You need help to return to the rest of the world, my nephew, and I can arrange this for you. One month is all it takes, and you'll be your old self again."

Through the fog Achille wondered if he could ever be his old self ever again.

"You must do something because you'll run out of money soon enough, and I don't know what you can do to support yourself. You can't race cars as you are, and you can't work in the family business either, although that never suited you."

"You say one month," Achille realised.

"One month on one condition. You must leave Ilse."

"No I can't!"

"Until she came into your life...."

"It wasn't her."

"That's my condition." Uncle Hercules leaned forward, up close. "I want to help you Achille, so I ask that you think about this. I'll return on Friday and we can talk again."

Uncle Hercules stood, and they departed on polite but distant terms.

"I heard that," Ilse said from the bedroom doorway. "You should listen to your uncle."

Achille turned around. "I'm not losing you," he said.

"Your uncle's right. We can't go on as we are."

"But what will you do?"

Ilse held his arm while looking into his eyes, as she often did. "I'll go home to my parents in Frankfurt, and when we're both better we can rejoin, and we'll be as we once were."

"You'll rejoin me here?"

"This is our home."

Achille hugged Ilse and pondered that if they separated for a month, he could love Ilse like when they first met. That would be worth it.

On Thursday, Ilse left by train to Frankfurt. On Friday, Achille was dressed and ready when he invited Uncle Hercules into his apartment, where they sat in the armchairs.

"Ilse has gone home to Germany," Achille said.

"Are you ready?" Uncle Hercules asked.

"I'm ready."

"Good. We can go."

They went downstairs and Uncle Hercules's driver headed north out of Milano, to cross the border at Como. He drove into the Swiss Alps and through the small town of Meiringen, to arrive at a grand manor in the midst of beautiful parkland. It was a building big enough to be a hotel. A nurse in a crisp, white uniform took Achille's bag and showed him to a small, windowless room. The nurse told Achille to change into the white trousers and a white shirt folded on a table, and later she retuned to take his other clothes away.

A middle-aged doctor in a long, white coat entered the room. "Buongiorno signore Varzi," he said.

"Buongiorno Doctor," Achille replied.

"I'm Doctor Bianchi and I would like to call you Achille during your stay here."

Achille nodded.

"You know why you're here, and we'll do all we can to help you return to old self. Have you ever run out of morphine and felt what it's like?"

Achille nodded and he remembered it well. "Once for a short while and it felt terrible."

"This is how it will feel in the first days of your treatment here, or even worse. You'll suffer cramps, nausea, vomiting, chills and fevers. This will be bad for you but this will pass, and then the real work begins. Your body will crave morphine weeks or even months after you finish here, and we'll do all we can to help you fight these cravings. As more time passes these cravings get less and less, and that's when you're cured. Do you understand?"

Achille understood the words but he didn't want to feel that way again.

"During your first days, when you feel at your worst, we'll be monitoring you, so you're in good hands. We'll help you get through your ordeal."

Achille thought about Ilse. "My companion is like me and she has gone home, alone," he said.

"Does she have support?"

"She has her parents."

"This will be hard for her but this doesn't mean it can't be done."

"Can I ring her?"

"You can't have contact with anyone outside until you finish this program. It's better for you, and it will be better for your companion if she isn't distracted."

Achille wasn't convinced, but he thought that if it worked and if he and Ilse were cured and back to where they once were, then it would be well worth it. "I understand," he said. "Do we start now?"

"We do."

Chapter Thirty Three

Paul sat at the kitchen table and turned over the pages of the latest edition of La Gazzetta Dello Sport, where a familiar name caught his attention. He read the article before putting the newspaper aside.

"What is it?" Pia asked.

"Rudi Caracciola and Alice Hoffman have just announced their engagement."

"Well, what a surprise!" She sat at the table. "Alice has wanted to marry Louis Chiron for a long time."

"But he didn't want to and Caracciola did?"

Pia nodded. "I wish them both good fortunes for the future, although I doubt if Louis Chiron will be so generous."

"There are some strange parallels with Alice and Ilse, and one will probably end well and one went very badly. Alice was older, of course, and better able to manage situations than a woman in her twenties."

"Achille loves Ilse so much, although that love is fogged now."

"They didn't ski this year."

"We had a good holiday this January, but it wasn't the same without Achille, Norma and the racing drivers from Milano."

Paul agreed. "Being with Achille was good while it lasted."

"The bobsleigh runs and endlessly chasing those last seconds! And cards! Did he ever lose?"

"Not often. I hope he comes back to us as he was at his best. I have read about addiction, and once cured, normality does come back. All of it, as if it never happened."

"That's good news."

Paul hoped their friend would be as he once was and even able to resume his racing career. And Ilse too.

* * *

The driver left Achille at Via Camillo, 27 – it had only been a month and yet it seemed much longer. Achille went upstairs and unlocked a deadly still and cold apartment, where he felt very lonely. A long time had passed and surely Ilse was past her withdrawal and ready for a new life. He sat in the chair, dialled zero and asked the operator to put him through to Frankfurt, Germany, number 78925. The phone rang and a man answered with 'hello'.

"Herr Hubitsch?" Achille asked.

"Ya."

"Je m'apelle Achille Varzi et J'aime bien parler avec Ilse, s'il vous plait.'"

Silence for a moment and then Ilse spoke, and her soft, sweet voice sounded clear. Clearer than Achille had heard for many months. "How are you cherié?" Achille asked.

"I'm good. It was tough but I had help, and now I feel good. I feel alive."

"Me too. We're ready for anything."

"We are cheri."

"When can you come?"

"Tomorrow!"

"I love you and you know what will happen."

"I know and I can't wait! We'll be as we once were. We'll be better because we missed out for too long. We must never do that again, no matter what happens."

"The doctors said we'll suffer cravings, but can support each other."

"Yes, we can do this. Together we can beat this thing."

"In time I'll go racing again. Maybe even Auto Union, if they will have me."

"Mon cheri, you have changed. I'll catch a train and this time tomorrow we'll be together again."

"This apartment isn't a home without my Ilse."

"If you can wait one night, we can make it our home.

"Your parents must have been good to you."

"They were the best. After, when I felt better, I told them what happened. At the time it seemed so innocent, one good night's sleep, and then it went so bad."

They talked for two or three hours but Achille didn't notice the time and didn't care. Eventually Ilse's parents called her for dinner and that reminded Achille that he had to eat. He would go to Ristorante Bagutta and maybe his friends would be there. If not it didn't matter, because he only had to wait one night and he would be with Ilse, and life would be as it once was.

Achille was startled by the phone ringing. He answered 'pronto' and was even more startled when Ilse blurted 'they won't let me into Italy'.

"What do you mean they won't let you into Italy?" Achille asked, confused.

"I'm at the border at Chiasso, and when the soldiers checked my passport they said Mussolini has issued instructions that I'm not allowed into Italy."

Achille barely believed it; Benito Mussolini of all people. Surely a racing driver wasn't that important, or maybe he was. And then it came to him. "Go home to Frankfurt and wait for me."

"You'll come to Frankfurt for me?"

"Il Duce won't prevent Italy's top racing driver travelling to his next race."

"What will we do in Frankfurt?"

"You're the expert about Frankfurt ma cherié. We'll get a hotel room and then rent an apartment, because I've had enough of hotel rooms. But in the meantime. go home and when I arrive I'll call you."

"When?"

"Tomorrow."

* * *

The phone rang and Ilse answered with 'hello'; Achille hoped their stay in Germany was temporary and there wouldn't be any need for him to learn the language. She nodded and replied 'danke' and turned to look at Achille.

"Giovanni Canestrini wants to speak with you," she said and gave the handset to Achille.

"Ciao Achille," Giovanni said.

"Ciao Giovanni," Achille replied.

"How are you in Germany?"

Achille looked up at Ilse. "It's good here and we're both good."

"Do you want to race again?"

"Yes," Achille said without hesitation.

"On the twenty-fifth of next month there's a Voiturette race on a new circuit at San Remo. Carlo Trossi can arrange a works Maserati drive if you want it."

Achille paused. "Ilse must be able to come with me," he said.

Silence for a moment. "Yes, of course, I'll speak with Carlo and I'm sure we can arrange this."

"Grazie Giovanni."

"I'll speak with Carlo and we'll see you at San Remo. Ciao Achille."

"Ciao."

"What was it?" Ilse asked.

"I have a drive in a Voiturette race at San Remo next month, as long as you're allowed into Italy."

"Do you think they will let that wicked, German woman into the country?" she asked, smiling brightly.

"I have important friends."

"Then San Remo it will be."

Achille remembered the Riviera Ligure. A race there was one thing, but he needed to recover from bleak Frankfurt. "I'll get us both into Italy as soon as we can, and we should holiday somewhere pleasant." At one of his favourite, summer destinations. "Have you ever been to Venezia?"

Ilse looked at him, wide-eyed. "No," she said quietly.

"We could spend a few weeks at Lido di Venezia, which is a beach resort close to the city island. And then we can drive to San Remo which is a lovely place as well."

"That sounds wonderful amore mio."

Achille knew it would be wonderful and more.

The Circuito di San Remo was a short and simple track, with the start and finish line, and the pits, located on Via Roma overlooking the sea. The town of San Remo made a beautiful backdrop to a racing circuit, with tall palm trees on the open stretches before the circuit wound between lovely sandstone buildings. Voiturette racing for cars with an engine capacity of up to 1500cc supercharged was proving more and more popular in Italy with the ready availability of four and six-cylinder Maseratis and small-capacity Bugatti Type 51s, but that wasn't why Paul was in San Remo. Through Didi, Achille Varzi was making his return to racing in a works Maserati 6CM. Paul stood at the side of Via Roma opposite the pits, transfixed by what he saw. Achille preparing for his drive supported by Ilse doing what she loved; in the pits as part of the team. Sadly that was something denied to her at other races. But it wasn't that or the couple looking healthy and recovered from their addictions; it was the sheer, overpowering adoration that Ilse showed towards her man. To watch them together was incredible.

"What are you looking at?" Pia asked.

Paul turned away from his view of the pits and gazed at his beautiful, darling wife and felt a sudden rush of desire. He grabbed her, hugged her, kissed her and felt Pia stiffen before relaxing with his affections. Still hugging Pia he whispered in her ear. "I was watching Achille and Ilse together, over there."

Pia looked over his shoulder for a moment. "I understand," she said quietly.

"I would never put such a scene in a race report, but I am a writer and I do write well. I couldn't even begin to put words to a scene like that."

"It's truly beautiful to see them together like that."

Paul turned around to look at the pits on a divine summer's day with heat tempered by the sea only a few metres away. "If I could freeze time for Achille and Ilse and have this day last forever, I would."

Pia nodded. "You know I love you and I know you love me, but they go beyond love or adoration. It's a strong and powerful place but ultimately it can't last. Such strong feelings can't last without destroying them. It almost destroyed them once and it will do it again."

Paul thought about that. "Is it worth being destroyed for that intensity of love?" he asked.

It might be," Pia said.

* * *

Achille sat on one side of the table, Dr Feuereissen sat opposite and the translator sat at the end. It took three phone calls to arrange a meeting in Zwickau, but Achille knew he had a chance despite his history.

Dr Feuereissen," he said. "Mercedes-Benz has had a very strong year, and I can change this for you. Like when you first hired me you have one, top driver and the rest are second-rate. Bernd Rosemeyer has talent; Hans Stuck has lost his touch while von Delius, Müller and Hasse won't win races."

"You have lost your touch too," Dr Feuereissen said through the interpreter.

"I'm fully recovered, and two weeks ago I easily won the Gran Premio di San Remo."

"Are you still with Ilse Pietsch?"

"I am and Ilse is recovered too, and she was at San Remo when I won." Achille contemplated Dr Feuereissen finding Ilse in bed mid-afternoon with morphine and a syringe on the bedside table. "What I propose is that Ilse won't accompany me to the remaining races of this season, so I won't be distracted."

"We can offer you races at Livorno, Brno and Donington. No fee and you get half of prize money."

Achille was startled but it was a start. "That's acceptable to me," he said.

"Good. I'll arrange a contract and we can sign it this afternoon."

Achille had his Auto Union drive back, and he would make some money too. It was good.

Chapter Thirty Four

The 1937 Gran Premio d'Italia was to be held at the Circuito di Livorno where Tazio Nuvolari in the Alfa Romeo had performed well during the 1936 Coppa Ciano. Mercedes-Benz had entries for Rudi Caracciola, Manfred von Brauchitsch, Hermann Lang, while Dick Seaman was getting a race as one of their junior drivers. Auto Union had entries for Hans Stuck, Bernd Rosemeyer, H.P. Müller and a surprise return for Achille Varzi. Varzi had shown promise at San Remo and Paul hoped he could carry that form into a longer, Gran Premio. Ferrari entered Alfa Romeos for Tazio Nuvolari, Carlo Trossi, Nino Farina and Clemente Biondete, and there was a single Alfa Romeo entered by the factory Alfa Corse team for Giovan Guidotti.

Friday practice was wet with Nuvolari fastest, but on Saturday when times counted it was Caracciola fastest in the immensely powerful Mercedes-Benz, ahead of Varzi and Rosemeyer. Achille Varzi showed that he hadn't lost his deft touch behind the wheel of a racing car.

Race day was fine and there were many spectators, and too many for the facilities at Circuito di Livorno. Some got frustrated and invaded the edge of the track and had to be moved, which delayed the start. A spectator then fell from a tree and had to be taken away by ambulance, which further delayed the start.

Eventually the race got underway where Caracciola led from Lang, Rosemeyer, von Brauchitsch and Achille Varzi making a typically slow start. Stuck abandoned his car so it was taken over by junior driver Rudolph Hasse. Seaman passed Müller and then Achille for fourth. The race dragged on and Achille eventually finished sixth behind Caracciola, Lang, Rosemeyer, Seaman and Müller, which meant the smooth, fast and consistent Rudi Caracciola was European Champion Driver for the second time. Paul was disappointed to see that Achille was so exhausted by the end of the race that he had to be lifted from his car. He had a deft touch behind the wheel, but more than a year away from racing had sapped his endurance. Even bigger news was Hans Stuck was sacked by Auto Union shortly after the race ended, for driving inconsistently and abandoning his car in a number of events, including the race just finished. It was a sad ending to the career of the one-time Auto Union team leader.

* * *

Achille rested in the pits and slowly his strength recovered. But he felt ashamed that he couldn't race the full distance at speed, and was passed by Müller of all drivers. The driver he recently disparaged and yet was unable to race against him. It was a shameful, embarrassing performance.

Tonino planned to drive to Bologna and spend the night at the Hotel Cavour. They drove in silence through the evening and arrived at the hotel in near-darkness. They checked in, got keys and Achille was still tired. He glanced at his watch where it was near seven and he needed a bath.

"I'll meet you in the dining room in 30 minutes," Achille told Tonino.

Achille headed up the stairs.

There were few diners and Achille expected good service, but it didn't come. Normally he would have complained, but he felt he had no right to. How could he complain about people not doing their jobs properly when he didn't do his job properly? He had right to do that. He didn't feel hungry and ordered ragù alla bolognese while Tonino ordered tortellino.

After eating almost in silence, Achille still felt frustrated over his race performance and he needed to talk to his lover. Yes, he would do that.

"Do you want to play cards?" Tonino asked.

"I have a phone call to make. Later we can play."

Achille went to reception where the young man at the counter looked bored. "Do you know who I am?" Achille asked.

The man nodded slowly. "Achille Varzi."

"I must use your phone."

The receptionist put it on the counter, and Achille went to a nearby chair with the phone in his lap. He picked up the receiver and dialled zero. The operator answered with 'pronto'.

"Connect me to Milano, number 68234."

The phone rang and Ilse answered. Achille greeted her flatly.

"What's wrong?" Ilse asked.

"I drove a terrible race and I had to be lifted out of the car at the end."

"Don't worry Achille; it's been a long time and it will come back to you."

"It was shameful."

"My darling, don't be hard on yourself. I'm sure you tried your best."

That brightened Achille and he knew it was right to ring Ilse. "I need you with me when I race," he said.

"I would love to come but Dr Feuereissen would never allow it."

Achille sighed. "I know."

"Now tell me you won't do anything silly."

For a moment Achille wanted to do something silly, to take away the pain of failure. But he couldn't. "I can't darling; I don't have any with me."

"Don't even think about it."

"All I need is your love."

"You know I love you my darling, and I can help you to be stronger for your next race."

That brightened Achille even more. They talked for hours, and when Achille eventually hung up he was surprised to be alone in reception with the murky, grey light of morning visible outside. He had to wash and change but that didn't matter, because soon he would be home with Ilse.

They didn't reach Milano until early afternoon, and when Achille let himself into their apartment he knew it was wrong. Ilse was dull and listless and he recognised the signs.

"What happened?" Achille asked.

"Your phone call," Ilse replied.

"You shouldn't have."

"I know, but I couldn't help it."

Achille understood because he felt the same way, especially at that moment. "Come to me," he said and she did, and he held her in his arms.

"You're so big and so strong. When you hold me I feel protected and safe."

"I drove a bad race," Achille said.

"You shouldn't let that get you down."

"I know but I can't help it." Achille realised his next race would be better. "Come with me to Lucca," he said.

"I will."

"You mustn't take morphine again."

"It's very hard not to."

Achille knew how hard it was. At that moment he desperately wanted to take sink into delightful oblivion.

* * *

The following week Paul drove to Genova, and then along the coast to Lucca to view the Coppa Edda Ciano Voiturette race. Achille Varzi returned to Maserati and was leading the race when the engine of his car failed, allowing Didi to win. Ilse was there but no longer the bright young woman of a month before. She was there in body but not in spirit.

Chapter Thirty Five

Auto Union were in disarray at the Velká cena Masarykova in Brno, Czechoslovakia. They'd dismissed Hans Stuck, Rudolph Hasse was sick and unable to start, and Achille Varzi complained about a bandage on two of his fingers. Dr Glässer examined this and pronounced him fit to race, but he turned very slow lap times on Friday. At least Bernd Rosemeyer and H.P. Müller were healthy. Mercedes-Benz had the same four drivers as in Livorno, while Ferrari had entries for Tazio Nuvolari and Tonino Brivio. There were a number of private entrants, including Paul Pietsch in a Maserati, but he crashed in Friday practice and was unable to repair his car in time.

On Saturday, things went from bad to worse at Auto Union because Achille insisted he was unfit to drive and he had a train to catch, no doubt to get home to his beloved Ilse, and that was that. Paul recognised the signs. As an anachronism the grid positions were drawn by ballot, which resulted in a skewed grid on a narrow circuit where it was notoriously difficult to overtake.

A Voiturette race was held in the morning, which had been quite exciting, and then the big cars were assembled on the grid at 12:00 to start fifteen minutes later. On a 30 kilometre circuit with no intermediate timing points, it was a hard race to follow for any of the hundreds of thousands of spectators, and just as hard for journalists.

Rudi Caracciola and Manfred von Brauchitsch finished first and second after Hermann Lang crashed, killing two spectators and injuring 12 others. Race organisers told Neubauer to get Lang out the country immediately, and he was on his way to Germany before the race even finished. Only lap 11 out of 15, Rosemeyer left the track and damaged his car, forcing him to walk to the pits where he took over Müller's car to finish third. It was a confusing race made all the more tragic by the death and injury of those people watching from a prohibited area. Achille Varzi was back on morphine, and Paul knew that Auto Union wouldn't give him a third chance. Achille Varzi's racing career was over.

* * *

Racing on public roads had always been banned in Britain, and as a result the banked oval at Brooklands was the only British circuit for many years. At the instigation of the enterprising Fred Cramer, a racing circuit was built on land at Castle Donington near Derby, in some ways like a privately-owned Monza. Two Donington Grand Prix had been held with limited success, but for 1937 Mercedes-Benz and Auto Union were lured to enter the race. Given practice started on the Wednesday after Brno, Paul had no choice but to fly to the nearby Midlands Airfield and catch a taxi from there.

The five kilometre long Donington Park Circuit was impressive by any standards, being a tight, winding layout though parkland, with newly constructed pits and a decent-sized grandstand. Paul felt the tight track could be a leveller between the powerful Mercedes-Benz W125 and the lesser-powered Auto Union Type C. Again Mercedes had cars for Rudi Caracciola, Manfred von Brauchitsch, Hermann Lang and Dick Seaman while Auto Union had cars for Bernd Rosemeyer, H.P. Müller and Rudolph Hasse, with Achille Varzi not showing up as Paul expected. The only other entries were British voiturettes: ERAs, two Maseratis and a Riley.

Race day drew quite a large crowd estimated at 50,000, and they enjoyed an exciting race that afternoon. Rosemeyer and von Brauchitsch battled hard for the lead, which was only resolved when von Brauchitsch had a tyre fail and that cost him the race. Caracciola's one tyre-stop strategy didn't work out; Seaman and Lang both retired while Müller and Hasse were unable to come to grips with the circuit and finished fourth and fifth. It had been a fascinating race where Paul was sure English spectators would remember the noise and spectacle of those powerful silver racing cars for quite some time.

They next day Paul flew to Milano via Paris where he wasn't looking forward to his summer job of reporting on basketball games for Corriere della Mattina, but it was a necessary evil that paid their bills. At least he and Pia booked three weeks in January at Cortina d'Ampezzo, in their favourite Hotel Meuble Oasi.

Chapter Thirty Six

Two nights of fresh snow made Cortina d'Ampezzo look superb, and too good to waste on the downhill runs. Paul gazed out of the window of their room at smooth, unmarked whiteness.

"You ought to dress," Pia said from the bed.

"They can't see me up here," Paul said.

Silence for a moment. "You want them to see you. It's like bragging."

Paul turned around to face his lovely wife.

"I know you," she said.

"Do you want to ski cross-country today?" he asked.

"Yes amore mio."

Paul bent down and picked up her nightie and tossed it on the bed. But Pia got up and went to him to hug him. "They will see you amore mia," he whispered in her ear.

"It's like bragging," she said.

After breakfast they headed into soft, fresh snow for the long trek to Tre Croci Pass. It was early, nobody was up and they could have been the only couple alive in the world, although tracks in the snow showed otherwise. But part-way to the pass, they were alone and isolated.

They eventually came across a party of three at the top and Paul barely believed it; Tonino, his wife Luciana, Didi and his wife Lisette. They closed and the foursome looked like they barely believed it too. They greeted one-another with big smiles.

"It's a beautiful day," Luciana said.

"It is," Pia replied.

"How long are you here for?"

"We're here for another two weeks. We always holiday here."

"I thought your work was a holiday," Didi said.

"You know what its like," Paul said. "Endless drives, train journeys, taxis, hotels...."

Didi nodded. "I know well enough. A holiday is when you aren't on the move every second day."

Paul nodded.

"We're here for another week," Luciana said and then her face brightened. "Do you want to meet tonight?"

"Yes of course," Pia said. "We should play cards."

"Yes, we should."

They talked for a while before Tonino suggested they ought to leave for an early lunch. Paul looked around at the beautiful desolation. "We're staying here," he said.

"I understand," Tonino said. "Eight this evening at Hotel Cortina d'Ampezzo."

The threesome departed while Paul and his darling waited at the top of the pass; alone in the world. Not a sound or even a breath of wind to disturb peace and tranquillity. Eventually they headed back to Hotel Meuble Oasi for lunch in the warm, dining room. They played chess in the afternoon and Paul let Pia win again, or so he told her. After dinner they rugged up for the four hundred metre trek to a larger and fancier hotel.

"Did I tell you Tonino retired from racing when he married Luciana?" Paul asked while they trudged along the path.

"No you didn't but that's really nice to hear. He's a good driver, but he gave that up so the woman he loves won't become a widow."

"Yes."

"Racing drivers are very romantic."

Paul thought that was as much sexual in nature but he didn't want to explain this to Pia. At the Hotel Cortina d'Ampezzo they removed their outer layers to reveal Paul's new, charcoal-coloured suit and Pia's new beige evening dress. They went to the lounge and Paul momentarily contemplated playing cards with the Marquis Antonio Brivio Sforza and Count Carlo Trossi, but he knew them through his work and they were friends.

They greeted informally with 'ciaos' all round. Didi dealt cards for Tonino, Luciana, Lisette, Paul and Pia and the game of Machiavelli got underway, but as much as he knew these men and Luciana quite well, and Lisette less so because she didn't attend races, it wasn't the same and never could be. They played two hands and paused while Didi dealt with his pipe; a regular occurrence.

"It's not the same," Pia said.

Tonino nodded. "This is Achille's group and it's different when he's not here."

"Will he ever come back to us?" Pia asked.

"Only if we separate him from Ilse."

"They love each other so much."

"After Livorno, we spent the night at a hotel in Bologna and Achille rang her. He was still on the phone the next morning. Many times in hotels he's been on the phone to Ilse for three or four hours," Tonino continued.

"And Ilse's just as obsessed over Achille," Didi said. "She only has eyes for him."

"Who got them rehabilitated last time?" Paul asked.

"His uncle Hercules," Didi said.

Paul understood. In Italian families the oldest brother or uncle took seniority. "Can Hercules Varzi do this again?" Paul asked.

"He could, but we need to separate them."

"I don't think Ilse would harm the man she loves," Pia said.

"She may not want to harm him," Didi said. "But that's what happens."

Pia nodded thoughtfully. "Their love is too obsessive."

"There have been many stories, songs and plays about love, but none come close to the reality of the love that those two share."

"And their disaster that follows."

"There are just as many stories and plays about the disasters of love, and they don't come close to the disaster of our friend."

"With Achille it's all or nothing," Tonino said. "If he races he has to have the best car and be champion. If he plays cards he has to win. If he buys clothes they have to be the best quality and the most fashionable. And now that he's in love for the first time, it's taken over his life and there's nothing left."

Didi lit his pipe and leaned back, looking thoughtful. "He wants to race, and I can get him a drive for Maserati at Tripoli and other races. This should help."

"He needs rehabilitation," Pia said.

Didi puffed his pipe. "Let's get him racing, and when it turns bad, Hercules Varzi will realise that he has to help Achille again, and like before he will separate them."

That was a good plan. But it was a shame they were too much in love. Too much in love for their own good.

* * *

The second race of the new formula regulations was in Tripoli. For 1938, cars were limited to three litres supercharged, or up to four and a half litres unsupercharged, with a minimum weight of 850 kilograms. Auto Union were absent with their cars not ready, while Paul wondered how they would be able to cope with the death of Bernd Rosemeyer during a speed record run earlier that year. Mercedes-Benz had three entries for Caracciola, von Brauchitsch and Lang, and attempted to enter a fourth car for Seaman. Maserati debuted the new, eight cylinder 8CTF model for Carlo Trossi and Achille Varzi. The factory Alfa Corse team entered new, twelve cylinder Tipo 312 models for Nino Farina, Raymond Sommer and Eugenio Siena, and an eight cylinder Tipo 308 for Clemente Biondette, in place of Alfa Romeos previously entered by Scuderia Ferrari. An old Type 59 Bugatti for Jean-Pierre Wimille and a couple of non-supercharged Delahayes made up the large car class, while the field was padded with voiturettes running as a separate class but alongside the big cars.

During practice there was no surprise the three Mercedes were fastest, while Carlo Trossi was a couple of tenths quicker than Achille Varzi to be inside the second row of the grid. Paul caught up with Didi after Saturday practice.

"What do you think?" Paul asked.

Didi drew on his pipe. "Achille at his best is faster then me, but he's only three tenths slower. He surprised me."

"Grazie," Paul said, and he went away to write his article on practice. Many drivers expressed concerns about mixing fast and slow cars on a fast circuit, and Paul put that in his article too.

The race start was delayed by 30 minutes to allow Air Marshal Balbo to wander around the pits and talk with the drivers. Eventually the race got away to a scrappy start with the light turning green while the voiturettes were still forming up on the grid. On lap eight Eugenio Siena crashed when he closed to lap Cortese's voiturette class-leading Maserati, and sadly he was killed. Caracciola, von Brauchitsch, Lang and Trossi all battled for the lead, while Achille Varzi retired with a broken rear axle after running mid-field. There was another collision two laps later when Hartmann in a voiturette Maserati cut across the path of Farina in an Alfa Romeo, and Hartmann was badly hurt and unlikely to survive.

Trossi retired on lap 15 with rear axle problems, but while he was running he showed he had more pace than Varzi in the same car. Paul hoped that was enough to convince Achille that if he wanted to continue racing he needed help. In the meantime, the race continued where Lang won from von Brauchitsch and Caracciola. Given the tragedies, the post-race banquet was cancelled.

Chapter Thirty Seven

Achille sat at the bar in the Umberto Restaurant in Galliate contemplating his empty glass. He was home but not home. Achille heard footsteps in the background.

"Ciao Achille."

"Ciao Uncle Hercules."

"How was your race in Tripoli?"

"The axle of the car failed early in the race."

"The same thing happened to the car of Count Trossi while he was contending the lead. You were well back in the field."

Achille didn't care. "Carlo Trossi is a good driver."

"He's good enough to win races but he's not as good as you, Achille. He would never be a champion like you."

Achille turned to face his uncle. "Why do you want me here?"

"I want to get you back to where you once were, so you can support yourself through racing again."

"Treatment in a clinic?"

"Treatment in a better clinic with a program for four months, and support for as long as you need it."

Achille's money was running low. "This will cost a lot," he said.

"You don't have to be concerned about the cost."

There was another issue; the most important issue. "Ilse?"

"I've heard people say she's to blame for what happened and I have heard other people say she isn't. The truth is none of us know what happened, but the other truth is you both end up in trouble. I know how strongly you feel about her, but you're not good for each other. You should let her go for her sake."

"I love her," Achille said automatically.

"There's no pressure on you, Achille, but when you feel the time is right you can contact me and we can arrange your treatment."

Achille had many things to think about. What his uncle said about racing, which was true. Life without Ilse. What would Ilse do?

"I'll help you, Achille, if you want me to. Ciao Nephew."

"Ciao Uncle," Achille said.

Achille contemplated his empty glass while the footsteps receded.

* * *

Achille woke feeling down, as usual. He reached to the table and grabbed the vial and syringe, drew ten milligrams and plunged the syringe into his leg. He lay in bed and slowly, steadily he felt better and better and better. No longer grey, he felt at peace. Warm, calm, relaxed.

Ilse murmured and squirmed while Achille knew how she felt. He grabbed the vial and syringe, drew ten milligrams, and he handed the syringe to her. In bed she injected and soon she would feel the sweet bliss of nothingness. They lay in bed and held hands as they often did in the morning, because after the bliss there was no desire for anything more than holding hands. And even though he didn't want it, Achille missed it. It wasn't as good but still he missed it. He wondered if Ilse missed it too. In a way he missed a lot of life, and sometimes what he missed didn't seem to matter, and other times it did. That morning was one of those times when it mattered and Achille wondered why. He suspected it was after talking to Uncle Hercules.

Achille slowly rolled out of bed, pulled on his gown, and pushed under the door was Corriere della Mattina and La Gazzetta Dello Sport, and there he saw the heading: 'Nuvolari to debut for Auto Union at the Nürburgring'. He read the article and, frowning, he read it again. Tazio Nuvolari was to commence practice on Thursday for the Gran Premio di Germania. Tazio Nuvolari was to drive *his* car. Tazio Nuvolari would win in his car, if not in Germany then other races.

"What is it Achille?" Ilse asked from behind.

"Nuvolari's to race for Auto Union," Achille said.

"Of course he is. All they have are Kautz, Hasse and Müller."

"That's my car."

"It was your car Achille."

Achille turned around and she was very beautiful, and then he remembered Uncle Hercules. He had no money and he couldn't live on love, and he couldn't race and earn a living the way he was. "I need treatment," Achille said quietly.

"Because Nuvolari has your car?" Ilse asked sarcastically.

"Because we can't go on like this." He remembered Uncle Hercules's observation that they weren't good for each other. Achille could get treated but he knew it would end the same as the last time. "We need to break up," he said quietly.

"Why?"

If he could live with Ilse and love her properly, he would. But he knew he couldn't. One always failed and dragged the other down. "We love each other but we can't live together. Surely you want a life that's more than oblivion?"

"But not without you Achille."

It was him; it was his fault. He wasn't good for her. "With me it will end up the same."

"It doesn't have to."

"It will. I want to let you go so you can live a normal life."

"I can't live without you," Ilse pleaded, but Achille knew it was the other way around. She couldn't live with him.

"I love you Ilse and I want you to go," Achille said calmly. "Your parents were good for you last time and they will help you again, I'm sure. I don't want you to be like this."

"You don't know what I want!"

Achille loved her and he always would. And because he loved her he would set her free. Anything else was selfish. He stood. "I must make a phone call," he said.

"Achille!" she screamed.

Achille went to the other bedroom and sat at the desk. He picked up the phone as Ilse staggered into the room and collapsed to the floor. She grabbed his ankle, sobbing while he dialled the number.

"Don't do it Achille," she spluttered.

The phone rang – Uncle Hercules answered 'pronto'.

"Uncle Hercules," Achille said. "I'm ready."

Chapter Thirty Eight

Paul couldn't wait to get home and get things arranged. Sudetenland of Czechoslovakia was ceded to Germany and the Donington Grand Prix was re-scheduled for three weeks time. He went inside where Pia cooked pizzoccheri. He kissed her cheek and she turned around.

"You're happy," she said.

"Crisis has been averted and Donington is scheduled for the 22nd. Do you want to go to the race?"

"It's a long way."

"You haven't been to England before, and you might not get a chance again."

"Why would I want to go to England? It's too Anglo."

"I'm half-Anglo or have you forgotten?"

"Which half?"

"The funny half."

"You do have a dry sense of humour."

"That's Anglo."

"I didn't know Anglos were funny."

"I thought ironic humour was Australian, until I went to England and realised they're similar to us."

"Then we can go to Donington and sample Anglo humour while we're there. How will we get there?"

"It's up to the agent but I think a train to Paris, a train to Calais, a ferry to Dover or somewhere like that, a train to London and a train to Derby."

"That's a lot of trains."

"We must spend a few days in London to sightsee."

"I'm not so sure about 'crisis averted' though."

Paul thought about that. "It's averted for now but you're right to be worried. First we had an Axis of cooperation between Italy and Germany...."

"Who would want to cooperate with that lunatic Adolph Hitler? I'll never forget seeing the newsreel of him carrying on the way he does."

Paul remembered when they were last in Paris and saw a film of Hitler shouting at an audience, and the audience going crazy in response. The sort of film not shown in Italy for obvious reasons. "Well, we do have an Axis, and that was followed by German annexation of Austria, which the Austrians seemed to be pleased about. And now this, although the Czechs were not so pleased about being invaded. Nonetheless crisis is averted but I don't think this is the end of the matter."

"Nor I. What will we do if it goes badly?'

Paul had thought about that. "I can't be forced because Italy has conscription once at age eighteen and that's it, so I suppose I'll have to find other work. Italy isn't war-ready in the way that Germany, Britain or France are, so I hope that whatever happens on the other side of The Alps, common-sense prevails on this side."

"What do you mean 'not war-ready'?"

"Italy has a big army but not much in the way of tanks or artillery, a good navy and no air force, except for a collection of biplanes. It's good enough to defeat Ethiopia but that's about the extent of it."

"Well I hope that common-sense does prevail, although we have no say in the matter." Pia cocked her head again. "Do you regret becoming Italian?"

"And not living in Milano with you? Never!"

"But...."

"I know what you mean. Australia is tied to Britain, so if Britain and Germany go to war, Australia will be at war."

"So it's the same, more or less."

"Probably more rather than less. In Australia they expect you to go overseas and lay down your life where Italy has a different perspective on things."

"Italy has quite a few different perspectives to Anglos."

"I know, I'm half-Italian. The cultured and refined half."

"The modest half."

"That too."

* * *

After Tazio Nuvolari's win at Monza, Paul thought Tazio had a good chance to do well at the tight Donington Park Circuit, especially as the European Driver's Champion for 1938, Rudi Caracciola, was sick and unable to race. In practice on Thursday, Nuvolari didn't disappoint, even after colliding with a stag. Paul waited for the final practice on Friday to see if Mercedes drivers could match the pace of the Auto Union. Pia was disparaging about a country which didn't allow a race to be run on a Sunday, which Paul agreed with. It was an antiquated concept for the twentieth century, and it meant many potential spectators would be working on the day of the race.

Hermann Lang, the fastest of the Mercedes-Benz drivers, scored pole from Tazio Nuvolari, Manfred von Brauchitsch and Dick Seaman, who continued his fine form after winning in Germany mid-year. On his way to their rental car Paul was startled to be intercepted by two men in quality dark suits who came alongside, one either side.

"Paolo Bassi," one said.

"Paul Bassi," Paul corrected.

"We would like to talk with you."

"Talk away."

"Privately."

Paul sighed. "I have to type my practice article and telegraph it, so I'm rather busy."

"Your hotel, tonight at seven."

"Do you know which hotel?"

"Room nine."

Paul thought that was odd. The two men peeled away and blended into the spectator crowd, as best they could while dressed in that way. Paul reached the car where Pia leaned against the mudguard. "Who were those men?" she asked in Italian.

"I don't know," Paul said. "They're going to meet us at our hotel, tonight at seven."

"That's strange."

Paul unlocked the car to drive to their less than luxurious accommodation at The Rangemoor Park Hotel, which was as good as Derby provided. There he set his typewriter up and wrote his article, while grateful the telegraph office was just along the street.

He returned and waited, and right on the church bell chiming there was a knock at the door. Paul got up and let them in, except there was nowhere to sit but on the bed. Paul sat, they stood by the door, and Pia stood in the corner of the small room with her arms crossed and glaring at them.

"Can I have your names please?" Paul asked.

"Our names are of no consequence."

"Then why are you here?"

"We know about your past and we might have need for your assistance in due course. This depends on how attached you are to your new home."

It started to make sense. "In case of war?"

"If the worst comes to the worst."

"I'm no fascist."

"Would you be capable of assisting His Majesty's Government in gathering information?"

"Spying?"

"If you say yes to this, then we'll talk some more, and if you say no then we'll leave and this matter will not be raised again."

As far as Paul was concerned there was a right side and a wrong side, and Mussolini and Hitler were the wrong side. If war broke out then, was the right side. "I will say yes," he said.

"Yes is good."

"This is spying."

"You could call it this."

"That's dangerous."

"If you were to cooperate with us and if you were caught, you're not covered by prisoner of war conventions. Most likely you will be tortured and executed."

"I understand. Can I ask my wife?"

Silence and one whispered to the other and then they nodded in harmony. "Your wife must be a part of this if you are to succeed, so you must ask her."

"Se c'è la guerra, vogliono farci fare la spia per loro," Paul said.

Pia nodded. "Perché tu sei Australiano?"

"Si. Spiare per l'Inghilterra?"

She nodded. "Si."

"È pericoloso e si potrebbe essere torturato o ucciso."

"Sono d'accordo"

"We understand," the man said. "Grazie signore e signora. When the time comes we will contact you. We must go."

They opened the door and left the room,

Now it was time to eat at the less than salubrious dining room of the Rangemoor Park Hotel. And then a good night's sleep for a race on Saturday.

Tazio Nuvolari led off the grid while team mate H.P. Müller made an excellent start from the second row into second place. Nuvolari built up a half-minute lead before he pitted on lap 26 to have spark plugs changed. Nuvolari then resumed fourth behind Müller, Lang and von Brauchitsch. It wasn't until the mid-race stops that Lang was able to get past Müller, while Nuvolari had a quick stop and moved into third place. Lang quickly built up a massive lead while Nuvolari entertained the crowd with his attempts to keep pace, throwing the Auto Union through the curves with abandon. He passed Müller into second while Lang suffered a broken windscreen and had slowed. Nuvolari passed Lang on the straight with seven laps to go, and Seaman passed Müller into third.

Tazio Nuvolari was a popular winner with the crowd, while the brave Hermann Lang collapsed when he got out of his car at the end of the race; such was the effect of the wind blast. Local driver Dick Seaman was a popular third place, of course.

On the way back to his car, Paul contemplated the previous evening's visit by who he assumed to be MI-6. He hoped his services wouldn't be called upon, but if it happened they must do the right thing.

Chapter Thirty Nine

Nurse Durante woke Achille and left a copy of La Gazzetta Dello Sport. He washed, shaved and dressed and then sat to read that Tazio won at Donington, which was his second win in a row. Achille was pleased. Tazio was a competitor and a friend while Achille had a soft spot for Auto Union, who only had a fraction of the resources of Mercedes-Benz and none of their racing experience, and yet were competitive and won many races. That news was a good start to his day.

The weather at Modena was rather lovely when they went outside for exercise, and later Achille had a one-on-one therapy session. There Achille went deeper into his previous recovery and relapse, which was brought about by Ilse's response to his extreme disappointment to the race at Livorno. More than ever Achille realised that, although he loved Ilse and always would, he made the right decision to leave her and not just for himself. Achille wondered how she fared. Momentarily he considered that he was being tended to while she lost everything. That was tough.

As days and weeks passed, Achille felt stronger and stronger, and he knew that every day was a day closer to recovery. Time was the healer, and only with time would the terrible cravings eventually fade. Eventually the time came for Achille's release from The Villa Igea Clinic, recovered but not cured because he would never be cured. Uncle Hercules sent a car, where Achille and Nurse Durante were driven to Achille's villa near Galliate. There he was home and ready to face the world. But first he had to face himself, and he thought the best way to start was to go hunting. It had been many years.

Christmas Eve was in Soncino and Daniela had good news for everyone. She was two months pregnant and Paul knew that after two daughters, Clara and Maria, the men in the family would hope for a son. Paul didn't care as long as their child was healthy. The two sisters didn't see each other so often, given Pia was either dress-making for models, especially for the new season, or travelling.

Daniela and Pia sat in the corner of the sitting room where it was quiet. So quiet that Paul heard every word.

"Do you want a boy?" Pia asked with one hand on Daniela's stomach.

"I don't care," Daniela said. "But this will be our last."

"Are you sure?"

"Yes. I heard Paul talking about England and Donington, wherever that is, and Monza of course and then Bern, which I think is in Switzerland, and I thought you go to these places."

"I do."

"I wish I could see more of the world than Milano and Soncino."

Silence. "I would like to have a family of three children, but that's not going to happen. I love Paul and I like travelling with him and helping with his articles. So it's a good life for me."

"We always wish for the things we can't have."

"That's true. Next year in July, no that's not going to work. I thought you could come with us to Livorno for the Coppa Ciano but it's the wrong time for you. You would like it there; Livorno is pretty."

"Some other year."

"You don't need to travel all the way to England to have a good holiday. There are many lovely places in Italy. Italy is the most beautiful country in the world. You must come with us when you can."

"I will."

"You can come out from where you're hiding Paul," Pia said.

"I wasn't hiding," he said.

"Of course not."

"If you had a choice...?"

"I pick you amore mio."

Paul checked his watch. "It's nearly time ladies."

Nearly time for midnight mass, as was the tradition. Another tradition was Christmas in Soncino with the Donati family. Even though they couldn't have children, they would always have Daniela and her children and the rest of the family.

* * *

Achille heard knocking at the door and Nurse Durante went to answer it. The commotion that followed brought good memories as Achille stood and waited.

"I waited for an invitation that never came," Norma said. She went to Achille and kissed his cheek. "How are you?"

"I'm good, I'm really good."

"Are you ready to face the world?"

"That was the mistake I made last time. This time I'll take my time, and when I'm ready, I'm ready."

"Are you ready for Norma Colombo yet?"

Achille nodded. "I'm ready and it's been a long time."

"We have a lot to make up for."

Achille knew what she meant and she was right, as she often was right. Achille left Nurse Durante behind and closed the door to his bedroom. It was more than time.

Achille lit a cigarette and gave his packet and lighter to Norma who lit one as well. Achille contemplated the quilt and sheets strewn all over and that brought back memories. Good memories.

"Do you want to tell me anything?" Norma asked.

"It's good to have you back," Achille said.

"It's good to be back."

Achille sat up and leaned against the bed head. "Whatever you may think, don't blame Ilse. It wasn't her fault."

"How long had we been together? Seven years? We were young when we met."

"I was young and something happened a few years before; another German woman. That's what brought us together. But it was destined not to last, unlike us." Achille slid down the bed and embraced Norma. We'll always be Achille and Norma."

"Yes we will, amore mio."

Chapter Forty

The year 1939 started with foreboding and became one near-crisis after another. In March, Germany and Romania signed a treaty which virtually ceded the economy of Romania to Germany. A week later, Britain and France guaranteed the sovereignty of Poland, a country which Germany had designs upon. And a week after that in early April, Italy invaded and conquered Albania which ended in a forced union with the Kingdom of Italy. War seemed imminent.

On the motor sport front, more and more racing in Italy and France was run to Voiturette regulations of 1.5 litres supercharged. Alfa Romeo developed a new Voiturette, the Tipo 158 with a straight eight engine, where that car debuted in August 1938 at the Coppa Ciano. Since then the Tipo 158 had proven to be fast but sometimes fragile. Maserati 6CM voiturettes were almost as fast and more reliable, so Voiturette racing had become quite interesting. The most lucrative race of the season remained the Gran Premio di Tripoli, which in 1939 was run to Voiturette regulations. There Mercedes-Benz had a surprise. Paul heard about the testing of a new Mercedes Voiturette at Hockenheim a few weeks before, although racing often revealed flaws that testing would never uncover.

Mercedes entered two W165s for Rudi Caracciola and Hermann Lang, featuring V-8 engines. Alfa Romeo entered no less than six Tipo 158s. There were four works Maseratis, including new 4CL models for Giovanni Rocci and Carlo Trossi, a special, streamlined 4CL for Luigi Villoresi, and an older 6CM for Franco Cortese. These were backed up by four Maserati 6CMs for Scuderia

Ambrosiana, six for Scuderia Torino and eight private 6CM Maseratis.

The weather for Thursday practice was dreadful even by Tripoli standards, with a hot wind blowing sand from the desert, limiting visibility and putting sand on the track. Paul noted that Alfa Romeo team manager, Meo Constantini, was afraid his cars would overheat so he lessened the cooling system pressure. Friday practice was less windy when Villoresi set fastest lap in the Maserati streamliner. On Saturday things went bad at Mercedes-Benz. For some time Paul had noticed that both Rudi Caracciola and Manfred von Brauchitsch barely acknowledged the existence of former mechanic Hermann Lang and sometimes were rude to him, despite Lang being the faster driver. Or perhaps it was because the quietly-spoken Lang was faster, especially over the past year where Caracciola was clearly overshadowed for speed, despite being consistent enough to win the European Championship. On Saturday Mercedes team manager Neubauer told Lang to practice on fresh tyres while Caracciola remained in the pit. Caracciola then exploded at both Neubauer and Lang before angrily storming off. By then Lang had disappeared, to be found with his wife Lydia who was crying. There was a long, quiet discussion that eventually resulted in Mercedes director Max Sailer getting involved, and Paul guessed that the Langs had enough of Caracciola's tantrums. Eventually Hermann Lang was persuaded back into his car where he set a time for second place on the grid towards the end of practice.

"I didn't like the way Rudi behaved," Pia called from the bathroom.

Paul sat on the side of her bath. "I think all the top drivers are a bit like that," he said. "If you're not tough and maybe even mean, then you won't be three-time European Champion."

"Tazio's not like that."

Paul thought about that. "Out of the car he isn't, but in the car I'm sure he's as mean as any driver." Paul remembered someone close who certainly was mean. "Who was the hardest on the track?"

"Achille; he bangs wheels and cuts other drivers off."

"He's hard off the circuit, especially with waiters and waitresses."

"So that's why he's twice been Italian Champion?"

Paul grabbed a sponge. "Lean forward and I'll wash your back."

"Grazie amore mio. Special things like that will get you everything that your heart's desire."

"Promise?"

"As soon as I finish this bath."

Race day was extremely hot, where Hermann Lang made a great start while Luigi Villoresi in the streamlined Maserati followed before falling back and pitting at the end of the lap with gearbox problems, but the car had also suffered an engine failure. Trossi's new Maserati retired on the first lap with another broken engine. Lang built up a massive lead, no doubt spurred by Caracciola's behaviour the day before, while the Alfa Romeos suffered overheating problems and all but one of their cars retired by lap 16 out of 30. By then tyre and refuelling stops were underway, by which time many drivers suffered from dehydration and some were quite disorientated. Lang won his third Gran Premio di Tripoli by easing off so he wouldn't lap Caracciola, while Emilio Villoresi finished third in the sole, surviving Alfa Romeo.

Since they'd previously been to Germany the persecution of Jews and Gypsies had gotten worse, with government-organised riots and looting of Jewish property and synagogues the previous November. Once the rioting and looting was over, many Jews who could leave Germany did. Against that background the 1939 Eifelrennen was run in May, staying at their usual Ringhaus Hotel along with most drivers and team managers. It was a small field of 13 cars although Auto Union were racing for the first time that season.

After checking in, Paul accompanied Pia to the dining room where he was surprised to sit in the table adjacent to Dick Seaman and his young wife, Erica Popp, the daughter of the managing director of BMW. Paul couldn't help himself.

"Good evening Mr Seaman," he said in English.

"Pardon? Oh, you speak English!" and he laughed. "Good evening; I've seen you around."

"I'm Paul Bassi, an independent journalist, and my wife, Pia Bassi."

"Good evening to you both, and this is my wife, Erica."

"Good evening Erica, and I hope you speak English."

"I do," she said in a light accent.

"So you're...?" Dick Seaman asked.

"I'm Australian of Italian ancestry and speaker of enough languages to get by."

He laughed. "I understand, yes, and you're married to an Italian woman. We have something in common."

"We both are married to beautiful ladies from our respective new homelands."

"Oh Mr Bassi!" Erica exclaimed.

"I won't intrude other than to wish you good luck for this weekend."

"Thank you."

Paul sat while Pia probably gathered enough of that conversation.

"I know what happened," Pia said in Italian.

"There's nothing he can tell me other than he'll try his best, so I didn't ask."

"What do you think?"

"Herman Lang will take some beating, but Dick Seaman won the Grand Prix here last, so you never know."

A waiter approached so Paul picked up his menu. German food wasn't his favourite.

In fine weather, Lang scored pole from Nuvolari, Caracciola, Seaman and von Brauchitsch. The race was a battle between Lang and Nuvolari, where Lang won by only 11 seconds showing Tazio hadn't lost his touch. Seaman burned his clutch at the start and retired at the end of the first lap.

That wasn't the end of the matter because Caracciola, who never was in contention to win, although not so far behind in third place, climbed out of his car and threw his cap and goggles at team manager, Alfred Neubauer. Age or possibly stiffness and pain from several bad crashes had blunted Rudi's speed, and clearly he was looking for a scapegoat. Of course, Mercedes-Benz was to blame for giving Lang a faster car.

The Nürburgring's usual weather was transplanted to Spa-Francorchamps for the Grand Prix de Belgique. Race day had intermittent showers and sometimes heavy rain, where on lap 22 out of 35, race leader Dick Seaman slid off the road at Club Curve and his car bounced into two trees. The force of the crash knocked Seaman unconscious while fire broke out. A brave soldier and two brave marshals eventually released the steering wheel and dragged Seaman from the inferno. In the meantime the race went on although everyone lost the heart for it. Lang pitted to report the bad news to his team before going on to win, while Hasse eventually finished second in his Auto Union.

Dick Seaman briefly regained consciousness that night, just before he died, while Paul was disappointed they only spoke the once. Although it was reported that Dick Seaman's mother disapproved of his marriage to Erica Popp, Paul was sure that if the world went to war, Mr and Mrs Seaman would have quietly migrated to England.

From there it was Reims in France, the Nürburgring and terrible weather as usual. Beautiful Livorno and Pescara, and Daniela gave birth to her daughter who she named Gia, and next came Bern in Switzerland. Then Germany invaded Poland.

Chapter Forty One

Achille contemplated the Alfa Romeo Tipo 158 standing next to the pits at Monza – a remarkably neat racing car. He walked around the car, taking in all of its details. The latest version of Monza with only one chicane would suit it. He put in his earplugs, fastened his linen cap, put on his goggles and gloves and climbed behind the wheel. In the background Meo looked on while the mechanic applied the starting motor. Achille eased onto the wide straight and accelerated up to Curva della Roggia and the old, road circuit. Around the Lesmo bends and onto the back straight before hard braking and a sharp left and right onto the former, banked circuit. Up to speed and onto Curva Sud before braking hard for the chicane, and then onto the main straight again.

The next lap was at racing speed and the Alfetta responded nicely. Achille completed five laps, increasing speed each time. It had been a long time since he raced a car. Faster and faster until Meo put out the 'In' sign and Achille completed the lap at part-speed before stopping at the pits. He raised his goggles, climbed out of the car and lit a cigarette. Meo walked across with the clipboard in his hand and Achille looked at it. Fast enough at 2 minutes 43.

"Do I have the drive," Achille asked.

Meo nodded slowly. "Yes Achille, as we agreed; 6,000 lira a month and half of prize money."

Norma closed while beaming brightly. The Alfetta was a lovely car and he would win many races with it, assuming there was racing to be had.

In the background Paul Bassi slid off the counter and walked to the group standing beside the red racing car. "Congratulations Achille," he said.

"What are you up to these days?" Achille asked.

"I'm working for Corriere della Mattina, and Pia's returned to dressmaking. I'll attend all races."

"Journalist in Italian now?"

He nodded. "Yes I am and now I must go. Good luck to you both; ciao."

"Ciao Paul. We should go too. Ciao Meo."

"Drop by the racing department to sign your contract," Meo said.

Achille walked with Norma to the car park. "Now that I have a real job, there's nothing preventing us from getting married."

"There isn't," Norma said.

"So Norma Colombo, my companion of many years. Will you be my wife?"

She took his hand. "Yes Achille."

Achille was pleased with that.

* * *

Italy was at war. It took a while but eventually it happened, no doubt on the back of the German successes in France. Paul contemplated his priorities while he walked the last few blocks to their home. It was the fault of Adolf Hitler, war-mongering Germans and Mussolini taking advantage of the situation. But if it wasn't for Germany, war would never have happened.

He climbed the staircase and let himself in, and Pia turned off the radio. "You heard?" she asked.

Paul nodded. "We need to drive to Chiari this weekend. Mario knows a farmer who will look after our car."

"We must look after your racing car."

Paul nodded. "We need to put it away safely, given there's no petrol other than what's in the tank. But when this is over we can use it again."

"I hope this war won't be long."

"There's another thing. Next month on the twenty-seventh we're catching a train to Galliate. There's a wedding there."

"That's great news on a bad news day."

"It is."

"Norma's attractive with a lovely personality, and she could have any man in Italy as her husband, but instead she waited for Achille. I know why."

"Why?"

Pia smiled. "Like Ilse. Like many women if they could."

That confused Paul somewhat.

Italy's campaign against the south of France went surprisingly well, although the French surrender to Germany on June 24 meant the end of that battle. In North Africa, things didn't start well with the British advancing into Libya and Air Marshal Balbo killed in a plane crash. The Italian army advanced about 100 kilometres into Egypt and began building a series of fortifications. In his role as journalist Paul attempted to report the facts dispassionately, which wasn't hard given early successes. What Paul didn't like was all day in the office in Milano. He wasn't suited to that.

Saturday was an opportunity to sleep in, only Paul was surprised to hear knocking at the door. He slipped on his gown and went to greet a well-dressed gentleman carrying a Gladstone bag, where this gentleman seemed familiar.

"Buongiorno signore Bassi," he said. "You may remember me," he continued in Italian. We met at Donington last year."

Of course Paul remembered. "Buongiorno signore...."

"Mario Toto."

"Who is it?" Pia asked, emerging dressed in her robe as well. "I remember you," she said.

"This is signore Mario Toto," Paul said.

"Buongiorno signore Toto," Pia said. "Sit, per favore."

Paul and Pia took armchairs and signore Toto sat at the sofa. "Like we discussed last year we need your assistance," he said.

Paul didn't hesitate. "I'll help you to defeat fascists."

"I will too," Pia said.

"Grazie signore e signora. The main campaign of the war is in North Africa to gain access to oil fields. Victory in North Africa will be the first step to the defeat of the Axis powers. One thing that could prevent us is Regia Marina attacking our supply convoys. So we need to know as much about Regia Marina as we can, from the major port of Napoli."

"Napoli!" Pia exploded. 'That's a city of thieves and whores. We can't go there! Why don't you get someone local?"

Signore Toto took Pia's outburst in his stride. "We need assistance from people who aren't fascist, aren't communist and who aren't associated with the Camorra."

That was obvious. "I understand," Paul said. "What do you want us to do?"

"We need you to monitor which Regia Marina ships are in port and report this to us. We bought an apartment near the port where it will be possible for you to monitor ships, using a telescope and silhouette drawings of each vessel. Then, three times a week, you mail coded letters to an address in Roma."

"Is this all?" Paul asked.

"For now."

"How do we survive in Napoli in the meantime?"

"You'll be given 1,000 lira a month for food and other expenses. We have an agent based in Roma, and Michele will visit you every week." Signore Toto placed his bag on the sofa and reached inside. He pulled out a sheaf of documents. "These are your new passports, identity documents and ration cards. To keep it simple you will be known as Paolo and Pia Amadio, and you're both from Roma. It's best that you be known as Paolo. Do you speak dialect?"

"I do," Pia said.

"Lombardian dialect is different to Neapolitan dialect, so don't attempt to use it. Roman dialect is different again, so if a Neapolitan talks in dialect to you, tell them you're Roman and you don't understand."

"They will pick my Lombardian accent," Pia said.

"This is a good point. You're originally from Lombardy and then you spent time in Roma." Signore Toto pulled out two train tickets. "These are for Monday." Next was a map. "This is a map of Napoli where your apartment is number 19 in Via Alessandra Volta, 22." Next some envelopes and a pad. "These are for you messages. Buy more envelopes in Napoli and always use this address," he said, holding up a pre-addressed envelope. "If you can't get envelopes, paper or stamps locally for any reason, Michele can arrange some. Waiting in your apartment are silhouette drawings of each naval vessel. Now, I need to teach you to code your letters. Coding is tedious, so it will take you the best part of a day to code your observations. Training in coding will take all day today and maybe part of tomorrow. Once you code your observations you should mail them, and always use different letterboxes. Now, because it's early, you should dress and eat breakfast and then we can start."

Paul wondered what he got himself into.

"Remember this could win the war," signore Toto said.

"Would you like coffee signore?" Pia asked.

"Grazie."

* * *

Every time Paul travelled south it was like travelling to another country. Ancient towns and villages little changed since Roman times. Small farms on hilly terrain with meagre crops or poor quality pasture, sometimes only good enough for grazing goats. Donkeys pulling carts, men on bicycles, little motorised transport and no farm machinery. And big, extended families, lots of children, men in shabby suits seemingly with nothing to do all day, women in black gathered together, urchins running about. From the window of the train he saw it all.

The railway from Roma hugged the coast with the uplands to the east. Through towns and cities until unmistakeable Mount Vesuvius beckoned the approach to Napoli. A populous city hemmed between mountains and the shimmering, blue

Mediterranean. Certainly easy on the eye, and with a broad, natural harbour protected by a man-made breakwater. Closer, the city was modern and yet ramshackle, with narrow streets crammed with utilitarian brick or stucco apartment buildings, many with clothing hanging from windows, little in the way of parks, gardens or even vegetation. Not so easy on the eye.

They arrived at the small but attractive Napoli Centrale Railway Station, and from there they crossed a broad avenue and headed almost due south to Via Alessandro Volta, 22, which was an ugly, multi-storey stucco over brick structure hemmed between a broad avenue and the port, made uglier by clothes strung from window to window to window. Paul unlocked the outside door where they trudged up many flights of stairs to the fourth floor, and then Paul unlocked a wooden door and entered a narrow corridor. Timber-framed glass doors led off the corridor into a narrow bathroom, a kitchen and eating area, a bedroom and a sitting room. The rooms were small and painted pink, except the kitchen which was mostly tiled at one end. Furniture was basic: timber bed and wardrobe, timber and fabric lounge chairs and a small sofa in the sitting room, and a timber table and four chairs in the kitchen. A radio in the sitting room with a clock on top was one concession to luxury. Pia went from room to room and returned to the corridor.

"I don't like it," she said.

Paul didn't like it either. "It's our sacrifice for the war," he said before going to the sitting room. There the window had the most amazing view over the busy port. "Look at this."

She handled the cheap, purple-coloured curtains before gazing into the distance. "This is a good view," she said, nodding slowly. "It's our sacrifice."

Paul went to the bedroom to reach between the mattress and the timber base and pull out about thirty cards: silhouettes of the ships of Regia Marina. In the wardrobe was a telescope. He held them – one in each hand.

"Tomorrow amore mio," Pia said wearily. "We'll unpack, make the bed, get something to eat and then we start tomorrow."

Chapter Forty Two

Identifying military ships from commercial freighters was hard enough, but identifying which military ship was harder. Paul came up with the idea of a map, sketching the layout of the harbour and where each vessel was berthed. There, one by one, they included or eliminated each one, and using the cards they managed to identify which was what.

They used a code based upon their poem Endymion by Keats, where it took about four hours to generate a message which seemed like a random series of characters, and then they interlaced their message into a letter using invisible ink. After that it was time to mail their precious espionage.

Paul bought stamps, posted the letter and then wandered through the nearby Poggioreale district which was a real eye opener. Narrow streets crowded by run-down buildings, with eyes at windows following every move. Self-consciously he thrust his hands in his pockets to appear casual while surrounded by an obvious criminal underclass. Men loitered in doorways observing the stranger walking along their street, while buxom and barely-dressed Neapolitan prostitutes loitered with less then subtle intent. Apartment blocks with shops at the ground floor: butchers, grocers, pharmacies and so on; no parks, no greenery; nothing. Scruffily-dressed street urchins noisily ran by, bumping Paul on the way through. Paul checked his pockets but his keys and wallet were safe. He emerged onto Via Gianturco Emanuele, breathed a sigh of relief and headed back to their apartment. Poggioreale was a district of thieves and whores to be sure.

The three observations a week took all day so the other four days were rather boring. They read books, played cards, played chess and Paul taught Pia to speak English, which could be useful given they worked for the British. She struggled with the concept of no gender except when necessary, sometimes, and also the randomness of English grammar after the precision of Latin-based languages. They walked the streets to identify things, had simple conversations and gradually Pia came to terms with the language.

There were twenty apartments at Via Alessandro Volta, 22, and over time Paul and Pia met their neighbours. There were five, elderly couples who called the building home, and several soldiers' wives struggling to make ends meet on a soldiers' pay. All apartments were one bedroom so only suited childless couples, either before having children or after children left home. Mario and his wife Cara were similar in age to Paul and Pia, and Mario worked at the electricity supply company.

Every week Michele came to Napoli, brought money and took away one of the letters, but he didn't know how successful their observations were. Paul met Michele in the downstairs courtyard at six on Tuesdays, given the outside locked door and the lack of door bell or telephone.

Christmas came and went, which wasn't a proper Christmas without going to Soncino. The story was they were in Australia for the duration of the war. Paul and Pia celebrated Christmas Eve at a restaurant followed by midnight mass at Saint Nicola from Tolentino.

Mid-afternoon a few weeks later, strange sirens echoed, and shortly after aircraft closed on the city. It was an air raid! The naval ships in the harbour opened fire which created a massive cacophony close to the apartment building – the ground literally shook. Bombs fell on the port and further east, and after about an hour it was over. It wasn't a surprise that the Port of Napoli was a target, so the question was where to go for safety. Air raid protection was surprisingly disorganised for a city which contained many targets of military significance.

Paul waited in the courtyard where all was quiet except for footsteps closing – Michele carrying his satchel.

"Ciao Paolo," Michele said.

"Ciao Michele," Paul replied. He reached inside his jacket and pulled out the letter. "This is it."

Michele put the envelope into his satchel. "They want more," he said.

"More what?" Paul asked.

"They want to know what happens before it happens."

Paul was confused about that. "How?" he asked.

"They want us to infiltrate Regia Marina and learn their secrets. Pia can do this, if you both agree."

"Agree to what?"

"Pia could seduce an important man and gather knowledge."

That made sense, although Paul didn't want Pia to seduce anyone. He doubted she would agree to it anyway.

"This is really important," Michele said.

"If this is important then you can ask Pia and let her make up her mind."

"You're her husband; would you allow her?"

Paul didn't want her to, and to imagine Pia making love with an old man in the hierarchy of Regia Marina would break his heart. But it was war and it would be wrong to reject the request purely on jealousy. "Come inside and convince us both."

"Grazie Paolo."

Paul unlocked the outside door and they climbed the many flights of stairs where he led Michele into their humble home. To the sitting room where Pia read a book, which she put down.

"Ciao Michele," she said.

"Ciao Pia," he replied.

"Michele has something to ask you," Paul said.

"As you know the Allies have been fighting in North Africa to gain access to the region's oil supplies, which is vital for any future invasion of Europe. To win in North Africa we must supply Allied armies with men, supplies and equipment, and this is done by shipping convoys through the Mediterranean. If Regia Marina can prevent these convoys getting through, the war in North Africa could be lost, and any chance of victory in Europe could be lost."

"We know this," Pia said impatiently with her arms crossed. "What do you want now?"

"The Allies need to know what Regia Marina plan to do before they do it, so we need to infiltrate their top command and obtain information. Ammiraglio Flavio Belloni is in charge of operational communications, and through him we can obtain every message sent to the fleet before its coded. Belloni has one weakness, he is a known philanderer and...."

"No!" Pia shouted. She jumped to her feet and marched towards Michele. "Lei boiata pirla picio! Non sono una puttana! She stood close with her hands on her hips and her face red.

"I understand," Michele said calmly. "There's another way. Ammiraglio Belloni has a secretary who handles his cables. If we could infiltrate Sergente Mara Pavesi, this could be just as good."

"How?" Pia snapped and then her face changed. "Oh," she said before turning around to look at Paul.

"Me?" Paul asked.

"It's possible. Mara Pavesi is single, about thirty-eight, and she's lived a sheltered life caring for her elderly parents. Her mother was thirty-eight when Mara was born while her father was ten years older. He died fourteen years ago and Pavesi's mother died about a year ago. As far as we know she's never had a relationship."

"That's ridiculous," Pia said.

"What?"

"Trying to seduce a good Catholic woman like her. I'll seduce the admiral."

"Are you sure?"

"As long as I can't fall pregnant, I'm sure."

"There are ways...."

"I know there are ways, just make sure I have access to them."
"I will."

Paul was shocked by this. "Are you sure Pia needs to do this?"

"Pia doesn't need to do anything, but if she succeeds we could save countless thousands of lives. Sons conscripted to war, husbands too, grieving mothers, grieving widows...."

"I offer no guarantees," Pia said. "He might not be interested in me, and even if he is, he might not reveal anything useful. But the least I can do is try. What do you know about him?"

Michele unzipped his satchel and removed a manila file, which he placed on the kitchen counter.

"You were prepared."

"There's also a file for Mara Pavesi."

Pia smiled while opening the file. "He's older than my father."

"Ammiraglio Belloni is age 57, married with four children, and the marital home is an apartment in the north-west at Chiaiano. He has a mistress, age 19, although she's more interested in his money than him. You at 28 should interest him, and make sure he knows you're married but separated by war, and you don't have children."

"Why?"

"You're more experienced at love than a girl age 19."

"I'm originally from a village, but for many years I've been travelling and socialising with women more worldly than me. To do this I need to be presented properly, I'll intercept the admiral and then we'll see what happens."

"He dines most evenings at Michelasso on Via Santa Brigida."

"With his mistress?"

"He doesn't dine with her. Pia, you have the looks, experience, intelligence and personality to do this."

"What if I discover something?" Pia asked.

"You and Paul can code a letter and mail it."

"What if it's important?"

"Telephone me on Roma 78966."

"I need money to buy dresses and shoes, and if I need to rework these dresses, I can."

Michele reached into his satchel to extract a bundle of lira notes which he handed to Pia.

"I know what I want," she said.

Paul was interested by that – Pia had become worldlier but there seemed to be more. Worse, though, the thought of Pia with an old fascist admiral was – revolting. Paul supposed that no matter how many lives they might save, he wouldn't be a man if he wasn't, well, jealous.

Chapter Forty Three

Pia fastened the black, lace garter belt, sat on the bed and carefully rolled flesh-coloured silk stockings and fastened them, and her new black satin pants. Next, her black pumps with 75 millimetre heels and a strap around her ankle. Finally, her black cocktail dress: body tight, off her shoulders and slit on the side from about mid thigh. She checked herself in the mirror – powder and lipstick in a subtle shade of red, and the dress highlighting the best parts of her figure. She took her black leather clutch and went to the living room where Paul clearly was surprised.

"That will grab his attention," he said.

"This is the intention but I'm not going to be an easy catch."

"Are you sure?"

"I'm sure."

"You don't look like you're wearing a bra."

"I'm not."

He pursed his lips. "You don't need to and it's – different." Pia crossed the room. "That's definitely not a bra," Paul said.

Pia was smaller-busted which had its advantages. "With luck we'll drink and talk and maybe I'll get another date, or maybe I'll go nowhere."

"Good luck anyway."

"Grazie."

Michelasso, in the centre of Napoli, was a short walk from their apartment, near shops where a woman could buy dresses to show off her figure, and buy the latest fashionable shoes. Pia walked past four tables outside, all diners' heads swivelling, to enter the restaurant, elegant and hushed, spacious and with many bottles of wine at the bar. Pia took a stool and put her clutch on the bar.

"Buonasera, I would like a Negroni, per favore."

He measured equal quantities of Vermouth Rosso, Campari Bitter and dry gin, added ice, mixed it, poured it into a glass, popped in a straw and gave it to Pia.

"Grazie." She sipped, most refreshing as she noticed in the mirror, the reflection of her target enter the restaurant. Pia turned side on while she drank, and turned her head to catch his eyes. He looked up and she saw it. She looked at her watch in an exaggerated way and tried to look annoyed. She sipped her drink until it was finished, and then a waiter closed.

"I'm waiting for my friend but he seems not to be here. I'll look outside for him."

Pia took her clutch, eased herself from the stool, and had to admit her heels made her hips sway, until she drew alongside where she dropped her clutch. She part knelt and part bent forward to pick it up, just as Belloni reached down. He picked it up and handed it to Pia.

"Grazie. It seems I've been stood up."

"That's a shame."

"I wasn't planning to dine alone."

"You can share my table."

"Grazie." Pia stood, walked around the table where the waiter took the chair. She sat, put her clutch on the table and the waiter laid a starched tablecloth across her lap. She looked up as the waiter set her place.

"My name's signora Pia Amadio."

"My name's Ammiraglio Flavio Belloni."

Pia shook his hand while the waiter placed a menu.

"I wasn't expecting to have beautiful company this evening."

"Grazie."

"You're not from here." Belloni asked.

"I'm Lombadian and more recently I've been living in Roma."

"I knew you were from the north with your fair skin and fine features – in fact you're the most beautiful woman in this restaurant. Would you like to share my wine?"

"Grazie."

He poured from his bottle of white wine. "This means you will have to order fish."

"I know."

"Cin cin."

Pia clinked his glass. "Cin cin." She returned to the menu to make up her mind and close it. The waiter approached and Belloni gestured to Pia.

"I'll have risotto and monkfish."

"I'll have squid and monkfish."

The waiter took their menus away.

"I can see you have dined in restaurants like this one."

"I'm well-travelled," Pia said.

He glanced at Pia's left hand. "Your husband must be wealthy."

"I was a journalist."

"And your husband?"

"He's not here." Pia sipped from her glass. "This is fine wine."

"They have excellent wine here. I come here most evenings."

"Oh I see, well, it's close to the port and naval headquarters."
Pia glanced at his cap on the table.

The waiter brought out their entrees, where the risotto was delicious with a glass of white wine. The squid looked equally delicious but Belloni knew the menu by heart.

"As I said I wasn't expecting beautiful company this evening. How did you come to be in Napoli?" he asked.

"Well, my husband's a journalist and he was sent here, only after a few months he was sent to North Africa as a war correspondent, and I moved in with a friend who has room in her apartment."

"What about your children?"

"I don't have children."

"How long is your husband going to be in North Africa?"

"For as long as the war lasts. How long do you think this will be?"

"Victory will take time."

"I expect it will. In the meantime, of course, I'm lonely."

"Yes, this is a price of war. Perhaps there's a way of easing your loneliness."

"Of course there is."

"How are you, financially?"

"I'm settled financially but I need other things."

He smiled. "Of course you do."

"And you?"

"My domestic situation isn't entirely happy, which is why I come here. In different ways we're both lonely."

"Yes, we are."

The waiter brought their main courses and Flavio poured more wine each. The fish was delightful which reminded Pia.

"I've travelled near and far, but no country I've visited has food and wine as good as Italy."

Flavio looked at her and smiled – yes, he understood.

Pia finished her meal, Flavio finished his, and now was important as Pia placed her knife and fork the correct way.

Flavio took her hand.

"I must admit, Pia, that you brighten this normally dull restaurant. I would like to get to know you better."

"I would like to get to know you, Flavio."

He lightly touched her cheek. "If you wish we can go somewhere discreet together."

Pia nodded her head while trying not to smile. "I would like to genuinely get to know you better, which will make further experiences more – worthwhile."

"I agree. Do you want to meet here again, the same time tomorrow night?"

"Yes, I would like this."

"Your friend who stood you up has missed out on a wonderful evening."

Pia allowed herself to smile. "In the end I had a wonderful evening so that doesn't matter." Pia put her hand on her clutch.

"Don't worry; this is on my account."

"Thank you." Pia went to stand only Flavio raced around to help with her chair. He put his cap on and walked beside Pia to Via Santa Brigida. She stopped to allow Flavio to kiss her cheeks while squeezing her hand. When she walked away, Pia knew he watched her.

* * *

Pia sat on the edge of the bath, legs spread while she used her Gillette to trim her hair into a strip, dunking the safety razor into water from time to time. To finish, she lightly brushed the razor over the rest of her hair to trim it shorter. Next, she stood to remove the cap from the bottle of white vinegar, poured some into the cap and then poured it over the rim of the cervical cap before squatting and pressing it into place. Before she tried the other day she never would have imagined suction would have been that strong, until she had to remove it.

Back in their room she dressed in the same underwear, stockings and shoes as the previous evening, again no bra while finishing with the other black cocktail dress with a V-shaped neckline plunging between her breasts almost to the waist, and held in place with strips of tape, and slit on one side to about mid-thigh. She went to the living room.

"It's hard to wish you good luck."

"I know, but this is a war that we must win."

"This is Germany's fault."

Pia left to walk to Michelasso where Flavio waited at his table with a bottle and his glass of red wine. He stood to kiss Pia's cheeks while squeezing her hand, and then he helped with her chair. The waiter draped a tablecloth and left a menu.

"You said you were well-travelled. Which was your favourite?"

"Italy's my favourite, of course, and the other Latin countries, France and Spain, come next. Germany is dreary, except for

Berlin, and England's awful." Pia searched for the right words. "Germany and England is like a death sentence – they have no joy of life."

"I've never heard it put like this but I've not met someone as well travelled as you. Grazie for your insights. I never expected to spend time with someone young, beautiful and yet worldly. If this isn't rude, how old are you?"

"I'm 28."

"Your's is a perfect age – youthful beauty yet experienced."

Pia looked at the menu, made her choice and closed it. The waiter approached and Flavio gestured to Pia.

"I'll have ravioli and veal."

"I'll have ravioli and veal, too."

The waiter took their menus while Flavio poured wine into Pia's glass.

"Cin cin."

Pia clinked her glass. "Cin cin." She sipped. "This is delightful, rich and woody."

"Yes it is."

"Now Flavio, what about you?"

Flavio sipped his wine. "I think, somehow, I'm not as interesting as you." He sipped more. "A wife and four children, where two are married with their own children. My wife and my two youngest daughters live in an apartment here. I have a mistress too."

"We haven't yet started, Flavio, but we will. I understand I'm second but I don't want to be third."

The waiter brought their entrees. Pia ate a little, which was delicious, and then looked at Flavio.

"Leave my mistress to me," he said.

Pia nodded her head as she ate more. "Is there Regia Marina in your family?"

"Yes, there is."

"How about your wife? Was she once your love?"

"It was more expedient than that."

Flavio might have married to get promoted – the Italian government and military worked like that. "This is a pity," Pia said. "You know, love and passion have a lot going for them."

"And yet you're here."

"My love isn't here and my passionate soul feels lonely." She looked into his eyes. "You never know where things might lead." Pia finished her entree and the waiter took her plate.

"I've never met anyone like you."

Pia knew that socialising with wives and girlfriends whose lives revolved around love and passion, open and unabashed, had changed her. This wasn't her choice but she knew there was no harm in it, unlike many. The words came to her. "Travel can change a woman," she said.

"Travel can make a woman worldlier."

The waiter brought out their main courses – the veal was delicious. Pia was going to become his mistress, of that she had no doubt, and she hoped in future she would return this restaurant, unlike the 19 year old. Their food was superb and their wine equally so as she sipped some. When she finished, Pia put her knife and fork just right.

"How was your meal?" Flavio asked.

"This is the best restaurant I have ever been to."

He smiled. "Now, if you want to go somewhere discreet, Pia, we can."

"Tonight we will."

Flavio came around to help with Pia's chair, and walk with her along the streets of Napoli to Pinto-Storey Hotel, where in reception Pia stood to one side while Flavio booked, and then they were free to go upstairs to room 15. Flavio opened the door, switched on the room light and put his cap on the hatstand. It was utilitarian, especially the simple, vanished timber furnishings. Pia pressed a light switch on the bedhead and turned the room light off – that was better as Flavio closed to hug and kiss; especially holding her bottom. He gently ran his tongue around Pia's lips; she let him inside and met that while her heart beat fast. Pia liked to rush into making love at the best of times as she eased away to unbutton her dress and ease it over her hips, aware of Flavio watching until he unbuttoned his uniform, and layer by layer discarded it while Pia removed everything except for her garter belt and stockings. Flavio's hair was receding, of course, and he was a little paunchy but not too bad as Pia eased close to allow him to hug and kiss, tongues touching and his hand on her bottom but actually his finger at her anus – interesting. He didn't press it in, just stroked which was delightful. Kissing, hugging and that which she'd never experienced before, and then Pia guessed what Flavio wanted, which would make her his special mistress. She kissed for a while before easing away.

"Sesso anale?" Pia asked.

"Si."

Pia picked up the phone. "Bring a small amount of oil or salad dressing to room 15."

A few moments later there was knocking on the door. Flavio slipped underpants over his erection to deal with that, and stripped off to look at Pia.

"You're remarkably attractive."

"Grazie."

He put the small bottle on the bedside table while Pia lay on the bed, face down.

"That's a lovely view."

Flavio spread Pia's legs to lie between, and then spread her cheeks to run his tongue over her anus – amazing! Pia couldn't stop herself from moaning at that truly delightful sensation. Over and over until Flavio eased away, pushed her legs almost together, knelt outside with his penis there, slick and slippery as it eased in, stretching her so much, filling her beyond full, and when he pulled back, like always it was like being pulled inside-out.

"How is it?"

"Delightful." He slapped her bottom as he fucked her – that sting was wonderful. "Do that again."

He slapped her twice while he fucked her, slow and steady, no hurry, relaxed.

"How is it?"

"Still delightful. And you?"

"Delightful."

He fucked her and fucked her, slowly and slowly, and then harder as Pia felt it faintly, and she moaned with it stirring, moaned more getting closer, more and more, closer and closer. She groaned as it burst free, endlessly and endlessly, lesser and lesser, but there could be more.

"Keep going."

He did as Pia felt it returning, moaning and moaning, building and building, right on the edge.

"Oh cazzo!" as she came again, lesser but still big. "Oh."

"You came."

"I came twice."

"I'm thirsty."

Flavio eased out and Pia felt hollow. He went to the bathroom, filled two glasses and gave Pia one. She sipped and put the glass on the table while thinking. She took the two pillows and lay over both with her legs together and had Flavio fucking her again, once more in no hurry although Pia wasn't going to come a third time. Endlessly and endlessly, steady and steady until he slowed right down and she felt him stretching and pulling her with each stroke, in and out, in and out until he groaned, deep and manly. Groaned and groaned and groaned. After a moment he eased out and Pia felt hollow again – hollow and wet.

"You were great – I knew exactly what to do."

Pia wondered how and then realised Flavio listened to her moans – clever. Actually, that was good. Flavio lay on his side while Pia got rid of the pillows, and, yes, that was good and she couldn't possibly fall pregnant. Flavio drank some water.

"We're great together," he said.

Pia didn't want to admit it but that had been good. She lay on her side with Flavio looking her over.

"You have a lovely bottom and lovely legs. How's your passion now?"

"My passion is satiated but I know this is temporary." Flavio slapped her bottom while Pia knew what he wanted. "We can have anale next time, if you like it," she offered.

"Do you like it?"

"I like it."

"You're about perfect in age, looks and experience."

"You're a man old enough to know how to satiate my passion." He smiled.

"Where do we go from here?" Pia asked.

"I have some things to arrange. Can you meet me at Michelasso tomorrow evening?"

"Of course I can."

Flavio slapped her bottom where Pia really enjoyed that stinging pain. Pia never imagined liking that but Paul would never do such a thing. Flavio did, only she trusted him to go so far and no further. So far, things had worked out well as Pia took her glass to sip more water.

* * *

Pia let herself into their apartment and went to the living room where Paul listened to the radio. He switched it off.

"How was it?" he asked.

"I'm now his mistress."

"How was that?"

Pia wondered how much to reveal, but she had to ease Paul's concerns. "He's a kind and gentle man; remarkably so."

"How do you feel?"

Pia wondered how much of that to reveal, until she remembered. "You made love before you met me, and I know you didn't love her and you weren't going to marry. This didn't stop it from being good."

"No, it didn't. So it was good?"

"Yes, it was good, but it wasn't love and never could be."

"I understand. You have done well, beautiful Pia, but let's hope this leads somewhere."

Pia knelt in front of Paul and looked into his eyes. "No matter what, I will love always."

He ruffled her hair. "I know amore mia."

Pia felt so horny but it was too soon, even after she bathed, but there was one thing. She went to their bedroom to undress and then to the bathroom where she took the cervical cap out, as always difficult with its suction. She rinsed it and put it in its container. She returned to the bedroom for her nightgown, only decided not to. It was still too soon after Flavio but perhaps in the middle of the night or tomorrow morning she and Paul could make love. Pia was sure they would.

Chapter Forty Four

Pia didn't have to dress up for Flavio, but she knew men lost interest when women stopped trying. She wore a new cocktail dress, sheer black over flesh-coloured tulle, making it look more revealing than it was, and pleated from her waist to her ankles, with her usual flesh-coloured stockings and black shoes, and a black velvet beret, worn at a jaunty angle. She hated leaving Paul at home alone while she went out to make love with Flavio, so this had better be worth it as she stepped down the endless staircase and walked to Michelasso. She was well used the al fresco diners watching her – men wanting her and their wives or girlfriends annoyed by that.

Flavio was at his usual table with a bottle and a glass, and Pia knew to wait until he helped with her chair. She sat and he poured her red wine.

"Cin cin."

"Cin cin." Pia clinked her glass and sipped. The waiter gave her a menu but she only glanced and closed it. The waiter closed.

"I'll have spaghetti and pork."

"I'll have spaghetti and pork, too."

The waiter took their menus away.

Flavio looked at Pia. "I know what you're looking for while your husband's away, but will you tell him when he gets back?"

"What he doesn't know won't hurt him."

Flavio laughed and Pia grinned.

"You're too worldly."

"Is there such a thing?"

"Not from my position or I suspect your husband."

"My husband loves me, I love him too, and you and I are, well, good together."

The waiter brought their spaghettis – delicious as always.

"This is a wonderful restaurant," Pia said.

"Only in Italy?"

"Oh yes; the joy of life and great food!"

Flavio laughed while Pia ate her entree – magnificent.

The waiter took their dishes, Pia sipped her wine, again Italy at its finest, and Flavio topped up her glass.

"I have an apartment where you can stay."

"Oh, grazie. This will be – convenient for us." She smiled.

"There's a maid, too."

"Oh, really?" Pia got over the shock while realising she'll have to be careful with her comings and goings.

The waiter brought out their pork – superb. That and the wine – magnificent. When they finished, Flavio helped with her chair and took his cap. Pia walked with Flavio west about a kilometre to reach a four storey apartment building in green-painted stucco over brick, one block from the sea. Flavio unlocked the door and they climbed stairs to the first floor corridor where he unlocked a gloss white door and held it open for Pia to enter an entrance area in light grey and polished parquetry floors with a staircase to a mezzanine level. Through a doorway was a living room in pale green with polished parquetry floors, a purple fabric lounge suite of a couch and two armchairs, and an empty bookcase on the right. Two pairs of French windows opened onto a balcony with a good view of the building opposite. Through a doorway to a small dining area with a table and three chairs, and beyond that a kitchen with benches, sink and range either side. and a fat older woman in black.

"Maria, this is signora Pia Amadio who you will be looking after."

"Buonasera, Maria."

"Buonasera, signora Amadio."

"Maria has a bedroom with her own bathroom upstairs."

"I'm going to my room now," Maria said.

"Now, come this way," Flavio said to Pia.

He led the way to the all important bedroom, in a different shade of green with a larger than usual bed, a gloss white wardrobe on the far side, two chairs and a small table. Windows gave a good view of the building opposite. It was rather small but that didn't matter while Pia contemplated the gloss white bedhead as Flavio closed to take her in his arms and soon enough they were kissing, tongues touching while he squeezed her bottom – he really had an attraction for that part of the female form. Pia eased away to draw the curtains, turn the room light off with the door part-open to allow light to spill in – much better as she undressed and lay her dress and underwear across one chair, and Flavio undressed and placed his uniform across the other. In no time they were hugging and kissing, tongues touching and his finger rubbing her anus which was delightful. They kissed for long enough while Pia liked the look of the bedhead – it was about right. She climbed onto the bed, knelt to hold it and looked over her shoulder.

"We can do anything you want or we can do this."

"We can do this."

"You need oil."

"I'll get some."

Flavio went to the kitchen, hopefully Maria wasn't around, and moments later climbed onto the bed, knelt behind and she felt his tongue there – amazing! Pia squeezed the bedhead while moaning with the incredible pleasure of that, feasting on her. After ages but never long enough, Flavio pulled away, eased his slick penis into her anus, as always stretching her beyond full. He started slow and then steady, no hurry as Pia enjoyed it, no hurry at all.

Then he went harder and Pia liked that. "Yes," she murmured as it sparkled. "Yes. More, more, yes." Closer, closer, "yes," closer still, right on the edge. "Oh cazzo!" as it burst into orgasm, faint and then bigger, endlessly, endlessly, fading but there was more. "Don't stop." Flavio didn't as Pia felt it again, "More, more, yes," as it closed. She moaned as it got closer, closer, closer still and groaned as it overflowed. "Oh yes," she sighed as pleasure washed through her.

"You came."

"I came twice."

Flavio eased out and left the room, hopefully Maria still wasn't around, and returned with two glasses of water. Pia sipped and put it on the small table. She lay on her front on the bed and put a thick pillow under her stomach. Flavio was comfortably able to enter, which was important because he would take a long time to come. Indeed he did, endlessly and endlessly while Pia enjoyed it, really enjoyed it, especially when Flavio eventually slowed, each stroke stretching and pulling her, delightfully slow, sweat dripping on Pia's back while she moaned – she moaned and moaned until Flavio groaned – groaned and groaned while she felt his wetness.

He stayed still for a moment and then eased out to lie on the bed and Pia got off the bed for his half-full glass of water, which he sat up to drink. Pia drank her water too.

"That was great," he said.

Pia didn't want to admit that, but then thought this will be a good time. "We have the rest of this war, as you know. How long do you think this will be?"

"This is in Germany's hands more than us, and all I know is Regia Marina."

"How is Regia Marina?"

"You mustn't tell anyone."

"I promise."

"We don't have enough fuel oil to operate our ships more than in a limited capacity. We have oil reserves in Tripoli, recently colonised as you know, but it will take some years to tap this and refine it into fuel oil. In the meantime, our bigger ships, especially our battleships and cruisers, are mostly limited to port."

"The North African campaign is to get access to their oil fields."

"How do you know this?"

"My husband's a journalist there. It is, though."

"It is, but it will take many years to tap those reserves and refine this into fuel oil."

Pia thought this through. "Does this affect the army and air force?"

"If it does it will be less than the navy which uses much more oil."

"How about the Allies?"

"That's mostly the British Navy and they get fuel oil from America, shipped across the Atlantic Ocean."

"This isn't good."

"This is between you and me."

"Of course."

"Those in Regia Marina, more senior than me, told Mussolini not to go to war because of the shortage of oil, but instead he dismissed them and appointed his supporters in their places."

Pia was quite shocked. "Grazie for your – candour."

"It's not often that I can discuss these problems."

"Well, we're good friends, as you know."

"I know." Flavio finished his water and put the empty glass on the bed. "I must go now." He rolled out of bed and gathered his uniform together to dress while Pia watched. He closed to kiss her.

"When next for us?" Pia asked.

"Are you interested in dinner and more tomorrow evening?"

"I am, of course." Pia wondered. "If you want something different to sesso anale we can do this."

"We'll see. Arriverderci."

That was no, Pia thought, while she watched Flavio leave her room. She didn't mind – to get anywhere she had to keep Flavio's interest, and seeing as he liked anale that was so much the better for her.

* * *

Pia woke, naked in a strange bed where she heard noises from the far end of the small apartment. Maria was up. Pia eased out of bed and went to the bathroom, tiled pale green and white with a shower, basin, toilet and bidet, and towels hanging. Pia used the toilet, ran the shower to get it warm and stepped inside which was refreshing while she washed. She turned the taps, stepped out and used a thick, white towel – most luxurious.

In her room Pia wasn't prepared as she dressed in her garter belt and stockings, her pants, her shoes with heels and her tight cocktail dress. She walked to the dining room.

"Buongiorno signora Amadio."

"Buongiorno Maria."

"Sit and I'll get your breakfast ready."

Pia sat on the chair facing the kitchen while Maria cooked pancakes and percolated coffee. She put a bottle of honey on the table, and then brought Pia's plate and coffee. Pia sipped, spread some honey and started, but she needed to know more.

"Pour a coffee and join me, per favore."

Maria did that and sat opposite.

"I'm Ammiraglio Belloni's new friend, as you know, so I'll be staying here. I have friends in Napoli so sometimes I'll be out, and I'll let you know if I'll be away at mealtimes. How is it that you're here?"

"I'm an old family friend of Ammiraglio Belloni, and in exchange for somewhere to stay I look after his friends."

Mutually beneficial – free rent and free meals. "How about your family?"

"My husband passed away a few years ago and my children are grown. I visit them when I can."

Pia glanced at her tight dress. "As you can see I wasn't prepared for this, so I'll leave in a moment to fetch what I need. Do you have a calico bag or something like this?"

"I'll get one."

Maria went to the kitchen and returned with a bag, and there was something else. "Do you have a pad and a pen?"

Maria placed both in front of Pia who wrote Flavio's revelation, tore the page from the pad, folded it and put it in the bag.

"Grazie for the pancakes and coffee."

Pia went to her bedroom where she put her clutch in the calico bag, and then noticed two, 100 lira notes under the bottle of olive oil from last night. She didn't need money, but if she was dining out she need another dress and maybe shoes, as she put that money in her purse in her clutch. Pia returned to the kitchen.

"I'm going out to get my things and I'm also shopping for clothes." Pia didn't know if Maria was Flavio's spy. "I should be back by lunchtime."

Pia walked east to Via Alessandro Volta, unlocked the outside door, climbed the endless stairs and let herself into their apartment.

"Paul?"

"I'm here."

Pia entered the living room. "I'm terribly sorry but he's got an apartment for me, and worse, it has a maid. So, I'm trapped except for now."

"He must love you."

"No he doesn't, but he likes me. I have something for you."

Pia reached into the bag to take the folded page which she handed to Paul, who read while frowning.

He looked up. "This is good although they might know this."

"I'm not sure if MI-6 has infiltrated Regia Marina, other than me."

"You might be right."

"I need to do something."

Pia went to the bathroom, removed her pants and extracted the cervical cap. She rinsed it and put it in its container, and put the container and the bottle of vinegar into the calico bag. She pulled her pants on and returned to the living room.

"I'll give your note to Michele when he's next here."

"I have a date with Flavio tonight which will be overnight again. I'm thinking this might be most nights, but if it isn't I have a fictitious friend who I'll stay with on those nights. Today I need to do a few things, so I'll only stay here a short while.

"How is he?"

Pia wondered how to frame this. "He's decent enough for me to like him, but don't forget that he's older than my father."

Paul laughed. "Of course."

There was one problem. "What will you do for meals?"

"Mostly I'll eat at trattorias."

"Oh, yes." Pia then had a thought that caused her heart to skip a few beats. "If he ever gets suspicious, I'm in trouble."

"Be careful, amore mia."

"I'll try."

But that was easier said than done when probing for information.

* * *

After a delightful meal, despite Pia running out of conversation having little in common with Flavio, she thought after last night's revelation she might be able to get more, if there was more. Regardless, she would try as she unlocked the outside door, they climbed the stairs and Pia let them into the apartment. Maria was nowhere to be seen so must be in her room as Pia crossed to her own bedroom, switched off the light and left the door open enough. And then she realised and went to the kitchen for the bottle of olive oil and two glasses of water which she put on the small table. By then Flavio had removed his uniform and closed on Pia to hug and kiss, tongues touching and grabbing her bottom of course.

"Cara mia, you have a lovely figure," he murmured.

They hugged until Pia eased away to remove her off the shoulder cocktail dress, shoes and underwear, as always leaving her stockings in place. They hugged and kissed, tongues touching and rubbing her anus which sparkled. Pia eased away and knelt low on the bed, her left leg pulled forward.

"Cara mia, that's beautiful."

Flavio climbed behind, put his head where there was plenty of room, and like every time his tongue was amazing. Amazing, amazing, until he moved away and she had a slick penis at her anus, stretching her and stretching her – incredible. Flavio started slow and steady as Pia's orgasm already stirred, maybe her body was more attuned to this. Moaning and moaning, Flavio fucking harder as a result. Moaning more as it closed, closer and closer, really close.

"Oh cazzo!" as it burst free. Endlessly, endlessly, less and less, gone. "Keep going."

Flavio did as it stirred faintly, then more insistent, moaning to encourage it, closer and closer, right on the edge – yes!

Still Flavio fucked. "Did you come?"

"Yes, twice."

Flavio eased out and Pia sat up to take the glass he gave her. She sipped while he drank about half of his. Flavio put their glasses on the table while Pia planned next and rolled onto her back and then onto her side with her legs partly spread, and Flavio knelt behind and slid in with his hand on her hip which forced Pia's legs together. Anale was tight but that was really tight as he fucked slowly and steadily. Fucking endlessly which was better, and then harder as Pia moaned, harder still, skin slapping against skin, so noisy. Noisy and noisy until he groaned and she felt his wetness. Flavio eased out and lay to one side with his body glistening with sweat.

"Are you alright?" Pia asked.

"Cara mia that was our best."

It was actually. "Yes."

"You have a lovely bottom, you know." Flavio slapped there which sparkled in delight – she never imagined pain would be pleasurable.

Pia got her thoughts in order. "I've been thinking about the fuel oil problem for Regia Marina This worries me."

"Another problem is our lack of radar. Do you know what radar is?"

"No."

"Radio waves are used to locate things that can't be seen, like a battleship at night, and this is displayed on a screen. Before the war, those in Regia Marina, more senior than me, weren't interested in radar because naval battles have never been fought at night. But the British have radar on their ships so they can fight at night.

Even worse is a battle strategy of laying smoke to obscure your vessels, except radar can see through smoke. We're now developing radar but it will take years to equip our ships."

This was interesting.

"This is between you and me," Flavio said.

"Of course."

"Grazie for listening to boring things."

"Grazie for sharing."

Pia knew Flavio's afterglow, perhaps amplified by her ready acceptance of anale, released his inhibitions and loosened his tongue. More luck her as Flavio looked relaxed and at peace with his world.

Chapter Forty Five

After Flavio left, Pia wrote a note outlining Regia Marina's lack of radar, and the next morning after breakfast she took this to Paul, and better that she was able to spend the day with her husband. The following evening, Flavio called around without dining out, and there they made love, anale of course. After, Pia wondered, following those two revelations, if there was more to be learned or if was she wasting her time. Then she supposed, no knew, that spying was mostly wasting time with the occasional revelation.

Pia settled into a routine of Flavio visiting her on Mondays and Wednesdays, and on Fridays meeting him at Michelasso and then returning to the apartment, and then spending weekends with Paul. She hadn't thought it was possible to cope with that much love, let alone enjoy it, but she knew the more love you had, the more you wanted. When she made love with Paul she encouraged him not to use his tongue first but instead to make love by slowing down and taking his time. To come by making love was more intimate and satisfying – truly they *were* making love. If Paul guessed what was going on, and he would have, he never said. Rather, he was pleased that Pia was pleased.

Even though Pia knew spying was mostly wasting time with the occasional revelation, she wondered if she could move things along. She cleared her head and thought she had to be subtly inquisitive and maybe important things would be revealed. MI-6 relied on her and she hoped this would work, even though it was dangerous.

* * *

Pia's favourite was on her knees holding the bedhead, and it wasn't until a few weeks passed that she realised Flavio always entered her from behind. Anale was possible facing each other, Paul had often done this with a pillow under her bottom, but first by accident and then by design Flavio always fucked from behind so Pia didn't see his face and he didn't see her come.

Pia eased away from their hugging and kissing to kneel on the bed, holding the bedhead, and Flavio feasted on her anus – gorgeous. After ages but never long enough, Flavio took his tongue away and Pia felt his slippery penis – marvellous. He held her hips while fucking slowly, then steadily, and when Pia moaned and murmured he fucked her harder, harder and harder while Pia felt it more and more, closer and closer.

"Oh cazzo!" as pleasure swelled through her, endless, endless pleasure. On and on, less and less, gone. "More." He fucked more as Pia moaned, willing it, feeling it close, closer and closer, right on the edge as it washed through her, softer and more subtle but still delightful. Less and less, gone.

"I've come."

"Twice?"

"Yes."

He eased out and Pia climbed off the bed to get their glasses of water. She drank a little, he drank a lot but his was harder work as Flavio put it on the table, beside Pia's glass, and more oil while Pia wondered. She knelt low on the bed, her left leg pulled forward and Flavio entered her to start for his turn, smooth and steady, endlessly steady, forever steady until he slowed and Pia just loved his penis stretching and pulling her, over and over and over until he groaned, deep and hard as she felt his wetness. Flavio eased out and lay on his side while Pia climbed off the bed to get his glass and hand it across. She sat cross-legged on her bed to sip her water.

"We're good together," Flavio said.

"Yes we are. How are you?"

"Something's happening."

"What?"

"Ammiraglio Iachino has been given orders to take the Vittorio Veneto to the Strait of Messina, accompanied by four destroyers: Vittorio Alfieri, Giusué Carducci, Gioberti and Oriani."

"You don't ever take your battleships out of port."

"How do you know the Vittorio Veneto is a battleship?"

Oops! "I just know."

"It is and you're right."

"You must tell me what happens."

"I will."

Pia glanced at his penis, flaccid and greasy. That didn't matter, he was good with it. She smiled – they were good because Flavio cared about her pleasure which made his pleasure more satisfying. He really was decent.

"I must go, cara mia. What are you doing when I'm not around?"

"I'm still learning English with my friend." Pia smiled.

"This could be useful one day."

"When I travel again, it will be."

Pia watched Flavio dress, he bent down to kiss and she rubbed his cheek. Pia waited until he left and then she removed her stockings and suspender belt, pulled on her pants, a day dress, flat shoes and her clutch to walk to the post office, long closed but there were telephone boxes in front. She opened a door, eased inside, opened her clutch took a five lira coin, lifted the receiver and dropped the coin in the slot. Pia dialled zero.

"Pronto."

"Get me Roma 78966."

The phone rang six times. "Si."

"Ammiraglio Iachino has been given orders to take the Vittorio Veneto to the Strait of Messina, accompanied by four destroyers: Vittorio Alfieri, Giusué Carducci, Gioberti and Oriani."

"Grazie."

The line went dead. Pia closed her clutch, opened the door and stepped onto the footpath. If Maria noticed, well, Pia felt restless and went for a walk.

* * *

That Monday evening, Pia let Flavio into her apartment only she knew something was wrong.

"Ciao cara mio and come to my room."

"Ciao cara mia."

Pia led the way and sat on her bed while he sat in one of the chairs.

"It seems something has happened," Pia said.

"It was a catastrophe, cara mia. It was as if the British navy expected our attack on their convoy and were well prepared. During the battle they slightly damaged the Vittorio Veneto and disabled a heavy cruiser, the Pola. But the real catastrophe was that night because they sank the Pola, they sank two other heavy cruisers, the Fiume and the Zara, and they sank two destroyers."

Pia's stomach churned. "How many died?"

"British ships took some survivors and we recovered others, but over 2,300 perished."

Pia's heart skipped and she felt sick. "Oh no, cara mio, that's tragic!"

"This is war."

"Yes I know," Pia said, while realising she might have been responsible for this. She tried to get her thoughts into order, thinking fascists had to be stopped, but that didn't help. One thing would help. "Cara mio; we must go to Saint Nicola from Tolentino, light candles and pray for their souls."

"This is a wonderful idea – yes we must. How is it that you're so good?"

Pia didn't feel good, but wearily accepted that many more would be killed before the forces of evil who started this were overthrown. She couldn't share this, except with Paul, who she would tell tomorrow. In the meantime she went to her wardrobe to find a dress more respectable for church.

* * *

Pia let herself into the apartment where Paul was in the living room, playing chess against himself. He looked up.

"Stay there, amore mio," Pia said as she sat in the other chair. "There was a battle where three Regia Marina heavy cruisers and two destroyers were sunk, and more than 2,300 died."

"That's terrible – how do you feel?"

"I went to Saint Nicola from Tolentino to pray and later I had trouble sleeping. I had nightmares of men drowning, and then I thought this is a war fascists started and never should have happened. But at other times I thought I caused this tragedy."

The room was really quiet. "This war never should have happened, like you said, and many more will die, as we know, so the only solution is to end it as quickly as possible."

"Can the Allies win?"

"America's on Britain's side so I believe the Allies will win. In the meantime, young men of all countries will die, like in this naval battle, until fascism is defeated."

That brought clarity. "I understand."

"I'm still doing my observations."

"I wish I could be with you, amore mio."

"This isn't a holiday and what you're doing is dangerous, but compared to many couples we're not so badly off."

For Pia that wasn't true. "I'm with that man."

Paul smiled. "I know you are but your heart is with me."

That was right. "Grazie."

"This war never should have happened," Paul said.

"I know."

Pia wasn't in the mood for intimacy but she needed something. "Can you hug me?"

Paul stood and Pia nestled into his embrace. Together they would help to defeat fascism.

Chapter Forty Six

Pia was certain, after Flavio shared so much, that if he knew anything important he would tell her. They made love on Mondays and Wednesdays, and dined out and then made love on Fridays, and each time Pia asked how Flavio was, to usually get a discussion about personal issues but not about the war.

Weeks drifted into months. Rationing of food, clothing and other essentials became ever-stricter which caused black markets to magically appear. Spring drifted into summer and hotter, but not unpleasantly so, especially with Pia's apartment close to the sea, where she enjoyed using the roof terrace and socialising with her neighbours under shady umbrellas while cooled by afternoon breezes. They knew Pia was a mistress but she didn't sense discomfort. Through Maria, Pia discovered it was a Neapolitan tradition in summer to take chairs and even tables out into the street each evening, where she overheard endless complaints about their many shortages and their men conscripted to the armed forces. Support for fascism, such that it was, waned, especially with two more air raids in July.

Autumn came, like Milano the best time of the year with summer's heat fading and winter's cool yet to arrive, and still nothing other than Flavio on weekdays and Paul on weekends. Two more air raids followed in November, fortunately with little damage. Food rationing became ridiculous, and with most restaurants closed and the rest too expensive, Flavio called by the apartment on Mondays, Wednesdays and Fridays, where Maria did her best with the rations she had, often bream, rice, vegetables and a glass of cheap red wine. Of course, after dinner Pia and Flavio made love.

Paul had a bigger problem, but he made arrangements to pool his rations with Mario and Cara and eat there, given they'd been told Pia was working away from Napoli each Monday to Friday.

By December the weather was cool enough to need steam radiators in the apartment. Most mornings after breakfast Pia went out to walk through the park, but that Monday newspaper stands had headlines about a Japanese attack on the United States at Pearl Harbour, wherever that was. Although propaganda, Pia bought a copy, took it back to the apartment and read about a torpedo attack the previous day which sank four battleships, goodness, damaged many more ships and killed more than 2,000 men. America and Japan, which was an ally of Germany and Italy, were at war, while Japan also declared war on Britain and most of the rest of the world.

Pia gave the newspaper to Maria while wondering if this would change things.

"What do you think, signora?"

"Soon, we might be at war with America."

"Surely America will want to defeat Japan after this?"

That was true. "Surely they will."

"If we try to fight America, we'll lose."

"I know."

"Do you want lunch now?"

"Yes, per favore."

Maria got busy in the kitchen to cook spaghetti with tomato, because there was little else. After, Pia visited Paul who knew about the Japanese attack , but whether that meant an expansion of the war in Europe was guesswork.

"I'm tired of week in and week out with nothing happening," Pia blurted out.

"This means nothing really is happening, because they don't have enough fuel oil."

Pia hit her forehead with the palm of her hand. "Stupido!"

Paul laughed while Pia thought about something. "Christmas Eve is a Wednesday – maybe Flavio wants to have dinner with me, like he usually does, but more likely he'll be with his family. If he isn't coming on Wednesday, I'll tell him that I'm visiting my friends and come here, and later we can go to Saint Nicola from Tolentino."

"As you know I don't have much in the way of rations for a Christmas Eve dinner."

"I know. In any case I'm certain we'll have Christmas Eve and Christmas Day together." That was enough. "Now I must go."

As Pia hoped, Flavio confirmed he was spending Christmas with his family, although they had little to eat. Pia said she would spend Christmas with her friends and be back on the 26th while Maria, of course, was going to see her family.

Pia walked to the black market not far from the port, and there the best was veal which felt fresh and tender. As well she bought an egg, crusty bread, two potatoes and a bottle of genuine red wine, which in total was expensive but you only live once. Breakfast was their usual pancakes, lunch pasta with tomato from their rations while dinner of crumbed veal with fried potato was delicious and filling. Later, Saint Nicola from Tolentino was packed but that was more the case in Napoli than in Milano which wasn't as devout.

Flavio reappeared on Friday while Pia wondered if he made love conventionally with his wife and anale with his mistresses, or just that he preferred anale, either how it felt or to prevent his mistresses falling pregnant, or both. That didn't matter – if Flavio wanted it, she would give it to him.

They settled into their routine of three times a week through the New Year with Pia not obtaining any information, but more worried that she couldn't do more than talk trivialities and then make love in various positions. If nothing else, Flavio got genuine pleasure from her pleasure so maybe, just maybe, Pia was actually good at making love. It was important that she keep at being Flavio's mistress because something important might be revealed.

Never in a million years did Pia imagine one day being the mistress of a man older than her father.

* * *

Friday, of course Flavio knocked on the door, and Pia let him in to get a kiss and then followed him to the dining room where Maria had pasta, parsnips and glasses of red wine each. Despite that miserable meal, Flavio was quite joyous; perhaps he was looking forward to making love.

"What did you get up to, today?" Flavio asked Pia.

"I bought some fabric and sewed a blouse. Maria helped me."

"I learned from Pia."

"Although I worked as a journalist I'm really a seamstress."

"I was thinking we've been seeing each other for almost fourteen months," Flavio said.

"I knew it was more than a year, and I expect it will be many more years before this war's over." Pia remembered she was married. "If I didn't have you, Flavio, I would be terribly lonely."

"You and many other wives."

"I know."

Pia finished her meal, such that it was, and drank the last of her wine."

"I'll wash our dishes and go to bed," Maria said.

Maria kept as much distance from their love-making as was physically possible, while Pia rinsed their glasses and filled with water to take to her bedroom. Flavio waited while she put them on the table next to the bottle of olive oil which was almost finished.

"I'll need to buy more of this at a black market."

"Do you want money?"

"No, grazie."

They were in a rut and Flavio wasn't going to keep Pia as his mistress when love-making were boring. Flavio was already naked while Pia undressed. She closed to kneel and take his penis, not in her mouth because she didn't like that, but instead she ran her lips along his shaft, she used her lips and tongue at the end which was sensitive, and then around the other side and then back. Pia looked up at him looking down at her as she worshipped his penis. On its own it didn't mean much but he knew how to use it.

"That's lovely," Flavio murmured.

Pia kept that up for a while. She eased away. "What do you want?"

"Sit on the edge of the bed."

Pia did, legs spread while he went there with his tongue for the first time – it was lovely. Truly, truly lovely while Pia moaned, squeezed her nipples and moaned. Flavio eased away, climbed onto the bed, and soon they knelt and kissed, tongues touching and Pia tasted herself, not for the first time. Kissed and kissed while Pia had an idea.

"Lie on your back," she said.

Flavio did while Pia smeared oil, and facing his feet she lowered herself over his penis, slowly so it didn't hurt as she swallowed him. Holding his ankles she rode him as he held her hips and dug his fingers into her bottom. Pia rode him until her legs began to cry enough. She climbed off, applied more oil and faced Flavio to ride him facing while he put his hands over her small breasts, not that he was worried about such things while she rode him a different way, and for the first time facing each other.

"How's this, cara mio?"

"This is good."

"You have to make me come later – I don't come this way."

"I'll make you come."

She ruffled his hair. "Of course you will."

Pia rode until her legs began to stiffen and ache. She eased off, rolled onto her back and put a pillow under her bottom. Flavio, kneeling with his legs spread, entered her and fucked her steadily and then hard. Pia felt it faintly, then insistent, then more, then ever more, moaning and moaning as she felt it so close.

"Don't stop, don't stop," as it got closer. Closer and closer – "Oh cazzo!" as her orgasm started faintly and then filled her, filled her and filled her, endlessly filled her, fading, fading, gone. "Keep going," as Pia already felt it coming back to her. Closer, closer, right on the edge. "Cazzo!" as it poured through her, endlessly, endlessly, less, gone. Pia sighed in near-exhaustion.

"You came."

She smiled. "I came twice."

Flavio eased away to allow Pia to get their glasses. She sipped a little, he drank a lot, and then she took the two pillows to fold in half and lay over with her legs part spread – his favourite as he straddled to ride her like a horse. Riding and riding, hard, harder, really hard and then he groaned and she felt his wetness. After a moment Flavio eased out while Pia got rid of those pillows, went to the table and got his glass which he drank. He put the empty glass to one side.

"That was great," Flavio said.

"That was great."

"At last something's happening."

"What?"

"Four destroyers: the Ascari, the Aviere, the Oriani and the Grecale have departed for Malta. Also the Littorio, cruisers the Gorizia, the Trente and the Bande Nere, along with four destroyers, have departed Taranto for Malta."

"The Littorio is a battleship, of course."

"Yes it is."

"I hope we have a better outcome than last time – you must tell me what happens."

"I will, cara mia."

"Now, have your recovered?"

He ruffled her hair so Pia dragged him down to kiss, tongues touching.

"You're the best," Flavio murmured.

Pia let Flavio go, he climbed off the bed and began dressing. Pia watched until Flavio bent down to kiss, and then he left the room. When Flavio left the apartment, Pia dressed in her pants, the skirt and blouse she wore that day, flat shoes and took her clutch. Pia went downstairs and walked to the post office where she entered a telephone booth, took a five lira coin, lifted the receiver and dropped the coin in the slot. Pia dialled zero.

"Pronto."

"Get me Roma 78966."

The phone rang three times. "Si."

"Four destroyers: the Ascari, the Aviere, the Oriani and the Grecale have departed Napoli for Malta. Also, the Littorio, cruisers the Gorizia, the Trente and the Bande Nere, and four destroyers have departed Taranto for Malta."

"Grazie."

The line went dead.

Pia eased out of the telephone booth while thinking if things went well she might be responsible for the deaths of thousands of Italian sailors.

* * *

Right on six, as usual for a Monday, Pia heard Flavio knocking. She walked to the door, released the locks and opened to get the greatest shock. She didn't know what it was until she saw his gun. Flavio pressed it against Pia's forehead while she eased backwards and he kicked the door closed with his foot.

"Maria, lock that. You, go to the living room."

Still with his gun pressed against her head, an automatic Pia supposed it was, she walked backwards to the living room.

"You're a spy."

"Me?"

Pia heard the click of the gun or automatic and realised this couldn't make things worse. "I am."

"Who for?"

"I'm a spy for British MI-6."

"How, why?"

"I'm married to an Australian journalist, we were contacted by MI-6 and they asked us to spy for them."

"Why did you agree?"

"Because it's right."

"You're a traitor to our country!"

Pia sneered. "Look at our country! You told me we don't have enough fuel oil and we never should have gone to war! Now we don't even have enough to eat!" There was more. "Do you know about Jews and Gypsies in Germany?"

"No."

"This started long ago when they were dismissed from government positions and other jobs like journalists, and no German employer would ever be allowed to hire a Jew or a Gypsy without being persecuted by Nazis. Jewish and Gypsy shops and businesses were smashed or confiscated, their books were burned, and those could get away did. Then, not long before the war, fascists here did the same to Jews and black Africans as a copy of Hitler and Nazis – you know this!"

Flavio took his gun from Pia's forehead. "I know what happened but I didn't know it was a copy of Germany."

"I knew one side of this war was right and one side was wrong, and I needed to be on the right side. I'm proud to have had this opportunity, and if you shoot me, I'll die a proud woman."

"You killed thousands of Italian sailors."

"Not me – Hitler and Mussolini killed them. Tell me I'm wrong!"

There was an awful silence. "I don't know what to do with you – what's your real name?"

"My name's really Pia and you don't need to know the rest."

"You were good."

"I know."

"Did you ever feel guilty?"

"Of course I did. But what choice did I have?"

"You had the choice of not being a spy and a traitor."

Pia remembered a conversation long ago with signore Toto. "If you want to deal with me, shoot me, but don't turn me over to the authorities. Will you do this?"

"Why?"

"Because I don't want to be tortured before I'm killed."

"Maria!" Flavio called. "Can you get string or twine and tie her wrists behind her back?"

Maria came into the living room to tie Pia's wrists with several loops of twine. While Maria did that, Pia wondered where those words came from. Did she really feel that? Deep down, of course she did.

Chapter Forty Seven

Pia watched Flavio pacing the small room, his brow furrowed. He turned to face her.

"You're the bravest person I've ever met."

"When you have right on your side, bravery goes without saying." Pia realised something. "Are you in trouble because of me?"

"I will be."

"I'm sorry, but in war there are casualties."

"Can you help me?"

Pia wondered if there were options and then it hit her. "Do you have savings?"

"I do."

"This is Napoli run by the Camorra – you should pay them to take you away."

"I have to take my wife and daughters or else they'll be punished."

"I hope you have enough."

"I hope I do."

"I don't know much about crime except you could get taken down, like any business transaction. The first Camorra you meet, don't give them anything, only when you're on the boat do they get your money. Oh yes, don't offer all of your money as a first bid because they will ask for more, and remember everything is negotiable – it's better for the Camorra to get some money for taking you and your family away than to get no money at all. Does all of this make sense?"

"How do you know this?"

Pia smiled to herself while she thought about her father's workshop. "Business and crime aren't that far apart. Do you think this might work?"

"I think this might work."

"I'm truly sorry this is happening to you."

"Did you like me?"

"Of course I liked you and I still do. I always will."

He shook his head.

"Are you going to kill me?"

"You had your reasons, and you're right when you say the real villains are Hitler and Mussolini."

"They will lose."

"I know." Flavio turned away. "Maria, can you cut the string?"

Maria came into the room with a knife to slice the twine.

"Maria," Flavio said. "Between the three of us, nothing has ever happened. This is now your apartment but I can't help with your expenses."

"Don't you worry about me, Ammiraglio Belloni; I'll work something out with my family. Perhaps someone can live here and we can share."

"Flavio," Pia said. "Do you know how to contact the Camorra?"

"No, I don't."

"Dress in civilian clothes, go to a black market and ask there. Remember, you need to speak to whoever's in charge."

"How about you, Pia?"

Pia knew she was alright. "Don't worry about me."

"Will you spy again?"

"This war is lost," Pia said to be ambiguous.

"I know."

Pia closed on Flavio to hug him. "I'm truly sorry."

"I know you are."

Flavio put his gun in the holster. Pia watched him leave the apartment while thinking she had to pack and get out of there.

* * *

Head down and carrying two calico bags, Pia strode to Via Alessandra Volta while alert for any sounds out of the ordinary, indeed, any sounds other than her shoes on concrete and her heavy breathing. Fortunately, nothing happened as she approached to unlock the outside door and let herself inside, where she felt safe. Pia paused for a moment, thinking it was odd that Flavio was suspected. A few times he told Pia general information and a few times he told Pia specifics, but nothing that wasn't known by many others in Regia Marina. How would they know, in the afterglow of sex, that Flavio told his mistress who was a spy? Especially that they hadn't come after Pia.

Pia climbed the stairs while thinking through risks and threats, where she opened the door and let herself inside. She went to the living room where Paul read a book. He put it down.

Pia sat on the couch to face him.

"Flavio Belloni is under suspicion and he guessed this was due to me. I told him to pay the Camorra to get him out of Napoli."

"How are you?"

Pia didn't want to worry Paul about having a gun held to her head. "I'm alright but the maid knows what happened. She might be trustworthy, she probably is, but I think we need to get out of this apartment and find somewhere else. If we're to stay in Napoli, Belloni knows my alias name so we need new identities."

"Are you sure we should stay here?"

"I'm not sure of anything except Belloni knows why I spied, and the maid knows too, and besides, ordinary people like the maid just want this war to be over. The main risk is if they find and arrest Belloni and he confesses, but as far as I know he doesn't know where I live. I can't guarantee this, though, so I know a cheap hotel where we can stay tonight and then we can find another apartment."

"Let's pack and go."

Pia packed her suitcase and followed Paul down the stairs to outside. She walked with Paul to the Pinto-Storey Hotel where she and Flavio started so long ago. All the way Pia was alert but heard nothing out of the ordinary.

Pia stood aside while Paul registered and was given a key, by coincidence to room 15. Pia sat on the bed with her suitcase and two calico bags beside; thinking for now she was safe. It was odd, though, that they suspected Belloni when so many knew what he told Pia.

* * *

Many had left Napoli which meant there were empty apartments everywhere and rent was cheap. Within an hour, Paul had the key to apartment two on the first floor of Via Solimena, 64, a brick and stucco building about two kilometres north of the port area, and typically Napoli meaning little in the way of greenery except for parks two blocks to the south and two blocks to the east. The two bedroom apartment had rooms opening off each other without the wasted space of a corridor, and it wasn't painted a ghastly shade of pink.

Via Solimena, 64 was three storeys with a closed haberdashery shop on the ground floor, and it contained six, two bedroom apartments. Other apartment buildings in Via Solimena had shops so essentials could be purchased locally, but of course there was little to purchase. It didn't take long to discover there were two couples, Mario and Aida and Santo and Gina, both with younger children, two soldiers' wives, Rosa and Leola, with older children, and an older couple, Lorenzo and Fabia, who had three sons in the army.

That evening, Paul walked to Via Alessandra Volta where Michele, of course, didn't know what happened. Not long after, Paul led Michele into their apartment.

"Ciao Pia," Michele said.

"Ciao Michele; sit, per favore."

He did. "How are you?" Michele asked.

"Well, I survived and I hope I helped."

"You helped a lot, and now that it's over, I don't know how you did it."

"Many women have done, and are doing now, what I did."

"You're right except you did it for so long."

"I'm sure I'm not unique." There were more important things. "Paulo and I need new identities."

"I'll arrange this and bring them as soon as they're available."

"We have to be known as Paolo and Pia because that's what neighbours here know us as."

"I understand." Michele looked around. "This apartment is better."

"It couldn't be worse than the other one," Paul said. "What do we do now?"

"There's an option for you," Michele said to Pia. "Officers of Regia Marina, especially from their submarine fleet, spend a lot of time at La Bar Danza Vittoria on Via delle Repubbliche Marinare. The women who work at the bar are beautiful and...."

"Do you want me to work there?"

"Serving drinks to officers and overhearing conversations."

Pia thought about that. "This is a good idea," she said. "I can overhear things, especially if they have a few drinks, and I'll earn money for rent. How can I get a job there?"

"You leave this to me. When I tell you they have a vacancy, you should see the manager, signore Bianchi, and nobody else."

"I didn't mind Flavio Belloni but I won't do anything like that with anyone else."

"Will you dance with an officer if he asks you?"

"Of course."

"I don't expect you will learn much, but every little thing helps."

"If what I hear is unimportant we can code and mail letters, and if it's important I can telephone you."

"Yes, do this. Those telephone calls helped a lot."

"It's a shame Belloni was suspected."

Michele didn't say a word. He stood, offered 'ciao' and left with a promise to return when their identity documents were available.

"I don't trust how he will make this job become available," Paul said when the door closed.

Pia guessed a beautiful woman will be accused of being a communist collaborator, and poor signore Bianchi will be looking someone to take her place.

Chapter Forty Eight

Via delle Repubbliche Marinare was a few hundred metres north of the port, while La Bar Danza Vittoria was an oasis of bright lights and congeniality amongst warehouses and factory yards, often brick with peeling white paint, surely the bleakest area of Napoli. Just before six, Pia entered to noise and bustle, the nightclub bursting with uniformed officers. A marble counter ran most of the length of the room, glasses and drink bottles behind, light grey tables opposite with five or six or seven at tables for four. At the far end of the counter were glass display cases, clearly for food but were empty, with a gelataria behind. Being Napoli the nightclub would serve pizza but such things were long past. Beyond the display cases and gelataria was a dance floor with a small band playing American-style dancing music. That was odd as Pia approached a waitress at the espresso machine.

"Buonasera – I'm here to see signore Bianchi."

"Go through that door to the kitchen and his office is to the left."

"Grazie."

The kitchen was nearly empty while the office was tiny.

"Buonasera signore Bianchi; I'm Pia Corradi."

"Buonasera Pia; come in."

She squeezed into the tiny space.

"What experience do you have of working in nightclubs?"

"I'm good with people, but as far as nightclubs go, nothing other than as a customer."

"Being a customer is a start, I suppose, and you are attractive."

"Grazie."

Signore Bianchi stood, reached behind the door and took out four coathangers with red and white dresses. "You're size 40."

"Yes I am."

He gave Pia one. "You can change in the toilet."

Pia changed into the short-sleeved dress: plain red with a white collar, white buttons and white at the end of the sleeves. It worked well with her flesh-coloured stockings and black pumps with 75 millimetre heels. She took her own dress to signore Bianchi.

"Can I leave this here?"

"Yes, you can. Now, your hours are six in the evening to two the next morning, Tuesday to Saturday, and you have a 30 minute break which you will see on the roster in the toilet. Do you know how to make cocktails?"

"I've seen it done but I've not made cocktails."

"Come with me."

Pia followed to the bar where there was a chart of each drink with prices and ingredients measured as millilitres, glass mixing jugs with stirrers, a stainless steel bucket of ice with a scoop and stainless steel measuring cups.

"I've seen how this is done," Pia said. "How big are the measuring cups?"

"One side is 30 millilitres and the other side is 60 millilitres. Can you make me a Negroni?"

Pia checked the chart – and measured 30 millilitres of each of Vermouth Rosso, Campari Bitter and dry gin, she added a scoop of ice, mixed it, poured it into a glass, and gave it to signore Bianchi.

"Very good. I suppose you know how to pour a glass of wine?"

"I do."

"Your job is to check on tables, take away unused glasses, bring drinks they order, get payment and generally look after things."

Pia glanced at the dance floor. "What if they want to dance with me?"

"This is part of your job. These are mostly submariners; they're at sea for lengthy periods of time and their chances of survival aren't good."

Pia felt her heart skip. "This is terrible!"

"You're a waitress, not more, and if I find you doing more I'll dismiss you. If they want more they can find what they want nearby."

"I understand." Pia was certain, after a few drinks and a few dances, they would find more. Men were different – they had an obvious need where women's desire was probably just as strong but seemed dependent on the man the circumstances, like when she first went away with Paul. By the time she got home she couldn't clear her thoughts from – love, and when she told Daniela she was going away with a male friend, of course Daniela understood and was able to help. With Flavio, Pia accepted that was her duty, but when it happened, she wanted love as much or more as he would have. Paul was lovely while Flavio was experienced.

"I'll leave you to get to know your colleagues, and ask them for help if you need to. It's better to ask than to get things wrong."

"Grazie signore Bianchi."

He walked away while Pia noticed the other hostess watching.

"Buonasera, I'm Pia."

"Buonasera Pia; I'm Maria. Take a tray and start at the tables over there and see what they want, other than you!"

The old Pia might have blushed but wartime Pia took that in her stride, as she took a round tray to the far table with six officers, each with rank and name embroidered on their uniforms, squeezed around.

"Buonasera; can I get you anything?"

"I want you!" and Capitano Aurelio laughed.

"I'm not available but I can get your drinks."

They wanted various cocktails and gave Pia money, where at the bar she checked prices to find what she had was correct as she put cash in the till. Pia mixed their cocktails according to the chart, with Maria watching, and took them to the table. Pia returned with their empty glasses and put those with others.

At the next three tables Pia did the same, and then she went back to the first, because she knew.

"I still want you!" and Capitano Aurelio laughed. "Do you want to dance?"

"I can dance with you."

On the way, Pia put the tray behind the bar, and on the dance floor he took her in his arms for a waltz, his hand quite firmly on her bottom, which Pia moved but back it went.

"Capitano; what's life like on a submarine?"

"It's like hell on earth at the best of times. I'm captain of the Squalo operating patrols against Allied supply convoys, with little success I must admit."

"I'm sorry to hear this."

"You're new here."

"This is my first night." She moved his hand but back it went. "I know what you want but this can't be with me."

He smiled.

The music ended and they applauded.

"Now, you can have your drink and I'll continue my work. Oh, good luck for the future."

"Grazie."

Pia fetched her tray, served more tables, danced with a lieutenant where she got broad details about his submarine, more tables and so the night went on. Maria closed.

"You can take a break, Pia."

Pia followed to the kitchen not busy apart from older women washing glasses, and there Pia met Loriana, Belina and Vissia, all smoking.

"Do you want one?" Vissia asked as she pointed her packet to Pia.

"No, grazie."

"You're not from here."

"I'm Lombardian. My husband came here to work, but then he was sent overseas as a war correspondent. His pay only goes so far."

"Do you have children?"

"No I don't."

"You're lucky."

"And you?"

My mother looks after our child when I work, and my husband's away like yours."

Vissia was young which meant only one child so far. Not long married, maybe to be widowed before this was over.

"There never was a good war or a bad peace," Pia said.

"That's true."

"The American, Benjamin Franklin, wrote this in 1783."

"So long ago and we still haven't learned."

"Some men never learn."

Vissia butted her cigarette. "I know."

After a while they returned to work with Pia encouraging more dances – it was a way of discovering information but she also enjoyed their desire. She moved their hands from her bottom and pretended not to notice how they squeezed her closer, but really it made her feel sexy.

* * *

Pia let herself into their apartment, switched on the dining room light, took a pad and a pen to write what she overheard and left the pad where Paul would have his breakfast.

Pia put away her dress and her uniform that she still wore, undressed and slipped into bed, well used to sleeping naked. What followed were the most amazing dreams – being hugged, kissed, making love, especially making love with Paul and with Flavio. She woke refreshed, got up, slipped on her gown and went to the dining room where Paul coded from her notes.

He looked up. "How was it?"

"It was good." Pia sat. "What I learned isn't important."

"Now that I'm not spying on the port, I thought I should get a job."

"Doing what?"

"I'm a journalist...."

"You can't write propaganda." Pia thought about Napoli in late March, 1942. "Most of the economy here is in ruins so I don't like your chances of getting a job in the private sector. Administration goes on, though, so you could get a job in the provincial council, which isn't political, if there are jobs going." Pia had an idea. "You could volunteer to help those less fortunate."

"Yes I could!" he exclaimed.

"There are many abandoned wives and widows where you can do husband-type jobs, from replacing light globes to helping with finances. This will also give you time to code my observations and, amore mio, because I work nights I want to see you." Pia dropped her head. "I know I'm selfish."

Paul put his hand under her chin while not realising she was pretending. "You've done so much and you continue to spy."

Pia smiled. "I know."

"Do you want coffee?"

"Yes, per favore, although coffee will disappear in the future."

"Well, it's rationed but still available."

Paul turned on the stove and got the percolator ready while Pia couldn't ignore those dreams. "After I drink my coffee, I want to bathe and then I want to make love."

"Of course."

Pia needed to be ravished but also she wanted to slow them down, the way Flavio did. She would get on top of Paul, he never came from that, and that way he would squeeze her bottom and she would see the desire in his eyes. Later she would come but being desired was what she really needed, as Paul poured her coffee and brought it to the table.

* * *

Pia worked Tuesdays to Saturdays with Sundays and Mondays special sleeps. Food was more difficult to obtain, more expensive and poorer quality. Bread was particularly dreadful: hard, coarse and tasteless. Meat became a rare luxury, while other goods like clothes and shoes disappeared from stores entirely. Many shop keepers closed down and boarded windows for the duration.

Pia wrote notes every morning before she went to bed for a few hours, and Paul then coded and mailed a letter. When she rose, Paul had either volunteered at Saint Vincent de Paul or he continued Pia's English lessons, and she felt she was getting quite good. Sometimes in their free time they played Scopa which reminded Pia of Achille and Norma. What was life for a racing driver who, because of war, couldn't race? That was a shame for all involved in the sport.

Often they made love because Pia often felt sexy.

Spring drifted to summer, people took chairs outside but few had the energy to complain about their miserable existences. If Benito Mussolini walked along Via Solimena alone, they would have killed him with their bare hands, but that was probably the case before the war started. In 1922 fascists took control of Italy by force, including police, military and newspapers, while jails became full not of criminals but political opponents. The ordinary Italian had no say, not then and not since, although for a long time they didn't realise newspaper and radio news was fascist propaganda. To be fair, Italy did better during the Great Depression than most countries, propaganda or not.

Summer passed to autumn, although Pia's favourite season didn't mean anything when it seemed like they were wasting time until the war eventually was lost. Pia worked, she doubted her spying was achieving much but she earned useful money, it passed the time, she liked her work colleagues, who liked Pia despite being from the north, and she liked and felt sorry for officers in Regia Marina, especially submariners.

That Tuesday, Pia danced with Capitano Alesi, not a submariner but with his hand on her bottom nonetheless. She moved it, for all the good that would do because he put it back again.

"You're beautiful, amore mia," he said.

"I don't know. How's your war?"

"Change is coming after stagnation for so long. Because the Allies have taken control of North Africa, we have been ordered to take our ships to Taranto."

"Oh, well, this is a big change. In Taranto, I hope they have a good nightclub like here."

"But no women as beautiful as you, amore mia."

Pia laughed as the song came to an end and they applauded.

"Now, you go to your table because I have work to do."

Pia checked on tables, brought their drinks, took away their glasses, and then noticed it was time for her break.

Pia used the toilet and then joined the others, smoking. She kept away from that as best she could.

"I could do with a man," Loriana said. "It's been too long."

"If you do, be careful," Pia said. "Do you know how to be careful?"

"Get then to pull out."

"That's one way, although there are risks if men get it wrong, while another way is sesso anale."

"No!"

"Oh no, it's not what you think. A man needs oil, of course, lay on your front, legs almost together, he kneels outside, stay relaxed – it's easy and it feels good."

"It can't be as good as...."

"For me it feels better and there's no risk."

Loriana laughed and butted her cigarette on the ashtray. "The things you learn. I need a man tonight!"

"I do too," Belina said. "Especially as there's a no-risk way to love that feels good."

"You have a great choice of men out there," Pia said.

"As long as we're discreet, yes we do, and I don't think we have to twist any mans arm to sesso anale."

"It's important to hug and kiss a lot, really relax, breathe really deeply, and if you do all of this and lie on your front too, it won't hurt."

"Alright, grazie."

"Let's get back to work," Loriana said.

Pia followed into the nightclub where they would dance with a man who interested them, tell that man to wait back and then go somewhere together. Pia decided to ring Michele with that information, which might or might not be important but that wasn't her decision. She kept herself busy until closing time approached and their customers drifted away. Pia made sure she was last away, where she walked to the post office, entered a telephone booth, took a five lira coin from her pocket, lifted the receiver, dropped the coin in the slot and dialled zero.

"Pronto."

"Get me Roma 78966."

The phone rang many times. "Si."

"Because the Allies have taken control of North Africa, all surface ships have been ordered to relocate from Napoli to Taranto."

"Grazie."

The line went dead.

Pia eased out of the telephone booth, and waked home along the quiet streets of Napoli in the early hours of the morning.

Chapter Forty Nine

Three weeks later came the biggest air raid of all and there was substantial damage to the port and to buildings nearby. Immediately the UMPA began work, and stairways leading to old, underground caverns appeared all over the city. By that stage, defeats in North Africa meant that Italy had all but run out of oil and it was no longer possible to deploy the ships of Regia Marina. Submarine operations continued while Pia continued to overhear fragments of information, but nothing that seemed useful.

Christmas came and it was even more subdued than the year before. Rationing took its toll and they had a meal of rice and a little meat, for there was little meat of dubious quality to be had. Somehow Pia smuggled home a bottle of red wine which they opened for Christmas Eve. Despite a half-decent meal and that special treat, she looked terribly sad.

"What is it amore mia?" Paul asked.

Pia said nothing but still looked sad.

"You mustn't keep it inside," he said.

"I miss my family," Pia eventually said. "And I worry for their children. They will be starving."

Paul remembered his nieces and nephews and they would be starving.

"The Allies might bomb Milano," Pia said. "It has industry."

"Antonio and Claudia and their family are safe in Soncino."

"But not Giorgio and Daniela and their family. He's Milanese and a fire-fighter, so he must stay and he must work. This is one time I'm glad we couldn't have children."

"Do you ever regret that we couldn't have children?" Paul asked.

"Every woman wants to have children but I don't regret what happened. We wouldn't have travelled together, we wouldn't have made so many friends, we wouldn't have skied every year and holidayed with our friends, and we wouldn't be here now helping liberate our country. Life would have been different but not better." She sipped her wine. "Do you wonder about your family?" she asked.

"The men of my family have been imprisoned in camps for being Italian. They're living in huts surrounded by barbed wire and separated from their loved ones. I'm the lucky one fighting for a good cause."

Paul looked up at Pia. "I worry for their children," she said softly.

"I know," he said. "So do I."

* * *

Sirens woke Pia who saw Paul was already up and dressing. She dressed too. They went outside, locked the door because there could be looters, went outside and descended the stairs into a long, narrow enclosure that in ancient times had been a water aqueduct. Wooden benches lined each side, while at the end was a tap, a sink and a shower in a curtained enclosure. They sat in silence alongside many neighbours while engines droned overhead and explosions were felt all around, and some explosions were close. So close that dust came down the stairway and they breathed gritty air. It was the biggest raid yet, it lasted for about two hours, and at the 'all clear' they emerged into a cold, sunny day. One building on

Via Solimena was turned into rubble while another was damaged but still inhabitable.

They picked their way through the mess and then Pia stopped with her hands on her hips. "Pourquoi font ils laissent tomber des bombes?" she said using French so she wouldn't be understood by those nearby.

"Ils ne laissent pas tomber de bombes sur nous, c'est accidentel," Paul said while pointing upwards. "C'est accidentel," he repeated.

American bombers flew at 10,000 metres and of course it was accidental. "Je sais," Pia eventually said.

They picked their way over rubble on the way home. There Pia was too agitated to sleep and too agitated to practice English, so they talked about the war and the future in French, because Pia hadn't used that language in recent times. And even though it was by far the biggest air raid, radio news mentioned nothing.

Another big air raid followed a few days later and then the air raids were daily. For weeks and weeks, drifting to months, sirens wailed, the population of Napoli traipsed down stairs into ancient caverns to wait in silence, always in silence, for the 'all clear' hours later. There they emerged hoping for the best but prepared for the worst. Some women shrieked when their homes were destroyed, because that meant they and their families only had the clothes they wore. Others picked through rubble for reasons Pia didn't understand, or maybe to find a trinket or a reminder of a life long gone. The infrastructure of Napoli collapsed; no trains, no postal service, little food rationed severely and terribly expensive. With no post there was no point in gathering intelligence, and without trains Michele was unable to travel from Roma to bring money.

Pia continued at her job for the money. They managed to survive because the rental agent was bombed and destroyed and they no longer paid. But they were always hungry and always waiting for the next siren.

Not everyone could get to a shelter in time and there weren't enough shelters for the city anyway. Sometimes shelters received direct hits and collapsed, maiming and killing those inside. After each raid, bodies were laid out to be collected. Sometimes whole families: husband, wife and children lay side-by-side next to the rubble that was formerly their home. As much as she hated to admit it, Pia became immune to tragedy.

Those who lost their homes could buy no clothes, so the clothes they wore deteriorated into rags. It was easy to tell the lucky from the unlucky by the way they dressed. Sometimes young mothers dressed in rags clutched babies in arms while Pia wondered how they survived. Pia sometimes worried about her nieces in Milano, for surely that city was bombed. Surely many cities in Italy were bombed. Surely many cities were bombed, tens of thousands were killed, injured and made homeless, and it was all the fault of fascists.

Pia lost track of weeks with only the change of weather into spring registering. Every day a siren, filing underground to wait in silence, and then emerging into more ruin. Always Via Solimena, 64 survived; they were enough distance from the port, and mostly the streets closer to the sea were destroyed. But even though they had shelter they suffered, she had to work all night so they could buy the little food that was available, and the hunger never left. Others were less fortunate, for there was little work and little money in Napoli – some even went into the countryside to scrounge anything, even eating flowers. Spring daisies were stripped bare by the hungry inhabitants of Napoli while others raided the town aquarium. Nothing that could possibly be eaten was spared.

The explosion of a ship in port during a raid caused terrible destruction, and even killed and injured some who were sheltering underground nearby.

Eventually, just before summer, a day passed without an air raid siren. By mid-afternoon many milled in the streets of Napoli and many strangers conversed in the streets of the devastated city. Pia was able to sleep and not go to work exhausted.

Sunday the twenty-fifth of July was a day she would never forget. The radio announced that Benito Mussolini had resigned and Pietro Badoglio was appointed Prime Minister. Such a thing was possible in Italy because it was a Kingdom and Parliament could move against a dictator who lost control, such as Mussolini. And they did. The radio announcement ended with the words 'The war goes on. Italy will be true to its word'.

The pandemonium outside was incredible, where every citizen of Napoli took to the streets to celebrate the downfall of the megalomaniac who destroyed his country. They ran outside and noisily celebrated the end of more than two decades of fascism, as only Italians could, with songs, dances, hugging strangers, removing fascist emblems, stripping soldiers of their fascist jackets and police throwing away their fascist badges. Despite the pent-up hatred, surprisingly there was no violence. Instead they celebrated the end of an era that had only survived through force.

And then nothing happened. Paul listened to the radio while Pia slept, with everyone in Napoli waiting for an armistice with the Allies, but it didn't happen. They went into the street and talked with neighbours where everyone was hoping for the end of the war, yet nothing happened. Ten days later air raid sirens wailed, they filed into the shelter and waited in silence, and they waited and waited because the raid lasted for four, long hours. The biggest raid ever. On and on and on, and eventually they emerged to incredible destruction. August the fourth and the biggest raid of all. The celebrations of July 25 meant nothing when faced with that catastrophe. Many thousands died that day, and many more were injured. As always, some were so badly injured that their lives were destroyed as surely as if they had been killed. To make things worse the water supply was damaged, which severely restricted supply.

La Bar Danza Vittoria had previously suffered with windows blown out and replaced with boards, but August the fourth destroyed the submarine base which spelt the end of Regia Marina in Napoli, and Pia found herself out of work. Fortunately in the absence of a landlord Paul had saved enough to tide them over.

Raids continued sporadically but none as big as August the fourth. The port area and nearby buildings were totally destroyed, many other buildings across the city were destroyed. There was no money, little food, many had no possessions and lived in the air raid shelters. The one concession to luxury was a cold shower without soap, before dressing in rags again.

September the eighth was a normal day with another air raid and later they listened to the radio. An armistice had been signed between Italy and the Allies and Pia wondered what came next. Italian and German forces occupied the city but to date had done little. Pia supposed the Italian Army would lay down their arms. But what of the Germans? The armistice didn't apply to them. What would the Germans do?

Chapter Fifty

Via Solimena was the place to be, and some even brought their chairs outside again. Via Solimena was where the news was to be heard, and the news wasn't good. Those in charge of the city and much of the Italian Army had fled, leaving citizens of Napoli and the German Army to share the city. The first clash happened two days later on the tenth, probably using firearms held in storage. In retaliation, Germans burned the Vittorio Emanuele III National Library and shot innocents nearby. Sporadic fighting continued, but worse was the news two days later that Mussolini had escaped from prison and fled north with his mistress, Clara Petacci. The same day the German commander, Colonel Walter Schöll, posted notices threatening resisters with death, implementing a curfew, and requiring all firearms to be turned in to German troops. None turned their rifles in, of course.

Italian soldiers were deported for forced labour, or in reality those soldiers who hadn't managed to discard their uniforms. A German tank opened fire on unarmed students protesting at the university.

On the twenty-third, orders from Colonel Schöll were posted for the evacuation of the entire coastal area up to a distance of 300 meters from the sea, displacing tens of thousands. More orders from Colonel Schöll were posted for compulsory work from all males between the ages of 18 and 30, and in the street that was universally agreed to be a euphemism for deportation to labour camps in Germany. All men were to present at German Headquarters on Corso Vittorio Emanuele on the twenty-fifth. Paul knew what this meant.

"What are you going to do?" Pia asked him.

"It's clear that few will volunteer to be taken away and worked to death."

"German soldiers will come after you."

Of that Paul had no doubt. "Yesterday Partisans captured weapons from the Italian Army at Vomero, which is close to here. We can add this to weapons they already have."

"You're going to fight the German Army?" Pia asked.

"I know how to use a rifle."

"I'm worried."

"It's clear this city of thieves and whores is ready to fight, and the least I can do is help them. If we lose, I'll be taken away and you'll never see me again, but if we can keep the German Army at bay for long enough to be liberated by the Allies, I can survive."

"Yes, I understand."

Paul slept fitfully that night and he was annoyed. If things were to progress to armed rebellion, he needed to be fresh, alert and ready. He made love with Pia the next evening, and she was sad as if it was their last time together. Paul hoped it wasn't, but he knew what he had to do. The Germans did it, all of it, and it was time to pay them back. After, contented, he moulded himself to the body of his wife and slept well.

Hardly anyone showed for deportation and Partisans captured more weapons. The next day German soldiers went into the city to take those who didn't present, and were greeted by an unarmed crowd who battled and jostled outnumbered Germans. German soldiers managed to take thousands of young men to Bosco di

Capodimonte. Paul knew the next day would be the key for him, and when German soldiers closed on Via Solimena it was time.

He hugged and kissed his beautiful wife. "If they take me away they will work me to death, so I have no choice. Wait for me."

"Be careful," she said.

Paul ran outside and sprinted around the corner towards Vomero, where he came across a group of Partisans with rifles and ammunition; just what he needed. He ran to them. "Do you have another rifle?" he asked.

"Who are you?" a young man with a few days' growth asked. "Are you one of us?"

"I spied for the Allies against fascists."

"Can you shoot?"

"Yes I can."

"Show me," he said, handing a rifle over.

It was much heavier than a twenty-two, but well-balanced. Paul slid the bolt and looked around and spotted a sign about 10 centimetres by 10 centimetres. Paul lowered the gun, aimed and gently squeezed the trigger. Compared to a twenty-two, the noise was deafening and the kick was substantial. Paul lowered the rifle to see the sign a nice, clean hole punched right through the middle.

"I once lived on a farm and we shot rabbits and foxes," Paul said. "What's happening?"

The man gave Paul two belts of bullets which he draped over his shoulders; one left and one right. "Bosco di Capodimonte," he said and Paul understood.

They ran towards the park but on the way they saw a column of German soldiers heading out of Campo Sportivo del Littorio. Left and right were damaged buildings and rubble where Paul ducked behind a small mountain of rock, slid the bolt, aimed his rifle and squeezed. The grey-uniformed solder fell as if he'd been hit with a bat. Paul slid the bolt, aimed, fired, slid the bolt, aimed fired, slid the bolt, aimed fired and then ducked down a lane to enter a building and run to the front to see German soldiers running all about while Partisans took cover in the rubble. Standing next to a glassless window, Paul fed four bullets into the magazine of his rifle before checking outside. Just beyond was a soldier on one knee aiming at a Partisan. Paul slid the bolt, aimed and fired. He couldn't miss from that distance. Other soldiers aimed at the apartment building as Paul knelt, slid the bolt, stuck his head up, aimed and fired before a barrage of bullets hit the building. Paul ran out the back, continued along the lane and into the street to face the column from the front. Protected by rubble he lay on his stomach, slid the bolt, carefully aimed and fired. That German soldier didn't stand a chance. That made six definite and one possible. From his vantage point Paul slid the bolt, lifted his head, aimed and fired. He ducked before bullets hit the rock and stone around him, and he felt strangely immortal even though sand and dust fell on his hair and got into his eyes. He slid the bolt, lifted his head, aimed and fired and knew he got one more, and more bullets hit the rubble and more sand sprayed into the air. Eight and one. He sat with his back to the pile of rubble and fed more bullets into the magazine while all around Partisans and German soldiers sniped at each other with the column pinned into a narrow street between apartment blocks. It was hopeless for them. Eventually those German soldiers had enough and retreated the way they came while still under fire.

Under fading light the Partisans gathered beyond the rubble and Paul was pleased he got ten and two.

There were 13 men, lucky 13, and names were exchanged. The leader was Elio, and there was Mario, Antonio, Rocco, Giovanni, Mario, Pascal, Vito, Bruno, Montel, Alberto and Lauro. All aged twenty through to about thirty, and all scruffy-looking as every inhabitant of the city was scruffy-looking. They wanted to know where Paolo was from, and were both surprised and pleased that an Australian-Lombardian had joined the fight to liberate Napoli. Paul didn't care who was from where; all he wanted to do was shoot Germans for what they did to the good people of his country. It was getting dark and too dark to fight, so a wine sack was produced and handed around, and Paul pictured Pia with her dismissal of Napoli as the home of thieves and whores. She was right, of course, but Napoli fought back.

Paul woke the next morning to the sound of gunfire in the distance. One or two of the Partisans were up and soon they all rose. Eyes were rubbed, water was sourced from deserted apartments to drink and to wash faces, and soon the band were heading towards Materdei, where they found ten Partisans with a German patrol under siege inside an apartment building. These partisans used rubble from a destroyed building opposite as cover, and sniped at German soldiers whenever they attempted to shoot from inside the building. A patrol was more than ten so the lucky 13 joined in and kept the German patrol pinned down for hours, with the front and back entrances covered so they couldn't get out.

Paul helped cover the back entrance by using a building opposite as cover, and he got one definite and one probable from soldiers attempting to fight their way out of the trap.

Another German patrol advanced from the south, severely outnumbering the Partisans. Rifle fire was split between the building and the approaching patrol while soldiers from the south returned heavy fire which pinned the partisans down behind their cover of rubble and buildings. With casualties growing the Partisans retreated through a narrow laneway to regroup, helping those wounded to escape the battle. Three Partisans had been killed and six injured with at least a dozen German casualties or maybe more. The dead were dead but the injured suffered; Paul saw it, heard it and felt it. It took time to evacuate the injured to the safety of Neapolitan women in apartments further to the east, and there the surviving Partisans, and Paul as an honorary member, had vegetables, rabbit or maybe horsemeat, and some rough, home-made red wine. During the night another group of Partisans arrived, some teenagers and some barely teenagers; all burdened with rifles and ammunition seemingly too big and heavy. Some smoked, even though they were much too young. Street urchins had joined the fight. Sleeping for the group of 50 or more was wherever there was space, until dawn.

There was talk of German soldiers in Piazza Giuseppe Mazzini just to the south, so that's where they headed. This was a small piazza on a crossroads and surrounded by buildings, but even though it was small Paul thought it was too open and too exposed. He dropped back and kept close to a building just along Corso Vittorio Emanuele, and shortly after more German soldiers protected by two tanks came along Via Salvator Rosa. Protected by their tanks these German soldiers opened fire while the Partisans sought cover wherever they could find it, including the base of the statue of Giuseppe Mazzini. The fighting was tremendous while Paul kept at a greater distance from the piazza than the other Partisans; sniping at solders from inside ground floor shops of an apartment building and keeping low when he reloaded his rifle. Some German soldiers realised where he was so they targeted these shops. Paul went upstairs, kicked down the door of an empty apartment and fired from there, where up high he had a good view and a good field of fire until Germans again targeted his position. Paul went up to the second floor and fired from there, and he had an even greater view and shot two soldiers who thought they were protected by their tanks.

Fifty Partisans didn't stand a chance against twice that number of German soldiers protected by tanks, but that didn't stop them trying. Paul couldn't abandon his comrades so he kept sniping, until Partisans were forced by sheer weight of firepower to abandon the piazza with about a dozen dead and 15 injured. They regrouped in a shop off a laneway further along Corso Vittorio Emanuele to get the casualties away from the battlefield. Some were walking wounded, some were badly injured and some were unlikely to survive. Again the survivors were fed and sheltered by Neapolitan women in nearby apartments, and while he ate Paul realised the hopelessness of the German situation. Outnumbered against an enemy who didn't wear uniforms, and who blended into streets, lanes and buildings as they pleased. German soldiers didn't stand a chance and it was only a matter of either time or reinforcements, and deep in southern Italy Paul doubted that the Wehrmacht had much in the way of reinforcements. Therefore it was only a matter of time, and Paul had thirteen and three. What was more amazing were the women who were able to feed a small army of fighters. At least twenty middle-aged women pooled all they had for the cause.

Napoli was ablaze. They woke to palls of smoke – Germans had torched many buildings. Paul realised the significance of that. They burned the city while they retreated, and the Battle for Napoli was won but not yet over. German artillery shelled areas of the city while rifle fire could be heard in the distance. The decision was to attack the German Headquarters in Corso Vittorio Emanuele, but that was relatively quiet. Paul was thankful for that. He wondered how soldiers fought wars for day after day and week after week when he was totally exhausted after three days of fighting, eating and sleeping. Some Germans emerged from inside the building so Partisans opened fire while Paul missed, showing how exhausted he really was. Partisans then moved to the port area and that was quiet too. Although there was sporadic rifle fire, the major part of the battle was over. Paul stayed with his group while the others mostly smoked cigarettes and told tall stories, mostly in dialect until they realised they had an Italian-speaker. At dusk they sought refuge, a meal, some wine, and a space to sleep. Paul slept on a hard, stone floor and he couldn't have slept more soundly if it was a soft, feather mattress.

"The Americans are here."

Paul woke with the rumour sweeping the city. Tanks only a few kilometres from the city and Germans were gone. Paul leaned against the wall, cradling his rifle with his half-empty ammunition belt at his feet. It was time to go home. He stood and said 'ciao' to each survivor in turn, and he headed towards Via Solimena, 64.

Paul knocked on the door of apartment two.

"Who is it?" Pia called."

"It's me," he said.

Pia ripped the door open and grabbed him so hard that Paul almost fell backwards with the burden of the gun and the ammunition belt over his shoulder.

"Amore mio, you're safe!" she exclaimed.

Paul put his rifle to one side and hugged his darling. "We're all safe amore mia."

"I heard the Germans are gone. You were so brave."

"I had no choice. None of us had any choice."

"But Neapolitans fought back and many don't."

Paul knew that was true. "Let me in," he said. "I need to get rid of this."

Pia stood back with her eyes wide. "You look like a soldier."

"It's a soldier's rifle. I got thirteen definite and three possible. I didn't see all of them fall."

"You killed thirteen!" Pia exclaimed.

Paul shook his head. "I shot thirteen but they wouldn't all have died." He looked into her dark eyes. "It's over now."

"I don't have much food for you."

Paul shrugged his shoulders. "It's alright; we're alive."

* * *

Olive-green trucks loaded with soldiers rolled along the narrow track between rubble. Neapolitans silently lined the road as if they had to see the liberation for it to be real. Paul and Pia lined the road as if they had to see the liberation for it to be real. Liberation was real but war wasn't over. The German response to the Italian armistice showed that it would be a battle to take each city and town further to the north. It would be perhaps years before Paul and his wife would return to Milano. For the time being, Napoli remained home.

A jeep rolled past containing a young driver and a middle-aged officer with many, colourful medal ribbons on his chest. The jeep pulled to one side just beyond where Paul stood, and the officer got out and looked around.

"Jeeesus," he said, rubbing the back of his neck while looking at the devastation. "Everything's in ruins."

Another jeep came from the opposite direction causing a degree of traffic chaos, given the narrow pathway between rubble strewn about. This jeep also contained a driver and an officer, and this officer was about the same age as the first but had many stars on the epaulettes of his uniform. The jeep pulled to the side with a sharp, squealing of brakes and the officer jumped out. The first officer saluted which was briefly returned.

"Harry," the new arrival said. "This is less about invasion and more about occupation."

"It is, sir," the first officer, Harry, said. "A lot here's been destroyed so we'll have to look after the locals."

"That'll be just up your alley. Look, find a place to base yourself and find out what the locals need."

"Do we have translators?"

"No, not yet. You'll have to find out, as best you can, and from there plan your priorities."

"Yes sir."

The second officer jumped into his jeep with gusto, leaving Harry rubbing the back of his head once more. Paul eased closer and the officer noticed. "I might be able to help you," Paul said in English.

"You speak English?" the officer asked with his eyes wide.

"I do, and my wife does as well."

"What's your name?"

Paul wondered which name and decided on the truth. "My name's Paul Bassi but I'm also known as Paolo Corradi. I worked for the British and they gave me a new identity."

"I'm Pia Bassi and also Pia Corradi," Pia said in her gorgeous, Italian-accented English.

"What'd you do for the British?"

"We spied on Regia Marina. What do you call it in English Paul?"

"The Italian Navy," Paul said.

"We spied on the Italian Navy until they ran out of oil," Pia said.

The officer rubbed the back of his neck again. "My name's Colonel Harry Miller and where'd you learn such good English?"

"I was born and raised in Australia and I moved to Italy about ten years ago."

Colonel Miller nodded slowly. "So this is why the British...?"

"Yes."

"Can you tell me what's happening here? No. Do you know where we can base ourselves?'

Paul did. "The old German headquarters on Corso Vittorio Emanuelle might be a suitable for you."

"Okay. Climb in and let's look at this headquarters."

Paul helped Pia get into the back of the jeep where he joined her, and Colonel Miller climbed in front. Paul gave the young driver directions and it only took a few minutes to drive there. Colonel Miller got out and scratched the back of his neck again. "The Germans might have booby-trapped this building so I'll get it checked out, and then we can use it. I reckon there'll be all sorts of interesting documents in there, too."

Paul joined the Colonel on the footpath. "Any building in Napoli could be booby-trapped, so this might be as good as you will get."

"I reckon you're right. Listen, you heard we haven't got any translators, and seeing as you both speak English, could you help out awhile?"

Paul looked at Pia. "Possiamo aiutarli per alimenti?"

"E caffè," she said.

"For food and coffee we can help you," Paul said.

"It's only army rations and army coffee, but we can do this. Next what I need is somewhere to stay."

Paul nodded. "Hotel Guiren?" he asked Pia.

"I don't know it," she said.

"Colonel, there's a small hotel not far from here and it's not bomb-damaged," Paul said. "I saw it the other day and it's in good order."

"Well then, let's go to Hotel Guiren and brew some coffee when we get there," Colonel Miller said. "How'd you know about these hotels and headquarters?"

"Did you hear about the uprising here?"

"Yeah."

"I saw these buildings when I fought during the uprising."

Chapter Fifty One

The army rations and army coffee were really quite dreadful, and the most wonderful food and drink that Paul had ever enjoyed. He didn't need to ask Pia, especially about the coffee.

Colonel Miller pulled up a chair and sat opposite with his battered, tin mug. "Now, what can you tell me 'bout this place?" he said before sipping some coffee.

"How do you say 'Napoli è città di ladri e puttane' in English?" Pia asked.

"There's no need to worry about that," Paul said. "The water supply was damaged in the big air raid last month, so that's a problem. There's little food, no jobs, no money and no clothing. There have been many air raids this year and you can see the damage. Also, Germans shelled parts of the city during the uprising. Underneath this city are many caverns which have been converted into bomb shelters, and homeless live in these shelters. They lost everything when their apartments were destroyed so the only possessions they have are the clothes they wear. The rest of us are close to starvation. Those who have no money scrounge food as best they can."

Colonel Miller nodded slowly. "I'll get the engineers to look at the water system and we'll get that going again. As for the rest it's gonna take time. Now for you two we have a file of suspected collaborators we must interview, and when the headquarters are safe we'll start with that."

Paul barely believed that. "Everyone here is a collaborator one way or another; it's the only way they could survive. Pia said Napoli is a city of thieves and whores, and she's right with that.

The Camorra consists of a number of families and they're always feuding with each other, and it's probable that false accusations of collaboration will be used to settle old disagreements."

"We still have to investigate. Do you still want to help?"

Paul preferred to deal with false accusations over starvation. "I'm not Neapolitan and neither is my wife, so we're best-placed to help you with this."

"There will be other things, and your background of living here but not associated with the locals will help."

There was knocking at the door and Colonel Miller left with an 'excuse me' and chatted quietly for a few moments before returning. "We've checked out the old German Headquarters building and it's clear, so we can start tomorrow. Is 0900 alright?"

"That will be fine," Paul said.

"Good. Report to the sentry and ask for me." The Colonel stood to shake hands with Paul and with Pia and then he opened the door.

Outside in the dusty, grimy corridor of a once-decent hotel, Pia sighed deeply. "I don't want to investigate the Camorra," she said in Italian.

"We're just translators and we'll get food and coffee. Colonel Miller seems decent enough and I would like to – encourage him to do more than investigate collaborators. Get food and essentials into the city to start."

"The Camorra will steal the food and sell it on the black market."

Paul knew that was probable.

* * *

Soldiers had rations, money and were, in Italian, allupato if not arrapato. Women had no money, no food but some were willing to trade. It was a sad to see younger, or older but attractive women taking young soldiers into ruined buildings or behind some rubble for a moment's intimacy, in exchange for a meagre ration of food. In the meantime Paul and Pia worked with Major Briggs and Major Davies to deal with accusers and suspected collaborators who were, universally, insulted that their good, family names had been desecrated in such a way. They got rather emotional in fact, and sometimes it was hard for Paul to keep a straight face while he attempted to translate the sense of injustice that such accusations brought.

One dark evening while they walked home to Via Solimena, Paul could have sworn there were footsteps in time with their own. And then footsteps approached from the opposite direction, until Paul and Pia were surrounded by six, burly men in dark clothes.

"Buonasera Paolo e Pia Corradi," one man said.

"Buonasera," Paul replied, echoed by Pia.

"You're helping Americans put our family into jail," he said in Italian.

"We translate English to Italian and Italian to English," Paul said. "Nothing more." That man closed where Paul saw the sparkle of a knife. "I told the American Colonel that many accusations about collaboration are false," Paul said. "All the Americans do is ask questions, write down answers, files will be completed and the men will be released due to lack of evidence."

"How do you know?"

"Because that's what's happened so far. For this, my wife and I are looked after, and the people of Napoli are also looked after."

"By you?"

"When I translate I could be more probing or less probing."

"And you are less probing?"

"You know I can't tell you this. But what I can tell you that you're better off with Italians translating and not American translators."

"Do they have their own translators?"

"They do but not here, because we volunteered."

"To look after yourselves."

The Camorra would understand. "Of course we look after ourselves, and we look after the good people of Napoli who drove the German Army away and stopped me from being taken to a labour camp. The good people I fought alongside for four days."

He stepped back and gave them some room. "Will you keep doing what you're doing?"

"Yes."

"I'm pleased that you look after Neapolitans."

"What's your name?" Paul asked.

"Giovanni Alessi."

"Buonasera signore Alessi."

"Buonasera signore e signora Corradi."

They dispersed as quickly as they appeared leaving Paul to lean against the building.

"You were brave," Pia said.

"No, not at all. You don't take these accusations of collaboration seriously?"

"No I don't."

"Then the truth doesn't hurt, except any accusations made by the family of Giovanni Alessi won't be taken seriously either. But we can't help this."

They continued on their way to Via Solimena. When they reached home they were surprised to see a gentleman waiting with an invitation to dine at Vadinchenia. They met with Giovanni Alessi, his wife or mistress Sophia, and enjoyed lobster accompanied with quality wine. They talked a bit, fended away questions about the specifics of their work for the British, other than they hoped it made a difference to the outcome of the war against fascism, and departed on friendly terms. Paul had no doubt the meal was intended to ensure that he and Pia continued with their ambiguous translations, but he was happy with this. It was up to the Americans to uncover solid evidence beyond accusal and denial. The lobster was far superior to U.S. Army rations.

From time to time buildings in the port area blew up because Germans left delayed-action mines. Some of the explosions were truly massive and the death toll of citizens and soldiers was tragic. In the midst of this was a German air raid on the port, and the wailing sirens meant traipsing down to underground shelters again. The next day there was a rumour that buildings within the evacuated 300 metres from the sea zone were mined to blow up that day, and that included the new American Headquarters. Every building was evacuated while servicemen retreated to Vomero. Paul took their rations and went home for the rest of the day, and by late afternoon the cataclysm hadn't happened so it was back to work the next day. Spasmodic German air raids continued, but with less frequency, and normality slowly returned to the city. More restaurants re-opened serving wealthy Neapolitans as well as British and American officers, and they needed to be wealthy given the prices being asked. For the rest a thriving black market of army food rations was available for those who could afford it.

Christmas 1944 was celebrated with serves of rations and a bottle of Chianti, courtesy of Colonel Miller. They attended Midnight Mass at Saint Nicola from Tolentino. All in all it had been a memorable year and things were slowly getting better. They had moved from the Dark Ages to Medieval Times.

Newspapers returned to the streets in January and life seemed even more normal. Perhaps it was normal in Napoli for there to be reports of widespread looting: including army blankets and uniforms, medicines, copper telephone cables, light poles, busses, trams and boats from the harbour. Paul assumed the busses and trams were stripped for useable components. Strangely the tailors of Napoli were able to fashion new clothing, dyed any colour the purchaser desired, and Paul guessed that looted uniforms were being re-made into civilian attire. If so then he wouldn't mind a change of clothes because what he had was rather shabby.

"I don't understand this place," Colonel Miller drawled in exasperation one morning. "It's a city of thieves and whores."

Paul smirked at that comment, first made by Pia. "It is a city of thieves and whores, but how many cities fought back and defeated German Army?"

The Colonel sighed. "You have a soft spot for this place?"

"I'm not Neapolitan but I do admire what they did, and there's more. With Napoli, what you see is what you get."

"What I'm getting are a whole bunch of soldiers infected with venereal disease."

"To reduce this you need to deal with the food shortage. There are few men, no work, no money and little food, all being sold on the black market at exorbitant prices. The women have to prostitute themselves to survive, and I'm sure for the survival of their children and extended families."

"There must be a way of stopping this."

"Every soldier you see with a Neapolitan woman could be paying for an hour or a night. What you must do is get the food supply sorted, and the need for prostitution for survival will abate."

"Yeah, I reckon you're right about that."

"This won't stop all prostitution, though. There are other items like wine, clothing, soap and all of this."

"Is there a way?"

"You're a soldier so what do you think?"

He shook his head. "Listen, I want to thank you and your wife for what you're doing here. It's really working out well. If there's anything we can do?"

Paul thought it wouldn't hurt asking. "This job is bigger than I first imagined, so payment for services would be nice."

"A couple of hundred lira a week?"

"Each?"

He paused. "Yeah, okay."

"Thanks Colonel."

The focus of translation changed from accusations of collaboration to vetting fiancees for American servicemen. One pre-requisite was the women couldn't be prostitutes, although Paul and Pia agreed they had to be prostitutes in order to meet their benefactors. Paul asked the question 'sei una prostituta' rather than 'eri una prostituta', to which the women could answer 'no', of course. What happened after that he had no idea, but if the women had Carabinieri records then the liaison was doomed.

Two German air raids followed on the fourteenth and fifteenth of March, and two days later Mount Vesuvius erupted and it seemed like Napoli was cursed. Smoke, ash and lava flows were clearly visible on the rim of the volcano which glowed red in the night sky. The next day the noise was louder and there were streams of fire shooting hundreds of metres into the air, looking particularly spectacular at night. A large lava flow headed towards Napoli which was ominous. Still the smoke, ash and cinders fell on the city until, over the next two weeks, the eruption gradually faded and the city was safe.

With the coming of spring the residents of Napoli spent more time in the street, including the tradition of bringing chairs and tables outside. The talk was of the successful advance of the Allied armies to the north, gradually pushing fascist Italians and Germans towards the Alps. In the midst of those battles were partisan Italians, which became a civil war between communist and fascist Italians.

Over the next few months Paul and Pia helped vet war brides, handle general queries and Pia amused herself by teaching young privates phrases in Italian, and telling them local customs so they could date local women. Although she really knew that soldiers a long way from home were wanting more than just to date the local women, teaching them Italian didn't do any harm. And then one of those privates mentioned that Colonel Miller was tired of the black market and was about to make a move on it. That piece of intelligence was backed up by Colonel Miller appearing out of nowhere and reminded Paul and Pia they had to be at work at 0900 tomorrow.

"He plans to raid the market tomorrow," Pia said while they walked home that evening.

Paul agreed. "He does, and he wants us to translate for him."

"I don't want to come between the Camorra and the U.S. Army."

"I don't either," and he wondered what to do. And then he remembered. "We'll go to Vadinchenia and see if we can find Giovanni Alessi and let him know."

"That's a very good idea."

They went to the restaurant and were lucky to find their man.

"Buonasera signore Alessi," Paul said.

"Buonasera signore e signora Corradi. How's life with the Americans?"

"That's why we came here. This is between you and us but the Americans are going to raid Via Forcella tomorrow."

Giovanni Alessi didn't show the slightest emotion. "Grazie," he said calmly.

"Buonasera signore Alessi."

They left him to sort whatever needed to be sorted, and went home to a meal of rations, some fresh rice that was on sale, and some red wine bought at that same black market. The next morning, just after they arrived at work, Paul and Pia were bundled into the back of a jeep, where five other jeeps with twenty or more

privates and a couple of sergeants, personally commanded by
Colonel Miller, headed for Via Forcella. There were the usual
trestle tables with a few items, all locally-sourced, and a few
prospective purchasers. The Colonel jumped out of his jeep and
marched up and down shaking his head. "Goddamn it!" he
eventually exclaimed, and it was back to Corso Vittorio Emanuele
and the rest of the day teaching American soldiers how to speak
Italian. Even though they didn't earn much, three meals a day and
a bit of spending money for not much effort was the best job that
Paul had ever enjoyed. The young, American soldiers were
pleasant, and they were all appreciative of a cushy posting in
occupied Napoli.

Christmas and New Year came while the advance of the Allies
and Partisans slowly dragged on, and on the twenty-fifth of April, a
significant date from Paul's Australian ancestry, Milano was
liberated. Three days later Benito Mussolini, Clara Petacci and
others were executed and then hung upside-down at a service
station in Milano. The same service station where, the year before,
fascists dumped bodies of fifteen political prisoners previously
executed. For the Partisans who executed the dictator and his
mistress, the hanging was retribution for the lives of those fifteen
martyrs, and fascists had often strung up executed partisans with
meat hooks, so the hanging was retribution for that. Two days
later Hitler and his mistress committed suicide, and two days later
war came to an end in Europe.

Chapter Fifty Two

Even thought it was three months after the end of war, Milano was tragic. The beautiful city centre was devastated by bombing raids, and countless thousands would have been killed or injured and countless more were homeless. His beautiful city destroyed, and those who survived struggled as best they could.

On the second of May, Pia had written a long and difficult letter. She had to explain to her parents that she didn't go to Australia; rather she lived in Napoli to gather intelligence for the Allies. Paul thought that term was clear and yet ambiguous. She assured her family that she was safe and well. Paul wrote a letter to his mother where he recounted his stay in Napoli and his gathering of intelligence, and that he was well and he hoped that she and the rest of his family were well too. Paul then wrote a letter to his friends Mario and Helena and briefly recounted the same, and received a reply that he must come to his home town and stay with them because they had room. Paul thought that was an excellent idea, especially as their house was a repository for their personal belongings.

Pia was relieved to receive a reply a few days later stating that Antionio, Claudia, Daniela and Giorgio had all survived, as had their children, although life had been difficult, especially for Daniela and Giorgio in Milano. And standing on the forecourt of Milano Centrale Station, the view of the devastation of the city was heart-breaking. Paul remembered arriving at that station a sunny day more than 11 years before, but now what he saw in July, 1945 was terrible. They set off past habitable buildings, damaged buildings and near-destroyed buildings to Via Teodoso, 46; the only habitable building in a street of rubble, as many streets in the city area had few, habitable buildings in streets of rubble. Unlike Napoli where damage was confined to the port and extended partly inland, the whole, central area of Milano was close to obliterated. Paul wondered why the British did that. Why did they bomb houses, churches, shops and cafes? Pia was more upset by the devastation around her; although Paul thought during their train journey she seemed – odd.

Daniela, Giorgio, and their daughters Clara, Maria and Gia shared a one bedroom apartment, crowded and clean. Daniela and Pia embraced and cried with relief and with joy, leaving Paul and Giorgio to make do as men do. The girls had grown and all three took after their beautiful mother, except they showed the puffiness associated with malnutrition. Paul knew that would pass in time. There were apologies that they had nothing to share and Pia said she wanted for nothing, which they didn't. Pia greeted each of her nieces in turn, but Gia was shy with an aunt who was a near-stranger. The other girls remembered Pia, and Clara recalled Christmases in Soncino.

* * *

"Pia," Daniela said. "Can you come to this room?"

Pia followed to mess everywhere while Daniela closed the door.

Daniela faced Pia. "We have been through a lot, I know, but something bigger seems wrong with you."

Of course it was bigger, and now the war was over her thoughts were worse. "British MI-6 asked Paul and I to spy for them in Napoli. At first it was easy but then they wanted me to seduce an ammiraglio. I didn't want to, and then I thought this would help win the war so I agreed. This wasn't hard for me; I think because Paul knew and the ammiraglio was decent. I discovered several things, I don't think they were important, but one thing I discovered resulted in the British being ready for a naval battle where many Italian ships were sunk and more than 3,200 died. Pia looked at Daniela. "I can't get them out of my mind. Later there was another big thing, but I don't know what came from this because soon after the ammiraglio knew it was me and he had to leave Napoli."

"Oh Pia!"

"How do I make my bad thoughts go away?"

"Come here."

Pia closed on Daniela who hugged her.

"My poor sister. Do you remember when you met Paul and you told me you were going away with him? I thought he must be special, more than taking you to see racing cars, and of course things could happen, or perhaps they should happen, so I told you what I knew."

"I remember, and yes, things happened that weekend. That was so long ago." Pia remembered not thinking her first time was really making love – little did she know. She remembered more. "The ammiraglio liked me and that relationship was never a problem, but I killed so many."

Daniela squeezed Pia. "It was terrible here, and I'm sure it was terrible in many other Italian cities. If you shortened the Italian war by just one day, you would have saved more than 3,200 Italian lives."

"Would I?"

"I'm certain." Daniela let Pia go, stood back and looked in her eyes. "I wish I had the chance to do what you did."

"Do you?"

"Yes I do. You're my little sister and always will be special to me, and special to all of us, especially the man who loves you. I can't make your hurt go away except that you did the right thing."

"I suppose I saved more lives than I killed."

"I'm certain of it. You were brave."

"He put a gun to my head."

"Did you think he would shoot you?"

"I don't know – I did at first but I talked him out of it."

"You've been through so much!" Daniela hugged Pia who felt her eyes get wet, and then tears ran. Ran and ran and ran. Eventually, there were no more tears and she realised she needed to cry after holding it in for so long.

"How do you feel?" Daniela asked.

"I feel better."

"If ever you feel upset, hug Paul, tell him everything again, and especially how you feel, and cry again. Do you promise?"

Paul would always help her. "I promise."

Daniela wiped Pia's cheeks with a handkerchief. Pia felt so much better, and next time she would do what Daniela said. Pia guessed she'd been in survival mode in Napoli for years, and now with the war over it hit her harder. In time, maybe it would go away entirely, but for now Pia had people who loved her and would help her.

Giorgio looked startled when he returned home a short time later. Pia knew it was time to leave that crowded apartment and told Paul they should go. They had to catch a train to Chiari.

* * *

Paul stood with his arms folded while Mario turned back the dusty, green canvas. There was his car: still shiny red and supported by bricks under the axles. He wondered.

"Your little racing car looks good," Pia said.

Paul nodded in agreement.

"You should change the oil," Mario said. "And the battery will be no good. New tyres would be better, if you can get them."

Again Paul nodded in agreement, but the car didn't seem so important any more. He wondered what it was, and it wasn't the car or even the first motor race to be held in Paris the next month, with many more promised for 1946. Alfa Romeo had stored their Tipo 158 Alfettas which were gathered together again. Many racing cars survived the conflict and drivers were ready, but that didn't seem so important any more. He had a job writing sports articles at Corriere della Mattina and travelled by train to Milano each day, which wasn't so bad. It took just over an hour each way. As part of his job he would attend Italian motor races and maybe others.

He had a job, he had his lovely wife and they were on the waiting list for an apartment in Milano but lived in Chiari for the time being. Once petrol and other parts were available he could drive again. He had everything he needed but something seemed to be missing. He wondered what it was. Never mind there was a family gathering in Soncino that weekend, and Paul looked forward to meeting the rest of his family. The distance wasn't far, 10 kilometres, and Alfredo, custodian of the Alfa Romeo Gran Sport, would oblige with a horse and cart.

The Donati family gathered on a lovely, sunny Saturday morning for lunch, albeit constrained by ongoing rationing. There were many noisy greetings of course, and Paul kept partly to the background at first. He was collared by his father-in-law who wanted to know about 'gathering intelligence' and Paul didn't know how far he ought to go, and there were many things he couldn't reveal anyway. He fended it off and dragged the conversation towards il quattro giornate di Napoli instead. As far as Paul was concerned, the future Repubblica Italiana should always remember the bravery of the men who liberated Napoli. His Papa didn't quite see it that way, of course.

The meal, padded with rice and potatoes, was pleasantly filling, especially accompanied by home-made red wine. Later Pia spent time with her nieces and nephews which Paul observed discreetly, and even though it had been many years, Aunt Pia quickly worked her way into the hearts of the girls and the boys. She was a natural with children and it was a shame they couldn't have children of their own. At least they had enjoyed travel, life and even helped liberate Italy from fascism.

On the way home in the cart Paul still thought about Pia and her nieces and nephews, but there was no answer to that.

"You were quiet today," Pia said, and Paul knew what she meant. He hadn't been quiet but he was quiet in the cart.

"You enjoyed meeting your nieces and nephews," Paul said.

"It's been a long time."

"I know."

Just then they passed a bedraggled-looking group of children being led alongside the road by two nuns, orphans, and Paul had the most amazing idea. "Do you want children of your own?" he asked.

"Of course I want children but we can't."

"We could adopt."

"Orphans from the war?"

"Yes."

She hugged him. "You darling man; how is it that you think of such wonderful things?"

"I'm just naturally wonderful."

"And modest."

"Always. No, seriously, are you interested?"

"Of course."

"When we have a home of our own."

"I hope our home comes soon because we can ease the suffering of...."

"Two."

"Why two?"

Paul thought about it. "We're older at thirty-three, so I think we need to be realistic."

"A girl and a boy."

"If you want."

"You would make a good father."

Paul was startled. "Why?" he asked. He never even contemplated how good a father he would be, or even what a good father did.

"You are decent, honest, hard-working and you would make a good example to any child, especially a son. What will you do about your racing?" Pia asked.

"Racing's not as important as a family," Paul said automatically. "No," he said, thinking it through. "I'll cover Italian races, of course, and some of the most important races elsewhere in Europe like Monaco and France. But not every weekend away."

"This will work."

"I'll report all sport including some motor racing."

"And most of this sport will be based in Milano?"

"Yes."

The cart rolled slowly on a lovely, late evening. Paul stretched out and Pia lay in his lap as he ran his fingers through her thick, black hair. Talk of racing brought back memories and there was one thing not yet resolved. "We should go to Galliate," he said.

"Yes we should," Pia said.

Chapter Fifty Three

Achille had just sat at the bar when he heard the door open and close followed by footsteps approaching on the bare floorboards.

"Ciao Achille."

Achille turned around to face the journalist Paul Bassi and his eternally beautiful wife Pia. They both looked good.

"Ciao Paul e Pia," Achille said. "How have you both been these past years?"

"A lot happened," Paul eventually said. "We spent the war in Napoli, which was for a good cause."

Achille wondered why they went to Napoli – he guessed Paul worked for either the Partisans or for the Allies. No, they both worked for the Partisans or the Allies. But why Napoli?

"How are you Achille?" Pia asked.

"Things turned out well for us. I had income from Alfa Romeo, I worked with my father, and Norma and I lived here."

"I'm glad to hear this. How's Norma?"

"She's good."

"How's everyone else?"

"Tazio's not well."

"That's too bad."

Achille still wondered what they did in Napoli while he fixed trucks, hunted with Gianni, played cards with Tazio, Didi, Tonino and others, and drove his Lancia with a gas generator. At least they didn't have to endure the destruction of Milano. Now, more important things.

"Are you going to follow racing again?" Achille asked.

"Not like before," Paul said. "Just major races. We have other plans."

"We're going to adopt war orphans," Pia said.

"That will be good for you," Achille said, where he thought they would make good parents to unfortunate children. "Do you want a drink?"

"Yes, per favore."

Achille ordered two Cinzano Biancos – they left the bar and went to a table.

"We were lucky," Pia said. "We did good work and managed to get by, and Paul taught me English so we were able to work for the Americans when they came. We did well out of this."

The door opened and closed and Achille heard more footsteps. "Ciao Paul e Pia," Norma said. "How are you both?"

"We're both doing well and glad to be back in Lombardy," Pia said. "I was telling Achille that we were lucky for these past years."

"I'm glad to hear this. I'll get a drink."

Norma was only gone a few moments and then she sat at the table, and Achille contemplated two and two. "Cards?" he asked.

Paul broke into the biggest smile. "You should know that's why we came here," he said. "Scopa?"

"Of course."

Achille reached into his pocket for the deck, and while he dealt the hands he contemplated that it had been a very long time.

* * *

Pia walked from room to room opening wardrobes, peering into cupboards and even opening and closing each tap. Paul leaned against a doorframe and waited with his arms crossed until she came to him.

"We can rent this?" she asked.

"We can buy this," Paul corrected. "We can borrow from the bank to buy this apartment, and pay back the loan and interest over twenty years."

"That seems like a catch."

"It's no catch. Loan payments are the same as paying rent; only at the end we'll own this."

"At least we have our furniture in storage with Mario."

"Yes we do."

She went to the window and looked across the street. Only a few buildings in Via Privata Moncalvo and nearby had survived, so the apartment was mostly surrounded by empty blocks, some blocks still with rubble to be cleared and a few, new buildings under construction. "Do you think it will be alright here?"

"We're only a few kilometres from the city centre and this street will be rebuilt, as will the streets nearby. In the meantime we can buy this apartment if you want it."

She turned around and frowned. "It's modern, and once we clean away the dust it will look good, and when the street is rebuilt it will be better. It has two bedrooms."

"It does. I think it's the nature of the destruction around here that has put other people off, so this is an opportunity for us as long as we recognise that what we see today isn't what we'll see in a few years time."

"This makes sense, and this is a modern apartment with all that we need. And one day we'll own it, so I think we should sign those papers. And then we can do the other thing."

That was a strange euphemism. "Once we arrange this as our home we can enquire about adopting?"

"Yes." Pia jumped up and sat on the kitchen bench. "We saw those orphans a few months ago when we travelled from Soncino to Chiari, and they're the sort of children we should look for. Children who need love and care that an orphanage can't provide, but who are from the country so they haven't been bombed or shot at. I think a mother who knows mothering can help a distressed child, but I don't know if I'm that sort of mother, and I don't want to make life worse for a child."

Paul thought that should enquire about the children they saw that afternoon.

Pia slid off the bench. "Let's go to the agent and sign those papers, and then we can catch a train to Chiari. Perhaps our friend Alfredo can take us for a ride in his cart."

Chapter Fifty Four

Achille leaned against the counter of the Alfa Romeo pits and looked across towards the grandstands. Packed grandstands for practice, and it seemed half the population of Torino had descended upon Parco del Valentino for the first motor race in Italy for many years. Race day was going to be big and he hoped he would win it, although Jean-Pierre's speed at Geneva was troubling. Achille wondered how Wimille was so fast with only a single-stage car. He wondered how he became so fast, or perhaps he always had speed but was held back racing uncompetitive Bugattis.

"Ciao Achille," a familiar voice said in greeting.

Achille turned around. "Ciao Paul e Pia," he said in reply, and he remembered something but couldn't recall what it was. He knew it was important but for the life of him he didn't know, and then he did. "Did you adopt a child?" he asked.

"Yes, we adopted Isabella and Guido, who are staying with my sister in Milano," Pia said.

"That's good for you," he said.

"Do you all have two-stage cars this race?" Paul asked.

"Yes, we all have two-stage superchargers," Achille replied.

"It should be a good race. Good luck and ciao."

"Ciao," Achille replied, and always wishing good luck hadn't changed.

* * *

The 1946 Gran Premio del Valentino was the first race run to Formula One engine capacity regulations of one and a half litres supercharged or four and a half litres unsupercharged. Alfa Romeo entered five Tipo 158s for Achille Varzi, Jean-Pierre Wimille, Carlo Trossi, Nino Farina and mechanic Consalvo Sanesi, who was favoured by left-wing unions. There were many Maserati 4CLs including cars driven by Louis Chiron, Raymond Sommer, Tazio Nuvolari and Swiss driver Christian Kautz. Farina set the fastest time in practice to start from pole position on the grid, ahead of Wimille, Varzi, Trossi and Sanesi.

It was a lovely, spring day on Sunday the first of September, as a massive crowd descended on the tight Circuito di Parco del Valentino on the banks of the River Po. At the drop of the Italian Flag, Farina was left behind while Achille took full advantage to take the lead from Wimille, Trossi and Sanesi, with Farina's car pushed away with a broken axle. The crowd cheered Achille Varzi leading the race, and cheered more enthusiastically than his pre-war heyday. Tazio Nuvolari passed both Sanesi and Trossi, with the groans showing that Sanesi was a crowd favourite as well. Achille and Wimille opened out a massive lead on the remainder of the field, until team orders were enforced for the two leading cars to hold position after their respective pit stops; although Wimille stayed right on Achille's car's rear and Paul wondered whether those orders were going to be followed. They were followed, but he doubted the two drivers really slowed that much to preserve their cars over the 270 kilometre race distance, with Wimille pressing the race leader all the way. Third, two laps behind, was Raymond Sommer in his Maserati.

While they walked to their own Alfa Romeo parked about a kilometre away, it seemed like nothing had changed despite five years of tragedy.

"Do you miss not going to all the races?" Pia asked.

"No," Paul said, while wondering if really he missed the noise, colour and excitement. "There aren't enough races to support me freelance so I don't have a choice."

"You don't like working five days a week though."

Paul agreed with that. "I don't," he said. "At least two of my five days this week have been spent in Torino with my beautiful wife, and I have Monday and Tuesday free.

"What's the next race?"

"Circuito de Milano at Parco Sempione on the thirtieth."

"We can walk there."

Paul sensed Pia had something on her mind.

"I would like to come to a few races with you," Pia said. She turned to look him in his eyes. "I want to be more than just a wife and mother. Sometimes I feel selfish."

"You're not selfish," Paul said. "You can work at a few races which isn't selfish."

"How can I work?"

Paul knew exactly how she could work. "Marco wants pictures with our articles, so you could be our photographer."

"I don't know anything.... No, I can learn."

"We'll find someone to teach you and you can buy your equipment."

"This might be expensive."

"We'll earn this money back after a weekend or two. You'll be paid casual rates for an eight-hour day, the newspaper covers your expenses and we can travel together."

"For a few weekends a year it will be like the old days, except I'll be a photographer."

"It will be like the old days."

"Maybe Achille will win the Circuito de Milano."

"Maybe."

At that race Jean-Pierre Wimille wasn't entered so Paul wondered if he was dropped by Alfa Romeo for pushing the speed of the race-winning cars at Torino. The format of the race in Milano was two heats and a final where Achille won heat one from Carlo Trossi and Tazio Nuvolari. Nino Farina jumped the start of heat two and the race was stopped and re-started, and Farina jumped the start again for which he received a one-minute penalty. Consalvo Sanesi won from Raymond Sommer and Farina. In the final Didi led at the end of lap one but was overtaken by Achille before Didi took the lead back, and Paul suspected that Alfa Romeo had 'given' the race win to Didi. Achille finished second ahead of Sanesi while Farina spun and then retired, apparently because Raymond Sommer passed him. Paul wondered whether Giuseppe Farina would be racing for Alfa Romeo in 1947.

Paul finished typing his article in the journalist's room above the pits, and then they walked to his work to drop it off for publication in the next morning's edition. They walked home after an interesting day's racing, and again it felt like things hadn't changed.

"What's on your schedule for next year?" Pia asked.

"Switzerland at Bern in June, Belgium if I can do it in late June, Reims the week after Belgium, Bari in July, and the Gran Premio d'Italia here in Milano, Venezia and the Grand Prix de l'A.C.F. at Lyon, all in September."

Pia nodded. I would like to go to Bern, because it's not so far to travel and it's an exciting circuit, here of course, Venezia and also Lyon because it's not so far to travel and it is the A.C.F. But you're on you're own for Belgium, Reims and Bari because that's asking too much of Daniela."

"I don't mind."

"Are you sure?"

"I'm sure."

"What about South America?"

Paul wondered what about South America and then he remembered. "A few European drivers like Achille Varzi, Luigi Villoresi and Carlo Pintacuda racing against unknown South American drivers isn't news, and even in my freelance days I couldn't have covered those races. So the drivers are welcome to enjoy South American sunshine while we endure winter, and we'll have to wait until Switzerland in June."

"It's summer there?" Pia asked, frowning.

"It's like Australia – hot in January and cold in June."

"Ah yes, of course."

Paul then remembered. "Why do you want to go to Venezia?" he asked.

"I haven't been to Venezia before and I would like to see the city."

Paul doubted a race at Lido di Venezia would be anything special, but he had to cover all Italian races, and it would be good to see Venezia. They reached home, climbed the stairs of the small building, their apartment upstairs and another downstairs, and opened the door for Pia to be stampeded by Isabella and Guido as if she'd been away for six weeks rather than six hours. She dropped to her knees and hugged them both, and Paul admired the happy, domestic scene. Daniela joined him.

"Grazie Daniela for helping," Paul said.

"It's no trouble Paul," Danielle said. "They're good children."

"I know." Perhaps they were lucky that there was an orphaned sister and an orphaned brother, aged four and two, and they were young, enthusiastic and ready to share love with parents who would love them. Or perhaps Pia was a natural born mother like her older sister.

"How did the race go?" Daniela asked.

"Carlo Trossi won from Achille Varzi, both driving for Alfa Romeo," Paul said.

"Do you know them?"

"Yes."

"Count Carlo Felice Trossi?"

"Yes. Now the next race is June next year."

"If I can help...."

"We can work it out when the time gets closer. It's a pity you missed out on Pescara and Livorno. You would have enjoyed visiting those cities by the sea and watching the races."

"And San Remo," Pia said from the floor.

Paul nodded and he remembered San Remo, Achille, Ilse and all that love. He wondered what happened to Ilse.

"I must go," Daniela said. "Ciao."

"Ciao Daniela," Paul said.

"Ciao Sister," Pia said.

"Now my two darlings," Pia said. "Mama has to cook us something for dinner. Papa will look after you now."

Paul was taken by Isabella to the bedroom where they both had spent the afternoon drawing pictures, and Paul sat on the floor with Guido on his knee while he was told all about her imaginary world. Later, Pia came to the door to announce their dinner was ready, and they adjourned to the kitchen for beef, vegetables and rice, along with wine for the adults. They listened to the news on the radio and then it was Paul's job to put the children to bed. He read a story that he'd read a dozen times before and it was still fascinating, and then he kissed them both and closed the bedroom door. Pia had also gone to bed, so he closed their bedroom door to find Pia sitting up and reading a book using the bedside lamp only. She put it down and removed her nightdress. Paul undressed and joined his wife and she slid down the bed and he went with her, and they kissed before he traced kisses lower and lower pausing at her breasts, and lower still and Pia squirmed with arousal. After a while of that, Paul moved to enter her while she wrapped her long legs around him to draw him deeper. He watched her dark eyes glistening in the light, and he watched her big, bright smile, and no matter how many times it was always special. He heard her moaning and moaning, closer and closer, still her eyes open when she came."

"More."

Always more as Paul made love to Pia, moaning and moaning, more and more and then she groaned.

"Did you come?"

"I came twice. Do you want me on my front?"

That meant her legs were sore. Pia rolled onto her front, legs almost together which she liked while Paul made love to her this way. But he was thirsty and Pia had glasses of water. He stopped and took a drink, by which time Pia was on her back again.

Paul slid into her and now it was his time as he kissed her and kissed her, and then turned his head away as he got closer and closer, ever closer and then came big, endlessly big.

Paul eased away lie beside Pia where she ruffled his hair which felt sweet.

"I knew you would make a good father," she said quietly.

Paul didn't think so. "It's nothing special," he said.

She ruffled his hair again. "It is special amore mio." Pia reached down to where she'd tossed her nightdress and slipped it on. "Buonanotte e dormi bene," and she kissed him lightly.

"Buonanotte e dormi bene."

Chapter Fifty Five

The weather for practice in Bern was cloudy but dry when Paul went to the pits to check what Alfa Romeo was up to. There were rumours of a more powerful model with a number of modifications and a bigger fuel tank for the higher fuel consumption, but after talking with team manager Battista Guidotti he discovered that car was not being raced. Paul glanced over the counter and noted that the cars allocated to Achille Varzi and Jean-Pierre Wimille had single pipe exhausts while the cars for Carlo Trossi and Consalvo Sanesi had twin-pipe exhausts seen the previous season. Just as Paul was about to leave the pits, Achille Varzi marched in and instructed Guidotti to make sure his car was as well prepared as the car for Wimille, and Guidotti, who was a decent driver and had driven all four cars during the previous day's practice, did his best to assure his driver. Achille then jumped the counter and inspected each engine. Apparently some Alfetta engines were better than others.

"Achille can't accept he's not the fastest," Pia said from her vantage point just outside the pits.

Paul nodded slowly in agreement.

"He's too proud to accept he's not the best anymore," Pia said to emphasise her point.

"If he wasn't proud he wouldn't be here as one of the top racing drivers of all time. His pride told him he was the fastest and nobody was going to get past, not even Tazio."

"That was then and this is now."

Paul agreed with that, and then thought it was ironic that the driver who learned more from following Achille Varzi for 15 laps many years ago had now become Varzi's nemesis.

"There are more pits to visit amore mia," Paul said. They discovered that Lugi Villoresi and Raymond Sommer, the two, best Maserati drivers, both had two-stage supercharging like Alfa Romeo now used. He wrote some notes and Pia took pictures of cars in the pits.

Wet weather threatened for Sunday but that didn't stop many thousands of Swiss flocking to Bremgarten. Indeed more spectators attended than the circuit could cope with, and they ended up sitting on the edge of the circuit which was dangerous. A mistake by a driver would result in the death and injury of tens or more spectators. The race was to be run in two heats and a final, where Trossi led the first heat just as rain began to fall. Trossi was well ahead of Varzi who seemed rattled by the crowds pressing close to the circuit edge, and his performance reminded Paul of a race at the Nürburgring when he accidentally hit a mechanic off the start line and was off the pace for the rest of the race. He was a sensitive man, which wasn't a criticism. Trossi then slowed to let Achille win the heat, but tragedy struck on the slowing down lap when a boy ran across the road and Achille hit him. Paul didn't know if how badly the boy was injured or even if he was killed, although there were rumours that the boy was killed.

Wimille won the second heat, while the two-stage supercharged Maseratis of Villoresi and Sommer were some seconds a lap slower than the Alfa Romeo. Sadly, Leslie Johnson in a Talbot struck and killed two spectators standing on the edge of the road. After that tragedy many drivers wanted the meeting abandoned, but the organisers were concerned about the reaction of the crowd. Paul wondered just how badly Swiss would react, but cars were readied for the final anyway.

Sommer got the jump at the start but was soon passed by Wimille and Achille, where the Frenchman opened a substantial lead and most likely Achille was still affected by the spectators at the edge of the track. Wimille eased back and Achille closed towards the end of the race, while Didi finished third ahead of Sommer and Sanesi. Then the crowd invaded the circuit, causing the cars to stop immediately rather than complete a slowing down lap. All in all it had been a tragic race meeting and Paul hoped that future racing at Bremgarten would be better controlled by the organisers.

* * *

Achille paced the hotel room; back and forward, back and forward. Wimille was fast, and worse that he wasn't likeable. When he obeyed pit signals, such as Torino, he did it with near-contempt. He did many things with near-contempt for the team and for the other drivers. Racing was a team sport, and Alfa Romeo first was the aim, not the betterment of any, single driver.

"You will wear a hole in the carpet if you don't stop," Norma said.

"Pardon?" Achille asked. "Oh, yes."

"Thinking about your team mate?"

"Yes."

"You mustn't let him get you down or else you will make a mistake."

"It's not that easy."

"Don't let your pride get in the way. You should have learned your lesson years ago."

Achille wondered what she was talking about and then he remembered a banquet in Tripoli. Norma was right, of course. "I'll race the best that I can."

"Nobody expects more of you than this."

Achille thought that was easier to say than to do, when Jean-Pierre Wimille did only three laps of Spa to set fastest practice lap and a new lap record. Belgium was Achille's victory, just as Milano the previous year had been for Didi, but he doubted Jean-Pierre Wimille would take notice of team orders. Achille had a battle on his hands.

The race was terrible. Wimille refused to follow team orders and Achille had no choice but to battle hard for the lead until the inevitable happened and he had a problem with his car, and lost a lot of time at the pits getting a brake pipe replaced. At least he made up time after that stop and finished second, and he was pleased that he raced as best he could.

* * *

Paul covered the race at Bari, won by Varzi from Sanesi in the two works Alfa Romeo 158s, and Balestero in an ancient Alfa Romeo Monza. Two months then passed before the Gran Premio d'Italia, where there was more interest from the Alfa Romeo pits than anything on the circuit. Five cars were initially entered, for the four usual drivers and a fifth car for a second mechanic Alessandro Gaboardi, who was apparently favoured by the left-wing unions just as Consalvo Sanesi found himself with a drive the year before.

The political pendulum had swung the other way and the communist Partisans Paul fought alongside in Napoli now called the tune. In practice there was no sign of Jean-Pierre Wimille and nobody was talking. Wimille didn't race at Bari, which wasn't a surprise for a minor race, but Paul was convinced that Wimille's failure to follow team orders in Belgium, harrying Achille to the point that Achille's car failed, irked the other, Alfa Romeo drivers. Especially as Achille Varzi, Carlo Trossi and Consalvo Sanesi got on well together, which was important for the team. With Achille Varzi and Carlo Trossi as their main drivers, Alfa Romeo would win anyway.

Sanesi showed good form on a new track at Milano and was fastest in practice, but in the race Varzi took the lead before allowing Trossi to win, and Trossi made the mistake of crossing the finish line with his hands in the air indicating that Achille was the worthy winner. The crowd responded by booing Trossi who was upset by that. These major races were degenerating into farce.

The following week at Lido de Venezia was better, given the absence of Alfa Romeo. Piero Taruffi won from Franco Mosters and Tazio Nuvolari, all in Cisitalias. A weekend in Venezia, all expenses paid, was a bonus, and it was good to see Tazio again, although he was sick and ought not to have been racing.

Chapter Fifty Six

Achille leaned against the rail of the ship and smoked a cigarette while contemplating the wake trailing off into the distance. Norma joined and Achille gave her his pack of Camels and his lighter. She lit one and handed them back while Achille returned to studying the wake of the ship. Leaving Europe and crossing the Atlantic on the way to Buenos Aires. Achille liked Argentina; he would like to retire there when he finished racing.

"Are you ready for Christmas on the ocean?" Norma asked.

Achille drew on his cigarette. "Christmas on the ocean isn't as good as with family, but I'm looking forward to visiting Argentina again. Would you like to retire to Argentina one day?"

"There are a lot of Italians there so it feels like home, only better. It's spacious."

Achille remembered driving from city to city along near-deserted roads, arrow straight from horizon to horizon. It was spacious.

Norma drew on her cigarette and then butted it on the rail before tossing it into the sea. She hooked her arm into his. "Let's go," she said. "It's time for Christmas dinner, even if it's not as good as with family."

Achille and Norma spent Christmas with mechanics Guido Bignami and Amerigo Zonca. Scuderia Milano dined at the next table: Luigi Villoresi, Nino Farina, Arialdo Ruggeri, along with their wives and companions. Jean-Pierre Wimille and his wife Christiane sat at another table on the other side of the dining room. New Year also passed at sea, and a week later they berthed at Buenos Aires in warm, clear and humid weather. While they caught a taxi to the L'hotel Palermo near Parco Palermo, the racing cars were unloaded from the liner including Achille's 1937 12-cylinder and Jean-Pierre's 1938 8-cylinder Alfa Romeos, with Achille's car purchased cheaply from Alfa Romeo. Achille checked in at reception, got a key, and they went upstairs to a room with a view over the park. Norma went to the window.

"I don't need to go to the circuit; I can see the racing from here," she said. "But I will go of course."

Buenos Aires was a thriving city of four million, with the central area built around a series of plazas with broad avenues radiating outwards. It was bustling and dynamic with many, modern, multi-storey buildings and even skyscrapers lining wide roads, which were necessary for the volumes of cars on the move. There was more to Argentina than buildings, roads and cars, and Parco Palermo was one of many public parks in the inner city. The city thrived and wasn't spoiled by the after-effects of war.

The race meeting was scheduled to have practice on Saturday, and two heats and a final on Sunday. The Automobile Club Argentino obtained two Maserati 4CL cars for local drivers Oscar Gálvez and Juan Manuel Fangio; but for two races only. Then dark clouds rolled over and the torrential rain set it, washing out the entire weekend. The Gran Premio del General Juan Perón was postponed to the following weekend, and the other races were also pushed back one week. This gave Achille and Norma time to meet with local, motor racing identities and gain an appreciation of life in Buenos Aires.

Back at Parco Palermo a week later, Achille had problems before practice commenced. It was only a short distance from the hotel garage so his mechanic Guido drove the Alfa Romeo to the circuit, but damaged the superchargers when the car bottomed on a railway crossing. Repairs took so long that Achille was unable to set a time, so he had to start from the rear of the grid for heat one on Sunday. He did well to finish second in to Luigi Villoresi who had a Maserati 4CL. Unfortunately the magneto failed on lap two of the final which forced Achille to retire at the pits. Villoresi won again.

It was time to load the car onto its rented trailer for the drive to Mar del Plata about three hours to the south, a busy city on the coast and popular with tourists in mid-summer. Achille and Norma stayed at the hotel as part of the Central Casino complex right on the waterfront, just behind a promenade pathway beside the beach. Nearby was the massive Grand Hotel Provincial, nearly finished.

The circuit was in parkland adjacent to the sea, and it was a simple layout and not particularly fast, where Achille's 4.6 litre Alfa Romeo was really too heavy and cumbersome to set fast times in practice. In the race Jean-Pierre Wimille initially led from Luigi Villoresi, Nino Farina, Achille and Juan Manuel Fangio. Villoresi, Farina and Achille got past Wimille easily enough, but Achille was surprised to have a lurking Fangio feint inside before out-braking him on the outside of a curve, and then Fangio set off after Farina who he passed as well. That put Fangio in third until he pitted. Villoresi slowed and Nino Farina found himself first from Achille in second, which was how the race finished. Achille was most impressed by Juan Manuel Fangio's smooth, precise and fast driving. He thought that Fangio could go a long way, and he heard that Juan Perón was keen for Argentina to make an impression in European motor racing. Juan Manuel Fangio could be the driver to do this.

After the race Achille went to the Automobile Club pits, where he sought out Juan Manuel and invited him for dinner at the Casino Hotel that evening at eight.

Away from the gaming tables in a dining room, Juan and his companion, signora Andrea Buerret, arrived on time. Greetings were exchanged and drinks were ordered, while Achille scolded the waiter because there wasn't a water bottle. Achille then asked if Juan ever considered racing in Europe and he said that he hadn't.

"There might be sponsorship opportunities from your government for the fastest Argentinean driver, and from what I saw today that driver is you. If you contact your club there could be funding for you to race in Europe."

"Grazie signore Varzi and I'll do this," the quietly spoken Juan Manuel Fangio said.

"Call me Achille. If you do go to Europe to race, the most important thing after being a competitive driver is to have the best car. You should only sign for a team or manufacturer who has the best car by contacting this team directly, or contacting the team through an intermediary. Over time you will build up your circle of contacts, and then you can use your circle of contacts to help you get the best drives."

"I understand."

"The best car in one year is not necessarily the best car the next year, so sign contracts for one year only. If you want to stay at a team for longer you can sign another contract, but if you want to leave to get a better drive, then you can leave without acrimony."

"I know you did this."

"That's right. I went from Bugatti to Scuderia Ferrari for a year, and then to Auto Union for a year. Auto Union was still my best chance so I signed a contract for a second year there. Once you get your contract, the most important thing is to get the team behind you. You are part of a team and their performance is your performance, so it's important to have your manager and your mechanics on your side. It's also important to show that you're number one, so you must be faster than your team mates. If you are the fastest, you will get the best equipment that your team can offer."

"My greatest rivals are my team mates?"

"Yes, absolutely. Mechanics work long hours for poor pay, and are often away from home for weeks at a time. Their reward is to see their car win, so the driver who brings their car home first will be their hero and he will get the best equipment."

"I understand."

"If you do come to Europe to race, contact me and we can put you up in our home in Galliate. It's a town close to Milano and Monza, and close to many circuits in Europe. It will be good base for your racing."

"Grazie Achille and I appreciate your offer."

Achille knew why he had to do this. "Racing has given me a lot over the years, and now it's time for me to give something back. My present to racing is to help a talented driver establish himself at the top level of European motor sport."

Drinks arrived and meals were ordered.

"What are your plans for the remainder of the series?" Achille asked.

"Signore Gordini has asked me to be team mate to Jean-Pierre Wimille."

"A Gordini isn't as fast as the Maserati you drove today, but more experience racing at this level will do you good. Don't be disappointed if you can't win with a Gordini."

"I can only go as fast as the car will allow."

That was Achille's philosophy for racing, and he felt that Juan Manuel Fangio had what it took to reach the absolute top ranks of European motor racing.

* * *

The next race was the Copa Acción de San Lorenzo at the Circuito de Parque Independencia in Rosario, about 300 kilometres north of Buenos Aires. Rosario supported President Juan Perón two years previously, but Achille had never been interested in politics. Argentina was prosperous and the people were happy, and that's what counted. Argentinean motor racing was competitive and there were talented local drivers, where Achille thought a good occupation for his retirement would be to open a racing driver's school in Buenos Aires, when the time was right for him. But before that he had a race to win, although the tight circuit didn't look like it would suit his car. And like at Mar del Plata, practice showed his big Alfa wasn't particularly fast. Juan Manuel Fangio joined Jean-Pierre Wimille at Gordini, and Oscar Gálvez drove his own Alfa Romeo 308.

Achille's car barely moved a few metres and he was out with transmission failure, so they pushed the car away quickly because it was a short, tight circuit and the field, led by Gálvez, thundered past less than two minutes later. Also slow away was Fangio but over the next few laps he passed six cars to be in fifth. By lap 10 Gálvez led Wimille and Fangio, who set a lap record in his chase of second place. Gálvez then retired and Fangio harried Wimille for the lead until forced to pit with overheating. Fangio retired allowing Jean-Pierre Wimille to win.

Achille knew his Alfa Romeo was better suited to the Circuito de Parco Palermo for the final race of the series, the Gran Premio de Eva Duarte Perón. Achille qualified fourth, and in the race Achille grabbed second behind Luigi Villoresi and ahead of Oscar Gálvez, until Villoresi pitted with problems. Achille then had a clear lead over Gálvez until the Alfa Romeo began to stutter and it seemed like his dreaded magneto problems had returned. Achille stayed out but the stuttering got worse to the point of being dangerous if the engine should cut out, so he pitted to retire leaving Oscar Gálvez to win. On the fast circuit, the Gordini of Fangio was uncompetitive and he finished well back.

Norma sat up in bed and reached across to the table and grabbed the pack of Camels and a lighter. She lit a cigarette before handing the pack and the lighter to Achille. "It was a shame your car failed today," Norma said. "You had it won."

Achille lit a cigarette. "It was a shame, but it wasn't the right car for the series."

"That's true enough."

"There wasn't anything better at Alfa Romeo, so.... But we sail tomorrow and proper racing starts in June."

Norma turned her head and looked at him. "Achille, I know you and I know how you drive. I know what you said to Juan Manuel the other week, but don't let yourself get dragged into a battle with Jean-Pierre. This could end badly for you."

"He's not a team player."

"You have won many great races, and you proved today that you could have won in an old car. Your turn will come."

Achille nodded in agreement, but he didn't want to fade away into obscurity.

Chapter Fifty Seven

Paul sat at the kitchen table to read the file. In the background Pia pretended to be cooking but he knew that wasn't the case.

"What have you planned for this year?" she asked.

"I have to do all Italian races, so that's Bari in May, Mantua in mid-June, San Remo in late June, the Gran Premio d'Italia at Parco del Valentino in early September, Monza in late October and a race in Salò a week later."

"Put me down for San Remo and Parco del Valentino, because that's a lovely circuit. Monza of course, and Salò is too close to miss out on."

"And I thought I will cover Switzerland, the A.C.F. at Reims, and I would like to see Monaco."

Pia turned off the stove and sat opposite. "Which will be the first race for Alfa Romeo?" she asked.

"Switzerland."

"I would like to go to Bern because it's a lovely circuit with a great atmosphere, as long as they keep their crowds under control."

"Any other races?" Paul asked.

"Reims is too far, and I would like to go to Monaco but that's asking a lot of Daniela."

"The Côte d'Azur...."

"I know. Maybe next year."

"So I'll drive to Bari, Mantua and Monaco, and then we both will drive to San Remo and Bern. I'll catch a train to Reims and then it's local from there."

"You don't mind, do you?"

Paul looked up. "Of course not; we're seeing five races together and I'll be away from Thursday to Monday for the others."

"Did I say five races?"

Paul nodded. "Remember we agreed for Daniela and Giorgio to take two weeks holiday, so that balances it out."

"They'll love visiting Lido di Venezia and then Pescara, Roma and Firenze."

"And we'll have a full house for two weeks, and cousins big and small will love this. I would like to get to Switzerland for scrutineering on Thursday morning, and watch the first practice session Thursday afternoon."

"To find out what is what?"

"Team politics are as big a story as the race."

"So we'll drive there on Wednesday and drive home Monday?"

"Yes."

"I must get back to cooking."

Pia turned the stove back on, and Paul wrote notes for the agent to book his accommodation for the first three races. He knew where he wanted to stay.

"What are you doing Papa?" Isabella asked.

"Mama and I are working out what motor races we'll see," Paul said.

"Does that mean that Guido and I will be staying with Aunty Daniela again?"

"You don't mind, do you?"

"Of course not! I like Clara, Maria and Gia."

Paul guessed her older cousins spoiled Isabella.

"Can we go to a motor race Papa?" Guido asked.

Paul turned around to look at his son aged almost four and wondered. "Pia?" he asked.

"Like father like son," Pia said. "We can all go to Monza."

Paul agreed, even though Monza would always have a mix of happy and bitter memories.

"Grazie Mama," Guido said.

Paul wondered, like Mario passing the baton onto him, that one day his own son might become a motor sports journalist.

* * *

Paul had just signed the register at the Bellevue Hotel when he heard Norma greet Pia, which the whole hotel would have heard. Paul put the room key in his pocket and turned around to greet Achille and Norma as well.

"How are you both?" Norma asked.

"We're both well," Pia said. "How are you?"

"We're good."

"How was South America?" Paul asked.

"There's too much to tell you about here," Norma said. "Would you like to have dinner together?"

"Yes, we will," Paul said while thinking it would be like old times, even if those good, old times could never be repeated.

"We'll see you at seven."

"Ciao Achille e Norma," Paul and Pia both said.

"Ciao Paul e Pia," they replied.

Achille and Norma went to reception while Paul escorted Pia from the delightful, spacious reception through the lovely, glass-roofed lounge and up the stairs lined with thick, red carpet. It was a beautiful hotel.

The Restaurant La Terrasse was delightful on a summer's evening, open on one side and overlooking the city and parkland beyond. Achille, Norma and Didi had just taken their seats on the terrace when Paul escorted Pia to meet them, and Pia looked right at home in a black evening dress. They greeted each other, Norma with great exuberance of course, and then they waited until the drinks waiter came, where Achille scolded him for being slow. Unflustered, the waiter took their orders.

"How was South America?" Paul asked.

"Very good," Norma said. "Achille would like to retire there when the time is right."

"As you know Tonino is organising a World Championship of Drivers, and I'm sure Argentina will be part of this championship," Achille said. "I'm also sure there will be opportunities for Argentinean drivers in this championship, and this is an opportunity for me."

"The World Championship of Drivers is worthy after what we did to each other," Paul said.

"It's a way to bring the world together again, and a way to further motor sport."

"One thing that's common throughout the world is motor sport."

"This is true."

"Achille discovered a driver already," Norma said.

"Juan Manuel Fangio is older at thirty-six, but he only raced gran premio cars for the first time in January," Achille said. "He was fast and I believe he has what it takes. We'll help him however we can."

"If he comes to Europe?" Paul asked.

"When the World Championship starts, Juan Manuel Fangio will be hard to beat."

Paul thought that Juan Manuel Fangio must be a special driver to become Achille's protege. It also showed that Achille was coming to the end of his driving career.

Drinks arrived and again the waiter was again scolded for being slow. Soon after orders for meals were taken, and Paul was glad the newspaper paid their expenses.

"How's your family?" Norma asked Pia.

"Isabella and Guido are staying with my sister who lives close by," Pia said.

"That's lucky for you."

"This is one of my favourite circuits, especially with the city and this hotel so close to the track, and I like coming here."

"What have Alfa Romeo planned?" Paul asked.

"Didi, Jean-Pierre, Consalvo and I have been entered," Achille said. "And we have a special car for practice."

Didi didn't look well – pale and drawn. Meals arriving stifled conversation. The food was superb, as the food was always superb at that restaurant. In neutral Switzerland it was like a world war had never happened. It was a pity the rest of the world hadn't seen sense.

"I remember when we met a while ago and you said you were in Napoli," Achille said.

Paul didn't want to clarify that, at all. "It wasn't anything," he said quietly.

Later they went to the bar to play Machiavelli and drink more Cinzano, while Norma and Pia talked in dialect, as usual. They always got on well together. Didi was quiet, though, and he looked sick. After a few hours they called it a night with Achille winning at cards, showing some things never changed.

"What do you have planned for tomorrow?" Pia asked while they climbed the grand staircase to their room on the first floor.

"Well, I know Alfa Romeo's plans," Paul said. "So I'll time the cars and write an article, and telegraph it after the first day of practice, and you can take some pictures. Now amore mia...."

"Ha! I should have known."

Paul thought there was something decadent about making love in hotel rooms all across Europe, especially in the luxurious Bellevue Hotel.

* * *

The big, roofed grandstand was empty on a wet Thursday afternoon for the first session of practice, but the pits opposite bustled with activity.

"I'm going down the road to Jordenrampe," Pia said.

"Enjoy," Paul said.

"It's a good spot for photography in the open past the trees. And raining of course, but it's Bern so we're used to this."

Beyond Alfa Romeo the entry list was light, with Luigi Villoresi and Alberto Ascari entered in updated Maseratis, supported by

Luigi Fagioli, Nino Farina, Christian Kautz and Bira in older 4CLs. There were a couple of Talbot-Lagos, including an entry for former great Louis Chiron, and two Ferrari sports cars stripped of mudguards. Former Alfa Romeo team manager Enzo Ferrari was making and selling his own racing cars and Paul wondered where that would lead. Hopefully competition for Alfa Romeo at some time in the future.

Paul sat in the grandstand to view the activity. Achille took his car out on the wet circuit and recorded decent times, as did the other Alfa Romeo drivers, but the wet circuit equalled things out because Villoresi in a Maserati was quicker than Sanesi. Achille was slower than Wimille until he came into the pits. He got out of his car and talked with team manager Battista Guidotti. Mechanics got to work in the drizzle and changed rear dampers in about twenty minutes. They fired the car up and Achille went out and did three moderately quick laps before piting and switching the car off. After a brief talk with Guidotti he climbed into the unused car numbered with rough, hand-painted 28s; presumably the special car. He left the pits just as Wimille closed, and Achille followed Wimille around Bethlehem curve and out of sight. Next past was Louis Chiron and he disappeared out of sight as well.

Less than three minutes later Wimille flashed past the pits and there was no sign of Achille or Chiron. Then Kautz pitted his car and climbed out to talk with his crew. Other cars came in one after the other while Paul was trapped on the wrong side of the circuit and unable to find out what happened. One by one the Alfa Romeos pulled in and shut down, and practice came to an end just a few minutes early.

Pia trudged up the hill in her waterproofs with her camera bag around her neck, and shaded by her big, floppy waterproof hat. She went into the grandstand and straight to Paul.

"Achille's dead," she blurted and then burst into tears.

Paul's heat sank and he immediately grabbed Pia and held her, and she cried and cried until, it seemed, she could cry no more. She pulled away and looked blank.

"Wimille came past and I turned and saw Achille coming out of Eicholz sideways in trouble, and them right rear of his car hit a timber wall and the car bounced off that and hit the opposite wall with the left front, and he kept fighting it and lost of lot of speed until it slid onto a grassy bank, and then slowly rolled over and slid upside-down along the road and back onto its wheels where it threw Achille out. Louis was behind so he pulled over and ran to Achille on the road. I saw it in his eyes so I turned around and walked away."

Paul barely believed it. It was Achille's first actual driving error, and sadly it would be his last.

"I don't like this sport any more," Pia said.

Paul hugged her again. "Remember Achille for the good man he was and the amazing things he achieved. Remember that he wouldn't have wanted to live his life in any other way."

"Even though he died?"

"Achille Varzi was not a man to do things in life by half-measures, and I can't think of anything that would have brought him the satisfaction he got from racing cars. Even though he died, he lived a life of excitement and adventure."

"Norma...."

"Leave her to grieve with the team."

"I hope they race because that's what Achille would have wanted."

Paul hoped that Alfa Romeo would race in Achille's honour.

* * *

At Norma's insistence, Alfa Romeo races. Jean-Pierre Wimille initially led until he had to pit with overheating problems, letting Carlo Trossi into the lead. After his stop, Wimille closed on Trossi but couldn't or wouldn't overtake, which meant one of Achille Varzi's closest friends won that tragic race.

Chapter Fifty Eight

As soon as they got back to the hotel, Paul made a phone call. He knew he needed to for Pia's sake. On Tuesday in Galliate he was glad he made that call because the numbers who descended on the town to pay their respects were truly massive. Relatively few could attend the service and accompany the coffin to Achille's final resting place, where the final address would be read. While they walked, surrounded by thousands, Paul gave Pia a sheet of paper which she read before placing it in her bag. The words meant a lot and they would be published, and those who followed Achille's career would understand.

Perhaps you were destined to die, Achille, because in your driving there was something of that genius which is one of Nature's greatest mysteries, and Nature strives to destroy those who come too close to her. Beethoven was struck with deafness when he seemed about to transcend man's powers of musical expression. Galileo was blinded when he tried to probe infinity and its laws. Leonardo da Vinci's hands were crippled when he was about to come nearer to perfection than any man before him. And you too, Achille, were destroyed when you sought to cross the known frontiers of man-made speed.

Now you are preparing for another race, the last great race. A race without danger, without care or sorrow.......

They walked to the station to catch one of the special trains to Milano. In the compartment surrounded by strangers, Paul sat close to his wife.

"How do you feel?" he asked.

"I feel at peace now," she said.

"What do you think of the sport now?"

"You were right that terrible day. Achille Varzi wouldn't have lived his life any other way, and he packed more into forty-four years than the rest of us could experience in two lifetimes."

Paul knew that was true but there was more. There will always be brave, skilled and talented men to race cars, and to compete to be a World Champion when that happens. And there will always be hundreds of thousands who attend races to watch their heroes who seemed larger than life, and many millions more will follow the sport. A sport of skill, teamwork, bravery and sometimes terrible tragedy.

Epilogue

Achille Varzi competed in 139 races, winning 33. After his death his family supported the career of Juan Manuel Fangio who became one of the most successful racing drivers of all time, winning five World Driver's Championships in seven years, and 24 World Championship races from 52 starts.

Count Carlo Felice Trossi was already suffering from a brain tumour when he raced for Alfa Romeo in the late 1940s. He died on the 9th May, 1949 aged 41.

Jean-Pierre Wimille continued to race successfully until he was killed in a practice accident at Parco Palermo in Buenos Aires on the 28th January, 1949, aged 40.

Rudi Caracciola spent World War Two in Switzerland, racing once at Indianapolis where he crashed. He returned to racing in Europe but crashed again. He died on the 28th of September 1959 aged 58, prematurely aged by his many crashes.

Louis Chiron continued racing into the World Championship years becoming the oldest driver to compete in a Formula One race. He died on the 22nd of June 1979 aged 79.

Tazio Nuvolari didn't formally retire from driving but the deterioration of his health meant his appearances became more and more sporadic. He was partially paralysed after a stroke in 1952, and he died on the 11th August, 1953 after a second stroke. He was aged 60.

Norma Varzi died on the 15th of March, 1975 from lung cancer aged 69.

Ilse Pietsch married opera singer Franz Fehringer during World War Two. She died on the 4th of May, 1969 in a Hospital in

Weisloch, a few kilometres south of Frankfurt, of an unknown illness. She was 58 years old.

The 1936 Gran Premio di Tripoli marked a turning point in the life of Achille Varzi. Nobody will ever know what happened behind the scenes, but it's possible either the Fascist Party of Italy or Auto Union decided an Italian driver should win that race held in an Italian colony, and Air Marshal Balbo, who was a motor racing enthusiast, was upset that his great race was turned into a farce. Most accounts have Ilse at the hotel but we know this wasn't the case, and those accounts have her already drug-addicted but Paul Pietsch later confirmed this wasn't the case.

Always when a champion driver crashes and is killed, a lot of thought goes into what might have happened because Varzi should have been able to catch and hold that slide. Theories include Varzi being blinded by spray from Wimille's car just ahead, Eicholz had overhanging trees and the track surface was extra slippery from sap dropped there, the spare car he drove had more power which caught him out, and even a muscle spasm from his morphine addiction a decade before. The end result of Varzi's death was crash helmets were made mandatory.

The Formula One World Championship consists of 24 Grand Prix races staged world-wide, including the traditional circuits of Monaco, Monza and Spa-Francorchamps. Typical circuit attendances are 100,000 each race day while television audiences are more than 500 million unique viewers.

www.ingramcontent.com/pod-product-compliance
Lightning Source LLC
Chambersburg PA
CBHW071144020726
47502CB00002B/262